Praise for the novels of Patricia Kay writing as *USA Today* bestselling author Trisha Alexander:

"This marvelous story is full to bursting with winning characters, special moments, and, most of all, hope, faith, and the rejuvenating power of love."   —*Romantic Times*

"A beautifully written, compelling story . . . once you pick it up, you won't be able to put it down."
          —Georgia Bockoven, author of *The Beach House*

"[An] intriguing story of love at first sight."
          —*Houston Tempo Magazine*

"There are deep questions about relationships and serious character growth evident in this story, which is also warm, sensuous, and excellent entertainment."   —*Rendezvous*

"A warm, tender, beautifully written love story with an emotional punch that only Trisha Alexander can deliver."
          —Amanda Stevens, author of
          The Bodyguard's Assignment

"One of those rare love stories that explores a difficult issue with honesty and realism."   —*The Romance Reader*

Also includes a special preview of Patricia Kay's *The Other Woman*!

The WRONG CHILD

Patricia Kay

BERKLEY BOOKS, NEW YORK

THE WRONG CHILD

A Berkley Book / published by arrangement with
the author

PRINTING HISTORY
Berkley edition / December 2000

The Penguin Putnam Inc. World Wide Web site address is
http://www.penguinputnam.com

ISBN: 0-425-17770-X

BERKLEY®
Berkley Books are published by The Berkley Publishing Group,
a division of Penguin Putnam Inc.,
375 Hudson Street, New York, New York 10014.
BERKLEY and the "B" design
are trademarks belonging to Penguin Putnam Inc.

PRINTED IN THE UNITED STATES OF AMERICA

10 9 8 7 6 5 4 3 2 1

This book is dedicated with love to the members of the sanctuary choir of St. John Vianney Catholic Church in Houston. Being a part of the choir and getting to know all of you over the past four years has been one of the great joys of my life.

Acknowledgments

A heartfelt thank-you to the following persons, without whom the writing of this book would have been much more difficult: Tess Gerritson, author and former internist, and Dr. Joseph D'Ambrosio, Baylor College of Medicine, for their expertise and advice concerning the medical aspects of this story. Alaina Richardson, Jan Freed, and Marilyn Amann, for their willingness to read and offer comments and suggestions on the final draft of the story. And a special thank-you to my terrific agent, Helen Breitwieser, who had such faith in this project; and to my editor, Cindy Hwang, who had the vision to see its potential.

Prologue

Helen Palmer couldn't remember ever feeling this tired. Her weariness went bone-deep, so that even the effort of putting one foot in the front of the other was almost more than she could bear.

She sighed heavily. It was 12:40 A.M., and she'd been on duty since ten-thirty the previous morning. For a sixty-four-year-old woman, fourteen hours was far too long to be on her feet. She thought longingly of home, where she should be warmly tucked into bed next to Leonard, her husband of forty-two years.

But this wasn't a normal day. The snow had started falling before dawn, and by ten o'clock, they'd had eight inches with no end in sight.

The nursing supervisor had called Helen, begging her to come in early. "I know you're not on until three, but half my people haven't made it in, and we desperately need you," she'd said. "You're the only one who lives close enough to walk."

So Helen had come in to work an hour later. She was appalled at how shorthanded they were, a situation that worsened as the day wore on. By that evening, the entire county was socked in with the worst winter storm the Texas Panhandle had seen in fifty-some years. The roads were mostly impassable, the county's lone snowplow entirely inadequate for the massive job of cleaning the snow that still fell heavily.

At eleven, when yet another shift failed to arrive, and Helen should have gone home—wanted nothing more than *to* go home—she knew she couldn't leave. There were two women in labor and no other nurse to assist in the delivery room or to take care of the infants when they decided to make their appearance. Even in the best of times, Cyrus Hurley General Hospital didn't have a surplus of nursing staff, and this February night was hardly the best of times.

So Helen had stuck it out, somehow overcoming her exhaustion and successfully helping an equally exhausted Dr. Slater with both deliveries, which had taken place within minutes of each other—one right before midnight, the other shortly after. She had then brought the babies here to the nursery where she would care for them until someone, God willing, showed up to relieve her.

You can do it, she told herself. *You've made it this long. You can take a nap when the babies go to their mothers.*

Feeling half-sick with fatigue, she opened a drawer and removed two plastic name bracelets. She had already printed out the newborn identity information for the two girl babies. All that was left to do was insert the information into the appropriate slot and fasten the bracelets to the babies' wrists. Normally, the bracelets would have been put on the moment the babies were delivered, but since nothing about the last fourteen hours had been normal, there had been no one to prepare the bracelets ahead of time.

As Helen, bracelets in hand, walked toward the babies, a wave of nausea gripped her. She clutched the edge of the counter that held stacks of diapers and the plain white blankets they used to swaddle the infants. She swallowed, willing away the nausea and accompanying dizziness. When the spasm passed, she took a deep breath and finished preparing the bracelets, then walked on unsteady feet toward the first bassinet. Reaching down, she loosened the corner of the blanket, which was wrapped burrito-style around the infant, and gently withdrew the little girl's left hand. She wrapped the identity bracelet around her tiny wrist, snapped it into place, then turned it so she could read the inscription: "BERNARD/GIRL"

Helen blinked. Frowned. Looked at the baby's wisp of

dark hair. *Wait. That's not right. The Bernard baby didn't have any hair. This is the O'Connell baby.*

She reached for the baby's wrist again. And just as she did, excruciating pain speared her between her shoulder blades and radiated into her chest, then upward, engulfing her left jaw and nearly doubling her over.

She staggered backward.

Leonard . . .

As she collapsed onto the tile floor, the bracelet that read "O'CONNELL/GIRL" fell from her lifeless hand.

One

Eleven years later . . .

Abbie Bernard sat back on her heels, looked at all the boxes she still needed to unpack, and swiped a tired hand across her sweaty forehead. In her years away, she had forgotten how muggy and just plain miserable summers in Gulf coast Texas could be. And it was only mid-June. By August the weather would be sweltering. For perhaps the dozenth time that week, she wondered if she'd done the right thing in moving back to Houston.

She would have been content to stay in the east Texas town of Lucas forever. Yet she knew Kendall deserved a more stimulating environment and the diverse opportunities only a sophisticated, cosmopolitan city like Houston could offer. Still, for many years Abbie had resisted her mother's efforts to get her to move back to her hometown, only succumbing now, when it was time for Kendall to start middle school.

A big reason for Abbie's change of heart was Kendall herself. If ever a child craved family, it was the precocious, irrepressible girl who seemed so well adjusted to outsiders. Abbie knew this was a perfectly normal reaction to the fact that her daughter had, for all intents and purposes, grown up without a father.

Even so, moving back had been a hard decision. Abbie

cherished her independence, an independence she knew might be difficult to maintain once the physical distance between her and her strong-willed mother was eliminated. But in the end, what was best for Kendall had been the deciding factor. After all, Abbie was a grown woman who had been on her own for a long time. Surely she could handle her mother now.

An added bonus to the move was the wealth of possible clients for Abbie, who was a freelance researcher and fact checker. She'd been lucky in the past. Her first client—a publisher headquartered in Austin—had come to her by chance, as so often happened with businesses that weren't planned but just seemed to evolve. But if Abbie had learned anything in the past dozen years, it was that change was inevitable. Yes, she had enough clients now to support herself, but that could change overnight. Living in Houston would give her many more options.

However, all other considerations aside, it was going to be hard to get used to a big city again when she was accustomed to living in a small town of fewer than ten thousand. The Houston freeways alone were daunting. Abbie was grateful she worked out of her home and would not have to contend with them on a daily basis, since she did most of her traveling on the Internet, with only an occasional foray to the local library.

But if Abbie still had some reservations about the move to Houston, her adventurous eleven-year-old did not. Thinking of her daughter, Abbie smiled. Kendall was her miracle. The most wonderful child any woman could ever hope for. Bright, beautiful, talented, outgoing—her daughter was everything Abbie was not. From the moment the tiny infant had been placed into her arms, Abbie had marveled that she had produced such a child. She still marveled today.

And she was sure her mother did, as well. Abbie sighed. Katherine Wellington had been disappointed in Abbie from the day she was born.

The trouble was, Katherine had wanted a son. Herself the daughter of a Texas Supreme Court judge and the granddaughter of a U.S. senator, Katherine had had visions of a son who would follow in those esteemed footsteps. At the very least, she'd hoped for a daughter who would be a credit to her in the twin arenas of politics and society—her two great passions. Unfortunately for Katherine, Abbie hadn't shown an interest in or aptitude for either domain. Unlike her cousin Pamela, who was the daughter of Katherine's sister Marjorie, the young Abbie had been shy and bookish, preferring her make-believe world to the real world outside her doors. Throughout her growing-up years, she had been a trial to her mother, disappointing her at every stage of her development. And when she'd married Thomas, Katherine had been thoroughly disgusted.

"He's a nobody," she'd scoffed. The fact that Thomas Scofield Bernard was a brilliant scientist already making a name for himself in his chosen field of archaeology meant nothing to Katherine. Who outside of scientific circles even cared?

"Why *couldn't* you be more like Pamela?" Katherine had lamented.

Abbie couldn't remember how many times she'd heard the same question. It wasn't as if she hadn't tried, at least when she was younger. But she simply hadn't been interested in the things that interested her mother and her aunt and her perfect cousin.

But when she produced Kendall, Abbie had finally done something right. Katherine doted on Kendall. "A chip off the old block," she was fond of saying. "A Vickers through and through." She insisted Kendall looked just like her own grandmother had looked, although from the few pictures Abbie had seen of her Great-grandmother Vickers, she hadn't been able to discern much of a resemblance. She hadn't voiced this opinion to her mother, though. Abbie knew better. Once Katherine Wellington made up her mind about something, woe to anyone who disagreed with her.

Still thinking about her mother, Abbie slit open the top of a carton marked "KITCHEN" and began unwrapping her everyday dishes. A moment later she heard the slap of Kendall's sandals coming slowly down the hall. Typically, Kendall would have skipped or danced her way into the kitchen, but lately she hadn't been quite her usual effervescent self. In fact, Abbie was more than a little worried about her.

She looked up as Kendall entered the room. "Hi, sweetie. Did you get your stuff unpacked already?"

Kendall shook her head. "Nuh uh, I got too hot." Her normally bright complexion looked pale and her green eyes, usually so animated, had a tired cast. "Is there any Coke?" Her thick, curly black hair was tied back with a scrap of red ribbon, but wet tendrils had escaped. Beads of perspiration dotted her forehead.

"Oh, honey, I forgot to buy any. I'm sorry. I made some iced tea, though. Want some of that?"

"I guess." Kendall opened the refrigerator and peered inside. Except for the essentials, it was mostly bare.

Abbie watched her daughter as she took out the plastic jug containing the tea, then looked around uncertainly. Abbie smiled. "Up there." She pointed to the cupboard where she'd put the tumblers.

After Kendall poured herself a glass, she sat at the kitchen table. Even dressed as she was, in an old pair of white shorts and a soiled-from-unpacking Spice Girls T-shirt, she looked lovely, Abbie thought, a lump of pride and love filling her throat. There was none of the awkwardness so common in prepubescent girls, but then, Kendall had the natural grace of a dancer and the kind of presence and poise that couldn't be taught. As Abbie studied her daughter, Kendall leaned her cheek on her fist.

There must be something wrong with her. This ennui simply wasn't like her, and it had gone on for far too long now. Abbie tried to push away the thought that niggled in the back of her mind. The one that said, *What if there's something seriously wrong with her?*

"You know, Kendall," she said slowly, "I'm a bit concerned about how tired you've been feeling lately. It might be a good idea for me to take you in to see the doctor."

"But I don't have a doctor here."

"True, but you're old enough now that you don't really need a pediatrician anymore, so I thought I'd just call the doctor who used to take care of me when I lived here. His name is Dr. Joplin, and he's really nice. I think you'll like him."

Kendall shrugged. "Okay."

If Abbie hadn't been worried before, her daughter's ready acceptance of her suggestion would have certainly triggered alarm, because, like most kids, Kendall disliked going to the doctor.

"I'll call him right now, then."

Ten minutes later, an appointment with Dr. Joplin scheduled for the following Monday, Abbie hung up the phone and sat down at the table. "All set."

Kendall nodded. Dispiritedly, she traced a pattern in the condensation on her glass.

Abbie frowned. "Sweetie . . . I know you're tired, but is there something else bothering you?"

Still looking at the glass, Kendall shrugged again.

"You know you can tell me anything," Abbie said gently. "Are you sorry we moved?" When there was still no answer, she continued to probe. "Missing Bernie maybe?" Bernice Walters was Kendall's best friend.

Kendall's throat worked.

"Oh, honey, you know you can call her anytime you want. And she's coming here to visit in August."

Finally Kendall raised her eyes. There was a bleakness in them that tore at Abbie's heart. "I know. That's . . . that's not . . ." Her voice trailed off.

"Well, what then? Please tell me, Kendall. How can I help you if you won't tell me what's wrong?"

A long moment went by. "Why doesn't Dad ever come to see me?"

To her friends, Abbie was considered the calmest, most reasonable person they knew. It took a lot to make her angry, but Kendall's plaintive question and the pain behind it caused such a storm of rage within, it was all Abbie could do to keep it tamped down.

She wanted to say the reason Thomas had all but ignored Kendall from birth was his monumental self-centeredness and his unshakable belief that his work was the most important thing in the universe. She wanted to tell her daughter that she should put him out of her mind, because if he was stupid enough not to realize Kendall's worth, it was *his* loss. She wanted to say she loved Kendall enough for both of them, that if necessary, she would lie down and die for her, and that neither one of them needed Thomas in her life.

What she said was "Honey, I'm sure he wants to come and see you. It's just that his work keeps him so far away." It was a lame excuse, and Abbie knew it, but what else could she say?

"He could at least *write* to me once in a while, couldn't he?"

"He does write to you sometimes," Abbie pointed out gently.

Kendall's lower lip trembled. At that moment, Abbie wanted to kill Thomas. How could he? How could he neglect his daughter so shamefully?

The last time Thomas had communicated with her had been on her birthday in February, and then all he'd done was send a card and a check. And from her glimpse of the card, Abbie knew Thomas hadn't even signed it himself. The handwriting was too neat and feminine. It had probably been his assistant who had taken care of the twice-yearly chore for him, for the other time Kendall heard from her father was Christmas.

And yet his disinterest wasn't completely unexpected. He had been furious with Abbie for getting pregnant in the first place. Remembering, she surged up from her chair, needing to get away until she had her anger under control. "I'll be right back. I need to go to the bathroom."

Once she reached the privacy of the bathroom, Abbie let the memories come. She would never forget the day she told Thomas about her pregnancy. She had been so happy. She and Thomas had been married for three years. Three blissful years during which Abbie served as Thomas's research assistant. They had shared everything. So his reaction to her news was a shock.

"I thought you were on birth control pills," he said tightly, his dark eyes hard with anger.

"I-I was," Abbie stammered, frightened by the look on his face. "B-but you remember what the doctor in London said, don't you? He advised me to stop taking them. I told you."

Abbie hadn't known brown eyes could look icy, but at that moment, Thomas's eyes were glacial. "Surely you're not stupid enough to think birth control pills are the only form of birth prevention, Abbie."

Abbie knew it would be useless to explain that most of the time, she *had* used her diaphragm, but a couple of times, in the passion of the moment, she had forgotten. Thomas was like her mother in that he did not brook forgetfulness, nor did he suffer fools gladly. And in this case, he would certainly have considered her a fool.

"How far along are you?" he snapped.

"A-about six weeks, I think."

"Fine. I'll make arrangements for you to fly to London. You can have the abortion there."

Abbie stared at him. An abortion? He wanted her to get rid of their baby? Instinctively, she put her hands in front of her stomach. "I can't do that," she said quietly. "I could never do that."

"You surely don't expect me to drag a kid around from site to site. I don't even *like* kids." And saying that, he swung on his heel and walked away from her. For days afterward, he barely spoke to her.

Abbie told herself he would come around. Lots of men thought they didn't like kids. Lots of men thought they didn't want kids. But once their babies were born, they changed. Thomas would change, too.

Luckily, Abbie had an easy pregnancy. She was able to continue traveling with Thomas, and gradually their working life resumed its smooth cadence. She told herself that she was right. Thomas *was* coming around. She ignored the misgivings she felt over their personal life, the fact that once her pregnancy became pronounced, Thomas lost interest in any kind of physical intimacy.

Abbie felt the loss keenly. Even more than the physical closeness, she missed the emotional closeness, for almost imperceptibly at first, then in a more pronounced way as her pregnancy advanced, his withdrawal from her encompassed all the areas they had once shared.

By the time she had given birth to Kendall, their marriage was over in all the ways that counted. Still, it had taken Abbie two years to admit there was no hope. Two years in which she had seen Thomas a grand total of six days, because he refused to allow Kendall to travel with them, and Abbie refused to leave her behind. And since their divorce, not only she, but Kendall, had not seen him at all. His only contact with his daughter was his twice-yearly card, although he had been rigidly punctual about sending his child support check.

Of course, Abbie thought dryly, sending a check required nothing of Thomas that he cared about, for money was simply a means to an end for her former husband. He didn't even have to make the effort to write or sign the checks. From the beginning, he had had his banker take care of that chore for him. So promptly on the first of each month, his child support money was wired to Abbie's checking account. Once, when Abbie had complained to a friend about Thomas's neglect of Kendall, the friend said Abbie should count her blessings.

"He leaves you alone, he doesn't interfere in Kendall's upbringing, and every month he sends the money he's supposed to send. What more do you want?"

Returning to the kitchen and seeing her daughter's woebegone face, Abbie thought how wrong her friend had been. She would welcome Thomas's interference, because at least then Kendall would know her father cared. Maybe Abbie should try one more time, even though the last letter she'd written Thomas about taking a more active role in Kendall's life hadn't garnered an answer. She'd vowed then she'd never stoop to begging him again. Still, what was more important? Abbie's pride? Or Kendall's happiness?

Reaching across the table, Abbie squeezed Kendall's hand. *Damn you, Thomas. Damn you to hell.* Desperately, she cast about for something to say that would make Kendall feel better. Finally she resorted to an old ploy. In a playful voice, she said, "Did you know that on a ship the watch changes six times a day?"

For a moment, Kendall didn't respond, and then slowly,

she raised her head. Her mouth twitched at the corners. "I don't even know what a watch is."

Abbie grinned. "A watch is the portion of time when part of the ship's crew is on duty. They watch out for possible dangers."

"You mean like the iceberg in *Titanic*?"

"Exactly."

"I'll bet I'm the only person in the world whose mom knows so many—"

"Useless bits of information," Abbie finished, laughing.

"I was going to say *interesting things*."

"That's because you're loyal."

Kendall nodded, a faraway look in her eyes. She was obviously back to thinking about her father. Finally, she sighed. When she looked at Abbie, there was a hopeful expression on her face. "Maybe I'll send Dad that new drawing I did."

"That's a great idea," Abbie said heartily, even as she continued to inwardly curse Thomas and think how much he didn't deserve a daughter like Kendall.

Kendall picked up her glass. "I guess I'll go back to my room and do some more unpacking."

"Okay. And if you want, we'll go out for pizza tonight."

Abbie's suggestion was rewarded with a smile, and for a few seconds at least, Kendall looked like the Kendall of old.

Two

Today Logan O'Connell was working at home, because Erin had a cold and didn't feel like going to his mother's. His mother had been pinch-hitting for Serita, their housekeeper, who was in Guatemala visiting her sister this month. Logan's mother had offered to come to the house, but the truth was, he liked being here. And as an architect who owned his own firm, he could work at home just as easily as at the office.

Patrick, his thirteen-year-old, had been away at camp for the last two weeks, and he liked the opportunity to spend time with Erin, just the two of them. When Patrick was around, Erin was overshadowed by the sheer force of his more extroverted personality. Not that she seemed to mind, Logan thought gratefully. Although it would have been normal for her to be jealous of her older brother and his accomplishments, she wasn't. Instead, she idolized him, and he was protective toward her. Logan was lucky, and he knew it. He had two great kids who loved him and loved each other.

Logan glanced over at the couch where Erin lay curled up against several pillows, their calico cat Mitzi snuggled beside her. Erin was watching *Grease* on video for perhaps the hundredth time. He smiled. She had inherited his love of movies but not much else. Sometimes he teased her, calling her his snow princess because she was so fair and blond, whereas he and the entire O'Connell family were lusty Irish, with black hair and bright blue eyes. Patrick looked just like him, and sometimes, when the three of them were together, people thought Erin was a friend of the family rather than the daughter.

"She obviously takes after the Chamberlains," Ann had always said whenever anyone pointed out the differences between Patrick and Erin.

Yes, Logan thought now. Erin fit the picture of a delicate English rose much more than she did the vigorous Irish lass. But that was okay with him. Everything about Erin was okay with him. Even her shyness and lack of self-confidence didn't bother him the way they bothered Ann's sister Elizabeth, because Logan figured those characteristics would help keep Erin from growing up too fast.

Just then she looked his way and, catching him studying her, said, "What's the matter, Daddy? Is something wrong?"

He smiled. Worrying about him was something she had begun to do since her mother's death three years ago. "No, worrywart," he teased. "Just wondering if you were hungry. You didn't eat much lunch."

She nodded. "I *am* kind of hungry."

"Want me to fix you a sandwich? Or some of that soup Aunt Elizabeth brought over last night?"

At the mention of his sister-in-law's name, Erin's eyes brightened. "I want some of the soup."

As Logan, followed by Rex, the yellow Labrador they'd had for ten years, headed for the kitchen, he thought how typical Erin's answer was. Anytime there was a choice involving her mother's older sister, Erin would choose the thing associated with Elizabeth.

Since her mother's death, Erin had become closer and closer to her aunt. Logan guessed this was normal. After all, being with Elizabeth made Erin feel as if some part of her mother was still there for her. Hell, he'd felt the same way for a while. Normally, he would be glad that Erin had someone like Elizabeth in her life. Trouble was, he had a feeling Erin hoped he and Elizabeth would eventually marry.

He took the homemade chicken soup out of the refrigerator, ladled some into a bowl, then put the bowl into the microwave. While the soup heated, his thoughts returned to the growing problem of his sister-in-law.

He was afraid Elizabeth harbored the same hope as his daughter. A couple of times lately, she'd hinted as much. Logan had always pretended not to understand, but he knew there would come a day when he could no longer pretend. And then what?

Suddenly, the way it had so many times over the past three years, pain engulfed him. Pain and an aching loneliness. He closed his eyes. *Ann.* He still missed her as much as he ever had. From the moment he'd met her—so effervescent, so full of life—he'd known she was the one for him. Since that day, he had never wanted any other woman. And yet, at forty, he knew he was far too young to spend the rest of his life alone. Still, Elizabeth wasn't the solution. He cared for her, even loved her he guessed, but not the way a man should love a woman he was going to marry. He loved Elizabeth in the same way he loved his own sister, Glenna. Maybe he was being weird, but the idea of Elizabeth as a wife almost seemed incestuous.

It was a shame he felt this way, because if he were to marry Elizabeth, it would probably make a lot of people happy. Not just Elizabeth and Erin, but, he imagined, Ann's parents and even *his* parents, who had loved Ann as much as they loved their own daughter.

But marrying Elizabeth would not make him happy. Not in the ways he had been happy with Ann, and knowing what was possible, how could he settle for less?

Yet Erin and Patrick needed a mother—especially Erin. Maybe he expected too much. Maybe the kind of affection he felt for Elizabeth was enough for a second marriage. Maybe the kind of love and communion he'd experienced with Ann was a once-in-a-lifetime thing, and he was being naively romantic and unrealistic to think he could have the same kind of relationship again.

The microwave dinged, causing Rex to cock his ears, then walk hopefully to his empty food bowl.

"Okay," Logan said. "You're hungry, too." He fed the dog, then put the now-heated soup on a tray, accompanied by some crackers and a glass of milk, and carried it into the living room. Erin had anticipated him and put up one of the TV tables. As he set the food down, the doorbell rang. "Be right back," he said, giving Erin a smile and heading for the front foyer.

The massive double doors at the front of Logan's award-winning contemporary house had wide glass panels on either side, and it didn't surprise him to see Elizabeth standing on the doorstep. Since Erin had been sick, Elizabeth had taken to stopping by on a daily basis.

"Hi," she said, giving him a bright smile when he opened the door. "I was in the neighborhood, so thought I'd come by for a minute."

As usual, she looked perfectly put together. Her blond hair, cut short, was flattering to her oval face, and she wore just the right amount of makeup to enhance her large gray eyes and fair complexion. She had a good sense of style, too, just as Ann had. Today Elizabeth wore a two-piece turquoise dress with ivory stockings and matching ivory pumps. A good-looking, smart, successful real estate agent, she was the kind of woman most men would be proud to call their own.

She walked in and laid her purse on the walnut refectory table that stood against one wall of the large foyer, then toed off her pumps. "Ah," she sighed. "That feels better."

For some reason, this unconscious familiarity rankled Logan. Immediately, he was ashamed of himself. After all, Elizabeth was family. Why shouldn't she feel free to remove her shoes in his home?

Standing on tiptoe, she kissed his cheek. "How's our patient doing?" Her perfume, faintly exotic, drifted in the air.

"A lot better. Right now she's eating some of your soup."

Elizabeth smiled. "Good." She began to walk toward the back of the house, Logan following. He couldn't help noticing how her hips swayed just the right amount to be enticing, and how the several-inches-above-the-knee length of her skirt exposed a flattering amount of her shapely legs. He wondered if there was something wrong with him that he could see this, even appreciate it, and still feel no desire for her at all.

"Aunt Elizabeth! Hi!" Erin's face broke into a delighted

smile as Elizabeth walked into the sunny living area that sprawled across the back of the house.

"Hi, honey." Elizabeth planted a kiss on Erin's head. "Feeling better today?"

"Uh-huh."

"Good. Maybe by the weekend you'll feel well enough so that we can go shopping. You're going to need new clothes for your trip to Vancouver next month."

Once again, Logan felt a prickle of irritation. He knew Elizabeth meant well and that she felt a woman was needed to do justice to a shopping trip for Erin, and he was sure she was right. Even so, he wished she didn't sound so proprietary. At the very least, she should have asked him if he minded her taking over the responsibilities that had been Ann's and were now his.

Almost as if she'd read his mind, she turned to him and said, "You don't mind, do you, Logan?"

He shrugged. "No, of course not."

Rex, wanting attention, planted himself next to Elizabeth. She ignored his thumping tail and baleful eyes.

"Rex," Logan said. "Leave Elizabeth alone." He knew Elizabeth didn't like animals, even though she wouldn't admit it.

The dog finally gave up and plopped down next to Logan's drawing table. For the next fifteen minutes, Elizabeth chattered away, and Erin hung on every word, hero worship evident in her expression. Logan quickly got bored and returned his attention to the drawing he'd been working on before Elizabeth had arrived.

"What do you think, Logan?"

He looked up. "Sorry. What did you say?"

Elizabeth smiled. "No, I'm the one who should be sorry. You're working, and we're bothering you."

"No, you're not. I just didn't hear what you said."

"I said I thought Erin was old enough now to start wearing a bit of lipstick and eye shadow."

"What? That's ridiculous!" he said before he could stop himself. "She's way too young for makeup."

Elizabeth's eyes widened at his tone, and Erin's face fell.

Logan was immediately sorry he'd answered so sharply, but Elizabeth had taken him off guard.

"Now, Logan . . . ," Elizabeth said. "All of Erin's friends are wearing makeup."

"I don't give a rat's ass—" Logan broke off. He made it a policy never to curse in front of his children. In a quieter voice, he said, "I don't care who else is doing what. I think Erin is too young for makeup." *And if Ann were here, she'd say the same thing.*

"But, Daddy," Erin said, "Shauna and Tiffany *both* wear makeup. They even wear mascara. And Shauna even has her ears double pierced!"

The double piercing had been a continuing source of conflict in the O'Connell household for several months, with Logan adamant on the subject. He thought girls nowadays grew up too fast, and he had no intention of allowing his daughter to become one of them. His feeling was, the longer a child could remain a child, the better off that child would be. "I told you, Erin," he said quietly, "just because other people are doing something doesn't mean you should do it. It's much better to be a leader than a follower."

Erin looked at her aunt for support. Elizabeth looked as if she were going to continue the argument, but wisely she didn't. Instead, she rose to her feet. "We'll talk about this another time. Right now, I've got to get back to the office. I have an appointment at five-thirty, and it's already almost five."

Logan had to bite his tongue to keep from saying something that he wouldn't be able to take back, but it really pissed him off that Elizabeth seemed to think she was the one calling the shots in this family.

She bent down to give Erin a good-bye kiss, after which Logan walked her to the front door. After putting her pumps back on and retrieving her purse, she looked up at him. "I know you don't like the idea, Logan," she said softly, "but Erin has to grow up sometime."

"I'm not trying to keep her from growing up. I'm trying to keep her from growing up too fast. There's a difference."

"I understand that, but at this age, it's important to be like the other kids. Erin isn't exactly filled with confidence, you know, and making her different from the other girls will just make her feel more inadequate."

Although his annoyance hadn't faded, Logan conceded that what she'd said had merit—yet something in him continued to resist. "She's only eleven years old."

"I know, but a little pink lipstick isn't going to turn her into a femme fatale." When he didn't answer, she sighed. "Will you at least think about what I've said?"

"Fine. I'll think about it."

She smiled and patted his cheek. "Good." Then, as if she'd just thought of it, she snapped her fingers. "I almost forgot. Jack and Mary Lou can't go to the ballet Saturday night, and they gave me their tickets. It's *Swan Lake*. Do you want to go?" Jack Turner was Elizabeth's boss, and he and his wife were avid balletomanes.

Ever since Elizabeth had started issuing invitations, Logan had mostly accepted, but today he wasn't in the mood. "I'm sorry, but Patrick's coming home Saturday, no telling what time, and I want to be here."

Almost imperceptibly, her lips tightened. But she quickly got her anger—if that's what it was—under control. Her laugh was relaxed, her words light and teasing. "I know. You're a doting father. Of course, you want to be here. I guess I'll just have to find some other handsome man to escort me."

"I'm sure you won't have any trouble doing that," Logan said just as lightly. "They are probably lined up at your door right now."

Elizabeth rolled her eyes, gave him a little finger wave, and walked out the door. "See you."

After he'd shut the door behind her, Logan knew he'd better do something to discourage Elizabeth—and soon.

Elizabeth drove on auto pilot, barely seeing the towering oaks and palatial homes bordering Memorial Drive and its environs as she made her way from Hunter's Creek Village, where Logan lived, to her office near Town & Country.

Damn, she thought in frustration, tapping her perfectly manicured pink nails against the steering wheel. What was she doing wrong?

She had thought, once Logan was over his first shock and grief at Ann's death, that it would be natural for him to turn to her. After all, who better? She was Ann's sister, and she had loved Ann, too. Elizabeth was the logical person to give him comfort and sympathy. They would comfort each other.

And then, in a normal progression, comfort and sympathy would become more. Eventually, Elizabeth had been sure, Logan would see that she was eminently suited to be the next Mrs. O'Connell—the perfect woman to mother his children and share his life . . . and his bed.

For a while, Elizabeth's scenario played out exactly the way she'd hoped. Logan *had* turned to her, and she *had* given him just the right amount of understanding and tender, loving care. They'd cried on each other's shoulders and talked about Ann for hours. But now that the healing process had run its course, instead of becoming closer to Elizabeth, Logan seemed to be pulling away.

The way he'd acted today was a perfect example. Not only had he resisted her efforts to help out in getting Erin ready for the Vancouver trip—a trip Elizabeth had vainly hoped would include her—but he had declined her invitation to the ballet.

Why? she wondered. She didn't for a minute believe that he'd really felt he had to be there for Patrick. Patrick hadn't been gone that long, for God's sake! No, Logan had used Patrick's return as an excuse, and a not-very-subtle one at that.

She sighed heavily.

She had to figure out a way to reverse things, because she had no intention of losing Logan to some other woman.

Not again.

Remembering, her jaw clenched. She had met Logan first. It was the summer after her graduation from college, and he'd been working an internship downtown in the Esperson Building, where she had just started her first job with a property management company. She kept seeing him in the elevator. Who could miss him? He was downright gorgeous: tall and trim, with thick black hair, intensely blue eyes, and an irresistible smile. Not to mention a perfect profile. All the other women in the elevator eyed him, too, as Elizabeth was sure they did anywhere he went. But he seemed oblivious to their covert glances. She had liked that about him. Most drop-dead handsome guys she'd known over the years had been arrogant, playing their good looks for all they were worth.

For weeks, Elizabeth had tried to figure out a way to get him to do more than smile and say hi. The problem was, they were never alone. If only he'd worked on the same floor, she might have managed it sooner. As it was, it was the end of July before she got her opportunity. Her boss had asked her to work late, and it was seven-thirty before she could leave for home. When the elevator stopped at her floor and the doors slid open, the car had a lone occupant. Logan.

Elizabeth still remembered how her heart had accelerated in excitement. "Well, hi!" She gave him her most brilliant smile. "I see someone else has been working late, too."

His answering smile was friendly.

The doors closed and the elevator began its descent.

"By the way," she said, turning to him. "I'm Elizabeth. Elizabeth Chamberlain. I work for Byerson Property Management." She started to say her office was on the twentieth floor, but caught herself in time. He already knew that since she'd gotten on the elevator at the twentieth floor.

"Logan O'Connell," he said. "I'm working for Whelan Architects up on twenty-nine."

She liked his voice. It was low and sexy. "It's nice to meet you, Logan." She stuck out her hand, and he took it. Her mind worked frantically as she tried to think of something else to say that would keep him talking to her even after the elevator reached the street level. And then inspiration hit her. "I don't mind working late, except that I get *so* hungry." She touched her stomach for emphasis.

"Yes," he agreed. "Me, too."

"I was actually thinking of walking over to Luther's for some barbecue. Want to come?"

He seemed taken aback, and for agonizing seconds, Elizabeth was sure he would say no.

Then he'd smiled and said, "Sure. Sounds good."

So they walked over to Luther's and had their barbecue

and talked. She learned that he was studying to be an architect at M.I.T. and that he had two more years to go before he would graduate.

"Oh, so you're still in college. Somehow I thought you were older."

He smiled. "I am. I didn't start college immediately after high school. I worked a couple of years."

She also learned that he'd been born and raised in Houston and came from a fairly large family, with three brothers and a sister. And she learned he was completely unattached. She decided midway through the meal that she wanted him, and that somehow, some way, she would wangle a date out of him before they parted for the evening.

But no matter how many hints she dropped, he didn't rise to the bait. After they finished their meal, and it was time to leave, she decided it didn't matter that she had never before had to ask a man out first. What mattered was seeing Logan O'Connell again.

"Well, I feel a lot better now," she said on the way out the door.

"I do, too. Thanks for letting me tag along with you."

"I was glad of the company. I hate eating alone."

He chuckled. "That's because you didn't grow up in a big family. I actually like eating alone."

Damn, she thought. She was getting nowhere.

They were only half a block from the lot where she'd parked her car, and she realized it was now or probably never. "You know," she said slowly, "my folks just moved into a new house and they're having a party Saturday night to christen it. Why don't you come?"

"Thanks, but I—"

"Don't say no. You admitted you've been away from Houston for so long you hardly have any friends left here, which tells me you don't have much of a social life."

He shrugged.

"Come on," she urged. "Say yes. My parents throw great parties. It'll be fun."

When he said yes, she wanted to skip to her car, but she restrained herself. "Okay, I'll type up directions and bring them to your office tomorrow."

She had no way of knowing that inviting him to her parents' home was a terrible mistake. That instead of taking the first step in the kind of relationship she wanted, she would lose him before ever having him. She'd been kicking herself for years, imagining how different things might have been if she'd only cemented her relationship with him first.

But how *could* she have known that he would fall for Ann? It wasn't as if Ann were better looking or sexier than Elizabeth. In fact, Elizabeth was much prettier than Ann and always had been. And she'd certainly been more popular with men, so there was no way she could have been forewarned about what was going to happen that night. So Ann was an artist, and she could talk Logan's language. Big deal.

Yet from the moment Logan was introduced to Ann, it was as if Elizabeth did not exist. Elizabeth put a good face on it, though. What other choice did she have?

The following morning, when Ann asked if Elizabeth minded that Logan had asked her out, saying, "I won't go if you *do* mind." Elizabeth had laughed. "Why should I mind?" she'd said offhandedly. "It's not like I'm in *love* with him or anything. Why, I barely know him." Then, for good measure, because she'd *die* before allowing Ann to know how much she actually did care, she added, "I felt sorry for him, if you want to know the truth. He doesn't have many friends."

But she could have been in love with him. She could *easily* have been in love with him. It had hurt to see them together, and slowly, the love Elizabeth felt for Ann had corroded, to be replaced by resentment and envy.

She'd never let on, though. She'd played the part of the loving sister to perfection, because if Elizabeth was anything, she was proud.

Ann and Logan and their in-your-face happy marriage were the reason she'd married Cliff, a marriage that was predestined to be a disaster. They were also the reason that, in succeeding years, she'd continued to become involved in relationships that never had a chance of working.

No, she would not lose Logan again. Most people didn't get a second chance, but she had. So no matter what it took, this time she planned to win.

Three

"When are you taking Kendall to the doctor?"

Abbie, who had been stitching the hem of some yellow-and-white striped curtains she was making for the kitchen, looked up at her mother. Katherine stood a few feet away, one hip resting against the kitchen counter while she drank a glass of ice water. As always, she was impeccably dressed and made up.

"On Monday."

Katherine nodded thoughtfully. "Good. She might have mononucleosis, and that's nothing to fool around with."

"I know," Abbie said. *Or she might have something worse.* The fear she'd been trying to bury resurfaced as she guided the material carefully under the needle of the portable machine.

"And we definitely want her well for her interview with Lois Caldwell," Katherine continued.

Abbie let up on the pedal, and the sewing machine stopped. "Look, Mother," she said slowly, "I haven't made up my mind yet."

"What do you mean?"

Abbie suppressed a sigh. "I told you," she said patiently, determined not to lose her temper. "I purposely bought this house because it's close to Jefferson Middle School."

Katherine's eyes narrowed. "How you can even *think* of sending Kendall to a public school is beyond me. There's absolutely no comparison between Caldwell and the Houston public schools, and you know it. Why, the public schools don't even offer *art* in the lower grades."

"That's not true. Jefferson has a full-time art teacher. I checked."

"You checked! Well, I checked, too. That art teacher has to service all the grade levels. Each class gets two hours of her time per week. That's not exactly cutting edge, now is it?"

This time Abbie didn't try to stop herself from sighing. Her mother was obviously in her take-no-prisoners mode.

"Don't be difficult, Abbie. Kendall deserves the best, and Caldwell *is* the best. It's where Pamela went to school, and it's where you *should* have gone to school. Where you *would* have gone if your father hadn't been so hopeless when it came to money." Now Katherine's voice turned bitter, the way it always did when the conversation shifted to John Wellington, Abbie's charming but financially inept father.

"But thank goodness there's enough money to send Kendall to Caldwell," her mother finished triumphantly. Ten years ago, when Abbie's grandfather died, Katherine had inherited one-third of the Wellington estate, which, though not riches, was a comfortable nest egg for her. And the fact that she was willing to spend a good portion of it on Kendall— when most women her age would be worrying about their own futures—spoke volumes about her feelings for the child.

"It's not a question of money," Abbie said. "I'm certain, if I insisted, Thomas would pay her tuition. I'm just not sure I want Kendall in that kind of insulated environment." Abbie wanted her daughter to meet all kinds of people, from all kinds of backgrounds. In fact, in Abbie's opinion, that was one of the positive aspects of living in Houston, which had a large population of people from many different racial and cultural backgrounds.

Her mother set her glass down. "Just because you have the ridiculous idea it's somehow noble to mingle with the lower classes, do not hamstring your daughter's future opportunities by insisting she adhere to your misguided principles."

Abbie took a deep breath. She had always hated confrontation. But she couldn't let her mother's remarks pass. "I don't happen to believe my principles *are* misguided."

Katherine opened her mouth to answer, but Abbie forestalled her. "I'm not going to argue with you about this. It's my decision to make, and if I decide I want Kendall to go to public school, that's where she's going to go."

Katherine stared at her. Abbie prepared herself for the tirade she knew was coming, but she was saved by the sound of her daughter's footsteps in the hallway beyond.

"Hi, Gran," Kendall said with a happy smile as she entered the kitchen.

She looked better today, Abbie thought, but then, she'd slept more than ten hours last night.

Kendall walked over to her grandmother and gave her a hug. "I didn't know you were here."

The anger faded from Katherine's eyes. She smiled and hugged Kendall back. "Hello, sweetheart. I only got here a few minutes ago."

Abbie and her mother might differ about many things, but in this one area, they were in accord: they both loved Kendall with all their hearts and wanted only the best for her. Unfortunately, their ideas of what was best were sometimes poles apart.

"I was just telling your mother that I've set up an appointment for you with Lois Caldwell, the director of the Caldwell School," Katherine said, keeping a possessive arm around Kendall. Her eyes, as they met Abbie's, dared Abbie to say something derogatory.

Kendall's gaze had also flickered to Abbie. She was an intelligent child. Although Abbie hadn't made an issue of the subject, saying only she thought Kendall would be happier remaining in public school, Kendall obviously sensed the silent tug of war. Not wanting to place her daughter in the middle of her disagreement with her mother, Abbie simply smiled noncommittally.

"You will love the school," Katherine continued. "In fact, if you're not doing anything special right now, we could drive over and I could show you the grounds."

"Well, I was still unpacking," Kendall began uncertainly, looking at her mother again.

"The unpacking can wait," Katherine said. "You've got the rest of the summer."

"I know." She looked at Abbie again.

"Maybe afterwards, we can stop at the mall."

Kendall's eyes lit up. Unlike Abbie, she loved to shop. "Cool. Can I go, Mom? Please?"

Sometimes Abbie could have cheerfully strangled her mother. Stifling another sigh, she said, "Yes, you may go." She knew that by the time Kendall came home, the battle would probably be lost, and Kendall would be convinced that attending the Caldwell School was what she had wanted all along.

After Kendall and Katherine left, Abbie forced herself to finish the curtains and hang them, then she decided she might as well take advantage of her time alone and indulge herself with a long bubble bath and a much-needed pedicure.

She had just finished adding the bath crystals to the water and was starting to undress when the phone rang. She debated ignoring it, but it might be Charlotte Post, and Charlotte did not take kindly to being ignored. She was Abbie's major client, responsible for the lion's share of Abbie's income. A *New York Times* bestselling novelist whose books routinely sat in the number one position for weeks on end, Charlotte wrote lengthy sagas that kind reviewers had described as wordy soap operas and unkind reviewers had described as cliché-ridden opiates for semi-literate women. Charlotte told Abbie once that it never bothered her when reviewers disparaged her books. "Those that can, do," she said disdainfully, "and those that can't, review." Abbie had grinned, wondering if the Charlottes of the world—so self-possessed and confident, so sure of their own self-worth—were born that way. God knows, Abbie could have used a little more of those qualities.

When Charlotte was working on a book, she called Abbie anytime of the day or night, saying things like "Tomorrow I'll be in Berlin. I'll need everything you can get me on the city, especially the Wall." Then, if necessary, Abbie would work all night gathering every fact and figure she could find so that Charlotte would have enough material to work on the next day's scenes.

Charlotte wasn't supposed to be writing a book this summer, but she could have changed her mind. And she hated getting Abbie's answering machine.

Sighing, Abbie turned off the water and headed for the phone.

"Abbie! Hi! I was afraid I was going to get the machine."

Abbie smiled in relief. It wasn't Charlotte. Instead, the voice at the other end belonged to Laura Kaminsky, who, ever since high school, had been Abbie's best and dearest friend. "Hi. I didn't expect to hear from you until tomorrow. Are you still in San Francisco?"

"Nope. We finished a day early, so I came home. I missed Rich."

Laura was an auditor for an accounting firm in Chicago and traveled extensively She was recently engaged and very much in love, something she'd laughingly said she'd never thought would happen to her.

"So how are things going? You settled in the house yet?"

Abbie sat on the bed, leaning back against the headboard. "I still have some unpacking left to do, but nothing really important. Just pictures and photo albums and stuff like that."

"Well, that sounds like you've made good progress. And what about Kendall? Does she like the house?"

"She seems to."

"Is she still acting peaked?"

"Yes, I'm afraid so." Abbie went on to explain about the doctor's appointment.

"Good. I'm glad you're taking her to the doctor."

"Me, too."

"And what about Mommy Dearest?"

Abbie grimaced. "What about her?"

"You two getting along okay? Or has she already started browbeating you?"

"She's trying."

"What's it about this time?"

"Kendall. What else?"

"Listen, girl," Laura said when Abbie had finished telling her Katherine's ideas about the Caldwell School, "you stick to your guns. Because if you don't, if you let your mother have her way about this, you'll never win another battle again. And there *will* be more battles."

Abbie sighed. "I know."

"I wish you'd have come to Chicago instead of Houston."

Now Abbie smiled. "I know." Laura had done her darndest to persuade Abbie to move closer to her instead of back to her hometown.

They talked for at least thirty more minutes, catching up on everything that had happened since they'd last touched base. Finally, Laura said, "Well, I'd better go. Rich is coming over for dinner, and I have to go food shopping. You know, the way to a man's heart . . ." As always, at the mention of Rich, her voice took on a huskiness that Abbie envied.

"You already have his heart," Abbie pointed out.

"Sometimes I can hardly believe it."

Laura was one in a million. Big hearted, sensible, generous, kind, loyal. What she wasn't was beautiful or sexy, and for most of her life men hadn't been able to see beyond that lack of physical beauty. But Rich had. For that reason alone, Abbie knew she would like him. "Rich is the lucky one, you know."

Laura didn't say anything for a moment. "Oh, Abbie, I'm so happy. I want you to be happy, too. I wish you could meet somebody like Rich."

"I thought Rich was the most wonderful man in the world. I doubt there are two. Besides, I'm perfectly happy the way I am." That wasn't true, and she was certain Laura knew it. Abbie missed being married. She missed the closeness and the companionship. And, if she were being perfectly honest, she missed the sex. But what was the point of whining?

"Okay, okay, I'll mind my own business. And on that note, remember. Stand firm with your mother."

Later, Abbie thought about Laura's advice. It was good advice, but Abbie had a feeling it was the kind of advice that was easier said than done.

Katherine smiled in satisfaction as she steered her Cadillac expertly around the curves of lower Memorial Drive. "So what do you think, Kendall? Isn't the school just as beautiful as I said it was?"

Kendall nodded. "Uh huh. It seems like a *really* nice school."

"Believe me, sweetheart, you will be *much* happier there, among girls like you, than you would be at that other school." Katherine made sure her tone when she said *that other school* expressed her low opinion of it.

"But Mom said—"

"Your mother will change her mind," Katherine interrupted firmly. "Especially if she knows Caldwell is where you want to go." She reached over and patted Kendall's hand. "Now, don't you worry about it. Grandma will take care of everything."

She would certainly take care of Abbie. How she, Katherine Abigail Vickers Wellington, had ever given birth to such a daughter was one of the great mysteries of her life. For years, Katherine had secretly wondered if there could possibly have been a mistake made. Maybe she'd been given the wrong child in the hospital.

From day one, Abbie had been a trial to Katherine. As an infant, she'd been colicky and cried all the time. As a toddler, she'd been clingy and whiny, afraid of her own shadow. As a teenager, she'd been a bookworm, socially inept and uncommunicative. And as an adult . . . Katherine mentally rolled her eyes. As an adult, her daughter was impossible. Take the way she looked, for example. With a bit of effort, Abbie could be quite striking. After all, she had a lot to work with: lovely blond hair, good skin, nice features, and she was naturally slender. But would she make the effort? No. She rarely used makeup, she persisted in wearing her hair the same boring way she'd worn it for years, and she had abominable taste in clothes.

Kendall, however, was another story.

Katherine gritted her teeth. There was no way Katherine was going to let Abbie ruin Kendall's life the way she'd ruined her own.

Glancing over at her granddaughter's perfect profile, Katherine smiled. She had great plans for Kendall, and the Caldwell School was a crucial first step. It was so important that Kendall meet all the right girls from the best families. Why Abbie couldn't see how important this was, Katherine would never understand. Sometimes she thought her daughter purposely took the opposite side of any subject they discussed. Why this should be so, Katherine didn't know, but the reason didn't really matter. Because regardless of anything Abbie said, this was one argument Katherine intended to win.

Pushing Abbie from her mind, Katherine went back to the much more pleasant pastime of her plans for Kendall's future. After the child's graduation from Caldwell would come a glorious debut, which Katherine was perfectly prepared to pay for herself. Then just the right university, which would prepare Kendall for a brilliant career and an equally brilliant marriage.

Once more, Katherine glanced at her lovely granddaughter. Why not? Why shouldn't Kendall have it all? She was certainly beautiful and smart enough.

Katherine's heart swelled with pride. Kendall was everything Katherine had wanted to be herself. Everything Abbie *should* have been and wasn't. But none of that was of any consequence now. Finally—*finally!*—Katherine would show them all. Especially her oh-so-superior sister Marjorie. No longer would Katherine have to sit there during symphony board meetings and listen to Marjorie boast about Pamela and her accomplishments without having anything to say in return. Oh, it had galled Katherine to be forced to listen year after year while Marjorie gloated. To smile and pretend. To swallow her disappointment and envy.

But no more.

From now on things would be very different. Because Kendall, her darling Kendall, would shine brighter than all of the Wellingtons and Vickerses and Thayers put together. And nothing Abbie said or did was going to stop that from happening. Not so long as Katherine had one breath left in her body.

Two hours later, the Cadillac's trunk laden with packages from several of the Galleria's nicest stores, Kendall and her grandmother were headed back to Kendall's house. Right now her grandmother was talking to her mom on the cell phone she carried everywhere. From the conversation, Kendall could tell her grandmother was mad at her mother again.

A familiar ache swept through her. She wished her mom and her grandmother got along better. She loved both of them, and she hated it when they disagreed, especially when what they disagreed about had to do with her. Her mom and her grandmother were all the family she had, and she didn't like to make either one of them feel bad. Most of the time she tried as hard as she could to please them both, but this time, she knew somebody was going to be upset, because she couldn't go to both schools.

Now she felt disloyal to her mom, because she really *had* liked the looks of the Caldwell School. It was so beautiful, not like a school at all. The buildings were redbrick, and there were great big trees and all kinds of flowers around the grounds, and there was a huge activity area and soccer field. Kendall loved to play soccer. Most of the time she played forward, and she was really good at it. Last year, in Lucas, her team had won the district championship. She felt sure she could win a place on the Caldwell team.

And that wasn't all. Her grandmother had said the Caldwell School had a great art department. Although Kendall had lots of interests and enjoyed doing all kinds of things, drawing was her favorite activity. She already knew that when she grew up, she wanted to be an illustrator or a cartoonist. Maybe she could even get a job with the Disney studios. That would be so cool.

She also loved music, and her grandmother had said the Caldwell School had the best music department of all the schools in the city. The senior choir had won some kind of big competition last year and had gotten to go to Germany to perform. Kendall had sung in the children's choir at her church in Lucas, and it was lots of fun. Maybe, if she went to Caldwell, she could be in the junior choir.

If only her mom wouldn't feel bad about it if Kendall said she wanted to go to Caldwell. She frowned, thinking about the differences between the schools. The day before, her mom had driven her by Jefferson to show her where it was located. Yesterday, Jefferson had seemed fine, but today, comparing the plain brown building that sat in the middle of a lot with no trees and surrounded by a chain-link fence to the pretty school they'd just left, well, there wasn't any comparison.

Kendall sighed. She wished things could be simple. She wished her mom and her grandmother both wanted the same thing. Still, her grandmother had said not to worry, that she would take care of everything. Maybe that was best. Just leave everything to her grandmother. Decision made, she laid her head back and closed her eyes, a sudden weariness overtaking her. In minutes, she was sound asleep.

Four

Abbie heard the phone ringing when she opened her car door. Thinking it might be Nat Gabriel, her newest client, she grabbed her purse and raced across the garage and into the kitchen. The portable phone sat on the kitchen counter. She punched the Talk button and said a breathless hello.

"Abbie? It's Dr. Joplin."

"Oh. Dr. Joplin. Hi."

"Just wanted you to know the results of Kendall's blood tests have come back."

"Already?" It was only Wednesday, and he had said the results of the blood work might take as long as four or five days, depending on how backlogged the lab was.

"Yes, and it's what we thought. The test shows both her hemoglobin and hematocrit to be on the low side."

"Which means?"

"She's moderately anemic."

Abbie hadn't even realized she'd tensed at the sound of Dr. Joplin's voice until she felt her body relaxing in relief. "Thank goodness. I was worried it might be something much more serious."

"Yes, I was afraid you might be."

"I'm surprised though. I can't remember anyone in our family ever being anemic."

"Anemia isn't something you inherit, Abbie."

Abbie could almost hear the smile in his voice. She smiled sheepishly. "So what do we do about it?"

"Well, the most common cause of anemia is iron deficiency, so we'll start her on an iron supplement. You should also watch her diet, get her to eat as many iron-rich foods as you can. I'll have Janet mail you a list. Then, in about six weeks, bring her in again, and we'll do another blood test. Make sure her levels are up to where they should be."

"Okay, great. What about activities? I was about to find a dance teacher for her, and she's always been active in sports. Can she still do those things?"

"She can do anything she feels up to doing. I'd keep an eye on her for the first couple of weeks, though. Don't let her get overtired. Other than that, I see no reason to curb her activities. Now, where do you want me to have Janet call in the prescription?"

She gave him the number of the Walgreen's closest to their house.

"Now, don't worry about her, Abbie. She's going to be fine."

Abbie smiled. "I admit, I do feel much better. I know I'm kind of overprotective, but she's pretty special. You know, my only chick and all."

"Well, who can blame you? She's a lovely child."

"Thank you."

"I didn't realize she was adopted, though."

Abbie blinked. For a moment, she was speechless. "Wh-where in the world did you ever get that idea? Kendall isn't adopted."

He was silent for so long, fear snaked down her spine.

"You're saying you gave birth to her?" he finally said.

"Yes. Of course I gave birth to her!" Again there was silence. Abbie's heart began to beat faster. "Is . . . is there something wrong? I thought you said Kendall was just anemic."

"With any other patient, I probably wouldn't have known," he said slowly, "but because it's *you* and you gave blood to Martha that time when there was a shortage of type O blood—" He stopped abruptly. "I'm sorry. I know I'm talking in circles. I'm sure there's a logical explanation for this."

"Logical explanation for *what*?"

"Based on the results of Kendall's blood work—which show her to be type AB blood—it would be impossible for you, with your type O blood, to be her biological mother."

"What? What on earth are you talking about?" Abbie knew her voice had become shrill, but he wasn't making any sense. Of course she was Kendall's biological mother!

"Abbie, please calm down and listen for a minute, okay? In order for Kendall to have type AB blood, she had to get an A gene from one parent and a B gene from the other. Since you have neither, if this was *really* Kendall's blood type, she couldn't be your biological child. But since we know she *is,* there's nothing to be upset about. The lab must have made a mistake. Kendall's blood got mixed up with someone else's blood. It's never happened before, because this lab is very reliable, but I can't think of any other explanation."

Abbie expelled her breath. Of course. That was it. How silly of her to get upset. A mistake had been made. The lab had screwed up.

"It *is* an odd coincidence, though," Dr. Joplin continued thoughtfully, "that the blood analysis we *did* get showed anemia . . . since that's also what we suspect is Kendall's problem."

"I don't care how odd it seems." Abbie was beginning to get angry. "Kendall is my daughter. After all, I should know. I'm the one who labored for hours at that godforsaken hospital in the middle of a blizzard to bring her into the world."

"Now, Abbie, I didn't say you were wrong. I just said it's odd, that's all."

As quickly as it had come, her anger evaporated. This mixup wasn't Dr. Joplin's fault, so there was no sense in her getting mad at him. "What do we do now?" she said in a calmer voice.

"We need to take another blood sample. Can you bring Kendall to the office first thing in the morning?"

"She'll be there."

That night, Abbie couldn't sleep. She wasn't really worried. After all, she knew the truth. She *had* given birth to Kendall, so there was no reason to worry. Although, as Dr. Joplin had said, it *was* odd that the blood test results—belonging, as they did, to some other person—showed anemia, too, but coincidences happened all the time. This was just some crazy coincidence, that was all.

The next morning, telling Kendall that someone at the lab had messed up her blood test, Abbie drove her daughter to Dr. Joplin's office and watched while the nurse drew blood from Kendall's right arm.

"Good girl," the nurse said when she was finished. "Not even a whimper." She pressed a cotton ball against Kendall's arm, then raised it. "Hold your arm up a minute, hon, until I get a Band-Aid on it."

Abbie watched carefully as the nurse labeled the tube containing Kendall's blood. She wanted to make sure there were no problems this time around. Satisfied, she stood.

"We'll call you when the test comes back, Mrs. Bernard," the nurse said. "But it probably won't be until Monday."

It was difficult getting through the weekend without thinking about the blood test, because now Abbie once again had the nagging worry at the back of her mind that what was wrong with Kendall might be more serious than anemia. To take her mind off the problem, Abbie kept herself as busy as possible and, in the process, introduced Kendall to some of the attractions of Houston. They spent Saturday at the Contemporary Arts Museum, which Kendall loved. On Sunday, after church, they ate lunch at Chili's, another favorite place of Kendall's, then went to Tinseltown to see a movie. It was a good weekend, and Kendall even seemed a little perkier.

Even so, on Monday, Abbie was on pins and needles until, at three o'clock, Dr. Joplin's nurse called. "Mrs. Bernard?"

"Yes?"

"Dr. Joplin asked me to call you and see if you could stop by later this afternoon."

Abbie swallowed. "Stop by? Why? Is something wrong?"

"He said to tell you he'd just like to talk to you in person."

Abbie closed her eyes. Oh, God. Maybe Kendall had leukemia, and he didn't want to tell her on the phone. Her hand shook as she gripped the receiver tighter. "I, um, sure. Wh-what time should I be there?"

"His last appointment is at six. Could you come about six-thirty?"

For the next three hours, Abbie was a wreck. Thank God Kendall was spending the day with her grandmother, because Abbie knew she never would have been able to hide her anxiety from her daughter. "Please, please, God," she bargained, closing her eyes, "I'll never ask you for anything else if you'll just please let her be all right."

The hands of the clock seemed to crawl, but finally it was time to leave.

Her stomach felt queasy as she entered the doctor's office.

"C'mon back," Janet, the receptionist, said when Abbie rang the bell signaling her arrival.

A few minutes later, Abbie sat in Dr. Joplin's office, nervously twisting a tissue in her hands as she waited for him to join her.

Thankfully, she didn't have to wait long.

"Hello, Abbie," he said a few minutes later. He sat down behind his desk.

Abbie searched his face for a clue as to what he might be going to tell her. She wanted to know, yet she was afraid to ask. *Please, God . . .*

"Well, Abbie," he said, tenting his hands, "we've gotten the results of the second blood test."

Her throat was so dry, she had trouble speaking. "And?"

"And they are identical to the first test."

She licked her lips. "Which means?"

"Which means Kendall *is* anemic."

Abbie let out her breath.

"However . . ." He sighed heavily. "I don't know how to tell you this, Abbie, but there was no mistake with the first blood test. This second test shows the same thing. Kendall's blood type is definitely AB. And yours, as you know, is definitely O. I'm afraid the truth is irrefutable." His voice was gentle. "You cannot be Kendall's biological mother."

Abbie sat in stunned disbelief, his words spinning crazily in her head. *The truth is irrefutable. There was no mistake.*

You cannot be Kendall's biological mother. Her heart pounded. Her brain wanted to deny it. She wanted to shout at Dr. Joplin. Shout at the world. This wasn't true. It couldn't be true. She didn't care what Dr. Joplin said. There had to be some mistake.

And yet . . .

How many times had she marveled at the miracle of Kendall? How many times had she wondered how she, or Thomas, for that matter, had ever produced such a child?

She thought about Kendall's black hair. How no one in her family or Thomas's had hair of that color. She thought about Kendall's green eyes and her own light blue ones and Thomas's dark brown ones. She thought about Kendall's artistic talent. Her athletic ability. Her charm and vivaciousness. All so different from her parents.

"H-how could this be?" she finally managed to say. "I had a baby. I'm not crazy. Y-you can examine me. You'll see that I've had a child."

Dr. Joplin's eyes were soft with sympathy. "Abbie, my dear, I know you're not crazy, and I don't disbelieve you. I don't know how this happened. Is it possible that you somehow were given the wrong child? Where, exactly, was Kendall born?"

Abbie remembered the tiny hospital and the terrible storm that night. She remembered the poor, harried nurse who assisted in the delivery room and how shorthanded the hospital was. She also remembered how that very same nurse had died of a heart attack in the nursery that night. How thankful everyone was that nothing bad had happened to the unattended babies in the time between her fatal attack and the discovery of her body hours later.

Dr. Joplin listened quietly to her story. "And she was the only nurse on duty? Both in the delivery room and later, in the nursery?"

"I think so. Yes, I'm sure of it."

"And there were only two babies born that night?"

"Yes. Two . . . two girls, they said." *Oh, dear God.*

"Did you see Kendall right after she was born? Get to hold her or anything?"

Abbie slowly shook her head. "I-I saw her, but only for a

moment. The . . . the other woman, she was ready to deliver, and . . . the nurse, she had to go help out there. She said she'd bring the baby back after she'd had a chance to clean her up. But she didn't and they were so shorthanded and everyone was so tired, I hated to make a fuss. I thought . . ." She swallowed. "I thought, *It's okay. I'll see her in the morning, when everything's calmer.* I was . . . I was exhausted myself."

Bitterly, she remembered how Thomas had refused to stay with her that night. How he'd dumped her at the hospital and then gone to find a hotel or motel room, because they had been on the road—driving from a speaking engagement he'd had in Abilene—when she'd gone into labor two weeks earlier than she was supposed to.

Dr. Joplin twirled his gold Cross pen and stared off into space. "I can see how, under those circumstances, a mistake might be made."

"What am I going to do?" she whispered. Her mind churned crazily. She couldn't seem to take it all in. Kendall. Her Kendall. Not hers at all. She slumped back into her chair.

"I won't attempt to play God," Dr. Joplin said. "It's your daughter and your life. It's up to you what you do with this information."

For a long moment, neither spoke. Abbie looked down at her hands while she struggled to get her chaotic emotions under control.

"Abbie."

Slowly, she raised her eyes.

"Here." He held out a slip of paper. "This is a prescription for an iron supplement for Kendall."

Abbie had forgotten all about the anemia. Hand trembling, she took the prescription, stuffing it into her purse.

"Whatever you decide to do," the doctor said, "if you want my help, all you have to do is ask."

She nodded numbly.

"And Abbie? If you do decide not to say anything, you can count on me not to say anything, either."

Somehow Abbie whispered her thanks. Somehow she managed to walk out of his office without falling or making a spectacle of herself. And somehow she drove herself home without getting into an accident. But all of it was done in a daze, her only coherent thought thankfulness that Kendall was scheduled to spend the night with her grandmother, because there was no way she could have faced her daughter.

Her eyes filled with tears.

But Kendall *wasn't* her daughter. She belonged to someone else. Two someone elses.

Abbie slept little that night. Over and over, she struggled to cope with the shattering knowledge that Kendall, her beloved Kendall, was not really hers at all.

What was she going to do?

How could she ever tell Kendall?

And her mother!

Abbie shuddered. Dear God. Her mother. Katherine would be devastated. Completely devastated. She thought the sun rose and set in Kendall.

I can't. I just can't do it. I can't tell them.

On and on her thoughts whirled.

Toward dawn, she reached a decision.

Dr. Joplin had said whether she disclosed the truth or not was her decision. So if she said nothing, no one ever had to know. She and Kendall could go on just the way they had been for the last eleven years.

Yes, she thought just before dropping into an exhausted sleep, that's what she would do. After all, wasn't Kendall her daughter in all the ways that really mattered?

Five

"Logan?"

Logan propped the portable phone on his shoulder while he continued to shade the final pen-and-ink drawing of a new recreation center that he had designed for a local church. "Hey, Glenna. You're back." His sister, a family therapist, had been attending a conference in Boston over the weekend. "How was it?"

"Actually, quite good. There were some valuable workshops."

"Why are you back so soon? I thought you were going to go up to the Vineyard and visit Marianne." Marianne Braun was Glenna's college roommate and lived on Martha's Vineyard. The two women tried to spend time together at least once a year.

"I was, but Megan had one of her allergy attacks, and you know how hopeless Paul is about that kind of stuff. I figured before everything fell to pieces, I'd better get home. I can see Marianne another time."

Logan shook his head in amusement. Glenna's husband was one of the nicest men he'd ever met, but he was the stereotypical absentminded professor who couldn't cope with everyday life. Logan considered it one of the great ironies that his super-organized, super-anal older sister had married someone so completely her opposite. But maybe those differences were the major attraction between them.

Maybe super-anal people needed a partner they could take care of.

"Anyway," she went on, "I'm home, and Megan's back on track."

"What was it this time?"

"We're not sure." There was an undercurrent of worry in her voice. "I just hope she doesn't have to go through the allergy testing again."

Logan made a commiserating sound.

"So how's Erin?"

He laid his pen down and leaned back in his chair. "She's much better, too. Back at Mom's this week."

"When does Serita return?"

"Next week."

They talked a few more minutes, then Glenna said, "I'm going home early today, making a big pot of chili. You want to bring the kids and join us for dinner? Kevin and Debbie are coming." Kevin was one of Logan's brothers. The other two, Regan and Tim, lived in Los Angeles and Denver, respectively.

"Sure. That sounds great."

"We'll have appetizers about six, let the kids swim for a while, then eat, okay? But come as early as you like."

"All right. We'll try to get there by five."

He was just about to hang up when she said, "Um . . . Logan? Do you want me to invite Elizabeth?"

He frowned. "What brought that on? Why would I want you to invite Elizabeth?" He knew he sounded irritated, but damn it, her question *had* irritated him.

She hesitated for a moment. "No special reason. It just seemed as if you were spending a lot of time with her, and I thought you might want her included." She was now talking in her soothing let's-not-get-excited therapist's tone.

"Well, I don't."

"Okay. No problem," she said breezily. "See you later."

After they had hung up, Logan swiveled his chair around and stared out his window. At fifteen floors up, he had a great view of the surrounding area. His office building was located near Woodway on Post Oak Lane, which still retained quite a few of the trees that had given it its name.

Damn. He'd thought only Erin and Elizabeth were thinking in terms of a different kind of relationship between him and his sister-in-law. Now it was obvious other people were thinking along those lines, too. Well, he'd just have to set his sister straight and tell her to pass the word along to anyone else who might be speculating that Elizabeth was on her way to becoming the next Mrs. O'Connell. He'd been right when he'd decided it was time to do something about the situation, because if he didn't, if he just coasted along, things would only get worse.

While he mulled over possibilities, his phone rang again. Almost as if she'd known she was in his thoughts, it was Elizabeth calling this time. "Where were you last night?" she said immediately after greeting him. "I stopped by and no one was home."

"I took the kids out to eat."

"Oh. I wish I'd known. I would have loved to go with you. I haven't seen the kids in nearly a week." Her voice carried just the right amount of wistfulness.

Logan's jaw clenched. He wondered if she practiced her intonations, if they were cleverly designed to make him feel guilty. He immediately regretted the unkind thought. Elizabeth might be hopeful regarding their relationship, but she had never given him any reason to think she was calculating.

"It was a spur-of-the-moment thing," he said.

"Well, how about tonight? Why don't you bring the kids over and we can order in some Chinese or pizza? I have that new Playstation they've been talking about."

"Thanks, Elizabeth. We can't. We've already got plans."

"Oh?"

Logan knew she expected him to elaborate, but in his new determination to steer their relationship back toward a more casual footing, he kept silent.

She sighed. "Oh, well . . . Guess I'll have to wait until this weekend."

"This weekend," he repeated, puzzled. "What's going on this weekend?"

"Now, Logan, don't tell me you forgot Mom's birthday?"

Damn. He *had* forgotten Celia Chamberlain's birthday. "Yeah, afraid so," he admitted. "Thanks for reminding me."

"I planned to shop for her gift tomorrow. Want me to get something for you to give her?"

"No, that's not necessary."

"I know it's not necessary. I want to do it. I know you're awfully busy, and I don't mind helping out."

"You're busy, too," he pointed out. "We've been taking advantage of you, and it's got to stop. It's time for the kids and me to stand on our own two feet."

"You're not taking advantage of me! I love—"

"Elizabeth," he interrupted, "I appreciate everything you've done, but I'm serious about this. We have to learn to get along on our own sometime." And then, before she could object and therefore prolong the discussion, he added, "But thanks for the offer. Listen, I've got a meeting in five minutes, so I've got to hang up. See you this weekend."

He had a hard time ridding his mind of the problem of Elizabeth, especially after her phone call, but he finally managed to get his concentration back where it belonged and kept it there until four o'clock, when he began to clear his desk in preparation for leaving.

Just as he was ready to walk out the door, a phone call came from Jasper Hendrickson, president of the local chapter of the American Institute of Architects. Logan grimaced with frustration. Hendrickson was a windbag. Normally Rebecca, Logan's secretary, would have fielded his call, but she was out sick today, and the temp didn't know any better and put Hendrickson through. So it was almost five before Logan drove his BMW out of the underground garage and headed toward his mother's house.

He found Erin and Patrick waiting impatiently.

"Finally," Erin said.

"I thought you were coming home early," Patrick said. "We've been ready for an hour."

"I know. I'm sorry. Let me just go say hi to Gran, and we'll be on our way."

Logan found his mother rolling out piecrust dough in the kitchen. At his entrance, she looked up and smiled. "Hi, Mom," he said, walking over and kissing her cheek. Faint traces of Beautiful, her favorite perfume, clung to her skin, which, at sixty-four, was remarkably youthful looking.

"The kids give you a hard time about being late?"

"Not too bad." He studied her affectionately. Mary Margaret O'Connell was a throwback to a different age. Plump and motherly, she had never worked outside the home, had without complaint raised five children, and seemed completely contented with her life.

"What are you looking at?" she said, dark blue eyes twinkling. "Do I have flour on my nose?"

In answer, he gave her another kiss. "No flour. You look gorgeous, as usual."

"Oh, go on with you." She swatted at him, but he could see the compliment pleased her.

"See you tomorrow," he said, waving good-bye.

Glenna and Paul and their totally unexpected but much-adored chick, Megan, who would turn five in August, lived only fifteen minutes from the senior O'Connells, in an old established Memorial neighborhood deep in the wooded area off Piney Point Boulevard. Their home, which had been built in the early sixties, was a solid brick ranch style with hardwood floors, higher than average ceilings, and lots of charm. Glenna loved it and spent long hours gardening and puttering in the yard. She said working with dirt and plants relaxed her and made her forget about the stresses of her work.

Logan smiled as he pulled into the circular drive in front and saw the "Yard of the Month" sign. If he wasn't mistaken, that was the second time this year his sister's home had been so honored. Pine needles crunched underneath the tires as he slowed to a stop and parked. Megan must have been watching through the big front window, because the front door opened before the car doors closed.

"Uncle Logan! Patrick! Erin!" Megan's impish face wore a huge grin as she rushed forward to fling herself first at Logan, then at Patrick, who was her favorite. Her dark pigtails, tied with bright blue ribbons to match the trademark O'Connell eyes, bounced as Patrick swung her around, saying, "Hello, stinky."

"I'm not stinky!" she shrieked, but she clearly loved his teasing.

Logan's eyes met Erin's. They both smiled.

A few minutes later, all four were outside on the shaded deck, where Paul was doing bartender honors and Glenna was bustling about, setting out a bowl of queso dip and chips and a tray of cut up vegetables and yogurt dip. Everyone greeted everyone, with much hugging and kissing, and for the second time that day, Logan thought how much he loved his family and how lucky he was to have them. "Where're Kevin and Debbie?" he said.

"They'll be here," Glenna said. "Debbie couldn't get away early." Debbie was a lawyer who worked for a big firm downtown.

After changing into their bathing suits, the kids stuffed their mouths with chips, then raced to the pool.

"Don't run!" Glenna and Logan said at the same time.

While the kids frolicked in the water, the three adults sat in cushioned chrome deck chairs and slowly drank the margaritas Paul had made. "Good margaritas," Logan said.

"Thanks," Paul said. "Making margaritas is one thing I do well, at least." He looked at his wife.

Glenna gave him a fond smile. "You do many things well."

Paul shrugged. "You only say that because you love me."

"Darn right I do." She leaned over, and they kissed.

Logan had to look away. The kiss wasn't much as kisses go. Just a quick peck—the kind of kiss that said *I love you, and you know it, so we don't have to make a big deal of it out here in public,* but nevertheless, it was painful to watch, because Logan no longer had someone with whom to share that kind of kiss. He no longer had someone with whom to share any kind of kiss. He wondered if he would ever be able to witness another couple's love and devotion without feeling this gnawing emptiness inside.

Thank God for the children, he thought, determinedly turning his mind to the positive aspects of his life. Especially Erin. He loved Patrick wholeheartedly, but Patrick didn't need him the way Erin did. Patrick was self-confident and would soon be self-sufficient. Already, at thirteen, he was showing signs of becoming more and more independent. It wouldn't be long before he would be off to college and on his own. But Erin was different. She was vulnerable, the kind of child who needed a lot of encouragement and support.

He watched her now, hanging back, the way she always did. Patrick and Megan, kindred spirits, were noisy and aggressive. They splashed each other and tried to duck each other, Megan holding her own even though she was so much younger. Erin laughed at their antics, but rather than participate, she watched.

He wondered if she would be different if Ann had lived, or if her lack of self-confidence was an ingrained thing, something she'd been born with and would have to work to overcome. Then again, what did it matter why she was the way she was? Probably she *would* be different if Ann had lived, because he was sure the trauma of her mother's death had at least exacerbated the problem. But cause wasn't important. What *was* important was working to keep her life as stress-free as possible and continuing to praise and encourage her, so that eventually she would develop pride and confidence and become the kind of woman he knew she could be. *I won't let her down,* he vowed.

"You certainly are quiet tonight," Glenna said, breaking into his thoughts.

"Oh, sorry," he said.

"Is something wrong?" His sister's eyes, more green than blue, were altogether too shrewd behind her black-framed glasses.

"No. What makes you say that?"

Glenna shrugged. "I don't know. You just seemed so serious."

"That's what happens when your sister is a psychologist," Paul interjected. "She's constantly studying you. Like a bug under a microscope."

Logan smiled. He knew Paul was giving him an out if he didn't want to talk about what was on his mind. But suddenly he did. "I was thinking about the kids. About whether or not they'd be different if Ann had lived. Especially Erin."

Glenna nodded thoughtfully, her gaze turning toward the

children. "That's one of those things it's impossible to know for sure, but given the kind of woman Ann was, I'm sure she would have been a strong influence on Erin." Then she turned to Logan and smiled. "But you're doing a wonderful job with her."

"I'm trying."

They were silent for a while. Then Glenna said softly, "Do you think you'll marry again?"

"I don't know. I've been thinking about it lately," Logan admitted. "Trouble is, I compare every woman to Ann, and nobody measures up." Their eyes met, and Logan knew both he and his sister were thinking about Elizabeth. "I'm not sure anyone ever will."

Glenna reached over and squeezed his forearm. "You just haven't met the right person yet."

Logan nodded, but he wasn't convinced. Finding someone who could love and accept his children and whom they could love and accept in return might be an impossible task. He might do well to resign himself to being single, at least until the children were grown, because their happiness and well-being was the most important thing in his life and always would be.

Suddenly tired of thinking about the subject, he attempted to change it by saying, "Know what? I need another margarita."

By the time Paul had poured Logan another drink, Kevin and Debbie had arrived, and the subject of Logan's love life was dropped. But at odd moments throughout the evening, Logan caught Glenna studying him speculatively, and he suspected she was still thinking about their discussion.

His suspicion was confirmed as they were saying their good-byes. She hugged him the way she always did and said sotto voce, "If you want to talk, you can always call me."

"Thanks."

But he knew he wouldn't call her. There was nothing she could say or do to change things. The void in his life was his problem, just as Elizabeth was his problem. And when you came right down to it, what was the big deal, anyway? He was making mountains out of molehills.

After all, he and the kids were doing okay. Yes, they all missed Ann, and he guessed they always would, but they'd survived. And they would continue to survive. The important thing was that they were a family, and together they could and would lick anything.

Six

Somewhere a baby cried. The sound was soft, mewling, frightened. Abbie desperately wanted to go to her. To pick her up and cuddle her. To tell her everything would be all right. That she wasn't alone anymore. That Abbie would take care of her, now and always.

But something held her back. Abbie fought against the restraints, yet she couldn't break away, no matter how hard she tried. As she struggled, the baby's cries grew fainter and fainter, until they disappeared completely.

Abbie awakened with an aching sense of loss, just as she had for the past three mornings. It was Wednesday, two agonizing days since her world had been thrown into chaos.

Her bedroom was still dark, the only light coming from the red glow of her digital clock. She glanced at it. 4:35. Two hours before she normally started her day. Sighing, she closed her eyes, although she knew she would not go back to sleep.

The memory of her dream drifted in her mind. It didn't take a brain surgeon to figure out what it meant. "My baby," she whispered. Tears seeped from under her closed eyelids.

On Monday, her decision not to tell anyone about the mistaken switching of the two babies had seemed like the right thing to do. The only thing to do. And as far as Kendall and Abbie's mother were concerned, it was still the right thing, Abbie was sure of it.

But every time she thought about the other baby, the baby of her flesh and blood, she felt a gnawing emptiness and was riddled by uncertainty—an uncertainty that was rapidly becoming unbearable. If only Abbie knew where her child was. If she was happy. If her home was a loving one, with parents who cared for her.

Abbie thought of all the cases of child abuse she'd read about in the past ten years. They were so horrifying. What if her daughter was in an abusive situation? It was possible. Anything was possible.

Oh, God. She had to stop this. She was making herself crazy. Sitting up, she reached for her cotton robe which hung from the newel post at the foot of the bed. Taking care not to make any undue noise—she did not want to wake Kendall, who slept in the next bedroom—she walked into her bathroom, snapped on the light, and splashed cold water on her face. For a moment, she stared at herself in the bathroom mirror.

She looked awful. Pale and haggard. As if she were sick. Which wasn't so far from the truth. She *was* sick. Heartsick. Closing her eyes, she massaged her temples, where a dull pain augured the beginnings of a headache.

How unfair life could be! Why was it that innocent people were so often hurt? As always, there was no answer to this question. Wearily, she opened her eyes, shut off the light, and headed toward the kitchen.

Fifteen minutes later, having downed two Advil and a glass of apple juice, she walked outside with a mug of fresh coffee and stood on her back deck. This deck and the yard beyond were two of the three main reasons she had bought this particular house, which was located in an older west side neighborhood, instead of one of the dozens of others the realtor had shown her. The other two reasons were the larger-than-normal third bedroom, which Abbie had set up as her office, and the proximity of the middle school she planned for Kendall to attend.

The deck extended twelve feet into the yard and was encircled by a waist-high railing dotted with flower boxes that spilled over with impatiens, pansies, and phlox. Built-in benches ran along each side, and the entire deck was shaded by a slatted wooden roof that filtered the sunlight and would keep the deck cooler and pleasant even in the hottest months.

At the moment, moonlight slanted across the surface of the redwood, which shone with dew. Stepping carefully in her bare feet, Abbie walked to the far railing. In the predawn quiet, she could hear the rustlings of the mockingbirds and doves who hung out in the big camphor tree that shaded two-thirds of the yard, and farther away the hum of a neighbor's air-conditioner. Somewhere in the distance, the faint wail of a siren punctuated the air.

The breeze felt pleasant against her bare arms. Abbie guessed the temperature to be in the low seventies, although the forecast predicted that later it would climb into the nineties.

She slowly sipped her coffee, unsuccessfully trying to keep her mind from returning to the subject that had consumed it the past few days.

"All right," she muttered. "If you have to think about this, try to think logically, the way you do when you're researching a subject, instead of emotionally, the way you have been."

She knew her decision to keep this horrendous mistake a secret was the most sensible course, because to expose what happened the night the babies were born would tear too many lives apart. If only she could leave her decision intact and go on with her life.

The trouble was, after the torture she'd gone through the past couple of days—a torture that showed no signs of abating—she knew she couldn't.

The bottom line was, she had to know about her daughter. She had to know the child was all right or she would never be able to rest again.

Be honest. It's more than knowing. You need to see her. You need to know what she's like.

Was it possible to do that—to see her—without telling anyone? Could Abbie find out where her child was, what she was like, if she was happy, without anyone knowing?

For the first time in days, something besides anguish and pain stirred in her veins. Slowly, a plan began to form. She remembered how the weekly paper in Lucas used to list all the local births, including the exact time each baby was born.

She'd be willing to bet the Hurley paper was the same way. It should be a simple matter to find out the names of the babies born at Hurley General that night.

Suddenly, she was excited and felt better than she'd felt in days. She wished it wasn't so early or she would go inside and call the newspaper immediately. Now that she'd made the decision to do so, she didn't want to wait another minute.

But wait she did. At nine, showered and dressed for the day, she headed to her office.

Five minutes later, armed with the newspaper's number from Directory Assistance, Abbie punched it in.

"Hurley Herald," drawled a young female voice. "How may I direct your call?"

Abbie had thought about what she would say before calling. "I'm not sure," she said. "I need some information that would have appeared in your paper about eleven years ago."

"Oh, okay. I'll let you talk to Janie. She's the editor. She can help you."

A few moments later, another young female voice said, "This is Janie."

"Hi, Janie. My name is Gail Wellington, and I'm a freelance writer." None of that was really a lie, Abbie rationalized. She *had* written a couple of articles when she and Thomas were married, and Wellington was her maiden name. "I'm doing an article about the hospital there in Hurley, and part of it will concentrate on that big blizzard you all had back in February of eighty-seven and how the hospital personnel handled the crisis."

"I'm sorry, Miss Wellington, but we can't afford to buy freelance—"

"No, no," Abbie interjected, "that's not why I'm calling. I just need some information."

"What kind of information?"

"I need to know the names of all the babies born that night."

"Oh, okay. That should be easy enough. Can you give me the exact dates?"

"February seventh and February eighth."

"Hold on a minute. I'll pull the paper for that week."

Long minutes went by. Finally, Janie came back to the phone. "Here we go," she said. Abbie could hear papers rustling. "There weren't many. Two on February seventh. Two on February eighth."

Abbie's heart beat faster.

"Ready?" Janie said.

"Yes."

"On February seventh at ten-forty A.M. a boy was born to Mr. and Mrs. Cole MacAllister. The second baby was a girl and was born late that night, at eleven fifty-eight P.M., to Mr. and Mrs. Thomas Bernard."

Abbie held her breath.

"On February eighth, the first baby arrived at twelve-fifteen A.M. A girl, born to Mr. and Mrs. Logan O'Connell."

The last baby was a boy, and he wasn't born until the evening of the eighth. Abbie didn't even bother writing down the information. She already had what she needed.

After thanking the helpful Janie and hanging up, Abbie attempted to bring her breathing and heartbeat back to normal. She stared at the paper she held in her trembling hand. *O'Connell.* The name would be forever branded in her brain.

Taking a deep breath to steady herself, she once more called Directory Assistance. It didn't surprise her that there was no listing for a Logan O'Connell in Hurley, but it did disappoint her. After hanging up, she thought a few minutes, then flipped through her Rolodex until she found the name she wanted. Quickly, she dialed the number. It rang only twice before it was answered.

"Bob? Hi. This is Abbie Bernard. We met at that seminar in Florida last October. I'm the one who works for Charlotte Post."

"Oh, yeah, sure. Hi, Abbie. How ya doin'?"

"I'm doing fine, but I really need a favor. You told me your group can find anyone anywhere?"

"Yep. That's what we do."

"Well, I desperately need to find this man and his wife. A Mr. and Mrs. Logan O'Connell." She told him about the birth of their child and the fact that they weren't listed in the Hurley directory. "I know it's not much information to go on."

"Hey, I've started with less."

"If you can't find out where they are now, at least try to find out where they lived when they had the baby."

"Okay, let me see what I can do. I'll get back to you."

It was the following morning before she heard from him.

"I've got what you wanted," he said.

Abbie swallowed.

"Your guy lives in Houston. He's an architect. Got a company listed in the phone directory."

After giving Bob her grateful thanks, Abbie unearthed the business section of the Houston phone directory. Sure enough. There it was. "Logan O'Connell, architect." Her heart beat harder as she stared at the name. His office address was on Post Oak Lane in the Galleria area. From where Abbie lived, that was only about a twenty-minute drive. Incredible. Who would have ever guessed that the O'Connells lived in Houston? Abbie marveled at the vagaries of fate.

Tapping her pencil against the directory, she thought about contacting Logan O'Connell at work but decided against it. That would be a last resort, because if she *did* contact him at work, she might not be able to finagle a way to see his home. To see her daughter.

Mentally crossing her fingers, Abbie found the residence section of the telephone directory and looked up O'Connell. There were a lot of them listed, but no Logan. There was one L. O'Connell, though. Abbie looked at the address, then got out her key map. Just as she'd thought, the address was way across town. She couldn't imagine that the L. O'Connell listed was the one she wanted, but it was best to be sure. She would call.

"Hello?" It was a young female voice.

Abbie's heart skipped. Could she be talking to her daughter? "May I speak with Logan, please?" Abbie managed to say in a voice that *sounded* calm, although she was anything but.

"Who?"

"Logan. Logan O'Connell. Isn't this his number?"

"Nuh uh. You've got the wrong number."

"I'm sorry to have bothered you," Abbie said, trying to quell her disappointment.

It looked as if she was going to have to call his office whether she wanted to or not. She picked up the phone again.

"Logan O'Connell's office," said a cheery voice.

"This is Abbie Bernard. May I speak with Mr. O'Connell, please?" Abbie had decided a businesslike approach was best, and she willed her voice to sound forceful, even though her palms were sweating and her heart was back to beating its erratic tattoo.

"I'm sorry, Miss Bernard. Mr. O'Connell is working at home today. Would you like his voice mail?"

"No," Abbie said in the tone her mother always used when she wanted something, "I need to speak with him *immediately*. Otherwise, I might just have to contact another architect for the job I have in mind. Let me have his home number, please."

The woman hesitated a moment, then gave Abbie the number.

After they'd hung up, Abbie pulled out her cross-reference directory, the one that matched phone numbers with the corresponding address. After that, it was easy enough to use her key map and discover that the address was in Hunter's Creek Village, about fifteen minutes from her home.

She looked at the map thoughtfully. Hunter's Creek Village was a wealthy enclave in the exclusive Memorial area of Houston. Abbie guessed there wasn't a property in the village worth less than three-quarters of a million dollars. So. The O'Connells obviously had money. For just an instant, doubt surfaced. Quickly, she banished it. Just because they had money didn't mean their home was a good one. Plenty of well-to-do people had dysfunctional—or worse—families. In fact, many times money caused more problems than it alleviated.

She picked up the phone again.

She took several deep breaths. There was no reason to be frightened. After all, she was the one in control here. She was the one who would make the decision. She did not have to say anything about her belief that Kendall and the child the O'Connells had raised had somehow been switched in the hospital nursery—unless she wanted to. First things first, anyway. What she needed to concentrate on now was getting an interview.

Calm now, she punched in the number. After several rings, an answering machine picked up. A man's pleasant voice said, "This is Logan O'Connell. At the tone, leave a message."

Abby hung up. She had suddenly realized it would be too easy for the O'Connells to say no to an interview if she made her request via the telephone. The thing to do was to go to their home, because it would be much harder to refuse her if she were standing there on their doorstep.

"Mom?"

Abbie started guiltily. A sleepy-eyed Kendall stood in the doorway. "Hi, sweetie. I didn't hear you get up."

Kendall yawned. "What're you doing? Working?"

"Yes," Abbie lied smoothly. "But I'm done now. Are you hungry? I could make you some pancakes for breakfast."

"Okay."

As the two walked to the kitchen, Abbie said, "Honey, I've got something I need to take care of today, something that can't wait, so after breakfast, I'm going to call Grandma and see if you can spend a few hours with her. Is that all right with you?"

Kendall nodded. "Sure. I like going to Gran's."

Later, when Abbie phoned her mother, Katherine was agreeable. "The only thing is," she said, "I'm getting my hair done this morning. How about this afternoon?"

Now that Abbie had a name and address, she didn't want to wait an hour, let alone half a day. But it didn't look as if she had a choice. "This afternoon is fine. I'll have her there at one."

Seven

"Ready?" Elizabeth asked.

After two postponements, she and Erin were finally going on their shopping trip. As it was, Elizabeth had had to juggle several other commitments to free up the day. But that was okay, because her relationship with Erin was a pivotal element in Elizabeth's campaign to become a permanent part of the O'Connell family. And, of course, she loved Erin, too.

Erin adored her; Elizabeth knew that. She also knew Erin wanted Elizabeth and Logan to marry. And Elizabeth reinforced that idea every chance she got. So this outing was not a hardship. It was an investment in Elizabeth's future.

Erin nodded happily. "I've been ready since nine o'clock."

"Yes, she has," Logan agreed. He started to ruffle Erin's hair, then stopped when she pulled away in alarm. "Sorry. I forgot. Girls don't like to get their hair messed up."

Erin's hair looked nice, Elizabeth saw with satisfaction. She'd been right to encourage the girl to get it cut short. When you had fine hair, it was a mistake to wear it too long. Or to wear it tapered the way Erin had been wearing it. Cut the way it was now—blunt and a swingy chin length—was perfect for Erin's face. As Elizabeth had suggested, Erin had pulled the sides up and back, and they were held by one of those big hair clips with teeth—*hair clutches* Elizabeth thought they were called—that the kids seemed to favor nowadays. This one was red to match Erin's red shirt. Unfortunately, the red wasn't terribly complimentary, because Erin's face was sunburned. In fact, her nose had started peeling. "When did you get the sunburn?"

"At Patrick's soccer game on Saturday," Erin said. "Dad forgot to bring sunscreen."

"I swear, you two need a woman around here," Elizabeth said with an amused smile.

"Serita will be back on Monday," Logan said.

Elizabeth gave him an arch look. He knew perfectly well she hadn't meant Serita. *You can run away from me all you like, Logan, but I'm not giving up.* "Where *is* Patrick?"

"He had an all-day swim meet."

"And you're working at home today?"

"Yes."

"Give your mother the day off?"

He nodded. "She had a doctor's appointment this afternoon."

"If you want to go into the office, I can stay with Erin this afternoon. In fact, how about this? On the way home I'll pick up some salmon or scallops and I'll cook dinner for everyone."

"Thanks, but that's not necessary. I like working at home once in a while. It's quiet. Anyway, I'm sure you must have work to do yourself."

"Nothing that can't wait until tomorrow."

"Why don't we wait until you two get back, then we'll see," he said. "Maybe we can all go out to dinner."

Now that her objective had been accomplished, Elizabeth smiled happily. "Okay, Erin, let's go. We've got a lot to do."

Logan stood at the door and watched as Elizabeth backed her Mercedes out of the driveway. He waved, then closed the door and walked back to his office, which occupied part of the right wing. His home was built in a U shape around an inner courtyard—a style he had always liked. The courtyard was paved in Mexican tiles and had a central fountain. A covered walkway extended around the entire U, in the manner of the Spanish haciendas he had seen in Barcelona and Madrid. Baskets of begonias and bougainvillea hung at intervals, and big clay pots filled with dozens of seasonal flowers dotted the sheltered enclosure.

During the year Ann was so sick, and afterward, when she was gone and Logan was trying to cope with her loss, his home had been his haven, its beauty a balm to his battered heart. Even now, when he no longer needed to hide from the world, he found it easier to think, especially when he was troubled, in its tranquil setting.

He stood in his office and looked out, his mind on Elizabeth. It was obvious his attempts to discourage her weren't working. Whether her failure to understand his message was deliberate or not, he couldn't tell. Sometimes he thought she knew perfectly well what he was trying to tell her. Other times, he wasn't so sure.

"Damn," he muttered. He was sick of the problem and wished it would just go away. But he sure didn't intend to ruin his day thinking about it. Since Ann's death he so rarely had a day alone, he intended to make the most of this one. That decided, he gave his full attention to the house plans now spread across his drawing table. Within minutes, he was fully engrossed.

Much later, the gnawing in his stomach alerted him to the fact that it must be lunchtime. He glanced at his watch, amazed to see it was after two. He'd been working steadily for more than four hours without a break.

He laid down his pen and stretched, rolling his head to relieve the sore muscles in his neck and shoulders. With the movement, Rex, who had curled up in a patch of sunlight near Logan's work area, stirred and opened a sleepy eye.

"Hey, boy," Logan said. "I'm starving. How about you?"

The dog made a sound halfway between a growl and a yawn.

"Well, let's go get something to eat."

Rex thumped the floor with his tail, then slowly unfolded himself and followed Logan across the hall to the kitchen. Logan filled the dog's food bowl first, then, chuckling because Mitzi, not to be outdone by the dog, had magically appeared in front of her bowl, shook some dry cat food into hers, too. Once the animals were contentedly eating, he opened the refrigerator and rooted around while he tried to decide what he felt hungry for.

He had just finished making himself a ham sandwich

when the doorbell rang. He frowned. He wasn't expecting anyone, so it was probably some sales type who had ignored the signs posted at the end of the street saying no soliciting was allowed. Well, he'd make short work of them.

With the dog following closely at his heels, Logan headed for the front door. The glass side panel revealed a tall blond woman standing on the doorstep, wearing a navy blue suit and carrying a briefcase. An Avon lady? Did they still sell Avon door to door? For just a minute, he considered turning around and ignoring her, but his innate good manners wouldn't let him.

He opened the door. "Yes? May I help you?"

She stared at him.

"May I help you?" he repeated more slowly. What was wrong with her?

"I . . . ," she began. She cleared her throat. "Sorry. I'm Abbie Bernard. And you must be Logan O'Connell." She shifted her briefcase to her left hand and held out her right.

Because Logan was a gentleman, he took it. Was he supposed to know her?

"I'm a freelance writer," she continued, smiling, "doing a story for *Lone Star Monthly* about Cyrus Hurley Hospital. The story is in commemoration of the hospital's fiftieth anniversary. Part of it will focus on the big blizzard of '87 and how it affected the hospital."

If she had stopped for breath, he would have told her he wasn't interested, but she barreled on.

"I know you had a daughter born there that night, and I wanted to get your take on the situation and maybe even—"

Now he *did* interrupt. "Look, if you'd called me first, I could have saved you a trip. I'm busy and I—"

"Oh, please don't say no. I promise it won't take long."

"I really am very busy right now." He started to shut the door.

"Well, if you don't have time to talk to me, maybe your wife . . . ?" The question hung in the air.

As always, at the unexpected mention of Ann, he felt a pang. "My wife died three years ago."

"Oh. I . . . I'm so sorry."

Her eyes, pretty light blue eyes—about the same shade

as Erin's, in fact—had softened in sympathy, as had her voice. For the first time since he'd opened the door, Logan took a good look at her. She was a nice-looking woman, slender and fine boned, with delicate features. Not beautiful, but attractive in an understated, quiet kind of way. It was obvious she'd tried hard to make herself look businesslike in her tailored suit, white blouse, and sensible low-heeled pumps. Logan almost smiled. Her efforts weren't entirely successful. In some way he couldn't have explained, she reminded him of a child playing dress-up.

Impulsively, he opened the door wider, hoping he wouldn't be sorry for this decision later. "Tell you what. I was just about to have lunch. If you don't mind watching me eat while we talk, I can give you thirty minutes or so."

"I don't mind at all." She smiled gratefully and followed him indoors.

Logan took her into the living room and gestured her to one of the comfortable chairs grouped around the slate coffee table. "Have a seat. I'll go get my lunch and be right back. Can I bring you anything? Ham sandwich? Soft drink?"

"That's very nice of you, but I'm not hungry. I'd love a glass of ice water, though."

"Coming right up."

He wondered if he was crazy to leave her alone in the living room. She was, after all, a perfect stranger. Maybe she'd cooked up that story about *Lone Star Monthly* so she could gain access to the house. Maybe when he went back into the living room, he'd find her holding a gun, and she'd rob him blind. He didn't think so, though. He was a pretty good judge of character, and Abbie Bernard just didn't strike him as anything but an upstanding, honest woman who was what she'd said she was.

When he returned to the living room, she wasn't sitting as he'd suggested. Instead, she stood in front of the great stone fireplace, intently studying the large family portrait that hung over the mantel. There was a strange expression on her face that puzzled him.

"Here's your water," he said.

She jumped.

"I'm sorry. I didn't mean to startle you."

"No, I . . . It was my fault. I was just so caught up in looking at your family. That's a lovely photograph."

"Thank you."

"How long ago was it taken?" There was an odd, strained note to her voice.

"It was taken more than four years ago." That was their last carefree Christmas, because four months later Ann had been diagnosed with her cancer.

"You have a son, I see, as well as your . . . daughter."

"Yes, Patrick. He'd just turned nine when that picture was taken. He's thirteen now." Logan couldn't help smiling. He was very proud of both his children.

"He looks exactly like you."

There it was again. That odd tone. Logan began to feel uneasy. Maybe there *was* something wrong with this woman. Many people had been fooled by a look of innocence before. This might be one of those times. "Yes," Logan said slowly. He walked over and placed his plate and glass on the coffee table. "Patrick is all O'Connell. Erin, on the other hand, looks like my wife's family."

"Erin? That's a lovely name. Is she . . . Is she at home today?" She finally moved away from the mantel, taking the chair he'd suggested on the other side of the coffee table. But she didn't relax into it. Instead she sat forward, knees together, as if she might jump up at any moment.

Logan picked up his sandwich and took a bite. "No, she's not home. She went shopping."

For the life of him, he couldn't figure out why she was so tense. He wasn't the type of man to frighten people. Especially not women. Most women acted like giggling idiots when they first met him—a reaction he had grown to hate. He'd been told he looked like Pierce Brosnan so many times that now, when he heard the comparison made, he wanted to puke.

And yet, the way he looked had been a benefit to him when he wanted to go to M.I.T. and his parents couldn't afford it. He had signed up with a New York modeling agency and earned enough money in a year and a half of modeling to pay for his entire education. But he hadn't enjoyed the work, and once it was over, he had resisted all efforts of the agency to lure him back, something they tried periodically.

"I see," she said, obviously disappointed. "I had really hoped to meet her."

He frowned. He was becoming more and more uneasy. "Why?"

"Because she was one of the children born during the blizzard, which is the focus of my story. Would you like to see copies of the articles I've written in the past? I have them in my briefcase. I'm sorry not to give you a business card, but my daughter and I just moved to Houston a couple of weeks ago, and I haven't had time to get any printed yet."

Even though he felt a bit foolish for his suspicions—after all, she did seem perfectly harmless—Logan said, "Sure, I'd like to see the articles."

"All right." She opened her briefcase and withdrew a manila folder. She handed it to him.

Inside he found two articles. One had been published in *The Archaeological Journal* and was about an expedition made by someone named Thomas Scofield Bernard.

"Thomas is my former husband," she said in explanation.

The other article had been published in *California Monthly* and was a profile of Charlotte Post. "How'd you happen to do this one?" he said.

"Charlotte is a client of mine. I do her research."

"Really? That sounds interesting."

She smiled and sat back, seeming more relaxed now. "What you really mean is, it sounds glamorous. Believe me, it's not."

He grinned. She was right. He handed the folder back to her. "So how can I help you, Miss Bernard? Or do you go by Mrs.?"

"Since I have a daughter, I go by Mrs., but I'd feel a lot more comfortable if you'd just call me Abbie."

Because Logan hated formality, he said, "All right, Abbie, and you can call me Logan."

She smiled. "Great. Okay, what I want to do is ask you some questions about the night your daughter was born."

"Shoot." He took a bite of his sandwich.

She returned the folder to the briefcase and pulled out a tape recorder. "Do you mind?"

"No." He continued eating while she switched it on and tested it.

"Okay, um, Logan—" She cleared her throat. "Can we start with how you happened to be in Hurley the night of the snowstorm? Did you live there then?"

"No. We lived in Abilene at the time. That's where I was working then. We'd driven to Amarillo the day before, and we were on our way back when the storm began. We thought we could make it home, but then my wife's water broke. The Hurley hospital was the closest. So that's where Erin was born."

She nodded intently. "I'll bet you were worried, it being such a small hospital and everything."

"I was worried sick," he admitted, "but it all worked out fine."

She asked him a dozen more questions about Erin's birth and the things that had happened that night. He didn't mind answering the questions, but he did wonder how anyone could possibly be interested in what he was saying or how the information related to the hospital itself. Still, she was the journalist, not him. He guessed she knew what she was doing. He finished his sandwich and glanced at his watch, not bothering to do it surreptitiously. Her thirty minutes were just about up.

"I'm really sorry not to meet your daughter," she said, getting the hint and turning off the tape recorder. "Do you suppose I could come back another time when she's here?"

Logan had started to answer when he heard the front door open and the sounds of Erin's and Elizabeth's voices. He smiled. "Looks like that won't be necessary, Abbie. Here comes Erin now."

Eight

Katherine couldn't have planned things better if she'd tried. Ten minutes after hanging up with Abbie that morning, she'd been on the phone to Lois Caldwell. And immediately after that, she had called Kendall and told her to dress up a little before coming over because they might go somewhere that afternoon. She'd decided it was prudent not to elaborate. Now, at three o'clock, she and Kendall were seated in the reception area outside Lois's office.

Katherine smiled down at Kendall. "You're not nervous, are you?"

Kendall shook her head. "No."

Katherine's smile expanded. "Good. Because there's nothing to be nervous about. Mrs. Caldwell is going to love you. You're just the kind of girl she wants in her school." Anyone with any sense would want Kendall to be in their school, she thought as she studied her granddaughter with undisguised approval.

She wondered if the green sleeveless dress and brown sandals Kendall wore had been her choice or Abbie's. No matter. With Kendall's gorgeous green eyes and tanned coloring, they looked wonderful. Of course, Kendall looked wonderful in anything she put on. She was just a naturally beautiful child, with an innate sense of style.

Kendall was actually beautiful enough to be a model, Katherine thought, but for once she was glad Abbie had such staid ideas, because modeling was not the kind of life Katherine wanted for Kendall. Oh, no, what she wanted—

She broke off the thought as Lois Caldwell's office door opened and the director walked out.

"Sorry to keep you waiting, Katherine. It was a phone call from England, so I had to take it."

"We didn't mind waiting." Katherine stood and smiled at her old friend. The two women had met years ago when both were serving on a charity bazaar committee for the March of Dimes.

Lois Caldwell was in her early sixties—a tall, athletic-looking redhead whose hair had grayed to the point that it now looked like pale apricot. She wore it short and brushed back. As always, she was dressed beautifully—if conservatively—in a dark brown pants suit paired with a pale yellow silk blouse. Also as always, her tortoiseshell glasses matched her outfit.

"And this must be Kendall," Lois said, turning her brown eyes in Kendall's direction. "I'm Mrs. Caldwell, Kendall."

Katherine's chest swelled with pride as Kendall, with perfect aplomb, rose gracefully and walked forward, extending her hand to the headmistress. "Hello, Mrs. Caldwell. It's nice to meet you."

The two shook hands gravely, and Katherine could see by Lois's expression that Kendall had already made a wonderful impression. Of course, Katherine had expected nothing less. After all, Kendall was her granddaughter, descended from a long line of lovely, confident, intelligent women, and blood would always tell.

"Shall we go into my office?" Lois said.

This was only the second time Katherine had ever visited Lois Caldwell's working domain, and she thought again how perfectly the understated but elegant wood-paneled office with the forest green carpeting and solid oak furniture suited the director. Lois took her seat behind her desk, and Katherine and Kendall sat in two of the four Queen Anne chairs grouped around the desk.

Lois folded her hands together and leaned forward, giving Kendall a warm smile. "So, Kendall, your grandmother tells me you're interested in coming to the Caldwell School this fall?"

Kendall nodded. "Yes, I think so."

Lois's eyes met Katherine's briefly, and Katherine was glad she'd decided to let the director know that there was some resistance to the Caldwell School on Abbie's part.

"She also tells me," Lois continued, "that you're a talented artist."

Kendall smiled in pleasure.

Lois went on to describe the art program at Caldwell, which was even more impressive and comprehensive than Katherine had understood. "What do you think?" she said at the end.

"It sounds great," Kendall said. Her eyes were shining. "Especially the computer graphics part. I don't know anything about that."

"It's interesting you should mention computer graphics because we're offering a special summer program called Introduction to Computer Graphics and we've got room for a couple more students. Maybe you'd be interested in joining us. The class starts next week and will go until August 1. It's every day from nine till twelve."

Excitement written all over her face, Kendall looked at Katherine. "Oh, Gran, do you think Mom would let me?"

"If you want to take the class, I'm sure your mother would have no objection." Abbie had better not object. Especially since she seemed to have no intention of giving up her work for the summer, as Katherine had thought she would. After all, the child had to do *something* until school started and she made some friends.

"Good," Lois said. "I'll put you down for the class and before you leave today, I'll give you all the information, including a permission slip that your mother will need to sign."

Katherine raised her eyebrows.

Lois, seeing the unasked question, said, "The instructor will take the girls on several field trips during the three-week course." She turned back to Kendall. "You know, Kendall, taking this course will be good for you, because not only will you learn about something that interests you, but you'll get to meet some of the girls who are already enrolled at

Caldwell, as well as a couple that will be newcomers in September. You'll also get a chance to see what our school is like firsthand."

For the rest of the hour-long appointment, Lois described other aspects of the school program, including athletics and music, both of which she knew from Katherine interested Kendall. She asked Kendall several questions about her former school—what she liked, what she didn't like, and why—and by the end of the hour, Kendall was talking to the director as if she'd known her forever. That didn't surprise Katherine. Lois had a way of talking to them that children responded to. She respected them, and they knew it.

At the conclusion of the interview Lois asked Kendall if she would mind waiting out in the reception area for a few minutes while she and her grandmother talked.

"Okay." Kendall got up and, after giving her grandmother a happy smile, walked out of the office.

Lois waited until Kendall was gone before getting up and shutting the door after her, then instead of returning to her desk chair, she sat in one of the Queen Anne chairs.

"I think she'll make a wonderful Caldwell girl," she said.

Katherine smiled. "I do, too."

"What about your daughter? I'm sensing she has some reservations."

"I can take care of Abbie."

Lois peered over her glasses. "Yes, knowing you, I'm sure you can." Then, more briskly, she said, "I'll need her school records, and even though I could call her former school and ask to have them sent, I really should have her mother's permission to do so."

"That's no problem." If Katherine had to browbeat Abbie, she would, because Kendall's entire future was at stake.

If Katherine had had this kind of opportunity when she was Kendall's age, her whole life would have been different. And maybe if it had, Abbie would have been different, too.

But none of that mattered now. It was all water under the bridge. Because in Kendall Katherine had another opportunity to get things right. And this time nothing was going to stop her.

Nine

If she hadn't been sitting down, Abbie was sure she would have fallen down. She turned slowly as Logan's daughter, accompanied by a striking blonde, entered the room.

"Well," said the blonde, "I wondered whose car that was out front." She gave Abbie a sharp look.

But Abbie had eyes for no one but the child. She gripped the arms of her chair as her heart galloped like a wild thing. It was unbelievable. Seeing Erin O'Connell's photograph had not prepared Abbie for seeing the girl in the flesh, especially since, in the photograph, Erin had only been seven years old. Looking at the child now was like looking at a photo of Abbie herself when she was young. Erin had the same coltish figure, the same pale hair, the same light blue eyes, the same shy expression.

Mine, Abbie thought, dazed. *My baby.*

"Erin, Elizabeth, I'd like you to meet Mrs. Bernard." Logan turned to Abbie and smiled. "Abbie, this is my daughter Erin and my sister-in-law, Elizabeth Chamberlain."

Afterward, Abbie was never sure what she said. She vaguely remembered getting up and shaking the sister-in-law's hand, but all else was a blur. The only person in the room who interested her was Erin. *My baby,* she kept thinking. *This is my baby.* Her insides were trembling with an emotion that was so much stronger, so much more intense than she had expected.

"Hello," Erin said, giving Abbie a shy smile.

When she imitated her aunt by holding out her right hand, Abbie's heart felt as if someone were squeezing it. And when her own hand closed around Erin's, Abbie had to fight against the tears that clogged her throat. Somehow she found the strength to answer in a voice that didn't shake. "Hello, Erin. It's nice to meet you."

"Mrs. Bernard is doing a story on the hospital where you were born, Erin," Logan explained.

How could he stand there, smiling and relaxed, and not see what Abbie saw?

"Why are you doing this story?" the sister-in-law said. Her gray eyes swept over Abbie.

Abbie knew Elizabeth Chamberlain was taking her measure. By the frosty assessment, she would be a much harsher judge than Logan had been. Abbie had better sound authentic and confident if she didn't want to make the woman suspicious. "It's an article for *Lone Star Monthly.* I've done a couple of things for them in the past."

"And when, exactly, will this article be published?" The sister-in-law continued to study Abbie carefully.

"I'm not sure. No . . . no publication date has been set." Abbie could have kicked herself for stammering. She avoided Elizabeth Chamberlain's too-shrewd gaze.

"How was the shopping trip?" Logan said.

Now Erin lost her shyness. Animatedly, she began to tell her father everywhere they'd gone and everything they'd bought. "Sit down, Dad. I'll show you."

"Whoa." He laughed affectionately. "We've got company right now. Why don't we finish up with Mrs. Bernard and let her get on her way, then you can show me, okay?"

"Okay."

They all sat down—Abbie in her chair, Logan in his, Elizabeth Chamberlain in another between them. Erin perched on the arm of her father's chair. He smiled up at her and put his arm around her. It was obvious to anyone observing that father and daughter were very close.

But he's not her father, and she's not his daughter. His real daughter isn't blond, and she isn't shy. His real daughter is vivacious and bubbly and, except for the color of her eyes, looks exactly like him. In fact, Kendall looked so much like Logan and Patrick that no one looking at them would—

Oh, my God. Kendall has a brother!

The realization was like a blow to the chest. Abbie guessed she'd been so rattled when she first entered Logan O'Connell's home and so focused on Erin, that she hadn't been able to think in terms of Kendall. But now she did, and her thoughts overwhelmed her.

How? How can this terrible thing have happened to us? That sweet child sitting there is my daughter. A daughter I've never held. Never kissed. And Kendall . . . my darling Kendall . . . who so desperately wants a father and a family . . .

For a moment, Abbie was afraid she was going to become hysterical. She felt completely unhinged. This horrible situation couldn't be real. She couldn't be sitting there in the presence of her flesh-and-blood child, acting as if nothing was wrong, that this was just a normal day and an ordinary interview for a magazine article.

Both Erin and Logan were looking at her expectantly. Abbie was afraid to look at Elizabeth. She was afraid the woman would see right through her and know immediately that something was very wrong.

Abbie knew she had to get out of there. Now. Even though she wanted so badly to talk to the child. But that wasn't going to be possible. As it was, she had to hold onto the arms of the chair to keep her hands from shaking uncontrollably. No, she couldn't stay. She had to get out of there. Otherwise, she might break down and say or do something crazy.

Drawing on reserves of strength she hadn't known she possessed, she managed to say, "Logan," in a more or less normal voice. "I-I'm afraid I'm not going to be able to stay. I really appreciate your talking to me, and . . . and Erin, it was so nice to meet you, but I, well, I'm not feeling well."

Swallowing against the lump in her throat, she picked up her briefcase and stood. Her legs felt unsteady, and she prayed they would carry her to the door. *Just let me get outside. Please, God, just let me get outside without falling apart.*

Logan, watching her, frowned. Concern clouded his eyes. "Is there anything we can get you?"

"No, no," she said, battling the panic that was growing more uncontrollable by the second. "I'll be fine. I'm just a little hypoglycemic."

"Are you *sure* you're going to be all right? You're welcome to stay until you're feeling better."

The sister-in-law had risen, too. "Logan, if she wants to leave . . ."

"I'll be okay, really," Abbie said. "I-I just need to get some air. I'll be fine."

He looked as if he were about to protest again, but Abbie forestalled him by walking toward the door. After a moment's hesitation, he joined her, saying, "I'll see you out."

Abbie avoided his eyes and managed to hold herself together until she reached the safety of her car. Even then, she knew she had to continue to hold on, because out of the corner of her eye she could see Logan O'Connell standing watching her from the open doorway. Her hand shook as she fumbled in her briefcase. Finally she found her keys. It took her three tries to get the proper key inserted in the ignition, and then she very nearly flooded the car before she got it started. Raising her hand in farewell, she pulled out of the drive.

Hold on. Hold on.

It was agonizing seconds before she turned the corner and was finally out of sight of the house. Shaking violently, she veered over to the curb and cut the ignition. Sobs tore through her, and she laid her head against her arms on the steering wheel and let them come.

"That woman was strange."

"In what way?" Logan wasn't sure why, but he was reluctant to admit to Elizabeth that he'd had his own doubts about Abbie Bernard.

Elizabeth tapped her finger against her glass of iced tea. "I don't know exactly. There was just something about the way she behaved. Are you *sure* she's really a reporter?"

"Yes, I'm sure. She showed me a couple of articles she'd written. Besides, what else could she be?"

"Oh, honestly, Logan." She gave him one of her I-can't-believe-how-naive-you-are looks, accompanied by an indulgent smile.

Logan bit back what he really wanted to say, which was that he was mighty tired of Elizabeth's superior tone and her constant implication that without her his life and the kids' lives would fall into chaos. "Okay, I admit it. I was swayed by a pretty face." He knew that was a cheap shot, but at the moment he felt she deserved it.

"Pretty face! Why, that woman wasn't the least bit pretty."

"Didn't you think so?"

Because he didn't defend his opinion, Elizabeth could hardly elaborate on hers without sounding mean and petty, so all she said was "No, I didn't." But there were two bright spots of color on her cheeks, and Logan knew she was angry. "For all we know, she could have been casing the house or something. Did you ask to see any *real* credentials? Like her driver's license? Why, anyone could say she was the author of some articles."

Logan's jaw clenched. If he hadn't been so irritated with Elizabeth, he might have answered her honestly, saying no, he hadn't looked at Abbie Bernard's driver's license, and that the reason he'd been so quick to believe the woman was that there was some quality about her, something in her manner that had appealed to him. And now that he thought about it, he could even identify what that something was. It was the sense that this woman, no matter how capable and mature she might be, no matter how many hard knocks she might have weathered, still retained some of the vulnerability associated with youth and innocence.

"Don't worry about it," he said. "Nothing happened, and now she's gone."

Soon after, the subject was dropped, but Logan continued to think about Abbie Bernard long after Elizabeth had gone home, and in the office the following morning, he was still thinking about her. He felt bad about the way she'd left. He shouldn't have let her go when she was so clearly not well. What if something happened to her? He wished he knew if she'd made it home okay.

By mid-morning, when he still hadn't gotten her out of his mind, he called Directory Assistance to get her number.

"I'm sorry, sir, there is no new listing for an Abbie Bernard," the operator said.

"What about Abigail Bernard or A. Bernard?"

"No, sir."

"Not even an unlisted number?"

"No, sir. I'm sorry."

Thoughtfully, Logan hung up the phone. Now, that was strange. He wouldn't have been surprised to find she had an unlisted number, but no listing?

Could Elizabeth have been right after all? No, he couldn't believe that. He felt he was a pretty good judge of human nature, and Abbie Bernard was not a liar. There was some logical explanation for the lack of a phone listing.

Telling himself to forget about her, that she had probably made it home just fine, that he was wasting time he couldn't afford to waste, he turned his attention back to his work. Yet as the morning wore on, his mind kept wandering back to Abbie. He wished he knew for sure that she was all right. Yesterday, even before she'd said she wasn't feeling well, she'd seemed so fragile.

"Oh, hell, why didn't I think of this before?" he muttered aloud. "I can call *Lone Star Monthly*. They'll have her phone number."

It only took a couple of minutes with Directory Assistance before he had the Austin number. A minute later he was connected with the magazine. He had to talk, and explain what he wanted, to four different editors. No one knew an Abbie Bernard. The senior acquisitions editor even said there was no article such as Abbie had described in the works. "Of course," he added, "some writers do articles on spec and then send them to us, but most of the writers we work with query first. They don't want to waste weeks or even months on something that might not be bought."

After they'd hung up, Logan sat there thinking. He hated to admit it, even to himself, but this latest phone call was disturbing. Maybe the woman *was* a liar, or worse, a possible burglar or con artist. Maybe he wasn't as good a judge of character as he'd thought. Maybe that air of innocence and that look of vulnerability that had appealed to him so much was just a very clever acting job. Maybe even the sickness she'd expressed had been fake, a way to get out of the house after she'd accomplished what she'd set out to accomplish. He thought back over the interview. Yes, he thought reluctantly, Abbie Bernard—or whatever her name was—*had* acted strange, especially in her desire to see Erin.

Erin! Alarm caused his flesh to break out in goose bumps as a horrifying thought crossed his mind.

Kidnapping.

What if, for some insane reason, Abbie Bernard had come to his house with the idea of kidnapping Erin? For it was Erin she'd shown the interest in, wasn't it? And if that was the case, maybe yesterday was just the initial foray to get the lay of the land. Maybe the woman who'd presented herself as Abbie Bernard had an accomplice and they would be back to finish the job. The smart thing to do was call the police.

He reached for the phone.

Ten

Elizabeth had floor duty Friday morning. Because the broker she worked for had a small real estate agency and was trying to keep overhead at a manageable level, they did not employ a full-time receptionist the way the larger agencies did. To offset this deficiency, Elizabeth and the five other agents who worked out of this office took turns manning the front desk and answering the phone.

Although sometimes Elizabeth resented floor duty, today wasn't one of those times. She had paperwork she needed to catch up on, and this gave her the perfect opportunity. Also, one never knew when one might pick up a client. It was surprising how many times prospective buyers called from the *Chronicle* ad or the agency's sign on the property, and if Elizabeth did her job right when she talked to the prospects, she might very well end up by becoming their agent of choice.

Unfortunately, the phone didn't ring much that morning, and she also didn't accomplish much in terms of her paperwork, because too often she found her attention drifting to Logan and the events of yesterday.

She had been so pleased when she'd finagled a dinner invitation out of him and she'd really been looking forward to the evening. So she was completely unprepared when she and Erin returned from their shopping trip and found Logan in cozy conversation with that Bernard woman. Elizabeth's antennae had gone on immediate alert, especially after Logan addressed the woman by her first name. That alone told Elizabeth something, and it wasn't something she was pleased to know.

Pretty!

Elizabeth couldn't believe Logan had referred to that woman as pretty. Why, she wasn't pretty in the least. She was completely colorless. God, that suit she'd had on! She couldn't have picked anything more unattractive to wear if she'd tried. It was obviously cheap. Probably bought off the rack at one of the discount stores, whereas Elizabeth, who *cared* how she looked, always shopped at Saks or Neiman's. Why was it so hard for some women to understand that when you bought clothes of quality you not only looked better but you actually got more value for your money?

And her hair! Elizabeth actually felt sorry for the woman. Fine hair like hers was impossible to style. It was bad enough when a child like Erin had hair like that, but at least *she* could use ribbons and barrettes to keep it under control. Now, if Elizabeth had been saddled with hair like the Bernard woman's, *she* would have gone to the best stylist she could find and had it cut and permed to make it look thicker and more fashionable. But there again, it was obvious the woman had no conception of what to do to make herself look better.

Her shy act hadn't fooled Elizabeth for one minute, either. Abbie Bernard was sly, not shy. How could Logan have been taken in by her? Elizabeth was willing to bet the woman wasn't a journalist at all. She might not be dangerous, as Elizabeth had suggested yesterday, but Elizabeth was sure she'd had some ulterior motive for calling on Logan. In fact, she wouldn't be at all surprised if the woman had researched Logan and his background and not only discovered how financially well off he was but that he was a vulnerable widower, as well. She'd probably used the supposed article as an excuse to meet him.

As if Elizabeth didn't have enough problems when it came to Logan and other women. Why, in their circle alone, there were at least three women she knew who'd had their eye on him ever since Ann's death. It had been all Elizabeth could do to ward them off.

God, she was sick of this. She was getting nowhere waiting for him to make a move. And the longer she waited, the more chance there was that he would meet someone else. Somehow, some way, Elizabeth had to make him see how perfect they would be together.

She thought about calling him. But what good would a phone call accomplish? She didn't really want to talk to him. What she wanted was to see him—alone. The fact that they were rarely alone was one of the major reasons their relationship wasn't going anywhere, she thought with a trace of resentment. Too often, the time she spent with Logan also meant the company of the children. And even though she loved the kids and wanted to be their stepmother, they were a definite hindrance when it came to romance.

Elizabeth sighed in frustration. Maybe she should enlist the help of her mother. If her mother would call and ask to have the kids for the weekend, Elizabeth could then try to get Logan alone, preferably in her home and not his. Yes, that would be perfect. If she could get him to take her out Friday or Saturday night, then come back to her house for drinks or coffee or something, she could change into that slinky black satin hostess gown of hers, and then surely . . .

Yes, but if she asked her mother to watch the kids, she'd have to admit to her mother that she wanted Logan. And then, in the end, if she didn't get him, her mother would know, and that would be intolerable. Bad enough she'd known Logan was Elizabeth's date the day he met Ann. Most mothers would have been sympathetic to a daughter who had been treated the way Elizabeth had been treated by Ann. Most mothers would have talked to the daughter who stole her sister's boyfriend, said it wasn't a nice thing to do, or something. But not Celia Chamberlain.

Elizabeth had always known her mother preferred Ann. From the day she'd brought Ann home from the hospital, when Elizabeth was three, Elizabeth had known. It never seemed to matter that Elizabeth was prettier and smarter and more popular. That she got better grades and more honors.

Even when she was elected Homecoming Queen her first year of college, who got the fuss made over them? Not Elizabeth. Oh, no. It was Ann her mother clucked over. Ann who got all the attention. You'd think no one else had ever fallen while skiing and broken a leg, for God's sake! Elizabeth felt furious all over again remembering how her spectacular accomplishment had had to once more take a backseat to something Ann had done.

And the day Ann had married Logan! Elizabeth would never, not if she lived a million years, forget that day. Why, her mother had acted as if Ann were the only woman who had ever snagged a man. Elizabeth might not have even existed for all the notice her mother took of her. She'd even acted as if Elizabeth had fallen and hurt her ankle on purpose so she couldn't walk down the aisle but had to be helped into the church ahead of time. It still stung to think how her mother had looked at her—that expression of blame in her eyes. As if Elizabeth had *wanted* to wear a cast! But her mother's behavior was so typical, it certainly shouldn't have surprised Elizabeth.

For some reason her mother disapproved of her, and no matter what Elizabeth said or did, that would always be true. A case in point was Elizabeth's decision to go into real estate. Instead of saying something positive, her mother had wondered aloud why Elizabeth had bothered getting her M.B.A. if all she was planning to do was sell real estate.

Elizabeth had never let on how these inequities and criticisms hurt. She'd just gritted her teeth and vowed to show everyone who the better person was, because she'd rather die than have anyone—especially her mother!—think she cared.

Remembering all this, she knew she couldn't call her mother. She'd have to figure out some other way to get Logan alone. She was lost in thought when the phone rang.

She picked it up. "Turner Realty."

"Elizabeth? Oh, thank God. I was hoping you were at the office."

"Mom?" Alarm caused Elizabeth's heart to beat faster. Her mother never called her at work. "What's wrong?"

"It . . ." Her mother's voice broke. "It's your father. He . . . he's had a heart attack."

"No!" Elizabeth cried, jumping to her feet. "Is he all right?"

"I-I don't know. They . . . they're working on him now."

Fear caused Elizabeth's voice to tremble. "Wh-where are you?"

"At Memorial City Hospital. Oh, Elizabeth, they're calling me. I have to go."

"Wait! Mom! Where in the hospital?"

"The emergency room."

"I'm coming over there right now." Elizabeth's mind raced. She felt stunned, hardly able to believe this had happened. Her father had always seemed so healthy. In fact, Oliver Chamberlain prided himself on how fit he was, bragging that he looked at least ten years younger than his sixty-three years, and he was right.

He didn't smoke. He wasn't overweight. And yet he'd had a heart attack. And it must be a bad one. Oh, God. What if he died? Her mind skittered away from the possibility. He would make it. He had to. Because she just couldn't imagine life without her father. Maybe Ann *had* always been their mother's favorite, but that fact had been bearable as long as Elizabeth had had her father. In his eyes, she was perfect. He had always been there for her, always made her feel special, and in return, she adored him. *Dad* . . . Tears blurred her eyes.

Trying to remain calm, telling herself over and over that he would be all right, Elizabeth called the answering service, then scribbled a note to Teresa Brunelli, the agent who had floor duty starting at one.

Halfway to the hospital, Elizabeth remembered Logan. He and her father were close. Logan would want to know. She fished the cell phone out of her purse. Thank God for speed dial, she thought, pressing the two-number combination for Logan's office.

He answered on the second ring.

"Logan, it's Elizabeth." Quickly, she explained. "Can you come?"

"I'll be there in twenty minutes or less," he said.

Elizabeth reached the hospital just twelve minutes from the time her mother had called her. Parking in the emergency parking lot, she raced inside. The triage nurse who manned the emergency waiting area took one look at her and said, "Are you Elizabeth Chamberlain?"

"Yes."

"Come with me."

Elizabeth followed the nurse back into one of the treatment rooms, where she found her mother, pale and puffy eyed, sitting talking to a doctor. No one else was in the room. "Mom," she said, rushing to her mother's side. "Where's Dad? How is he? Is he all right?"

"Oh, Elizabeth," her mother said in a strangled voice. Her eyes overflowed.

Elizabeth's heart stopped.

The doctor stood. "Miss Chamberlain?"

Elizabeth's gaze swung to meet his.

"I'm sorry." Compassionate brown eyes told her everything she needed to know, even as her brain denied the message. "We did everything we could, but we couldn't save him."

"No!" Elizabeth shook her head. "No."

"I'm sorry," he said again.

Her mind screamed in denial. No. Not Daddy. He couldn't be dead. He just couldn't be. There had to be some mistake.

"Elizabeth . . ."

Elizabeth swallowed. Looked at her mother. She knew she should do something. Say something. But she felt frozen. She simply couldn't believe her father was gone. These people had made a mistake. He just couldn't be dead. What was she going to do without him? He was the one who loved her best.

"Miss Chamberlain," the doctor said, "I know it's hard, but there are some decisions that have to be made immediately. I was just explaining to your moth—" He broke off abruptly, looking beyond Elizabeth.

Elizabeth swung around. Logan stood in the doorway. His eyes, questioning, met hers.

At the sight of him, something inside Elizabeth gave way. With a wrenching sob, she flung herself across the room and into his arms. "He's gone, Logan," she cried. "Daddy's gone. Now all we've got is you."

Eleven

Abbie knocked on the door of the guest bathroom, which had been officially designated as Kendall's. "Hurry up, Kendall. You don't want to be late on the first day of class."

"I'm almost ready."

Walking back into the kitchen, Abbie refilled her coffee cup. She felt like hell. Ever since Thursday, she hadn't slept well, and this morning her head was pounding. Consequently, she wasn't looking forward to the drive to the Caldwell School, which would probably take her at least thirty minutes each way, but she had to admit she was grateful Kendall would be gone every morning for a few weeks.

She smiled ruefully. A week ago she wouldn't have imagined she could possibly feel grateful to her mother for going behind her back and enrolling Kendall in a course, especially not one at Caldwell. But a week ago she had still been living in blissful ignorance. The problems she'd stewed over then seemed insignificant now, merely petty annoyances compared to the earth-shattering trauma she had endured since then.

For the past three days, she had hardly slept. Each night she lay in bed and prayed for the release of sleep, and each night it eluded her. Instead, her mind churned furiously. And daytime was no better. Thank God Charlotte Post was between books, because Abbie wouldn't have been able to concentrate on Charlotte's needs right now. It was taking all her energy just to keep up a normal front with Kendall and her mother, let alone having to deal with a demanding, self-involved client such as Charlotte.

If only Abbie could stop thinking about Erin. But no matter how she tried, the child's image remained burned into her brain. Abbie stood at the sink and stared sightlessly out the window above it. Erin was so like Abbie when she was young. It wasn't only that she looked like her, she had the same reserved personality and was probably just as lacking in self-confidence as Abbie had been at that age. The moment Abbie saw her, her heart had ached and she'd wanted to put her arms around Erin and protect her from the world.

Abbie wondered how Erin felt about the death of the woman she believed to be her mother. Did she miss her? Did she cry for her at night? Abbie's eyes misted at the thought.

"Mom?"

Oh, God. I have got to get a grip on myself. Forcing a smile to her face, Abbie turned. Kendall, back to her perky self, had walked into the kitchen. She looked darling in blue jean shorts, a navy-and-white striped T-shirt, and tan leather sandals. Her unruly curls were held back by a wide navy headband and there were tiny silver earrings looped through her ears. Looking at her, Abbie's heart swelled with love. "Ready to go?"

Kendall grinned, eyes shining with excitement. "Uh-huh."

"Let me pour this coffee into one of those thermal cups, then I'll be ready, too."

Kendall chattered the whole way to the school. Abbie was glad because it helped keep her mind away from the subject that had obsessed her the past week. So she listened to Kendall and tried to relax and enjoy the scenery. It had rained during the night, and the trees and lawns sparkled in the early morning sun. Every time Abbie returned to Houston after being away for a while, she was struck anew by how green everything was. It always tickled her that people who had never been to Texas—Easterners and foreigners in particular—thought all of Texas was brown, dry, and filled with cowboys, sagebrush, and cactus plants. That might be true of west Texas, but it was certainly not true of the Texas Gulf coast. Houston had a subtropical climate, and it was not uncommon to see yards filled with banana plants, plumeria, oleander—even palm trees. And as for cowboys, Abbie had to smile. The only time she'd seen real cowboys in Houston was during the trail ride preceding the annual Houston Rodeo and Livestock Show. Why, there were more young Turks in expensive suits than there were jeans and cowboy hats on the city streets.

Her mind thus occupied, it seemed like no time at all before they reached the school. Abbie parked in the side lot. She wanted to meet Lois Caldwell and had decided this was the logical time to do so.

"There's Miss Caldwell now," Kendall said as they entered the front door. She pointed to a tall woman dressed in a russet linen pantsuit who stood talking with another, younger woman and a girl about Kendall's age. Abbie stood a few feet away and waited until the director was finished and the other woman and her daughter had disappeared down the hall before approaching.

"Well, hello, Kendall," the director said, giving Kendall a welcoming smile. Her friendly brown gaze moved to Abbie. She extended her right hand. "And you must be Mrs. Bernard. I'm Lois Caldwell."

"It's nice to meet you."

The two women shook hands and appraised each other. Abbie reluctantly admitted that Lois Caldwell made a favorable first impression. There was none of the haughty, superior persona Abbie had feared. Instead the woman seemed completely approachable and down-to-earth. Suddenly Abbie was glad she'd worn her favorite sleeveless, blue flowered rayon dress instead of the shorts and T-shirt she usually wore on hot summer days.

"I'm so glad Kendall is joining us this summer," the director said. She gave Kendall another smile, and Kendall smiled back.

"Well, she's certainly excited about the course."

"Since it's about time for class to start, would you like to go back with Kendall and see the classroom?"

"I'd love to."

Abbie looked around as much as possible as she and

Kendall followed Lois Caldwell. Everywhere she looked, she saw clean, bright rooms filled with the latest in educational aids. Well, all it takes is money, she thought. After several turns, they reached a big, sunny room that faced the back of the school's property.

"This is our computer room," Lois Caldwell said. "We do all our computer courses here."

The room contained at least forty computers. Macintoshes, Abbie saw. Although she knew very little about computer graphics, she knew enough to be aware that Macs were considered the best for this type of work. There were already a couple of dozen girls in the room. Abbie glanced down at Kendall, who had moved imperceptibly closer to her. Even Kendall, as outgoing as she was, had her shy moments. Abbie squeezed Kendall's shoulder encouragingly.

From the back of the room, a young dark-haired woman in a yellow sundress emerged from behind a supply cabinet. "Oh, hello," she said, walking toward them. She looked at Abbie with friendly hazel eyes.

Lois Caldwell introduced Abbie and Kendall. "This is Lacey York, who will be teaching this class," she explained.

After they had exchanged greetings, Lacey smiled down at Kendall and said, "Come on, Kendall. I'll introduce you to the others. I especially want you to meet Heather, who's going into the sixth grade just like you. She's also a newcomer, so you'll have a lot in common."

Satisfied that Kendall was in good hands, Abbie said goodbye and, accompanied by Lois Caldwell, walked back to the front entrance.

"It was very nice meeting you, Miss Caldwell," she said as they reached the door.

"Thank you. I'm glad I've had the chance to meet you, as well. Your mother has had many nice things to say about you over the years."

Obviously Abbie's mother was less than honest with her friend, Abbie thought wryly. "Mom has had very nice things to say about you, too."

"And Kendall is a delight."

Abbie smiled. "Thank you. I think so, too."

"I do so hope she'll be joining us this fall."

"Well," Abbie hedged. "I haven't made up my mind yet."

"I understand. I'm not trying to pressure you, but I did want you to know how much we'd like to have her. And I do feel we can give her many opportunities that won't be found elsewhere."

"I appreciate that. And I'll think about it."

"Good. Now I know you probably have a lot of things to do this morning, so I won't keep you any longer."

During her drive home, Abbie tried to keep her mind focused on the school and the things Lois Caldwell had said, but it simply would not stay there, returning instead to the problem that refused to give her any peace. Only this time, unlike earlier this morning, it was Kendall and not Erin who dominated her thoughts.

She remembered all the times Kendall had asked about her father. How hurt the child was by Thomas's neglect. How she'd asked, more than once, if her father really loved her. Was it right of Abbie to keep her from knowing her real father? Especially when that real father was so obviously a nice man.

Well, if she were being totally honest, she'd admit that Logan O'Connell was more than nice. He was terrific: handsome, charming, successful. And a wonderfully devoted father. The complete opposite of Thomas, in fact. With a stab of yearning, Abbie wondered what her life would have been like if she'd married someone like Logan. What *Kendall's* life would have been like.

She thought about all the times Kendall had expressed envy of friends who came from large families. The wistful look in her eyes when she saw the camaraderie and friendly rivalry between brothers and sisters.

Once she'd asked Abbie if she'd ever thought of remarrying. Bemused by the question, Abbie said, "Why, honey? Would you like me to remarry?"

Kendall had shrugged. "I don't know."

"But you must have had a reason for asking the question," Abbie pressed.

"I-I just . . . I don't know . . . I thought it would be nice to have a brother or a sister, and maybe if you got married again . . ."

Abbie felt the same ache now that she'd felt then, for it was so obvious how much Kendall wanted to be part of something larger than just the two of them. And now she could be. For she not only had the kind of father she'd always wanted, she also had a brother. How could Abbie justify depriving Kendall of knowing them?

Dear God, please help me. Please tell me what to do . . .

If only Abbie knew what was best. If she exposed the truth, so many lives would be changed forever. A lot of innocent people would be hurt. Is that what she wanted? Wasn't it better to just stick to her resolve? Pretend she'd never gone to see Dr. Joplin? Say nothing about the switch of the babies? After all, Abbie could relax on Erin's behalf. The child was living in a wonderful environment, with a loving father, a brother, and lots of extended family. Couldn't Abbie be content with that knowledge?

If only she *hadn't* gone to see Dr. Joplin. No other doctor in the universe would have known about her type O blood or made the connection. The only reason he had was that his own daughter had the same blood type as Abbie and once, years ago, Martha had needed a transfusion and the blood bank was low on type O blood, so Abbie had donated hers. In this case, ignorance really would have been bliss.

That night, her dreams were dark and disturbing. Several times she awakened with tears on her face. A little after four, she finally gave up trying to sleep and tiptoed into the kitchen to put on the coffee. Later, as she sipped the hot brew and waited for daybreak, she wished there were someone in whom she could confide, because this secret was too much of a burden to carry alone.

But who?

Certainly not her mother. Even the thought made Abbie shudder. As strong as Abbie's mother was, she would not be able to handle the truth. Her love for and pride in Kendall was the dominant force in her life.

Who then? Who could Abbie talk to?

She thought about Laura. They'd never had any secrets from each other. When Abbie was going through such a bad time with Thomas, it was Laura whose shoulder she cried on, Laura who listened and comforted and advised. It would be such a relief to confide in Laura, to have the benefit of her sensible and objective views.

But what if, in the end, Abbie decided keeping silent was the only answer? If that was the case, would she *really* want someone else, even someone as close as Laura, knowing the truth?

No, she thought wearily. No. As tempting as it was to unburden herself, for the time being, at least, it was best to keep her own counsel.

Twelve

Oliver Chamberlain would be buried at Memorial Oaks Cemetery, and as was fitting for such a solemn, sad occasion, it rained on the day of his funeral.

Logan, dressed in a dark navy pin-striped suit, stood in the family room and gazed outside. The rain showed no signs of letting up. In fact, the sky looked darker and more threatening now than it had at six o'clock, when Logan had awakened after a restless night.

He'd dreaded the day. It wasn't so much that he dreaded it personally, just that he knew the funeral would be very hard on his children, especially Erin.

Next to telling the children about their mother, telling them about their grandfather's death had been one of the hardest things Logan had ever had to do. If only he could have found some way to soften the pain, but how could he? The raw truth was their grandfather was gone, and no amount of sugarcoating would change it.

Patrick, probably because he felt it wouldn't be manly to cry, had, after an initial grimace of pain, been stoic. Erin, though, Erin was another story.

Remembering her grief, Logan hurt for her again. She had gone to pieces when he told her, crying as if her heart would break.

"Oh, sweetheart, I'm so sorry," Logan had said, holding

her close. His eyes met Patrick's over her shoulder, and Patrick moved closer and patted Erin's back.

"Why does everyone I love have to die?" Erin sobbed. She clutched Logan tighter. "Daddy, please don't die, too. Please don't."

"Erin, honey, I'm not going to die," Logan said. His chest ached with her pain. "Not until I'm a very old man."

"Promise me, promise me," she cried desperately.

"I promise. I promise." He kept smoothing her hair and kissing her cheek, and Patrick, looking as if he wanted to cry, too, kept stroking her back. "I won't ever leave you."

She had finally calmed down, but for the past two days, she had followed Logan around like his shadow, as if she were afraid that if she let him get out of her sight, he would disappear, too.

"Mr. Logan."

Logan turned. "Yes, Serita?"

"I'm sorry to disturb you," she said in her heavily accented English, "but Miss Erin, she needs you."

"Is she ready?" Serita had been helping Erin dress for the funeral.

Serita nodded. "Yes, she is dressed."

"Okay. Thank you, Serita." Logan headed for the wing that contained the children's bedrooms. He stopped outside Patrick's door first and knocked softly. A moment later, Patrick, dressed in a charcoal gray suit, opened the door.

Logan gave his son an approving smile. "Good. You're ready. You look nice."

Patrick nodded solemnly. "Thanks, Dad."

"Why don't you go wait in the living room? I'm going to check on Erin."

"Okay, Dad." Then, "Dad? I think she's crying."

Logan squeezed Patrick's shoulder. "I'll talk to her." His heart was heavy as he approached Erin's room. Glenna had offered to stay home with Erin if Logan didn't feel she was up to facing the funeral. But Erin had insisted she wanted to go.

Wishing he knew what to do, Logan knocked on Erin's door, then opened it. Looking unutterably sad in her dark burgundy dress, Erin sat on the edge of her bed, her head bowed. Logan sat down next to her and put his arm around her. She leaned against him, but she still didn't meet his eyes.

"Erin . . ."

She sniffed.

"Sweetheart, you don't have to go, you know. It's okay to stay home. Your grandfather wouldn't mind." He could feel the tremors in her body. He waited, and when she didn't say anything, added gently, "Why *don't* you stay home?"

She took a deep shuddering breath and looked up. Her soft blue eyes were full of tears. "W-will you stay with me?"

"Honey, I can't. You know that. I'm one of the pall-bearers. But Aunt Glenna said she'd come and stay." Logan could see the conflict on her face as she considered his words.

She shook her head and stood. "No, I'm going with you."

"Are you sure?"

She nodded. "Yes."

Logan stood, too. "All right. If you're sure."

Later, as he sat in the front pew at St. Luke's with his mother-in-law and Elizabeth, his children on either side of him, he thought about how much sadness and loss his children had experienced in just a few short years.

He glanced at each of them in turn. They were such good kids and he loved them with an intensity he would never have believed possible. He knew all parents did not feel this way. He'd heard enough talk on the golf course or at cocktail parties about how much trouble children could be, but he had never felt that way about Patrick and Erin. From the day each was born, he had felt they were a gift to be treasured.

He and Ann had often talked about how lucky they were and had spent endless hours discussing their hopes and dreams for the children. Now he was the only one left to help ensure those dreams would come true.

Today especially, he felt the weight of that responsibility. If only he could protect them from everything bad for the rest of their lives. But that was an impossibility. The best he could do, the best any father could do, was to put their needs first. To provide a secure and safe place for them to grow and to let them know he loved them and would be there for them, no matter what.

Just then Erin stirred next to him, and as he watched, she slipped her right hand into Elizabeth's, who sat on the other side of her. Elizabeth turned her head, and for a few moments, her grief-stricken eyes met his. Then she slowly returned her attention to the choir, who had begun singing "Jerusalem, My Destiny," one of Oliver's favorite hymns.

He looked down at Erin's and Elizabeth's joined hands, and somehow they seemed symbolic.

To put their needs first . . .

Erin needed a mother, more now than ever before. Maybe marriage to Elizabeth was the right answer, after all.

Abbie hated rain. She sighed as she crept along in the slow-moving traffic on the Katy Freeway. Why was it so many Houston drivers couldn't seem to handle driving in the rain? Half of them were afraid to drive at a normal speed; the other half drove like maniacs. And the trucks! They were the worst, flying on the freeways at speeds that would have been dangerous during perfect weather, let alone with these slick roads. A huge tanker passed on her left, kicking up a monumental spray of water in its wake.

Thankfully, her exit was the next one. She put on her right blinker.

"Mom? Can we stop at Burger King?"

Abbie stifled a sigh. "Kendall, we had Taco Bell yesterday on the way home from school. You know you're not supposed to be eating junk food."

"Ah, Mom, just this once, *puh-leeeze*? I'm *starving*! I feel like I'm going to faint, I'm so hungry!"

Abbie couldn't help smiling at Kendall's dramatics. And it *was* way past their lunchtime since Abbie had had several errands to take care of after she'd picked up Kendall. "Oh, all right. But we're not going to do this every day."

"I know."

"And tonight, young lady, you're having both broccoli *and* carrots!"

Happy now that she'd gotten her way, Kendall grinned. "Okay."

Fifteen minutes later, the car filled with the aroma of hamburgers and French fries, Abbie turned off Briar Forest Drive and into their subdivision. The rain was still coming down in torrents. Her windshield wipers were turned on high and barely doing the job. As she turned right onto their street, Abbie could see the mail truck ahead.

"Looks like the mail's here." Abbie was expecting a sorely needed check from one of her clients. "I'll pull up close to the mailbox, okay? Can you reach out and get the mail?"

"Sure."

Abbie waited until she was right up next to the mailbox before lowering the window. Kendall stuck her hand in and pulled out a wad of mail. Even though it only took a few seconds, her arm was soaked, and Abbie hurriedly raised the window. Kendall leafed through the mail, which, from what Abbie could see, was mostly junk.

"Mom! There's a letter from Dad!" Kendall squealed. "It's addressed to you. Maybe he's coming to visit!"

Abbie grimaced. She doubted Thomas was coming to visit. More likely, he was simply answering her letter, because she had written to him two weeks ago, on the day after Kendall had been so upset. She made a noncommittal sound and, swinging wide, pulled into the driveway.

"Hurry up," Kendall said. "I can't wait to see what he says."

Abbie aimed the garage door opener. "I'm hurrying."

Loaded down with office supplies, the books they'd gotten at the library, and the food from Burger King, they made their way into the kitchen. Delaying the moment when she would have to read the letter, and wishing she could figure out a way to read it away from Kendall's too-observant eyes, Abbie slowly lowered her bundles onto the kitchen table.

Practically dancing with impatience, Kendall thrust the envelope bearing Thomas's return address in China under Abbie's nose. "Mom! Come on, open it! I want to know what he says."

Trapped, Abbie slit the envelope and removed the single sheet of paper. But when Kendall tried to read over her shoulder, she resolutely kept the paper folded. "Kendall, I know you're anxious, but this is my letter, honey. Now sit down while I read it, okay? You said you were starving, so why don't you start eating?"

Kendall looked as if she were going to protest, but she didn't. Instead she sighed and reached for the bag of food.

Abbie walked to the kitchen sink and filled a glass with water. She wasn't really thirsty, but she didn't want Kendall to see her face. Keeping her back to Kendall, she opened the letter. It was very short, only a few lines. Steeling herself, she read:

> *Dear Abbie,*
>
> *I received your letter yesterday. I told you years ago how I felt, and I haven't changed my mind. Kendall is your child. You wanted her. I didn't.*
>
> *I really must insist you refrain from bothering me with these kinds of demands again. I have been very fair over the years. Some people would say overly fair, and certainly extremely generous, and I do not appreciate your efforts to make me feel guilty.*
>
> *Please be advised that I have remarried. Kindly address all future correspondence to my wife, as she will now be taking care of all my business and personal affairs. Her name is Cynthia.*
>
> *Thomas*

"Mom? Mom?"

Abbie blinked, not sure how long she'd been standing there, staring at the hateful letter.

I really must insist that you refrain from bothering me. Please be advised. Address all future correspondence.

The words, so cold, so formal, so *Thomas*, hammered in her brain. How could she *ever* have loved him?

Carefully, she refolded the letter. Shoving down the rage that was like a gorge in her throat, she composed her face and slowly turned to face Kendall, whose eyes were bright with hope.

"Is he coming to visit?"

"No, sweetie, I'm afraid not."

Kendall's face fell. "Well, what did he *say*?"

Abbie started to lie, started to make the same excuses she'd made for years, but she stopped herself. Why should she keep hope alive for Kendall? It was cruel. "He said he wanted us to know he's gotten married again." Crumpling the letter in her fist, she thrust it into the pocket of her shorts.

Kendall stared at her. Abbie pretended not to see the emotions that flitted across her daughter's expressive face: disbelief, quickly followed by bewilderment, then hurt. She reached for the bag of food, saying brightly, "I'm hungry, too. Shall we eat?"

For a long moment, Kendall said nothing. And then, shocking Abbie, she threw down her hamburger and jumped up, overturning the plastic container of Coke she'd been drinking. The top popped off, and Coke flew everywhere. "I hate him!" Kendall cried. "I hate him! I hope he dies!" Weeping hysterically, she bolted from the room.

If Abbie lived a hundred more years, she knew she would never forget the gut-wrenching sound of Kendall's brokenhearted sobs as she ran down the hall and into her room, the door slamming behind her. Kendall didn't deserve this unhappiness. She certainly didn't deserve to believe that a selfish, cold-hearted, miserable bastard like Thomas was her father.

And it was only then, after all these days of indecision and agonizing, that Abbie knew what she must do.

"I'm sorry, Miss Bernard, Mr. O'Connell is not in the office today."

"Is he working at home?" Abbie kept her voice low, even though Kendall was still shut up in her room, and Abbie knew she couldn't hear her.

"No, ma'am. There's been a death in the family, so he's been out for a few days."

"A death!" Oh, dear God. Erin! Abbie's heart lurched in fear, and she could barely get the next words out. "I-I'm so sorry. Who . . . who was it?"

"His father-in-law. He, Mr. Chamberlain, that is, had a heart attack on Friday. They're burying him today."

Relief made Abbie's knees feel weak. She thanked the girl and hung up. Then she dug out the paper. She hadn't read it this morning because the rain had seeped under the plastic covering and soaked the outer sections. It was still wet, she saw, thinking she should have hung it out to dry somewhere. Quickly, she searched for the obituaries. Sometimes obituaries ran for more than one day.

Sure enough, there it was. "Oliver Chamberlain." She scanned it, then read it through more slowly.

Survivors were listed as his wife, Celia, and his daughter Elizabeth. Two grandchildren, Patrick and Erin O'Connell. Preceded in death by his daughter Ann Chamberlain O'Connell. Former engineer, retired from Shell Oil Company. Lifelong Houston resident. Member of St. Luke's Methodist Church. Volunteer with Citywide Food Project. Volunteer at Methodist Hospital.

As she read, the knowledge thrummed through her that this man was Kendall's grandfather.

Sadness pierced her. Kendall was such a wonderful child. And she'd never known a grandfather. Abbie's own father died when Abbie was a freshman in high school, and Thomas had been a late-in-life baby whose parents were both dead by the time Abbie met him. He'd told Abbie once that his mother had never expected to have any children, had in fact been married for twenty years before becoming pregnant with Thomas at forty-five.

"I was a great shock to them," he'd said. "They hardly knew what to do with me. After all, their ways were already set." He shrugged. "They provided food and shelter and after they died, there was plenty of money for my education. And when you come right down to it, that's all any child needs, anyway."

Thomas had been so wrong. Abbie had known it then, but when she'd tried to say so, he had told her to stop being so sentimental.

Poor Kendall.

All these years, she'd been so cheated.

Abbie sat for a long time, thinking. The death of Oliver Chamberlain had, in some inexplicable way, made her doubt her earlier decision to tell Logan O'Connell the truth.

What if he didn't believe her? What if he wanted nothing to do with Kendall and refused to allow Abbie to see

Erin again? Because if she were being entirely honest with herself, she would admit that she didn't just want Kendall to know her father. Abbie wanted to get to know Erin and for Erin to know her.

But maybe Logan wouldn't see things that way. Maybe he would throw Abbie out. And then what? Was Abbie prepared to go to court and fight him?

Everything in her shrank from the thought. The publicity, the notoriety—it would be horrible, especially for the children. She remembered the media circus and hoopla surrounding the last case of baby switching to come to light. She cringed thinking about the headlines in all the papers, the covers on *People* and *Time* magazine, the stories on "Inside Edition" and "Dateline." The way the press had camped out at both homes, giving none of the involved parties any peace.

Oh, God. Surely Logan wouldn't want that. He was much too nice a man. He would never want that.

But how did she know? She didn't really know Logan. Maybe he was not the man she thought he was. Maybe, if she told him, it would be the worst mistake she'd ever made. A mistake that could never be rectified.

Thirteen

"Hey, Erin, I'm goin' over to Josh's to swim. You wanna come?"

Erin looked up from the pictures spread out on her bed. Her brother, dressed in swim trunks and a Smashing Pumpkins T-shirt, stood in the doorway to her room. She shook her head. "Nuh uh."

"Ah, c'mon. Brianna's gonna be there, and she said to ask you."

Erin knew Brianna didn't really want her to come. Why would she? Brianna was almost thirteen and going into the eighth grade at Caldwell, whereas she, Erin, was only going to be a sixth grader next year. Brianna just had a crush on Patrick, that was why she'd said to invite Erin, because she wanted Patrick to like her. Erin would just be in the way. She'd much rather stay home. "I don't feel like it."

Patrick walked into the room and sat on the edge of the bed. "Hey," he said softly. "You feeling bad?"

She shrugged, unable to look at him, because if she did, she knew she would cry.

"Thinkin' about Gramps?"

To Erin's mortification, she could feel the tears welling. She bit down on her lower lip. She didn't want to start crying again. She was sure Patrick already thought she was a baby.

"I miss him, too," Patrick said, putting his arm around her, "but he wouldn't want us to be sad."

Erin took a deep breath. "I know. That's what Dad said."

"But if you *are* sad, you can always talk to Aunt Glenna about it."

Erin nodded. Her dad had suggested that, too, but she didn't want to talk to Aunt Glenna, even though she loved her and Aunt Glenna was really smart about things, being a psychiatrist and all. The reason she didn't want to talk to Aunt Glenna was that the thing Erin wanted to talk about was Aunt Elizabeth, and she didn't think Aunt Glenna liked Aunt Elizabeth. One time last year, when Erin had been at Aunt Glenna's house, she'd overheard Aunt Glenna talking to Uncle Paul, and what she'd said was that Aunt Elizabeth was like a bitch in heat when she was around Logan. Even though Erin wasn't exactly sure what "a bitch in heat" meant, she was pretty certain it had to do with sex and that it wasn't nice. She picked at a loose thread on her shorts. "Patrick?"

"Yeah?"

"Do you think Daddy will get married again?"

Patrick shrugged. "I don't know. If he meets somebody he likes, I guess."

Erin frowned. "I don't want him to meet somebody. I want him to marry Aunt Elizabeth."

"Yeah, I know."

"Well, don't *you*?"

Patrick shrugged again. "I haven't thought about it."

"Why not? Don't you like Aunt Elizabeth?"

"Yeah, sure, I like her. She's our aunt. But Dad and Mom, you know, they were real happy together. Maybe he doesn't want another wife."

"But Aunt Elizabeth wouldn't be just another wife," Erin pointed out. "She's Mom's *sister*. It would be like having Mom here again, don't you think?"

"I don't know," Patrick said again. He avoided her eyes.

Erin could tell he didn't agree with her, but he didn't want to say so. Maybe she hadn't explained things the right way. "I don't think Dad would ever want to marry somebody else. I mean, what you said was right. He and Mom were really, really happy, so he would want someone just like Mom. And there's no one else as much like Mom as Aunt Elizabeth."

Patrick seemed like he was going to say something else about Aunt Elizabeth, but then all he said was "Yeah, well, you could be right, but listen, don't get your hopes up, okay?"

"I won't."

"Good. Well, I'd better get goin'. Sure you don't want to come?"

"I'm sure. Anyway, I'm supposed to meet Allison this afternoon." Allison was her E-mail/chat room buddy. Most afternoons they met on-line and talked for at least an hour.

"Well, all right. See you later."

After Patrick left, Erin lay down on her bed and closed her eyes. Her dad had gone back to work today, and the house seemed so empty without him. Serita was there, of course, but Serita was just the housekeeper, and Patrick— well, Patrick was older and he had his own life. Besides, he didn't really understand how Erin felt. He tried, but he was a boy. A boy didn't need the same kinds of things a girl needed. And even though she *did* have Allison to talk to, it wasn't the same as having someone here. She'd never even met Allison, who lived in St. Louis.

That lonely feeling, the one that had started when her mom died, filled her chest and made it hurt. Her lower lip trembled, slow tears seeping from beneath her closed eyelids.

She missed her mom so much.

Mommy, why did you have to die?

The really scary part was that sometimes she couldn't remember what her Mom looked like. Today had been one of those days. That's why she'd gotten out all her pictures. And looking at the pictures had helped Erin remember what it had been like before her mom died. How much fun they'd had in the summer, when Erin and Patrick were out of school. Her mom had planned all kinds of things for them to do together, even when Patrick was busy with swim team or camp.

Sometimes they would go shopping or to the movies. Sometimes her mom would take her to the museums or the galleries—her mom had loved those places because she was an artist herself—and sometimes they would just be lazy and spend the whole day at the club pool. And if Erin wanted to invite a friend to go with them, her mom had never cared. Her mom had made the things they did so much fun.

Now there wasn't anyone to take her places except her dad, when he wasn't working, and Aunt Elizabeth, when she wasn't working. Most of the time, though, Aunt Elizabeth had to work. But if Erin's dad and Aunt Elizabeth got married, things would be different, because then Aunt Elizabeth wouldn't have to work anymore and she and Erin could spend all their time together. She knew Aunt Elizabeth wanted that as much as she did. Oh, she wished it would happen! Then she wouldn't feel lonely anymore, ever. And her dad wouldn't be lonely anymore, either.

Suddenly Erin remembered something her Grandmother O'Connell always said, that wishes weren't enough, you had to work to make those wishes come true.

Slowly, as she considered her grandmother's advice, Erin's tears dried, and the achy feeling in her chest went away. Of course. That's what she needed to do—work at making her dad see how perfect Aunt Elizabeth was.

And when he did . . . Erin smiled. Well, then everything would be wonderful.

Logan had hated leaving Erin and Patrick today, but he'd been out of the office for a week, and work was piling up. He told himself they would be okay. Next week the three of them were going to Vancouver, and with the exception of the few hours when he would be doing his presentation at the International Association of Architects meeting, they would have an entire week to do nothing but enjoy themselves and one another.

Trying not to worry, he settled down to work. At ten o'clock, deep into a design for a new children's clinic, he frowned in annoyance when Rebecca buzzed him on the intercom.

"Yes? What is it, Rebecca?"

"Mr. O'Connell, I'm sorry to disturb you, but there's a Ms. Abbie Bernard here to see you."

In the emotional turmoil of the last week, he had completely forgotten about Abbie Bernard. But now he remembered how he had been only seconds away from calling the police when he was interrupted by the phone call from Elizabeth saying her father had had a heart attack.

Although normally he would not see anyone without an appointment—especially not on a day when he was as swamped as he was today—he was too curious about what story the woman had concocted today to send her away. "Bring her in, Rebecca."

A few moments later, there was a soft tap on the door. "Come in." He stood as Rebecca ushered Abbie into his office.

Smiling, she walked forward. "Hello, Logan. Thank you for seeing me. I know I should have called first, but I was in the area and thought I'd just take a chance you could give me a few minutes."

If she was a liar, she was damned good at it, with just the right combination of assertiveness and diffidence.

"I'm afraid a few minutes *is* all I have," he said. "I've been out of the office for a few days and have a lot to catch up on."

"I know. I was so sorry to hear about your father-in-law."

He frowned. How the devil had she known about Oliver?

"I called here last week," she quickly explained, "and your secretary told me."

"I see. Well, thank you. It was quite unexpected and a terrible shock for all of us." He gestured to the corner, where a group of navy-and-gray plaid chairs were grouped around a glass-topped coffee table. "Let's go sit over there, shall we? Would you like some coffee or a soft drink?"

"No, thank you."

Once they were seated, he studied her. She looked very nice today—that black dress was flattering. And she'd done something to her hair, too. It was shorter and curlier. Looking at her, at those big, soft eyes and delicate features, it was hard to believe she was a con artist. And yet, how to explain what he had discovered?

She cleared her throat. "I, um, suppose you're wondering why I'm here."

He said nothing, having learned long ago that silence was

a stronger weapon than words when you wanted to best an opponent.

"You know, because I got sick that day at your house, I didn't get to talk to Erin the way I wanted to, and I was hoping maybe we could set up a time for me to see her."

He let a long moment go by, noticing by the way she kept fiddling with her purse that she wasn't quite as cool and collected as she'd like him to believe. "Give me one good reason, *Mrs. Bernard,* why I shouldn't get up right now and call the police."

The color drained from her face. "The police?" she said faintly. "Wh-why would you do that?"

"You know damn well why. I don't know what your game is, but you're no more a journalist than I am, and until I know *exactly* who you are and *exactly* what you want, I have no intention of allowing you within one hundred yards of my daughter."

Her mouth opened, but no sound came out.

"Don't bother denying it. I called *Lone Star Monthly.* They've never heard of you. I'm not even sure Abbie Bernard is really your name."

That statement seemed to galvanize her. Opening her purse, she withdrew a black leather wallet. "Here," she said, "look. Here's my driver's license. And here's my American Express card. And my social security card."

Logan studied the license and the cards. All were issued to Abigail Wellington Bernard. And that was definitely her picture on the license. Somewhat appeased, his voice was milder when he said, "Your driver's license says you live in Lucas." He handed the cards back to her.

"I told you. My daughter and I just moved to Houston a month ago, and I haven't had time to get a new license."

"Okay. So you gave me the right name. But how do you explain the fact that *Lone Star Monthly* doesn't know you?"

"Well, the thing is, I'm doing the article on spec. I did discuss it with one of the editors last year, but he's gone now. Still, I thought it was a good enough idea to develop it, anyway."

Everything she'd said sounded perfectly credible. Logan wanted to believe her, because despite his doubts, he couldn't help being drawn to her. And yet the doubts remained. "Maybe you're telling me the truth," he said slowly, "but I don't think it's the whole truth. There's something you're hiding from me. For all I know, you're a kidnapper. So there's no way I'll allow you to get near any member of my family until you can prove to me you're no threat to their welfare."

Her eyes met his. A long moment passed during which the only sounds in the office were the muted clicking of Rebecca's computer keys and the faint rumble of traffic fifteen stories below.

Finally she gave a long, tremulous sigh and looked down at her lap. "You're right," she said softly, "I haven't told you the whole truth."

He waited until she looked at him again. "Go on."

Once more, she opened her purse and withdrew her wallet. But this time she removed two photographs. Silently, she handed one of them to him.

The oddest sensation gripped him when he looked at the picture. It was a head shot of a beautiful young girl with dark curly hair, huge green eyes, and a brilliant smile. She looked—how was it possible?—so much like Patrick that the two could have been twins, except it was obvious, even in the photo, that the girl was younger, probably closer to Erin's age.

Something very close to fear crawled down Logan's spine as he slowly raised his eyes from the photograph to Abbie. Her eyes were filled with an emotion he couldn't identify, and yet it intensified his fear.

Silently, Abbie handed him the second photo. Now the fear erupted into full-blown panic, for this was a picture of Erin. Only it wasn't. Erin had never worn her hair in braids like that and she'd never been in a house like the one in the photograph.

"Who are these girls?" he demanded in a voice that sounded too harsh to be his. "And just what the hell are you trying to pull?"

She swallowed. "The first girl is . . . my daughter, Kendall. The second picture . . . that . . . that's me when I was ten years old."

He shook his head slowly. "I don't understand."

"I—" She bit her lip. Took a deep breath. "I know you don't. And I'm doing a very poor job of trying to explain it to you, but this is so hard." Tears filled her eyes. "You don't know how long I've been agonizing over this, trying to decide whether to tell you or not."

"Tell me *what*?" Her tears infuriated him, and he didn't know why.

"Please don't be angry." She made an obvious effort to get herself under control. "I'm trying. Kendall, my daughter, the girl in the first picture I gave you, was born at Cyrus Hurley Hospital in Hurley, Texas, a few minutes before midnight on February seventh eleven years ago."

It took a few moments before the significance of her words sank in. As soon as they did, shock rendered him nearly speechless. A few minutes before midnight on February seventh! Erin had been born a few minutes *after* midnight at the same hospital! He even remembered the doctor talking about the other baby he'd just delivered. Why, he even remembered hearing the sounds of the other birth taking place as he sat beside Ann and helped her through her labor pains.

Abbie's eyes pled for understanding. "Kendall is such a wonderful girl. Beautiful and talented. A really gifted artist."

Logan stared at her.

"I've . . . I've always been so proud of her and so amazed that someone like me could have produced a child like her," she continued in a soft voice filled with pain. "And then . . . and then two weeks ago today, I was given irrefutable proof that Kendall isn't my daughter."

Logan's heart beat in slow, painful thuds. Somehow he knew what was coming next.

"You see . . ." Tears ran down her face. "I'm convinced that somehow our two babies, yours and mine, were switched in the hospital. That Erin . . ." Her face crumpled, and it was a few seconds before she could continue. "That Erin is really my daughter, and Kendall is yours."

There was a great roaring in Logan's head. He jumped up and glared at her. "You're crazy."

She shook her head. "I wish I were, but—"

"Get out of here," he said through gritted teeth. "Get out of here, and don't ever come back."

She had fished a tissue out of her purse, and she swiped at her eyes, saying, "Logan, please, listen to me."

Because she showed no signs of obeying him, he reached down and grabbed her arm, hauling her up from her chair. "I said, get out."

"Listen, I can prove—"

Blindly furious, he picked up her purse and shoved it at her with such force she stumbled backward and would have fallen except for the chair. White-faced, she stared at him. Instantly, shame consumed him. "Christ, I'm sorry. Are you okay?" He reached out to touch her arm, and she shrank back. The shame deepened. He had never in his life touched a woman in anger until this moment.

Closing her eyes, she took a deep, shuddering breath. When she opened them again, she looked calmer. "Yes, I'm okay." Her blue eyes met his. "Do you still want me to leave?"

He ran his hands through his hair. "I . . . Jesus. I don't know what I want." Now it was his turn to take a deep breath. "No, don't leave. But before we continue, I think we could both use a drink."

While he poured them each a small amount of Remy Martin, he resolutely kept his mind empty. It was only after he'd handed her the snifter of brandy and they'd both taken a fortifying swallow that he allowed himself to think again. "You said you had proof of what you've told me."

She nodded.

"What?" The word came out as a croak. He cleared his throat. "What kind of proof?"

"I've had Kendall's blood tested. Twice. And both times it's shown that it's biologically impossible for me to be her mother."

"That's not proof that *Erin* is your daughter."

"No, but," she added calmly, "since I know I gave birth that night, and since I know my baby was a girl and that your baby was the only other girl born during that period, it's pretty obvious that our babies must have been switched. I mean, that's the only logical explanation."

He wanted to deny what she'd said. Just because Kendall wasn't *her* daughter didn't mean Erin wasn't *his*! He wanted to laugh and say it was all just a screw-up, that's all, and she had scared the shit out of him for no reason. He wanted to say this whole idea was the craziest thing he'd ever heard and there was no way—*no fucking way!*—it could be true.

And if he hadn't seen that picture of her daughter, that's exactly what he would have said. But the image of that beautiful child—so like Patrick and so like him—was impossible to ignore and even more impossible to deny.

And don't forget that other picture.

He swallowed. Yes, that Erin-like image would be burned forever into his brain, too.

"I know this is a terrible shock to you," she said. "Believe me, I know. I've been agonizing over this for two weeks now. I haven't been able to sleep. I haven't been able to eat. I haven't been able to work. All I've done is think and think. That such a thing could happen is just unbelievable. And yet it did."

Jesus, he thought. Jesus. Could this be true? Could it?

"You believe me, don't you?" She sat calmly now, her hands resting quietly in her lap.

He looked into her eyes, and he remembered how, that first day, he'd noticed that her eyes were the same shade as Erin's. And now that he was looking for them, he saw other similarities as well: the color and texture of her hair, the shape of her hands, that wistful, vulnerable expression that even now was etched across Abbie's face.

"Yes," he said, hearing the roughness in his voice. "I believe you."

Fourteen

Logan's words echoed around them.
I believe you.

After a long, agonizing moment during which their eyes were locked in mute misery, Logan got up and walked to the window. He stared out, seeing nothing. He would need proof himself—blood tests, DNA tests. He would never just take someone's word for it. Yet, down deep, in his gut, he knew that no matter what he did, in the end nothing would be different than it was right now.

Erin. Not mine. She's not mine.

Over and over, like a stuck tape, the words repeated themselves. Numbness enveloped him, as if essential body parts had frozen and might never again come to life.

"Are you all right?" The question was soft, concerned. He wanted to laugh. All right? He would never be all right again. Slowly, he turned and met Abbie's eyes. He shook his head dumbly. "I can't seem to think straight."

"I know. It's . . . it's such a shock."

Shock. Yes. Shock.

Erin.

Images swirled. Erin as an infant. How quietly she'd slept in the old-fashioned crib that was a holdover from Ann's babyhood. How he would tiptoe into her room at night just to look at her innocent face. How his chest would hurt from the love he felt as he touched her tiny, perfectly formed hand

and watched her little chest moving up and down as she breathed.

Erin.

The day she got her first pair of patent leather shoes. She'd worn them with thin white socks trimmed in ruffled lace. Her small face had been shining with happiness as she pranced around the room, showing them off. He and Ann had exchanged a look filled with amusement and love and a poignancy that neither could put into words, because it was the first time they realized their little girl would some-day grow up and leave them.

Erin.

Teaching her to ride her bike without training wheels. How she'd fallen before Logan could catch her. She'd scraped both knees and he'd held her and comforted her, then taken her inside, where he and Ann had cleaned them and kissed them and put Neosporin on them.

He remembered the day they'd gotten Rex. Erin lay on the floor, laughing hysterically, while the exuberant puppy cavorted around her, yipping and licking her face.

He remembered her first day of kindergarten. How scared she'd been. He and Ann had taken her to Caldwell together. Both had lumps in their throat when they waved good-bye.

Erin.

He remembered her devastation when Ann died. How her pillow was wet every morning for months afterward.

And lastly, he remembered how she'd cried and clung to him when he'd told her about her grandfather Chamberlain. How she'd begged him to promise he would never leave her.

Impossible. This is impossible.

He shook his head. "I . . . Look, I'm sorry. I need to be alone. I can't talk right now."

She nodded sadly. "I understand." She reached for her purse. "It's going to take time for you to absorb all this."

She was halfway out the door when some semblance of lucidity returned. "Wait," he said. "Give me your phone number. They said it wasn't listed when I tried to call you before."

"Oh." She grimaced. "I'm sorry. That's because I don't like advertising the fact I'm a woman. When the new directory comes out, I'll be listed as Bernard Research in the business pages." She opened her purse, pulled out a business card, and handed it to him. "I got some new ones made."

"Thanks." He shoved it into his pocket without looking at it. "I'll, uh, call you tomorrow."

She studied him for a moment. "Are you going to be all right?"

Mutely, he nodded. After touching his shoulder briefly in a gesture of comfort, she left.

When the door closed behind her, he sat down at his desk and buried his face in his hands. Thirty minutes ago the biggest worry on his mind had been whether his kids were coping without him at home today. And now . . .

Erin wasn't really his daughter. No matter how much he loved her and she loved him and Patrick, she didn't belong to them.

I could lose her!

The knowledge slammed into him like a physical blow. And just as if someone *had* hit him, pain followed, making it hard to breathe.

It was unthinkable. He *couldn't* lose her. She belonged to him. *But Abbie Bernard says she doesn't. Abbie says the blood tests prove she doesn't.*

The pain was joined by an anger so ferocious, he wanted to throw things. He wanted to hit something. He wanted to rail at the cruelty of fate.

No, no, no, no!

Wasn't it enough that he'd lost Ann?

Was he now going to lose Erin, too?

By the following morning, Logan was much calmer. His emotions had run the gamut from blind fury and denial to sorrowful but wary acceptance. And with that acceptance came clarity, which led to decision and a plan. The first order of business, he decided, must be confirmation of the blood tests Abbie had talked about, because even though he believed her, only a fool would go forward on something this important without concrete proof.

So when he arrived at his office, he called the number on the business card she'd given him.

The phone rang four times, then her recorded voice said, "This is Abbie Bernard of Bernard Research. At the tone, leave a message and I'll get back to you."

"This is Logan O'Connell," he said. "Please call me at the office."

While he waited, he tried to work, without much success. At nine-thirty Rebecca buzzed him to say Abbie Bernard was on the line.

"Hi," she said when he answered. "How are you today?"

"Better."

"Good. I-I worried about you all night."

He'd worried about her, too. Worried about what she wanted. What she might do. And yet . . . he might be wrong, but he didn't get the feeling she wanted to hurt him or Erin. "Thanks," he said cautiously.

"Did you sleep at all?"

"Not much."

"That's the way my first night was, too. It's . . . it's overwhelming, isn't it?"

"You could say that."

"I'm sorry I wasn't here when you called. Kendall is taking a summer art course and I drive her to school every morning."

Kendall. My daughter. It was a moment before he could answer. "That's okay. Listen, there are a couple of things I wanted to talk to you about."

"Okay."

"The first is your husband."

"My *ex*-husband."

"Okay, your *ex*-husband. Does he know what you suspect?"

"No. He has nothing to do with this. Nothing."

"Abbie, if this is true, if our daughters really *were* switched in the hospital, he has as much to do with it as you or I do."

"You don't understand. Thomas never wanted a child. He has ignored Kendall since the day she was born. If I were to tell him about this, he wouldn't care. He'd say it was my problem."

Her tone was expressionless, but he imagined this was

because she'd had a long time to reconcile herself to her former husband's rejection. Jesus. And this jerk was Erin's *father*?

"Believe me," she continued, "you don't have to worry about him. He's not going to make any trouble."

"All right." There were dozens of questions Logan wanted to ask, but he'd save them for later. "Let's drop that subject for now. The next thing is, I want to call your doctor and talk to him about the blood tests."

"Oh. All right."

"It's not that I don't believe you."

"No. No, of course not. I understand. In your shoes, I'd want to check my story out, too." She gave him the number. "Were you planning to call him this morning?"

"Yes. The sooner, the better."

"Of course. You're right. But give me about fifteen minutes, okay? I'll call his office and tell his nurse that I give my permission for him to release any information you want."

She was right, he thought ruefully. It was stupid of him to think he could just call. "I hadn't thought of that," he admitted.

"It's no wonder. You're still reeling from shock."

His mouth twisted in wry agreement. For a few moments, neither said anything.

Then she said, "Logan?"

"Yes?"

"Before we hang up, I just wanted you to know that somehow we can work this out. The last thing I want is to hurt anyone, most especially either of the girls."

Her unexpected assurance, and the sincerity he heard behind it, was nearly his undoing, but he managed to hang on to his composure and thank her.

When they hung up, he stared at the phone. We can work this out, she'd said.

But how? he wondered. How?

An hour later, Logan quietly placed the phone back into its receiver. So it was true. He had just talked with Dr. Joplin, who verified everything Abbie had told him. The doctor had even offered to fax the pertinent records to Logan—an offer Logan had gratefully accepted.

Before they'd hung up, Dr. Joplin suggested that Logan might want to have his and Erin's blood tested, too.

"Oh, I was planning to," Logan assured him.

"For legal purposes, you might even want to consider DNA testing," the doctor added.

Logan swallowed. For legal purposes?

The words reverberated in his brain.

For legal purposes.

Did Dr. Joplin think Abbie would go to court and try to get Erin away from him?

Surely not. Hadn't she said they could work this out? That hurting either of the girls was the last thing she wanted?

But she could change her mind. Now that the idea was planted, he couldn't get rid of it. What if she did change her mind? What if she decided she wanted Erin? Didn't the courts usually side with the mother?

Jesus.

The word was half prayer, half oath. He closed his eyes. What should he do?

After long minutes when his heart refused to slow down, and his brain was consumed by fear, he finally got a grip on himself. Dr. Joplin's suggestion didn't mean Abbie was going to do anything like going to court. It was just a sound suggestion, the kind of thing—if Logan had been operating on any level other than the emotional—he should have thought about himself.

Calmer now, he picked up the receiver again. It was time for step two.

Seven and a half hours later, as the lavender sky of early evening settled over the sultry city, Logan drove toward the west side address Abbie had given him. He had just dropped Erin at Glenna's house, saying he had a meeting and didn't want her to stay home alone. Patrick had gone to see a movie with a group of friends and was spending the night with one of them.

And now, with an increasing feeling of unreality, Logan

was on his way to meet the girl he still couldn't think of as his daughter.

"It's your turn, Erin."

Erin looked up. She and her Uncle Paul were playing a game of checkers, and she'd been daydreaming. She considered the board carefully, then moved one of her red pieces. Too late, she saw that she was going to get jumped. Twice, in fact.

"Sorry, pumpkin." Her uncle made an apologetic face as he captured two of her pieces.

Erin sighed. "It's okay." She had no real interest in the game, although normally she loved playing board games with her uncle.

"Hey." He reached over and squeezed her hand. "You're awfully quiet tonight. Anything wrong?"

She shrugged. When he didn't say anything, Erin looked up into her uncle's soft, kind eyes, and suddenly, she wanted to tell him. Her glance shifted to the kitchen doorway. She could see her Aunt Glenna unloading the dishwasher. Erin bit her lip.

"Tell you what," her uncle said. "Why don't we put away the checkers, then maybe you and I could go for a walk. Okay?"

Grateful that he'd understood without her having to explain and feel disloyal to her Aunt Glenna, Erin smiled and said, "Okay."

Ten minutes later, they were walking slowly down the winding, tree-lined street. It was just beginning to get dark, and the cicadas were really making a racket singing to one another. Erin kicked at a stone and thought about how to begin. "I miss my mother," she finally said.

"Ah, honey." Her uncle put his arm around her shoulder. "I know you do."

"My dad tries hard, but he just doesn't *know* some things." She looked up. "Do you know what I mean?"

Her uncle smiled. "Of course I do. We guys are pretty dense when it comes to knowing the things women want us to know."

"And he has to work all the time." Then Erin felt bad because it sounded like she was complaining, and that wasn't it at all. "I understand about him working, but still, it's *hard*. It's great when he works at home, but he can't do that all the time." She sighed. "Mom was always home, and we . . . we *did* things together. We talked about things, things I can't talk about with my dad . . . especially now, when I'm older . . ."

"Well, honey, I know it's not the same as having your mom, but if there are things you need to ask or things you need to talk about, you have two grandmothers and two aunts who love you very much."

Erin nodded. "I know."

"You can always call Aunt Glenna, and I'm sure your Aunt Elizabeth feels exactly the—"

"That's just it, though. I don't *want* to call someone. I want a mother! I-I wish my dad would marry my Aunt Elizabeth," Erin blurted out, "then I'd *have* a mother again."

For a long moment, her uncle didn't answer. When he did, his voice was quiet and thoughtful, the way adults get when they are going to say something you're probably not going to want to hear. "Erin, I know that's what you want. Probably your dad knows it, too. But marrying someone, that's a real big step in a person's life. You can't do it just because someone else wants you to, not even someone your dad loves as much as he loves you. I know you're only eleven, but you're old enough to understand. If your father married your Aunt Elizabeth just to please you and give you a mother, it wouldn't work. In the end, he'd be miserable, and so would your aunt. And, probably, so would you."

Erin wanted to say he was wrong. That her dad *would* be happy. That they'd *all* be happy. And yet something held her back, because she thought about the funny look that would sometimes come over her father's face when her Aunt Elizabeth said something he didn't like, or the way he acted around her sometimes, like he wished she would go home. She also remembered how he would sometimes forget to return Aunt Elizabeth's phone calls, even though her father never forgot anything.

She sighed again. Maybe her uncle was right. Maybe she should forget all about her dad marrying her Aunt Elizabeth.

"You want your dad to be happy, don't you, Erin?"

Erin had almost forgotten her Uncle Paul was there, she'd been so engrossed in her thoughts. "Yes, of course I do."

"Well then, honey, instead of wishing he would marry your Aunt Elizabeth, why don't you hope that one of these days he will meet somebody he can love?" her uncle suggested gently.

Erin knew what her uncle wanted her to say, but she couldn't do it, because if her dad wasn't going to marry her Aunt Elizabeth, Erin didn't want him to marry anyone. Just the idea of some strange woman coming into their house and trying to act like her mother made Erin feel sick.

No, her dad wouldn't do that. He'd loved her mom too much to marry some stranger.

But no matter how many times she reassured herself, now that her uncle had planted it, Erin couldn't get the thought out of her head. And it scared her. So that night, just before she fell asleep, she decided no matter what her uncle had said, she would keep trying to show her dad how perfect Aunt Elizabeth was for them.

Fifteen

Ever since her mother said she was expecting company for dinner, Kendall had been trying to figure out what was going on. Who was this man? Was he a *date*?

The idea excited Kendall. Her mom hadn't had a date in a long, long time. Kendall had almost given up hope. The last man her mother had gone out with was a science teacher from Lucas High School. He was okay, Kendall guessed, although nobody she'd have wanted her mom to marry. Kendall hadn't had to worry about that happening, though, because he didn't last long. And since then, there'd been no one.

She eyed her mom, who was standing with her back to Kendall while working on the salad for dinner. Her mom was wearing a red sundress—a *nice* sundress, not one she wore for everyday—but that didn't really mean anything. She would dress up no matter who the company was—that's just the way she was. But she was also wearing makeup— not just lipstick, but eye shadow and mascara. Her hair looked great, too, ever since she'd gotten it cut last week. Her hairdresser had also talked her into a perm, and now her hair curled around her face and made her look really pretty. Could this man be the reason for all these changes in her mom?

Not only that, her mom was nervous, too. She kept looking at the clock. And she wasn't humming. She always hummed when she cooked, because she liked to cook. Cooking made her feel happy, she said.

Tonight was definitely beginning to seem like a date. "So when did you meet Mr. O'Connell, Mom? I thought I knew all your friends."

"Oh, a couple of weeks ago." Her mom quickly chopped the carrots she'd arranged on the cutting board and tossed them into the salad bowl.

"But where?" Kendall pressed.

"Where what?" Her mom reached for a tomato.

"Mo-*om*, where did you meet him?"

"Um, it was while I was doing some research for a client." She cored the tomato, then began cutting it into chunks.

"So how old is he?"

"I'm not sure. Somewhere around my age, I'd guess."

"Oh. Well, is he married?"

Her mother finished the tomato, then turned around to face Kendall. "No, he's not married. He was, but his wife died."

That was good, Kendall thought. Not that his wife died. She'd never think someone dying was good. Just that he wasn't married. "Does he have—"

"That's enough, Kendall," her mom said, cutting her off in her I'm-losing-my-patience voice. "Instead of standing there bugging me, why don't you go wash up and fix your hair and put on your new shorts outfit? He'll be here soon, and you're not ready."

"I just wanted to know if he had any kids."

"Yes, he does. He has two, a boy and a girl. *Now* will you go get ready?"

"Okay, okay, I'm going."

As Kendall changed clothes, she kept going over her mom's answers. This *must* be a date. Because her mom hadn't said this Mr. O'Connell was a client, just that she'd met him while doing some work for a client. She began to daydream about the possibility of her mom getting married again, like her dad had.

Thinking of her dad, she frowned. She felt bad about saying she hated him and wished he'd die that day when her mom had gotten his letter. Kendall didn't really want him to die. She just wished he loved her the way other girls' dads loved them. What was wrong with her that he didn't love her? Kendall's mom was always telling her how special she was, but if she were *really* special, wouldn't her dad love her? Wouldn't he want to *be* with her, the way Bernie's dad wanted to be with Bernie?

Mr. Walters was so great. He didn't have an important job like her dad did. Mr. Walters just managed the Piggly Wiggly in Lucas. But who cared about important jobs, anyway? Mr. Walters helped coach their soccer team, and he went to church every Sunday with Bernie and her mom and brother and sister, and he helped Bernie with her math homework, and he talked to her and teased her. He even talked to Kendall and teased *her*.

He teased Bernie's mom, too. Wistfully, Kendall remembered how, at the Walters' house when Mr. Walters came home from work, he'd walk over to Bernie's mom and put his arm around her and kiss her cheek and call her "honey" and ask her how her day had gone. And he actually *listened* to her answer and said stuff back. Kendall liked that. Lots of times grownups didn't listen at all. They asked questions, and then when you answered, they said something like "Uh-huh" in this faraway voice, and you could tell they hadn't heard a word you'd said.

Then after he and Bernie's mom talked awhile, he'd come over to Bernie and pull on her ponytail and call her "Short Stuff" and ask about *her* day. And he'd listen some more. He was neat. Watching them all together, Kendall always got this lonely, achey feeling in her chest. She sighed again. She wanted to have that kind of family, too.

Well, maybe one of these days, she would have. After all, things were looking up around here. Especially now that her mom was dating again.

And yet the whole idea of a stepfather gave her a funny feeling. As much as she wanted a family like Bernie's, Kendall wasn't sure she wanted a stepfather. Sometimes stepfathers were mean and they didn't like kids. That would be awful!

But surely her mother wouldn't marry someone who didn't like kids. Besides, this man coming tonight *must* like kids. Hadn't her mom said he had kids of his own?

But that thought brought another. What if his kids were

horrible? What if her mom and Mr. O'Connell ended up liking each other and wanted to get married but his kids didn't like either her *or* her mom?

Suddenly Kendall remembered how her mom was always cautioning her against jumping to conclusions. *You're doing it again*, she thought. And because it wasn't in her nature to dwell on anything unpleasant for very long anyway, she pushed her worries out of her mind and headed back to the kitchen.

Abbie's neighborhood was pleasant. The homes were a mix of one- and two-story brick contemporary designs and, to Logan's trained eye, looked to be anywhere from fifteen to twenty years old. Most had well-kept yards, with lush St. Augustine grass and full, mature trees. Beds of begonias, freesia, and periwinkle along with an occasional scarlet hibiscus added bright splashes of color.

Her directions were easy to follow, and within minutes of entering the area, he found her street. Her home was about halfway down the block, an attractive tan brick one-story shaded by an enormous eucalyptus tree. Large clay pots filled with bright red impatiens stood on either side of the recessed doorway, which was paved with terra-cotta tiles.

Everywhere Logan looked, he saw Abbie's neighbors engaged in normal activities: walking, riding bikes, moving sprinklers, watering flower beds, talking to each other. They all looked as if they hadn't a care in the world, yet Logan knew some of them, at least, must have problems. Most families did. Yet he was sure none had a problem like his.

Suddenly all Logan wanted to do was turn around and drive back home. Pretend he had never met Abbie Bernard. Pretend he'd never heard her unthinkable story. Pretend he was normal, too, and none of this had ever happened.

But even if Abbie would agree to forget the whole unbelievable situation, he knew he never would. The picture she'd shown him of that beautiful child that she raised—*his* child, *Ann's* child—would haunt him for the rest of his life.

He took a long, steadying breath, pulled into her driveway, and cut the ignition.

Abbie, looking as unsettled as he felt, opened the door to him. "Hi." Her voice was as grave as her eyes.

"Hi."

"You ready for this?" She gave him a sympathetic smile.

His answering smile was rueful. "I don't know if anyone could ever be ready for something like this."

She nodded. "I know. Come on in." She led the way into a bright living area at the back of the house. Logan's eyes quickly scanned the room, taking in the comfortable-looking green striped sofa, the green leather side chairs, the light oak coffee table and end tables, the piano, the bookcases overflowing with books. But the room's furnishings didn't interest him. It was Kendall he wanted to see. Just as he turned to ask Abbie where she was, movement behind him alerted him to the fact that someone else had entered the room. Pulse quickening, he slowly turned.

Years later, he would always remember that moment when he saw his daughter for the first time. Her picture hadn't done her justice. She was so beautiful! Like Patrick, everything about her was vivid. She was dressed in a yellow-and-white shorts outfit that complemented her dark hair and tanned skin. Her eyes—Ann's eyes!—were bright and eager as she walked forward to meet him.

"Logan," Abbie said, "this is Kendall. Kendall, this is Mr. O'Connell."

Something hard and painful knotted in Logan's chest, and when she held out her hand, he actually trembled from the force of his emotions. "Hello, Kendall," he managed to say. "It's nice to meet you." The touch of her firm, warm skin was nearly his undoing. He swallowed. *This is my daughter. Ann's and my daughter!*

"Hello." She gave him an enchanting smile. "It's nice to meet you, too."

Logan knew he should say something else, but his brain seemed to have shut down.

"Why don't you have a seat, Logan," Abbie said, "and I'll get you something to drink. What would you like? A glass of wine? A beer? Or I could make you a drink. Let's see, I have scotch and vodka." She was talking too much and too fast, obviously trying to fill the breach and give him a chance to collect himself. "And Kendall, why don't you go out to the kitchen and get those little toasties out of the oven? Put them on that glass platter, okay?"

Kendall nodded happily and went to do Abbie's bidding.

Logan walked to the couch and sat down. He felt stunned. It had been one thing to acknowledge the fact of Kendall intellectually and quite another to see her in the flesh.

"Are you going to be all right?" Abbie asked softly.

He nodded. "I just need a minute."

"I know."

Their eyes met. In hers he saw compassion and understanding. Yes. Abbie knew exactly what he was feeling. "I think I'll take you up on that scotch."

"All right." She headed toward a tiny wet bar.

Logan heard the rattle of a pan as Kendall worked in the kitchen and the clink of ice cubes as Abbie prepared his drink. Homey sounds. Normal sounds. A stranger looking in the window would imagine that Logan, Abbie, and Kendall were a normal family, too.

"Logan?"

He looked up.

Abbie handed him a squat crystal tumbler half-filled with Scotch. "The worst is over now," she said softly.

A few minutes later, Kendall walked in carrying a dish of appetizers, and Logan realized Abbie was right, for the respite had helped him gain control of himself. So he was able to smile almost naturally when she walked over to offer him one.

"They're called mozzarella toasties," she said proudly. "I helped my mom make them."

She had rolled the *r* in mozzarella, which amused Logan. "Do you like to cook?"

"Uh-huh. It's fun. Mom says I'm a natural."

Abbie walked over to hand Logan his drink. "She is. She's not afraid of cooking, like so many people are."

"I can make meat loaf and spaghetti and pancakes," Kendall said.

"But not at the same time," Abbie said, laughing.

Kendall grinned. "My mom showed me how to make

homemade doughnuts, too. Those are *really* fun to make, and they're good, too."

Logan thought sadly about how much Erin was missing. If Ann had lived, she would have taught Erin to cook, too. As it was, Serita did all of their cooking for them. Logan cooked on the weekends, if they weren't eating out, but it was always something simple, like grilled hamburgers or baked chicken—nothing a young girl would find "fun."

"What else do you like to do, Kendall?" he asked.

"Well, my favorite thing is drawing."

"Is it?" He had always loved to draw, too.

"Uh-huh. But I like all kinds of art. I *really* like computer graphics."

"She's taking a computer graphics course at the Caldwell School this summer."

"Oh? Is that where you're going to go to school?"

"I don't—"

"We haven't—"

Abbie and Kendall both broke off at the same time. Abbie smiled. "We haven't decided yet."

"My grandmother wants me to go to Caldwell," Kendall said.

"It's a good school," Logan said. "My daughter goes there."

"She does?" Abbie said.

"How old is your daughter?" Kendall asked.

"She's eleven."

"That's how old *I* am!"

Logan's and Abbie's eyes met. "Yes, I know," he said.

"What's her name?" Kendall asked.

"Her name is Erin."

"So if I go to Caldwell, I'll be in her class."

Logan nodded. "Yes, I guess you will."

"My mom said you have a boy, too," Kendall said.

"Yes, his name is Patrick, and he's thirteen." *Your brother.*

For a few seconds, Kendall's expression turned wistful. She gave a little sigh. "It must be nice to have an older brother."

The yearning look on her face reminded him so strongly of Ann he almost lost his composure.

For a long moment, no one said anything. Then Abbie, in an obvious effort to lighten the atmosphere, said brightly, "Well, are you hungry? Dinner's ready."

Grateful for the distraction, Logan said, "I never say no to food."

Later, as the three of them sat around the oval oak table in the dining area, eating Abbie's excellent seafood casserole and salad and talking about everything under the sun, Logan wondered what was to become of them all. He remembered how, earlier, he'd wanted to turn around and go home, pretend none of this had happened.

He still wished it hadn't happened. But it had. He didn't need blood tests for him and Erin to prove that it had happened, either, although he still intended to have them done.

The only question now was what they were going to do about the situation. They would have to do something, because now that he had met her, he knew he would never willingly walk away from Kendall.

She was incredible. So bright and so pretty. At first—except for her green eyes—he'd thought she was all O'Connell, but as the evening progressed, he realized there was a lot of Ann in her. Her hands, for one thing. They were shaped like Ann's. And the way she laughed. Her laugh was *exactly* like Ann's. And certain expressions and ways of saying things. She was a living example that genes play a big part in who we are.

The dinner, which he'd imagined would be interminable, was, in fact, over too soon. Logan glanced at his watch. It was already nine o'clock. He wondered if his being there had exhausted Abbie and if he should leave. He didn't want to. He hadn't spent nearly enough time with Kendall. But he didn't want to overstay his welcome, either. He was just ready to suggest it might be time for him to go when Abbie forestalled him.

"Kendall," she said, "why don't you take Mr. O'Connell back to your room and show him some of your drawings?"

Kendall's eyes shone. "Would you *like* to see them?"

"I'd love to see them."

The drawings amazed him. Most were rendered in black pencil, but there were several done with charcoal and several others done in pastels. They were all wonderful, realistic yet imaginative. One in particular—a simple scene of a kitten lying on its back, paws straight up in the air—delighted him. He'd seen Mitzi lie that way dozens of times, and it had never failed to amuse him. "I like all your drawings, but I particularly like this one."

"It's my favorite one, too."

"Is it a picture of your kitten?" he asked.

"Uh-huh." Her eyes were sad. "We didn't have him very long."

"Why not?"

" 'Cause he got run over by Mr. Goldblum's car." She sighed heavily. "Mom said we should never have let him go outside." Her eyes met his. "But doesn't that seem *mean*? Making a cat stay inside all the time? Isn't that almost like being in *jail*?"

The earnest question and her obvious concern touched Logan deeply. "Maybe it seems like that to you and me," he said carefully, "but the world we live in was never meant for animals. We're showing them we love them by protecting them from cars and other dangers. Even Rex, our dog, is never allowed outside the yard unless he's on a leash."

She nodded thoughtfully. "That's what Mom said, too." Then she brightened. "She said we could get a new cat after we got settled here."

Logan smiled. "Good. I think every house needs a pet."

"Do you have a cat?"

"Yes, we do. We've had her for ten years, since Erin was a baby."

"*And* a dog?"

"Yes."

"What kind?"

"The dog is a yellow lab, and our cat—Mitzi—is a calico."

Her smile lit up her face. "I *love* yellow labs. My best friend, Bernie, she has a yellow lab. His name is Ben, and he loves the water. Every time we swam in her pool, he'd jump in with us. It was so much fun!"

Logan grinned. "I'll bet it was."

"Does your dog like the water?"

"Yes, but we don't have a pool. We *do* have a fountain, though, and he likes to run around in it."

"Oh, I'll bet that's fun to watch."

"Yes, it is. Tell you what. Maybe you and your mom can come over one weekend and you can see Rex for yourself."

"Oh, that'd be *cool*!"

They smiled at each other. Suddenly, her smile turned shy. "I like you."

His heart contracted. More than anything, he wanted to open his arms and hold her close. "I like you, too," he said softly.

"I think my mom likes you, too."

Something about her tone alerted Logan. *Uh-oh,* he thought. *She's viewing me as a prospective suitor for her mother.* "Of course," he said casually. "We're friends."

They talked for a few minutes more, then rejoined Abbie in the living room. Soon after, Logan said his good-byes. Once again, Kendall offered her hand to shake. "Don't forget," she said, "you said I could meet Rex."

Logan bit back a chuckle. "I won't forget."

"I'll walk out with you," Abbie said. "Kendall, you start getting ready for bed, okay?"

"Okay, Mom."

With sunset, the temperature had finally dropped, but the humidity hadn't, and it felt as if they were entering a steam room when they walked outside.

"Who's Rex?" Abbie asked.

"Rex is our dog. You saw him the day you were at the house. When I told Kendall about him, I told her I'd invite the two of you to come over one weekend and she could meet him." His eyes met hers. "That was okay, wasn't it?"

"Yes. That was okay."

Their unspoken thoughts hung heavily between them.

"She's a terrific kid, Abbie," Logan said finally. "You've done a great job."

She nodded wordlessly. Her eyes were very bright, and he knew she was close to tears.

He reached out, giving her upper arm a gentle, reassuring squeeze. "Don't worry. We'll work this out." With a pang, he remembered she had said the exact same words yesterday.

She nodded again.

"Next week I'm taking the kids to Vancouver, so don't be alarmed if you don't hear from me, okay?"

"Okay."

"I'll call you when I get back."

"All right."

He opened his car door. "Abbie?"

"Yes?"

"Thanks for tonight. I know it wasn't easy for you."

After a moment, she gave him a sad smile. "Who said life was going to be easy?"

Sixteen

Elizabeth taped and labeled the last of the cardboard boxes. For the past few days, she'd been helping her mother go through all of her father's clothing and personal possessions. They had sorted and stacked, deciding what to keep and what to give away. It hadn't been easy, yet Elizabeth knew it was a job that must be done, because the house was too big for her mother, too much for her to care for now that Elizabeth's father was gone, and she was planning to put it on the market. In fact, Elizabeth was going to list it, and as popular as the neighborhood was with young families looking for a larger home, she knew it would sell quickly.

Thank God her father had been meticulous about keeping up-to-date records. Every document of any importance was safely filed away in his safe-deposit box, so it was a simple matter to find insurance policies, investment records, and his will. He'd even made a list with numbers of bank accounts and credit cards.

He was just as organized at home. *The same way I am,* Elizabeth thought. Briefly, her eyes filled with tears. *Daddy,* she thought. *I can't believe you're gone.* Several times over the past two weeks she'd caught herself reaching for the phone to call him, then she would remember, and grief would hit her in a fresh wave. People said grief faded, that eventually days, even weeks and months, would go by without you thinking about the person you'd lost. Elizabeth wasn't sure that would ever happen with her father. She was sure she would always miss him and feel the tremendous gap his passing had left.

She sighed and looked around her. Tomorrow she would call Goodwill and schedule a pickup, although there were some things they planned to give to her father's friends, and there were several boxes earmarked for church charities. Those would have to be delivered personally.

She eyed the box marked "LOGAN." She planned to deliver that one personally, too. Not this week, though. Logan and the kids were in Vancouver this week. She sighed again, sitting back on her heels and thinking about the past couple of weeks. There had been a time there, right after her father died, when she'd felt as if she and Logan were finally going in the right direction. But then last week she'd barely seen him. She'd bet she wouldn't even have talked to him before he left if she hadn't called him. And then, when he got on the phone, he'd seemed distant and preoccupied. Why? What had happened to make him cool off? She had a sudden flash of fear and an image of herself, growing older, alone and lonely.

"No," she muttered. "No. It won't happen. I won't fail. Somehow I'll make Logan see how perfect we'd be together."

"What, dear? Did you say something?"

Elizabeth turned. Her mother, looking pale and tired, stood in the doorway. "No, Mom. Just talking to myself."

Her mother nodded. "Well. I just wondered if you were hungry. I made some tuna salad and there's fresh limeade."

Elizabeth got up. "I *am* a little hungry." She wasn't, really, but she knew if she didn't eat, her mother wouldn't, either. And Celia needed to eat. Her clothes were hanging on her.

Elizabeth was worried. Celia seemed disoriented. She spent much of her time wandering around the house, touching things and gazing off into space. And she kept forgetting things. Half the time she couldn't remember what had been said only minutes earlier.

She wasn't that old. Only sixty-five. Yet Elizabeth was afraid her mother could no longer live alone, even though the plan was that when the house sold, her mother would buy into a high-rise condominium.

Surely living somewhere like that, her mother would be okay on her own. But Elizabeth was scared. What if she wasn't okay?

I can't have her come to live with me. I just can't. Under the best of circumstances, Elizabeth wouldn't have wanted her mother living with her, and considering their relationship and her mother's recent behavior, these were far from the best of circumstances.

Following her mother out to the kitchen, Elizabeth told herself they would work something out. Maybe they could hire a companion for Celia. Or maybe her mother would snap out of her lethargy. Maybe this was just a natural reaction to losing her husband and it would pass just as her first grief had passed.

If only Elizabeth wasn't alone in having to cope with the situation. *Why couldn't I have had brothers?* she thought. *Somebody to take charge and give me a break!* And then another thought struck her. Instead of lamenting the problem of her mother, she should be welcoming it. Because now she had the perfect reason to confer with Logan, didn't she? After all, it would be only natural for her to turn to him, wouldn't it? He was just as much a part of the family as Elizabeth was. And Celia was his children's grandmother. He *should* be involved in any decisions affecting her.

Of course!

Elizabeth smiled for the first time in days.

Surrounded by spectacular mountains and calm, tidal waters, Vancouver was everything Logan had imagined it to be: dynamic, beautiful, progressive, and ethnically diverse. Like Houston, it was a fairly young city enjoying great prosperity and rapid expansion. Everywhere he looked, he saw new buildings springing up—great glass and concrete skyscrapers, mid-size office complexes, and smaller, Victorian or Asian-influenced shops, apartments, churches, and schools. He took dozens of pictures for his files.

The convention was being held at Canada Place, with half the attendees housed at the Pan-Pacific Hotel, and the other half at the Waterfront Centre Hotel. Logan and his children were staying at the latter, and from their twenty-first-floor window they had a magnificent view of the harbor and mountains. Erin loved to sit at the window and watch the big cruise ships sailing in and anchoring at the Canada Place pier.

"Where are they going, Dad?" she asked on their second day in the city.

"They're either getting ready to sail to Alaska or just coming back from Alaska, honey."

"Really? That would be neat, wouldn't it? To go to Alaska sometime."

The question gave Logan a pang. He and Ann had talked about a trip to Alaska several times but had always said they'd wait until the children were older and could appreciate its history better. "Yes, that would be neat."

"Maybe we could go next summer . . . and take Aunt Elizabeth with us. I'll bet she'd like to go, too."

One thing Logan did not want to do was discuss Elizabeth. So he made a noncommittal sound, then urged Erin and Patrick to get ready as the three of them were scheduled to join a walking tour to Gastown in less than thirty minutes.

But Erin, with an uncharacteristic doggedness, managed to bring up Elizabeth's name again and again throughout the afternoon. After a while, it was amusing to Logan to see how innovative she could be. When they stood looking at the Gastown Steam Clock at Water and Cambie Streets, waiting with all the other tourists for it to toot the Westminster Chimes theme, she said, "This clock reminds me of Aunt Elizabeth's clock, don't you think, Dad?"

"Seeing as how this is a steam clock and Aunt Elizabeth's is a pendulum clock, there's really no similarity between them," Logan said dryly.

"I didn't mean how they *work*. I meant how they *look*."

"I know what you meant."

Between her attempts to insinuate Elizabeth into his consciousness and his own relentless thoughts of the harrowing situation waiting for him when he returned to Houston, Logan couldn't relax and enjoy the afternoon or the succeeding days in the lovely city the way he had imagined he would.

He tried. But no matter what they were doing, the image

of Kendall refused to leave him. She should be there with them now. Yet, if she were, Erin wouldn't be. That was unthinkable. Erin was as much a part of him as his arms or his legs. Logan didn't care what any future blood tests proved or didn't prove, Erin belonged to him.

I can't lose her. I won't *lose her.*

The trouble was, now that he'd met Kendall, he wanted both girls.

He remembered how he'd told Abbie they would work things out. But how? How were they to work things out so that each would be satisfied, for if he wanted both girls, wouldn't Abbie— no matter how nice, how sympathetic and understanding she'd seemed—eventually come to the same conclusion?

And then what?

On and on his thoughts churned, a relentless barrage that refused to give him any peace or any answers.

On their last night in Vancouver, after both children were already asleep, Logan stood at the window and watched the lights of the city flickering below and on the calm, inky surface of the harbor. A deep melancholy seized him.

What was to become of them?

Since he'd left, Abbie hadn't stopped thinking about the evening Logan had spent at their house. Of course, she'd have been hard pressed to forget about him even if she'd wanted to, because Kendall kept bringing up his name.

The morning after the dinner, the first thing Kendall said when she joined Abbie for breakfast was "Last night was fun, wasn't it, Mom?"

"Yes," Abbie said, "it was." She ladled half the eggs she'd just scrambled onto Kendall's waiting plate, then put the rest on hers. She poured orange juice for both of them, then joined Kendall at the table.

"You like Mr. O'Connell, don't you?" Kendall said around a mouthful of eggs.

"I wouldn't have asked him for dinner if I didn't like him, Kendall."

"Well, I know, but what I mean is, you *really* like him, right?"

"I'm not sure I understand what you're getting at."

Kendall rolled her eyes. "Mo-*om.* You do too know what I mean."

Abbie sighed and put her fork down. "Kendall, Mr. O'Connell is just a friend. Just a friend. That's all."

Kendall's expression said she didn't believe Abbie, but she dropped the subject. Later, though, as they were driving to Caldwell, she brought up his name again. "What's the name of Mr. O'Connell's daughter?" she said.

"Her name is Erin. Why?"

"I just wondered. Have you met her?"

Abbie swallowed. "Yes, I've met her."

"What's she like?"

There was a lump in Abbie's throat when she answered. "She's very nice. Kind of quiet. Shy, probably."

"Did you meet Mr. O'Connell's son, too?"

"No, I didn't."

"What's *his* name?"

"His name is Patrick."

"I wonder what he's like," Kendall mused.

With relief, Abbie saw they were almost to the school. She flipped her turn signal on in preparation for steering into Caldwell's drive and didn't answer Kendall's last question. But Abbie knew their arrival at the school was only a temporary reprieve.

She was right. In the days that followed, Kendall brought up Logan's name at every opportunity, which always led to more questions. She didn't even try to be subtle about what she was doing.

Abbie wondered if Logan had picked up on Kendall's obvious interest in him as a potential husband for Abbie. God, she hoped not. The situation with the children was fraught with enough conflict. They certainly didn't need the added embarrassment of Kendall's clumsy attempts to matchmake.

Funny thing, though. Once the idea was planted in Abbie's head, she had a hard time getting rid of it. After all, Abbie was only human, and Logan O'Connell was an exceptionally attractive man. And his attractiveness was more than just physical. Watching him with Kendall, Abbie had been impressed again by how different he was from Thomas. And how perfect he was with Kendall. Yes, she could easily be interested in him. Very easily.

Well, she'd better get the thought of him out of her head, because she was not in the same league as Logan. A man that attractive would have his pick of women. And he would pick someone like that beautiful sister-in-law of his. He would never, in a million years, look twice at Abbie. Even when she was younger, she had not been the kind of woman who had interested many men. And when she *did* catch a man's eye, he didn't remain interested for very long, because Abbie had never known how to act around them. She either said too much or too little, and she was completely devoid of what her mother would label "feminine wiles."

Her dating years were horrible, one disaster after another. And then, just when she'd begun to think she would never meet anyone who would see past her insecurities, she'd met Thomas. She was a senior in college, and he was a visiting professor. She'd been infatuated with him from the beginning. Everything about him excited her. She loved the way he looked: tall, lean, with thick brown hair and dark brown eyes that made her feel special when they singled her out. His voice: rich, fluid, golden, flowing over her like honey as he lectured. And most especially, his intellect. He dazzled her when he talked about archaeology. She felt his passion, and it quickly became hers.

She researched the field, devouring as much information as her brain could hold. Before long, she was staying after class, and they would talk about some aspect of the day's lecture. Soon they were going out for coffee or sandwiches, and their talks spilled over into evening. It was only a matter of time—and not much time at that—before she was spending the night at his apartment.

Even now, after all these years and all her disillusionment with Thomas, she could still remember vividly how he had made her feel in those first, exciting weeks. Abbie had been a virgin, and Thomas had delighted in introducing her to the joys of sex. Abbie smiled grimly. Yes, seduction was one area where Thomas hadn't disappointed. Not then, anyway. Of course, he'd had a lot of practice. And because he had, he knew exactly which buttons to push.

She was bewitched, intoxicated, completely obsessed by him. In her eyes, he was perfect. And if he had faults, she justified them. His insistence on perfection and his disdain for those who didn't meet his standards weren't intolerant, they simply reflected a refusal to settle for anything less than the best. His self-involvement wasn't selfishness. It was simply a result of his brilliance and the important work he was doing and one of the reasons he was so successful in his field. One couldn't accomplish great things if one's focus was diluted by the mundane problems of others.

At the end of the semester and Abbie's graduation, she and Thomas were married in a quiet ceremony in the college chapel. Up till the morning of the wedding, Abbie wasn't sure if her mother would be there. In the end, she'd shown up, but she was clearly unhappy with Abbie's choice.

"Don't let her get to you," Laura whispered as she hugged Abbie good-bye that evening. "If you're happy, that's all that counts."

"Oh, I am," Abbie said. "I'm *so* happy."

And she had been. For a long time she had been. Because as long as she concentrated all her energies on Thomas, their marriage had flowed along beautifully, with never a ripple to mar its surface.

Then Abbie got pregnant.

She realized now that what happened next was probably inevitable. For a long time, she'd thought the wreck of her marriage could have been prevented if she'd only been smarter or sexier or more beautiful or more interesting.

In the end, though, none of those qualities would have mattered, because what Thomas demanded from her was complete and total attention, and that was the one thing he could no longer have once their child was born.

She sighed deeply, imagining how different not only her life but Kendall's life would have been like if Abbie had been married to someone mature and generous like Logan instead of someone as egocentric as Thomas. Logan, she was sure, had been, and still was, an ideal father.

Suddenly, she was very frightened.

Oh, God. What if Logan changed his mind? What if, when he returned from Vancouver, he decided he didn't want to "work things out"? What if, instead, he tried to take Kendall away from her? She trembled at the thought. Was it possible? Could he? He had so many resources, including family, influence, and money, and she had so few. It was true that years ago her family had been movers and shakers, but those years were long gone. If Logan decided to fight her for the girls, Abbie knew he would have an enormous advantage.

Well, she would not make it easy for him if he did try to take Kendall away from her. She would fight him every inch of the way, even if they ended up in the Supreme Court!

You're getting yourself all upset over nothing. Logan O'Connell is a decent man. He's not going to try to take Kendall away from you. He'd never do that—he's too nice.

Abbie thought about Logan again and again in the days after his visit. She kept remembering how sweet he'd been, not just to Kendall, but to her. *He won't hurt us. I just know he won't.*

But no matter how many times she told herself this, she knew she would be a fool to trust Logan completely. There was simply too much at stake.

Abbie and Kendall spent Saturday afternoon at the Museum of Contemporary Art, which was showing an exhibit of Ansel Adams photography. Afterward, they stopped for Mexican food at the Ninfa's near Greenway Plaza. At eight, tired and happy, they headed home. The excursion had been good for Abbie. It had taken her mind off Erin and Logan. But now, as they neared their house, her thoughts once again returned to the subject that had monopolized her life the past five weeks.

She wondered if Logan and the children were home yet and if he would follow through with his promise to call. And then she worried about what he would say when he did call. She wasn't even sure what she *wanted* him to say. She only knew that this limbo they were now in wasn't something she could bear for very long without going crazy. With that in mind, she hoped she would hear from him soon and that somehow, some way, they could work out an arrangement whereby each of them could have some part in the life of their biological child.

The message light was blinking on the answering machine when she and Kendall arrived at the house. Mentally crossing her fingers, Abbie pressed the Play button.

"Abbie? It's Logan O'Connell. The kids and I are back from Vancouver. Please give me a call when you get home."

When Abbie didn't immediately pick up the phone, Kendall said, "Aren't you going to call him, Mom?" Her eyes were wide with eagerness.

If it hadn't been obvious before, it certainly was now, that Kendall was entertaining thoughts of some kind of relationship for Abbie and Logan. Poor kid, Abbie thought. She has no idea what's really going on. "Yes, I'm going to call him, but not right this minute. I want to get out of these clothes first."

Entering her bedroom, she shut the door, listened to make sure Kendall had gone into her own bedroom, then picked up the phone. He answered on the second ring.

"Hi," she said. "It's Abbie."

"Good. I was hoping this was you."

His warm greeting gave her an equally warm feeling of gratefulness, which she immediately tried to quell, telling herself to remember what she had decided. *You are not friends.* "How was your trip?" she said guardedly.

"Nice, but you know, I didn't enjoy it the way I'd expected to. Trouble is, I couldn't stop thinking about everything."

A little ball of tension formed in Abbie's stomach. "No, I couldn't either."

They were silent for long seconds as each thought about their mutual problem.

"Abbie," he finally said, and there was something in his tone that caused the ball to knot tighter. "I think we should talk again, but before we do, I want to have DNA testing done. It's not that I don't believe you—"

"No, of course not," she interrupted. "Don't apologize. In your place, I'd feel exactly the same way."

"Good." He sounded relieved. "I'm going to ask Dr. Joplin

to handle the testing for me, because my feeling is the fewer people who know about this, the better."

"I think that's a good idea."

"From what I know about this kind of testing, it may be a couple of weeks before we'll have the results."

"Yes, I know." Oh, God. A couple more weeks of waiting. How was she going to get through them and stay sane?

"In the meantime," he continued, "why don't we assume the tests will show what we suspect to be true and agree to use this time to think about ways we might want to consider handling things once we have the final proof?"

"All right."

They agreed that Logan would call Abbie when he had the results of the test, then they said good-bye.

Abbie felt a profound sense of relief. Maybe she was a fool, but she *did* trust Logan. Every instinct told her he would never intentionally hurt her. *That's what you want to think, because you're attracted to him!* Well, maybe she was, but that was beside the point.

Later, though, as Abbie lay in bed listening to the sounds of the summer night and thinking about the future and what it would hold for all of them, she knew that even if she and Logan were able to reach some kind of reasonable, workable solution whereby they shared in the lives and upbringing of both girls, there were still going to be many rocky days ahead for all of them.

Seventeen

Elizabeth slammed down the phone.

"Whoa," said Rick Overstreet, who happened to be passing by her cubicle at that precise moment. He leaned his head inside and leered at her. "Hey, babe, who put the bug up *your* ass?"

Elizabeth almost told him to go fuck himself. Not only did she despise being called "babe," she couldn't stand Rick Overstreet, an overweight, overage Lothario who still thought he was God's gift to women. But she overcame the urge. Just because his vocabulary was routinely peppered with four-letter words didn't mean she should sink to the same level.

"Oh, just another arrogant secretary," she said coolly. "No big deal." She didn't turn around. And, as she'd hoped, seeing he wasn't going to get anything more out of her, he continued on his way.

Once he was gone, she allowed herself to think about the conversation that had just taken place. She hadn't lied when she said she'd been talking to an arrogant secretary, for that's exactly the way she had always characterized that little bitch who worked for Logan. The nerve of the woman, saying that Logan would probably be too busy to return Elizabeth's call this afternoon! Where did she get off making Logan's decisions for him?

Elizabeth drummed her fingers on her desk. As much

as she wanted to stay mad at Rebecca, she knew Rebecca wasn't the real problem. The real problem was Logan. He was avoiding her. It was now Thursday, and since Saturday night, when he and the children had returned from Vancouver, she had only spoken to him once. And if she hadn't called him, she probably still wouldn't have talked to him.

And that one conversation had been decidedly unsatisfactory. She'd called him on Sunday and told him all about her mother—how she was acting and how worried she, Elizabeth, was. And instead of being sympathetic, Logan had acted as if Elizabeth was manufacturing a problem where none existed.

"She just needs some time," he'd said. "You don't get over the death of a spouse in two weeks."

"I know that. But in the meantime, I'm worried about leaving her alone," Elizabeth had responded. "I thought maybe we could get together and talk about some possible options."

"Look, I really think you're overreacting. But I was planning to call your mother this afternoon, anyway, see if she wanted to come over and have dinner with us tonight. Let me see for myself how she is, okay?"

It wasn't okay at all, but what could Elizabeth do but agree? She'd tried to prolong the conversation, asking him about the Vancouver trip and anything else she could think of to keep him on the phone, all the while hoping he'd include her in the dinner invitation. Finally, she'd had to concede defeat, especially when Logan said he really needed to go and would talk to her later in the week.

She'd really expected him to call her Monday. When he hadn't by four o'clock, she called him. Rebecca said he was out looking at a site. Elizabeth left a message but didn't hear back. And when he finally did call back about noon on Tuesday, Elizabeth was out of the office. She'd called back, but he was out to lunch.

"A business lunch," Rebecca said. "I'm not sure when he'll be back."

"Tell him to call me at home tonight," Elizabeth said frostily.

"I'll tell him, but I believe he has plans for the evening."

Elizabeth gritted her teeth. She knew Rebecca didn't like her. Well, the feeling was definitely mutual.

Sure enough, Elizabeth hadn't heard from him last night, nor had he called her this morning. And now, to be told he was in a meeting and probably wouldn't be able to return her call today . . .

Why was he avoiding her?

Without warning, tears blurred her eyes, followed by a hollow feeling of hopelessness. For a few moments, she let herself give in to the emotion, but only for a few moments. Always more of a doer than a thinker, she quickly shook off her melancholy. *Where there's life, there's hope,* she told herself firmly. *Since when has a little setback deterred you from going after something you want?*

After all, it wasn't as if Logan were involved with someone else. Elizabeth just needed to be more creative, that's all. Figure out more ways to put herself in Logan's orbit. And she'd start immediately. In fact, if she didn't hear back from Logan this afternoon, she would take matters into her own hands and go over to his place tonight. She had a closing at four, but she should be out of there by five-thirty and could probably be at his place by six. She would probably even beat him home.

She smiled. Yes. That's exactly what she'd do.

Happy now, she turned her attention back to her work.

The blood work was done on Monday. Logan had expected it to be tough to explain to Erin why they were going to a different doctor than she was used to, but she didn't question his statement that their regular doctor was away on vacation, so her annual back-to-school physical would be performed by someone else this time.

"While we're there, I might as well have my cholesterol tested, too," he'd said casually.

"I'll put a rush on the blood work for you," Dr. Joplin said when he and Logan were alone. "But it will still take about a week to get the results."

"That's all? I thought it would take longer."

"It used to, but now there's a lab right here in town that does paternity testing. I'll send it there."

Then came the waiting.

Logan tried to keep from thinking about the test. It was hard not to, though, especially when he was around Erin. Every time he looked at her, he couldn't help but be reminded that, unless some miracle happened, she wasn't really his. That no matter how much he loved her and how much a part of his life she was, he *could* lose her.

Sometimes he still couldn't believe this had happened. How was it possible that everything you believed to be true could, in the blink of an eye, prove to be an illusion? That because of a twist of fate, entire lives could be uprooted?

What if he *did* lose her? It was possible. Hell, anything was possible. And if the newspapers and news shows were to be believed, it was entirely *probable*. Judges always sided with mothers, unless they were proven to be unfit, and Abbie certainly didn't fall into that category. No, if anything, she was an ideal mother. Anyone talking to Kendall for more than a few minutes would be able to tell she was a totally well-adjusted child. Whereas Erin had all kinds of insecurities and fears.

It didn't help, either, that during this period, Elizabeth kept calling and dropping in unannounced, either. Ostensibly, she wanted Logan's input concerning her mother, and to be fair, perhaps she really *was* concerned about Celia. But Logan didn't feel there was anything serious to be concerned about. Yes, Celia was sad and feeling lonely and frightened. But those were normal emotions for a woman her age who had been married more than forty-five years to a man as dynamic as Oliver Chamberlain had been. She just needed love and support and time to adjust. And Logan had told Elizabeth so, more than once. He knew Elizabeth was hurt because he seemed to treat the matter more lightly than she did. She probably thought he didn't care. He did care. Unfortunately, his own problem was all-consuming. He simply had nothing left emotionally to offer Elizabeth.

Finally the wait for the DNA results was over. On Wednesday, nine days after having the blood drawn, Dr. Joplin called with the results. "It's what you suspected," he said. "The DNA testing shows that it is genetically impossible for you to have fathered Erin."

Even though Logan had expected this result, to hear the words spoken aloud by the doctor, to know—*irrefutably*—that Erin was not his daughter, was still a knockout punch. For a second, he couldn't speak.

"Mr. O'Connell?"

Logan took a deep breath. "I'm here."

"Are you okay? I wouldn't have been so blunt, but I thought you were prepared for this result."

"I thought I *was* ready to hear this, but I guess I was holding out a thread of hope that somehow what we suspected wasn't true."

They talked a few minutes longer, then Logan thanked Dr. Joplin, adding, "I appreciate your discretion. It would be terrible if the press got wind of this."

"You can count on me. I don't want this to get out any more than you do. Remember that case last year?"

Logan remembered it all too well. He'd felt so sorry for the parties involved. The media had been like piranhas, camping outside the respective homes of the switched babies, feeding on the grief and anguish of the parents and grandparents.

He sat thinking for a long time after his conversation with the doctor. He turned the situation over and over in his mind. An idea had come to him a few days earlier—one he'd first dismissed as crazy. But now . . . knowing for certain that Erin was not his daughter . . . and that Kendall was . . . he wondered. Maybe his idea wasn't so crazy after all. In fact, maybe it was the only reasonable solution. But would Abbie see it that way?

Thoughtfully, he picked up the phone and dialed Abbie's number. "The results of the tests are back," he said without preamble.

"And?" The tension in her voice was unmistakable.

"It's what we expected."

For a long moment, neither said anything. "I guess we need to talk again," he finally said.

"Yes."

"But not on the phone."

"No."

"Why don't we meet for lunch next week?"

"All right."

"In the meantime, I was wondering if you and Kendall would like to come over Saturday night, say about five, and stay for dinner and the evening? It would give the kids a chance to meet."

She didn't answer immediately. When she did, it was obvious she was picking her words carefully. "Are you sure it's a good idea for them to meet right now? I mean, shouldn't we have some plan for the future first?"

"Are you saying there's a chance you won't want to be part of Erin's life?"

"Oh, no! No, I'm not saying that. I just . . . well, I guess I'm . . . afraid."

He decided honesty was best. "Look, Abbie, I'm scared, too. I love Erin. She's as much a part of me as my arms or legs. I don't want to lose her. But I can't walk away from Kendall, either. I want to be a part of her life, too. So the kids are going to have to meet sometime. And frankly, I think the sooner we get this initial meeting over with, the better."

He could hear her sigh. "You're right. Okay, five o'clock Saturday. We'll be there."

"Good. Okay. Here's what I plan to tell Erin and Patrick. I'm going to say you and I met after that day you came to the house, and during our discussion I discovered you have a daughter Erin's age who's going to Caldwell next year, so I thought it would be nice for the two girls to meet."

"Um, well, that would be okay, but we haven't actually decided on Caldwell."

"Oh. I thought you had."

"I know. The thing is, it's my mother who wants her to go there. I had planned on sending Kendall to public school."

"Public school? Look, if it's a matter of money, I'd be glad to—"

"It has nothing to do with money," she said, her voice cooling by several degrees.

He could have kicked himself. "Abbie, I'm sorry. I know I don't have any right to tell you what to do. I'm just prejudiced because Erin goes there, and I think Caldwell is the best school in Houston."

"Oh, I know." Her voice softened. "Undoubtedly, as my mother likes to point out, I'm just being stubborn. You and she are probably right."

He smiled. "So it's okay if I tell Erin what I'd planned?"

"Yes, it's okay."

Logan decided he would tell the kids that night at dinner that they were expecting company on Saturday. He would also talk to Serita and see if she'd prepare a casserole for him to serve. Normally when he entertained—which wasn't often—Serita cooked and served for him, but he wanted this to be strictly a family affair on Saturday. His feeling was, the fewer people involved, the fewer questions there might be.

Logan waited until he and the children were almost finished with dinner before introducing the subject. "Hey, guys," he said offhandedly, "don't make any plans for Saturday afternoon or evening, okay? Because we're going to have company."

"Oh? Who?" Patrick said around a mouthful of bread.

"Don't talk with your mouth full," Logan said automatically. Then, casually, he looked at Erin, whose eyes met his curiously. "Remember the woman who came to interview me about the hospital where you were born?"

"Uh-huh," Erin said.

"You were away at camp, Patrick," Logan explained. He returned his gaze to Erin. "Well, I've talked to Mrs. Bernard since then and it turns out she has a daughter your age who's going to be in your class at Caldwell this year. I thought it might be nice for her daughter to meet you, so I've invited them to come over Saturday and have dinner with us."

Erin frowned. "Why do they have to come here? Can't I just meet her at school?"

Logan had expected this reaction. Erin's shyness made it hard for her to meet new kids. "Well, honey, sure you *could* meet her at school, but Kendall—that's her name—doesn't know many people here yet. So it'll be a nice thing, you meeting her. Then you can introduce her to some of your friends. Remember how you felt when you didn't know anyone?"

She sighed. Nodded. "Yeah."

"Okay, then." He smiled at her. Now that he was over the first hurdle, he decided to tackle the second. "It'll be fun. You'll like her. She's a nice girl."

"How do you know, Dad? She might not be."

"Trust me. She is. I've met her."

It took a few seconds for Erin to snap to what he'd said. Then her eyes narrowed. "When did *you* meet her?"

"Remember the night you stayed at Aunt Glenna's? Before we went to Vancouver? The night I had a meeting?"

"Yes." The frown remained.

"My meeting was with Mrs. Bernard." Logan hated that he was telling less than the truth, but there was no help for it right now.

Erin looked as if she were going to say something else, and Logan braced himself.

But before she could, Patrick piped in with "So, Dad, this isn't really company for *me,* right? 'Cause Scott said something about us going to see that new Bruce Willis movie."

"It's company for all of us, Patrick," Logan said.

"Aw, Dad . . ." Patrick had a pained look on his face. "She's Erin's age, not mine. Why do I have to be here?"

Logan sympathized with Patrick's sentiments, but Kendall was Patrick's sister, whether he knew it or not, and it was important that Patrick be a part of this first meeting.

"Listen, son, I'm sorry to disappoint you, but I really want you to be here. You can go out with Scott another night, okay?"

Now it was Patrick's turn to sigh. After a few seconds, he said, "Okay."

Just then Serita walked in with a chocolate pie. "You are ready for your dessert, yes?" she said, smiling.

Logan gave her a grateful smile in return. And by the time dessert had been served, the children seemed to have forgotten about his announcement, and the subject was dropped.

Eighteen

"Wow," Kendall said. "This is a really *nice* neighborhood." Her eyes were wide as they drove through Hunter's Creek. "Mr. O'Connell must be *rich*."

Abbie put on her right turn signal. "I don't know if I'd describe him as rich. Besides, whether he is or not isn't important, is it?"

"No, Mom," Kendall said in her best parents-can-be-so-exasperating voice. "It's what's inside a person that counts."

Abbie smiled. "Well, it's true, honey."

"I know it's true, Mom, but what's wrong with just saying Mr. O'Connell must be rich? That doesn't mean I like him any better."

"Good. Because, you know, honey, you're going to be around a lot of girls who come from wealthy families if you're going to Caldwell this fall, but I hope it won't change—"

"You mean you've *decided*?" Kendall squealed.

"Yes, I've decided. If that's where you want to go, it's all right with me."

"Oh, *thank* you, Mom! Gran is gonna be *so* happy!"

Abbie's mouth twisted in a wry smile. "Yes, I'm sure she will be."

"Can I call her tomorrow and tell her?"

"Yes, you can call her." By now they had reached Logan's street, and within minutes, Abbie was pulling into the circular drive. She glanced at Kendall to see her reaction to Logan's home, and just as Abbie had imagined, Kendall's eyes widened in awe. It *was* a pretty spectacular house, but Abbie derived no pleasure from it. Unfortunately, his home, his entire lifestyle, was just one more area where Abbie couldn't hope to compete with him. She tried not to think this way, because so far he had said and done nothing to make her believe he would try to take Kendall away from her. And yet how could she help but worry? Logan O'Connell had everything going for him, and in comparison Abbie had very little.

He must have been watching for them, because no sooner had Abbie cut the ignition than the front door opened, and he walked out. Their eyes met briefly before his gaze shifted to Kendall.

"Hi," he said to Kendall.

"Hi!"

It hurt Abbie to see his smile. The longing in his eyes. The possessive way he dropped his hand on Kendall's shoulder. But what hurt more was the pure delight in Kendall's eyes. She was already smitten with him.

But isn't that what you wanted? For her to know her father? For him to love and appreciate her, and her to love him? Isn't that exactly what you want for yourself? To know and love Erin, and for her to love you back?

Oh, God. She didn't know what she wanted. She was so afraid.

"Let's go in," Logan said. "Erin and Patrick are waiting to meet you."

Abbie's stomach felt hollow as she braced herself to see Erin again. The three of them walked into the house, and Logan, still with that proprietary arm around Kendall, led the way to the family room.

The next few minutes were a jumble of impressions: the afternoon sunlight pouring through the patio doors, the fragrant aroma of something cooking, the excited panting of Logan's yellow lab, the tall, good-looking boy who rose politely from his seat as they entered the room. But overriding everything else, there was Erin. Abbie's heart contracted painfully as the child walked forward, an uncertain smile on her face.

"Erin, you remember Mrs. Bernard?" Logan was saying. Erin nodded shyly.

"Hello, Erin," Abbie said softly.

"Hi."

"And this is my son, Patrick," Logan continued. "Patrick, this is Mrs. Bernard. And this . . ." He gave Kendall a gentle nudge forward. "This is her daughter, Kendall."

"Hi," Kendall chirped. She smiled at Erin, then looked at Patrick.

He grinned down at her. Abbie could barely breathe as her gaze moved from one to the other. Kendall's brother. This was Kendall's brother. And, like Kendall, he was the kind of kid a person immediately warmed to, with a great smile and friendly, open face. Something knotted in Abbie's chest, and she fought to get her emotions under control.

"Well," Logan said heartily, "why don't we all sit down? Abbie, would you like a glass of wine? Or a soft drink? And what about you, Kendall?" There was a forced quality to his voice that told Abbie he felt just as off-kilter as she did.

Just knowing he was nervous made Abbie feel better. She said she'd take a glass of wine, and Kendall opted for a Coke. The dog, who had been circling her and sniffing, licked her hand.

Kendall laughed and scratched his head. "Look Mom, he's just like Ben, isn't he?"

"Yes," Abbie agreed, grateful for the distraction.

"Who's Ben?" Patrick said. "Your dog?"

"No," Kendall said. "We don't have a dog. But my best friend Bernie does, and her dog is a yellow lab, too. He's neat."

"Yeah, labs are cool dogs," Patrick agreed.

For a few minutes, they all looked at the dog, who had an expression of pure bliss on his face as Kendall continued to pet him.

"Hey, Kendall," Patrick said, "do you like Playstation? We've got a new game."

"I *love* Playstation, but my mom won't let me get one." Kendall gave Abbie a mischievous look. The acquisition of

Playstation had been a bone of contention for a while now, but Abbie had remained firm. She didn't want Kendall spending all her time playing games.

Patrick looked at Abbie. "Is it all right if she plays, Mrs. Bernard?"

The polite question told Abbie volumes about the way Logan had raised his children. "Of course."

"C'mon, then," Patrick said. "Get your Coke and we'll go back to the game room."

Kendall grinned. "Okay."

The two of them, talking and laughing like old friends, headed out of the room. Erin didn't move. The expression in her eyes was part hurt, part something else, something Abbie clearly understood because she'd felt enough of the same emotion when she was young, especially when she was with someone like Kendall, to whom everything—including friendship—seemed to come so effortlessly.

Patrick finally turned. He frowned. "Aren't you coming, Erin?"

Erin shrugged.

"Come *on*," he said, giving her a look that said *What's wrong with you?*

Slowly, Erin got up and followed him out of the room.

When she was gone, Abbie turned to Logan. She could see he was concerned.

"I worry about Erin," Logan said. "She doesn't make friends as easily as Patrick." He looked in the direction the children had gone.

"I was just like that when I was her age," Abbie said softly. "More than anything, I wanted to be popular and liked, but I never seemed to know the right thing to say or do. As a result, I was always at the tail end of things. An afterthought, if I was included at all."

Logan nodded. Silence fell between them. Then he heaved a sigh, saying, "Well, you turned out all right."

Abbie smiled. "Thanks. It was a hard road, though." Her smile faded. She remembered how her mother's obvious and constant disappointment in her had intensified those feelings of inadequacy. "You know, it's funny. My ex-husband was a real bastard. But in many ways, he was good for me. In the first years of our marriage, before I got pregnant, he made me feel special, and I gained self-confidence as a result. And then, when he rejected Kendall, I was forced to become independent and self-sufficient. Because of that, I discovered a strength I never knew I had."

"I still can't believe he rejected Kendall."

Abbie grimaced. "I know, I couldn't believe it, either, even though I knew he didn't want children. I kept thinking he'd change his mind once the baby was an actuality. But he didn't. He was totally self-involved, and having a child took too much away from him. He needed to be the center and sole focus of my universe, and once Kendall was born, he wasn't."

"Why did you marry him?"

"Ignorance. Naïveté. Stupidity. You name it. I was just so young—maybe not in terms of age—although I was only twenty-two. But in terms of social maturity, I was a virtual baby. I'd never had a real boyfriend until Thomas took an interest in me. It was a very heady thing, believe me. He was a visiting professor, and I was a student. Plus, he can be very charming when he wants to be. Oh, I was a sitting duck for someone like Thomas."

"When you say he rejected her, what do you mean, exactly?"

"I mean he hasn't seen her more than a half dozen times since she was born . . . and never since our divorce."

"Which was?"

"Nine years ago."

"Nine years," Logan repeated. "Does he ever write to Kendall? Call her?"

"No."

Logan stared at her. "How does Kendall feel about this?"

"About the way you'd imagine. She's hurt and bewildered. For years, I made excuses for him, but lately, well, I don't think he deserves any sugarcoating." Briefly, she described the letter Thomas had written about his new marriage, and how it had affected Kendall.

"Poor kid," Logan said.

"Thomas is why I decided to contact you, you know."

Logan frowned, not understanding.

"I didn't want Kendall to go through the rest of her life without ever knowing what a real father was like."

"What if I'd turned out to be just as bad?"

"Then I wouldn't have told you about her."

He mulled this over for a few seconds. "So you think we should tell the girls the truth?"

Abbie shivered. "I don't know." She had started to say something else when she saw movement out of the corner of her eye. She turned to see Erin entering the room, a dejected expression on her face. From the direction of the game room, Abbie heard peals of laughter.

"Hey, pumpkin," Logan said, "what's wrong?"

Erin shrugged. "Nothing."

"Why aren't you playing with Patrick and Kendall?"

Another shrug. "I don't want to."

"Erin," Logan said softly. "Kendall is your company. I think you should go back—"

"She's not *my* company," Erin shot back, her eyes suddenly mutinous, "she's yours."

"Erin," Logan said, "you know better than to talk like that. Apologize to Mrs. Bernard, then go back in the game room with *our* company."

Abbie's heart ached as Erin, face flushed with embarrassment, eyes bright with tears, turned to her.

"I'm sorry," she muttered.

"Oh, honey, it's okay. I understand." Abbie had meant for the words to be comforting and to take some of the sting out of Logan's reprimand. Instead, they seemed to have the opposite effect, for the look Erin gave her was filled with dislike.

When she was gone for the second time, Logan said, "I'm sorry. I've never known Erin to be rude."

Abbie bit her lip. "Maybe she senses something." She wanted to say she wished Logan had simply ignored Erin's behavior, let her work out her fears in her own way, but she hesitated to say anything that could be construed as criticism. After all, she wasn't a perfect parent.

Logan frowned. "I don't know. Maybe she does. She's a sensitive child, and we're very close."

"I can see that," Abbie said softly. Then, because the time

seemed right, and she was very curious, she added, "Was she close to your wife, too?"

"Yes. Very close." For a moment, his eyes turned bleak, giving Abbie a glimpse into a darkness he had obviously still not conquered. But after a few seconds, he gave himself a visible shake. "Sorry. Sometimes I actually forget. Then someone will say something, and it all comes back . . ." His voice trailed off, and he shrugged, giving her a half smile.

It was silly, Abbie knew, but his clear love for his dead wife had brought her perilously close to tears. She swallowed. "Would . . . would you mind telling me about her?" she asked softly.

"Not at all."

Abbie listened quietly, trying not to feel hurt by the things he said. She was glad Erin had had such a loving woman to mother her, even as she ached for all the years of her daughter's life that she'd missed.

"You loved her very much," she said softly when he'd finished.

"Yes." He sighed deeply. "We all miss her. But I think her death was harder on Erin than anyone else. For months afterward, she had terrible nightmares. She'd cry in her sleep."

"Has she . . ." Abbie hesitated. Maybe he would think she was criticizing him.

"Has she what?"

"Has she had any counseling?"

"That was the first thing we did. My sister's a psychiatrist, specializing in family therapy, so I was very aware of what needed to be done."

Just then a bell dinged in the kitchen, and Logan stood. "That's dinner. Excuse me for a minute?"

"Why don't you let me help you?"

He smiled. "There's not much to do. Just get the food on the table."

"I'll help anyway."

She followed him to the kitchen, which turned out to be bright and attractive and obviously decorated by a woman, with its red-and-white cherry-patterned wallpaper and red

pleated valances on the windows. The feminine decor softened the otherwise modern and utilitarian design of the room,
with its gleaming pots hanging over the butcher block cooking island and its white cabinets and white ceramic flooring.

"Salad's in the refrigerator," he said, heading for the oven.
Five minutes later, the meal was on the dining room table.
"Let's go call the kids," Logan said.

When they walked into the game room, it wasn't hard to
see that Erin might be there physically, but she wasn't taking part in the game. Patrick and Kendall sat side by side
on the floor, and Patrick had the controls while Kendall
watched and cheered him on. Erin was sitting apart, on a
futon, staring at their backs. Abbie's heart went out to her.
Her unhappiness was palpable.

"Dinner's ready," Logan said with forced cheerfulness.
He walked over and ruffled Erin's hair.

After a few seconds of grumbling on Patrick's part—he
wanted to finish his game—they all headed to the dining
room. Logan told them all where to sit. He was at the head
of the table, with Kendall on his right and Erin on his left.
Patrick sat next to Kendall, and Abbie sat next to Erin. Although Abbie understood why Logan had chosen this seat-
ing arrangement, she quickly realized it was just going to
exacerbate Erin's feelings of isolation.

Her analysis turned out to be uncomfortably accurate.
Throughout dinner, Patrick and Kendall talked animatedly,
while Erin ate silently. Logan and Abbie both tried to draw
her out, and if she were asked a direct question, she would
answer politely. But she contributed nothing voluntarily. As
soon as dinner was over, she asked to be excused.

"Erin," Logan said gently.

"Please, Dad. I-I don't feel good." She held her stomach
for emphasis.

The loneliness and pain in her eyes made Abbie want
to fold the child in her arms. She knew exactly what Erin
was feeling, because she vividly remembered the days she'd
been forced to be in her cousin Pamela's company. She
particularly remembered Pamela's thirteenth birthday party,
which Abbie's Aunt Marjorie had thrown at the country
club. There were thirteen girls invited, twelve of them

Pamela's friends. Abbie was the outsider. She remembered how she had watched them having so much fun together. She told herself she hated them, but down deep, she had known that wasn't true. She'd envied them and wanted to be like them, but she wasn't, and she never would be. They hadn't meant to exclude her. They simply hadn't noticed her.

Abbie met Logan's eyes. *Let her go*, she communicated silently. *If you force her, she'll hate me.*

After a barely perceptible sigh, Logan said, "All right, Erin. You may be excused."

Abbie knew how hard it was for Erin to look at Kendall and say, "It was nice to meet you, Kendall," then turn to her and say, "Good night, Mrs. Bernard."

"Good night, Erin." Her heart ached in sympathy, yet she was proud of the child, too, for remembering her manners.

"Night, Erin," Kendall said. "I hope you feel better."

"Thanks."

"I guess I'll see you in school."

After Erin left, Logan said, "Well, shall we let these two go back to their game, and we'll have our coffee in the living room?" Once more there was a note of false heartiness to his voice, and Abbie knew he was as concerned as she was about the disappointing way the evening had turned out.

"I think maybe we should be going," Abbie said. Erin's departure had left her with a feeling of sadness she knew she wouldn't be able to shake. Suddenly she wondered if her dream of getting to know her daughter, of building a relationship with her, would ever be anything more than a dream.

"Mom," Kendall protested, "Patrick and I haven't finished our game."

"Do you have to go already?" Patrick said.

Abbie couldn't help smiling at the youngster. He was such an appealing kid. Well, of course, she thought wryly. No wonder you like him. He's just like Kendall.

"You don't have to leave," Logan said. "It's still early."

"Well . . ." Abbie was torn. She wanted Kendall to spend as much time with her brother as she could, yet she knew how much pain Erin was in right now, and that pain wouldn't begin to go away until Abbie and Kendall were out of the house. "Just until you finish the game. Then we absolutely must go."

Grinning happily, Patrick and Kendall took off. Abbie helped Logan clear the table and then insisted on helping him clean up the kitchen.

"I really don't want any coffee," she said when he started to put on a pot. "I think Kendall and I should leave so you can go to Erin."

He nodded unhappily. "You're right. But listen, Abbie, don't be discouraged. It's going to take some time, but Erin will come around."

Abbie's eyes met his. "I hope you're right." She prayed he was right. Because if Erin didn't come around, if she *never* accepted Abbie, then what?

Nineteen

Logan knocked softly on Erin's door. When there was no answer, he eased it open. There were no lights on, and Erin lay motionless on the bed. She was still fully dressed, so he walked around to where he could see her face. Her eyes were closed. "Honey?"

She didn't answer. Either she really was sleeping or she was putting on a good act. Gently, he touched her shoulder. "Erin? You awake?"

Slowly, she opened her eyes.

"How are you feeling? Any better?"

"I don't know," she mumbled.

"Well, if you're going to sleep, maybe you should get your pajamas on."

"Okay." She sat up, avoiding his eyes. "Are they gone?"

There was no sense pretending he didn't know her meaning. "Yes, they're gone." Logan sat on the side of the bed. He smiled. "I'm glad you got to meet Kendall. She's nice, isn't she?"

She shrugged. "I guess."

"Erin . . ."

Her eyes finally met his. In them he saw bewilderment and something else. Defiance.

He was stunned. Erin had always been the most agreeable of children. Combined with her earlier rudeness in front of Abbie, her behavior was unprecedented.

"I didn't like her," she said.

Logan sighed. He knew he wouldn't get anywhere by pushing her, yet he couldn't seem to let the subject go. "Why not?" he asked quietly.

Another shrug. More eye avoidance. She picked at a loose thread on the quilt covering her bed. "I don't know. I just didn't."

"That's a shame," he said after a few seconds went by, "because I *do* like her, and I like her mother, too. I was hoping we could all be friends. You know, do things together."

She didn't respond, just kept picking at the thread. His heart sank. This wasn't going to work. He couldn't force Erin to accept Abbie and Kendall, especially since he couldn't explain why he wanted them all to get along. Who knew? Maybe she *did* sense something. Maybe she felt threatened by them. But he was certain those feelings would change, if only she knew them better. They were both so nice, he was sure they would win her over in time. Yet he knew if he suggested seeing them again, he would meet with nothing but resistance. "Well." He stood. "We don't have to talk about this tonight."

Once again silence greeted his words. He searched for something else to say that would ease this unaccustomed tension between them, but finding nothing, he kissed the top of her head, whispered, "Good night, sweetheart," and reluctantly left the room.

"So what did you think of Erin and Patrick?" Abbie said on the drive home.

"I really liked Patrick," Kendall said. "He was so nice, and lots of fun, too. You know, Mom, older kids, especially boys, usually don't want to mess with younger kids, especially girls. But he was really nice to me."

Abbie smiled. Yes, brother and sister had recognized a kindred spirit. "What about Erin?"

Although Abbie wasn't looking directly at Kendall, she could feel her shrug.

"She's okay."

"Just okay?"

"Mom," Kendall said with a sigh. "She wasn't very friendly."

"No," Abbie agreed. "She wasn't. But, honey, you know, some kids are just shy. I think Erin's shy."

"Yeah, well, I don't think she liked *me*."

"It's easy to think shy people don't like you, when the reality is, they just don't know how to be friendly. I was like that myself."

"I know, but that wasn't it. Trust me. Erin didn't like me." After a moment, she added, "I didn't like her, either."

Although Kendall couldn't know it, her words stung. It was almost as if she were rejecting *Abbie*, and even though Abbie knew this was a ridiculous thought, it was nevertheless there.

Kendall's pronouncement continued to weigh heavily on Abbie's mind for the remainder of the drive home and for hours afterward as she tossed and turned and tried to get to sleep. Tonight had been a disaster, for she was sure Erin felt exactly the same way Kendall did, only in her case, it was much worse, because Abbie was sure Erin disliked her as well as Kendall. When Abbie finally fell asleep, it was with a heavy heart.

It took Logan a long time to fall asleep. He kept rehashing the evening, wondering what he could have done to make it turn out better. He also wondered if his idea was complete idiocy. Maybe he should abandon it and try to come up with something else, because based on the way Erin had acted tonight, he wasn't sure she'd ever accept Abbie, on any terms.

And yet, if anyone could bring Erin around, he was sure Abbie could. Like Ann, Abbie was completely unselfish where her child was involved. Anyone could see she cared more about Erin's feelings and welfare than she did about her own. She would never rush Erin, no matter how much she might want to be acknowledged as Erin's mother. Given enough time, he was sure she could win Erin over the same way she'd won him over.

He smiled. She *had* won him over. Tonight, watching the way she gently tried to bring Erin into the conversation and the way she refused to take offense at Erin's behavior had banished any remnant of doubt he might still have harbored about her or her motives. She was a remarkable woman. She was also an attractive, interesting woman with a sense of humor—someone he felt he would like more and more as time went on.

Feeling once more reassured, he punched up his pillow and determinedly closed his eyes.

Erin hadn't slept well. She'd been too worried and afraid about why her dad had invited Mrs. Bernard and Kendall to their house.

She thought about how he'd said he liked Mrs. Bernard and Kendall and wanted them all to be friends. How he wanted to do things with them. Erin couldn't remember him ever saying anything like that before, about anyone.

Was he interested in Mrs. Bernard? Like as a girlfriend? The idea horrified Erin. She didn't have anything against that woman, but she sure didn't want her dad *interested* in her!

Erin chewed on her bottom lip. She eyed her phone. She had to talk to somebody, and she couldn't think of a better person than Aunt Elizabeth.

Elizabeth tried to ignore the ringing of the phone. She even went so far as to put her pillow over her head. She must have forgotten to turn on the machine last night. Damn these people! Were they trying to sell things on Sunday mornings now? It must be a sales type, because no one Elizabeth knew would dare call her at eight o'clock on a Sunday morning. All her friends knew Sunday was the only morning of the week she got to sleep late.

Furious, she snatched up the receiver. "Hello," she said in her coldest voice.

"Aunt Elizabeth?"

"Erin?" Suddenly fully awake, Elizabeth sat up. "Is something wrong?" Fear knotted in her stomach.

"I-I . . . No, nothing's wrong," Erin said in a small voice.

Elizabeth sank back against the pillows. Trying to keep the annoyance out of her voice, she said, "Why are you calling me so early then, honey?"

" 'Cause I really needed to talk to you about something."

Elizabeth could hear the child's unhappiness. She sat up straighter. "What is it?" With growing alarm, she listened to Erin's account of the previous evening. She could hardly believe it. Erin was right to be upset. Elizabeth was upset, herself. This development boded no good for either of them. When Erin was finished, Elizabeth said, "I'm glad you called me." She didn't for one minute believe Logan's tale about wanting Erin and the Bernard woman's daughter to meet.

"Then you'll talk to my dad?"

Elizabeth considered. This was touchy. "Let me think about it, okay? And in the meantime, you keep me posted, all right?"

"All right."

"And Erin?"

"Yes?"

"Don't worry, honey. Things will work out, I promise."

"Oh, Aunt Elizabeth, I feel *so* much better already."

After they hung up, Elizabeth decided she could no longer afford the luxury of sleep this morning. She had to get up and plan her strategy. Because it was obvious to her that her entire future was now at stake.

By the following morning, she had figured out a way to broach the subject of the Bernard woman so that Logan couldn't take offense. This time when she called Logan's office, Rebecca put her right through.

"Logan, I really need to talk to you," she said when he was on the line. "Can we have lunch today?"

"Look, if this is about your mother, can't it wait? I'm really bus—"

"It's not about my mother. It's about Erin, and it's very important."

"Erin?"

"Yes, but I don't want to talk about it on the phone."

"All right. I'll juggle some things. Where did you want to meet?"

"How about that little seafood place around the corner from your office?"

They arranged to meet at the restaurant at one to avoid the lion's share of the lunch crowd. Logan was always punctual, so Elizabeth made sure she got there a few minutes early. As expected, he walked in almost immediately after. Elizabeth's heart lifted at the sight of him, and for a moment, she forgot what she was there for. God, she was crazy about him!

"Hi," he said, giving her a kiss on the cheek.

They didn't talk until they were seated at a corner table. Even then they waited until their waiter had taken their drink orders. But once he was gone, Logan said, "What's this about Erin?"

She had carefully rehearsed what she would say. "She called me yesterday. She was upset."

For a fraction of a second, his frown deepened. Then, suddenly, his face smoothed out and he nodded. "I see. I suppose she told you about Saturday night."

"Yes."

He sighed and shook his head. "I don't know why I'm surprised."

"I hope you're not angry with her."

"Angry? No, I'm not angry. I am disappointed, though."

"Why? Because she confided in me? She's confused, Logan. She doesn't understand what's happening to her. Her world used to be secure. Now it seems as if everything is changing, and it frightens her. And the thought of you being interested in some strange woman is the most frightening of all."

"Is that what she said?"

"Not in so many words, but it doesn't take a genius to figure out why she was so bothered by your interest in the Bernard woman." Elizabeth kept waiting for him to laugh and say it was absurd for anyone to think he'd be interested in Abbie Bernard. When he didn't, she knew the situation might be even more alarming than she'd first thought. Was it possible Logan *was* interested in Abbie Bernard? Seriously interested?

"Look, Elizabeth—" He broke off as their waiter approached with their drinks. He didn't continue until they'd given the waiter their food orders and he'd departed once more. "What did you tell Erin after she told you about Saturday night?"

"I told her not to worry. That I was sure the only reason you had invited the Bernard woman and her daughter to come over was so Erin and the daughter could meet. They *are* going to be in the same class in September, right?"

"Yes, they are. And that is why I invited them."

Elizabeth was good at reading people, and something about Logan's reply didn't ring true. Yet Logan was one of the most honest men she'd ever known, and she didn't think he would deliberately lie to her. But her instincts rarely failed her, and right now they were telling her that although what he'd said might be true, it wasn't the whole truth. Something else was going on here, and if she hoped to ever become the next Mrs. O'Connell, she'd better get a handle on it before it spiraled out of control.

"You know, Logan, maybe it would help if I spent more time with Erin, at least until she gets over the loss of Dad." It wasn't deliberate on her part, but the moment she mentioned her father, her eyes misted. When his face softened, she realized she had a weapon she hadn't really utilized. "I miss him so much," she added softly. "And I know she does, too." Pressing her advantage, she added, "It would be good for both of us, I think."

He didn't answer for a moment, and when he did, his voice was resigned. "Maybe you're right. Maybe that *would* help."

After the lunch with Elizabeth, some of Logan's doubts resurfaced. He wondered if he should try to talk to Erin again, then decided against it. He needed more time to think about everything, to try to decide if his idea of a way to solve the problem facing him and Abbie had any merit at all or if it was completely nuts. He guessed most people would think it was crazy. And maybe it was, but he'd been over and over the problem, and the only solution he'd come up with was this one.

By Wednesday, when he still had no other viable solution, he decided he would at least broach his idea to Abbie. If she shot it down, then he'd forget it, and between them, they could try to work out some other plan. But if she agreed, then he would decide whether to try to talk to Erin or simply wait until the plan had been set into motion. So that afternoon, he called Abbie.

She picked up on the first ring.

"You sound upset," he said.

"Not upset. Just harried. Kendall's best friend from Lucas is visiting this week, and I'm trying to take them places as well as get some work done. I feel a little crazy, that's all."

"Yeah, well, I understand that feeling." He waited a moment, then said, "Listen, Abbie, I need to see you."

"All right."

"But I don't want to talk in a public place."

"Do you want to come over here?"

"That would be okay, but you said Kendall has company?"

"Yes, but they'll be gone tomorrow night. My mother is taking them to the ballet. You could come here then."

"Okay. That'll work."

They decided he should come at seven. "Do you like Chinese?" he asked as an afterthought. "If so, I'll pick up some on the way."

"That sounds good."

"Great. See you tomorrow night then."

Abbie could hardly wait for Kendall and Bernie to leave so she could get ready for Logan's arrival. She'd been on tenterhooks ever since his phone call. What did he want to talk about? Was he going to suggest they stop trying to see the girls? Surely not. But what then? Was he going to suggest they tell the girls the truth? Maybe share custody of them? Abbie wasn't sure how she felt about that. In one way, it would be the best solution, because they would be a part of both girls' lives. Yet how could she bear only having Kendall half the time?

She took special care with her appearance, even though she knew it really didn't matter what she wore or what she looked like. This wasn't a date. Logan O'Connell was only coming here for one reason: Kendall. Even so, Abbie wanted to look her best. She rationalized that if she looked good, she would feel more confident. And right now, she needed all the confidence she could get. God, she was nervous!

By seven she was a complete wreck. When the doorbell rang, it was almost a relief. At least she would soon know what was on his mind. Knowing was always better than imagining the worst.

Yet as tense as she was, she couldn't help noticing—and appreciating—how great Logan looked in a royal blue knit shirt, the exact color of his eyes, and casual khaki Dockers. The trouble was, he was too darned appealing. She wished she didn't like him as much as she did, because if he *did* suggest something she wasn't in agreement with, it would be harder to say no.

"Come on in." She tried to smile naturally. "Do you mind eating in the kitchen?"

"I prefer the kitchen, but before we sit down to eat, could we talk for a few minutes?"

"Sure. Let's go into the living room. Would you like a glass of wine?"

"Sounds good."

Once they were settled, Logan said, "I've been thinking about Saturday night ever since you left." He drank some of his wine.

"I know. Me, too."

His eyes met hers. "I'm not going to beat around the bush. I think I've come up with a solution to our problem."

Abbie's heart gave a great thump. He sounded so *serious.*

"You might think it's totally crazy."

Abbie stared at him, afraid to hear what he had to say and afraid not to.

"If you think this is nuts, just say so, okay?"

"Logan, just tell me."

He met her gaze evenly. "All right. Here goes."

Abbie held her breath.

"I think we should get married."

Twenty

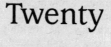

Married!

Abbie stared at Logan, too stunned to speak. Of all the things he could have said, she had never expected anything even remotely like this.

He grimaced. "I've shocked you."

Abbie finally managed a rueful smile. "You could say that."

"I know this idea has come out of the blue, and that it *is* pretty drastic, but before you say no, can I tell you why I think us marrying is a good idea?"

Abbie nodded. Her mind was whirling.

"First of all, I think we're in agreement that we want what is best for the girls."

"Yes," she said faintly. Married. She could hardly take it in.

"And I also think you feel the way I do. I love Erin, and I don't want to give her up. And you love Kendall, and you don't want to lose her."

Abbie swallowed. "No."

"But I also want to be fully involved in Kendall's life, and I think—despite the fiasco the other night—you feel the same way about Erin."

"Yes, I do." This time she answered more strongly.

"Good." He smiled reassuringly. "I think we both recognize that Kendall needs a father, and Erin needs a mother."

"Yes," Abbie agreed. Her first shock had worn off, and in its place, a tiny seedling of excitement was growing. Married to Logan. Kendall to have the family she'd always craved. And Abbie to have both her daughters.

"So we have common goals," Logan continued. "However, I don't see any way to accomplish those goals unless we live with the girls . . . or we share custody of them." His eyes probed hers. "I don't want to do that. Not only do I, personally and selfishly, not want to give up even one day with Erin, but I don't think it would be in the girls' best interests. I think it would cause both of them needless trauma, and to tell you the truth, I'm not sure it would work." He grimaced. "Don't get me wrong. This is not a criticism of you in any way, but if we tried to do something like that, it would be especially hard on Erin. I don't know if she could handle it."

Abbie sighed. "You're right. Sharing custody crossed my mind, too, but I don't like the idea. I'll be honest with you. I was afraid that's what you were going to propose."

"So considering everything, marrying and becoming one family seems the only logical solution to the problem."

"But don't you think a marriage between us might cause even more problems?" She didn't want to raise this particular objection, but it had to be said. "I mean, we don't . . . have that kind of relationship."

"I know. But I think we can make it work." He smiled. "I like you, and I think you like me."

Her pulse skipped. Oh, yes, she liked him.

His smile faded, and his expression became serious again. "I also respect you and the job you've done raising Kendall, which tells me we have the same values."

Abbie nodded again. Her mind was jumping around wildly.

"I know marrying me is asking you to give up a lot. Your independence. Your own home. The possibility of meeting someone you can fall in love with."

"You'd be giving up many of the same things," she pointed out, managing to talk in a calm voice, even though she was anything but.

"Not really. I miss being married. Having someone to

share my life with. And quite frankly, I don't expect to fall in love again." A brief sadness flickered in his eyes. "I think what I had with Ann was a once-in-a-lifetime thing."

Abbie knew it was ridiculous to be envious of a dead woman, but she couldn't imagine anything more wonderful than to be loved the way Ann O'Connell had been loved, especially when the man in question was Logan.

He gave her a long, thoughtful look. "I want you to know that if you agree to marry me, I won't expect anything more of you than to be a good mother to the children and a pleasant companion for me."

Did that mean no sex? Abbie could feel her face heating and once again inwardly cursed herself for her tendency to blush.

"I also respect your commitment to your career, and I wanted to reassure you on that score. I wouldn't expect you to give it up. In fact, I've already got an ideal room that you can use as an office. It'll be totally private, totally yours. You can have your own phone line put in. Whatever you'd need."

"I-I don't know what to say. You've obviously given this quite a bit of thought, but I'm still kind of flabbergasted."

"I know, and I apologize. I wish we had the luxury of time, but I don't want to wait to be a part of Kendall's life. I've already missed too much of it. But I realize you need some time to think this over."

"Yes." She swallowed. *Say it.* "B-but before I can make a decision, there's something else, something important, that I need to know." No matter how embarrassed she might be, she simply had to ask the question. She wet her lips. "Would . . . would you expect us to have a . . . physical relationship?" The moment the words were out, she wished she could take them back. But since she couldn't, she figured she might as well follow through as matter-of-factly as possible, so she forced herself to maintain eye contact without flinching. It wasn't easy, because just the thought of a sexual relationship with Logan made her feel weak in the knees.

"That would be up to you," he said slowly. "I hope you'll want to eventually, because . . ." Now he smiled, his eyes reflecting his amusement. "I don't know about you, but it might be tough to go without sex for the rest of my life."

She couldn't help laughing, even though she was still terribly embarrassed. She didn't dare think of the implications of what he'd said. Not yet. Not until she was alone and didn't have to worry about revealing too much.

"Seriously." His voice sobered. "I know it might take some time, but yes, I would hope we could make our marriage as normal as possible." He reached across the table, covering her hand with his. "Abbie, I want to assure you of something. If we marry, and whether or not we have a physical relationship, I will be completely committed to you, in every way. You would never have to worry on that score."

As she looked into his eyes, something stirred deep inside her. "Yes," she said softly. "I would be the same way."

He squeezed her hand. "Good. Now, what do you say we eat before our food is stone cold? Later we can talk some more if you like. Or, if you'd rather, I'll go, and you can think about everything in peace."

They didn't talk while eating, and Abbie was grateful. Her mind was too chaotic to be able to make casual conversation. Instead she put on a Pavarotti recording and simply listened to the music.

When they were finished with their meal, Logan said, "Do you want me to leave? Or do you want to talk some more?"

"Actually, I do have a few more questions."

"Ask away."

"If I say yes, when would you want to get married?"

"As soon as we can make the arrangements."

"Would you want a civil ceremony? Or a religious ceremony?"

"I think a civil ceremony is the best way to go, because it could be handled quickly, with no questions asked."

She nodded. "Yes, I see what you mean. What about family? Would we tell them beforehand?"

He shook his head. "No. Then we'd *really* have questions. I don't want to answer questions, do you?"

Abbie thought about her mother. About Laura. About Kendall. Well, Kendall wasn't a problem. She would be pleased. Actually, Laura would be pleased, too, but only if she thought Abbie had found someone who would love her as much as Rich loved Laura. Abbie didn't know about her mother. Katherine *should* be pleased. After all, Logan O'Connell would be considered quite a catch by anyone's standards, and Katherine cared about things like that. But you never knew with her. She had always found fault with Abbie's choices, so she just might have objections to Logan, too. Abbie sighed. "No, I don't want to answer questions." She looked at Logan. "What about the children? You don't think we should keep it a secret from them, do you?"

"I don't think we should tell anyone until it's a done deal, not even the children."

"But won't that be an awful shock to them?" Abbie couldn't help thinking about Erin and what her reaction would be to the news. "I don't think Erin likes me."

"It's going to be a shock to the kids no matter how we do it," Logan said. "But if it's an accomplished fact, they'll have no choice but to adjust." He idly picked up the salt shaker and turned it around in his hands. "You know, Abbie, even if we don't get married, the kids will eventually still have a huge shock when the truth comes out. So isn't it better to start now? Get them used to each other and the fact that, like it or not, we're all tied together and we always will be?"

Long after Logan had gone home, Abbie kept thinking about his last question. They *were* tied together. So why not join forces? It would certainly solve the biggest problem they faced. And it would certainly be no hardship to marry Logan. She was already attracted to him. If she were honest, the only reason she hadn't wanted to admit the attraction before this was the belief that he could never be interested in her. But obviously he was. Maybe not in the way she might want him to be, but she could live with that.

Couldn't she?

When it came right down to it, what would she be missing if she married him under these circumstances? He was offering her everything except a wild, romantic love. But Abbie already knew that kind of love didn't last. At best, that first chemistry and I-can't-live-if-he-doesn't-love-me kind of feeling turned into a deeper, more committed but less hectic caring and respect. At worst, all the good feelings disappeared and you discovered the person you were married to was someone you didn't even like very much.

As he'd pointed out, they already liked each other. And they respected each other. And they had two extremely important reasons to make their marriage work.

The following morning, Abbie waited until she knew Logan would be in the office. Then she called him.

"Good morning," he said.

"Good morning."

"Did you sleep well?"

She smiled. "Not really. My mind was too active."

"Yeah. Mine, too."

Abbie took a deep breath. "I've made a decision."

"And?"

"If you haven't changed your mind, then, yes, I'll marry you."

Things moved quickly once Abbie gave Logan her answer. On Monday morning they went to the county clerk's office and applied for their marriage license. The waiting period in Texas was seventy-two hours, which meant Thursday was the soonest they could marry. Logan arranged for Judge William Dickinson to marry them.

"I designed a house for him," Logan explained, "and we've gotten to be friends. I thought it would be less impersonal with him officiating than it would be in some JP's office."

So on Thursday morning, wearing a new, pale aqua linen dress and carrying a small nosegay of pink baby roses that Logan had thoughtfully provided, Abbie and Logan were married. The judge's two clerks acted as witnesses.

Abbie's stomach felt hollow throughout the ceremony. The entire scene seemed surreal, a blur of images and sounds: Judge Dickinson's sonorous voice, the beatific smile on the face of the youngest clerk, the bright August sun slanting through the smudged windows, the dust motes dancing in the air, the drone of traffic outside the courthouse. But most unreal of all was the handsome man in the dark blue suit standing next to her—the man who in the space of minutes would be her husband.

As they said their vows, Abbie's voice trembled. *In sickness and in health. Till death us do part.* The gravity of the words, the absolute commitment being promised, could not be taken lightly. Today her life was changing. And whether it would be for better or for worse, she didn't know. She hoped, and she knew Logan hoped, that the change would be a good one for them all.

When it was time for the rings to be exchanged, Abbie held out her hand. When Logan slipped the ring on her finger, she nearly fainted. The day before they'd picked out plain gold bands, but the ring now glittering on her left hand was anything but plain. A wide platinum band containing four rows of diamonds, it was breathtaking—the most beautiful piece of jewelry Abbie had ever owned.

She knew her mouth must be hanging open, but Logan just smiled and squeezed her hand.

"You may kiss the bride," a beaming Judge Dickenson said after pronouncing them married.

Abbie's heart skipped as Logan, giving her another reassuring smile, drew her close and kissed her lightly. His lips felt wonderful, soft yet firm. "It's going to be okay," he murmured before releasing her.

She watched in a daze as the clerks signed the marriage certificate. Then the judge congratulated them, and he and Logan talked casually for a few minutes. Abbie used the brief respite to try to settle herself down. She kept looking at her ring, which sparkled brilliantly in the sunlight.

Mrs. Logan O'Connell.

She could hardly believe it. Everything that had happened in the past week seemed like a dream. Maybe it *was* a dream. Maybe, any moment, she would wake up and find herself back in her old life, the one she'd had before making her momentous discovery about the girls.

And yet was that what she wanted? To go back to that old life? Weren't the possibilities for the future with Logan far more enticing than what her old life had offered? And not just for Kendall, but for Abbie herself?

Before long, Logan thanked the judge, and Abbie, rousing herself from her dreamlike state, added her thanks to both him and the clerks, who grinned delightedly. Once the niceties were out of the way, she and Logan said their good-byes and soon were on their way.

They had decided earlier that they would have a cele-bratory lunch. Once their lunch was over, Logan would drop Abbie off at home, she would change clothes, pick up Kendall who was going to be at Abbie's mother's, then Abbie and Kendall would head for Logan's, where together, Logan and Abbie would break the news of the marriage to their chil-dren. The actual move to Logan's home would begin on the weekend. The only decision about the immediate future that Abbie hadn't made was what to do about her house. She knew it would be financially unwise to try to keep the house, yet she was uneasy about putting it up for sale. What if things *didn't* work out with Logan? Well, she didn't have to decide anything right now. A few weeks or even a few months wouldn't make that much of a difference.

"I've made reservations for us at Brennan's," Logan said as they left the courthouse. "I hope that's okay."

Abbie was pleased that he was treating this occasion as something special. Perhaps the reasons for their marriage weren't conventional, but marriage itself was something she'd always considered to be one of life's most solemn and hallowed events. That her first marriage had ended badly had not changed this view.

They walked to the nearby lot where he'd parked his BMW. Once they were settled in the car, she thanked him for the ring. "I was absolutely stunned when you put it on my finger."

He smiled. "Good. I surprised you."

"Well, yes. After all, we'd already picked out those bands."

"That was just a ruse. I needed to know your ring size and didn't know any other way to find out." He started the car and gave her a sideways glance. "I hope you like it."

"Like it! I love it. I've never seen a ring quite so beau-tiful. But you didn't have to do this, Logan. I certainly never expected it."

His eyes met hers. "If you were the kind of woman who did expect it, I probably wouldn't have done it."

His statement warmed her and allayed some of her doubts about the future. He was such a thoughtful, generous man. Her heart lifted, and her fears began to melt away. Even the daunting task of telling their families—especially their children—didn't seem half as scary as it had earlier.

Surely, she thought, working together, they could overcome any obstacles in their path. For the first time in many weeks, she almost felt happy.

After dropping Abbie at her house, Logan headed home. Things had gone well today, he thought with satisfaction. And even though he was still apprehensive about the children's reaction when they told them about the marriage, he felt hopeful that between the two of them, he and Abbie would be able to make a go of things. They had to. He refused to even consider the possibility that this blending of their families might not work out.

Erin's reaction was his biggest concern. Patrick might be surprised. He might even be upset. But any negative feelings wouldn't last long. Erin, though . . . she would be a problem. Even if they were to tell her the truth, Logan didn't think it would make any difference. She was going to resent Abbie. But eventually Abbie would win her over.

Abbie. He smiled, remembering how pleased she'd been by the roses he'd given her and then again, by the ring. She was the kind of person you wanted to do things for, someone he would have liked no matter what the circumstances. If she hadn't been, he'd never have been able to conceive of marrying her, no matter what the reason.

And even though sex had had nothing to do with his proposal of marriage, he had to admit that in the past few days he'd been thinking more and more about what it would be like to make love to her. After all, he was human. And he'd been celibate for a long time. And she was very attractive.

He wanted this marriage to work, he realized, not just because of the children, but because he was lonely. He'd meant what he said when he'd told Abbie he liked being married. It would be good to have someone with whom to share his life again.

We're going to make this work, he vowed. *No matter what happens, we're going to make it work.*

Twenty-one

Abbie was already out of the car and on her way to the front door of her mother's house when she remembered the ring. Hastily, she pulled it off her finger and dropped it into her purse. Her mother had eagle eyes. No way she wouldn't notice the ring.

When Kendall had gathered up her belongings, Abbie turned to her mother. "I really appreciate you picking up Kendall today."

Katherine smiled down at Kendall. "It was no trouble at all."

Abbie had been in her mother's good graces ever since her decision to send Kendall to the Caldwell School. This beneficent attitude wouldn't last, Abbie knew. Sooner or later, she would do something to incur her mother's disapproval once again, and they'd then be back to their familiar contentious relationship.

Abbie grimaced inwardly. This morning she had probably already done the deed that would bring Katherine's censure back in full force, for even if her mother approved of Logan—which Abbie was sure she eventually would—Katherine would not take kindly to the fact that the marriage had been accomplished in secret. In fact, Abbie could imagine in vivid detail what choice things her mother would have to say when she was told.

"Well, Kendall," Abbie said. "We'd better be going."

"Okay. Bye, Gran."

"Good-bye, sweetheart. Don't forget. We're going to the symphony on Sunday."

"Don't worry. I won't forget. I can't wait."

Katherine came outside with them and watched as they got into the car and backed out of the driveway. Then she waved and walked back into the house.

"Mom," Kendall said when Abbie got to the end of the street and put on her left blinker, "you're supposed to go right."

"Yes, if we were going home, but we're not going straight home."

"Where are we going?"

"To Logan's house."

"Really?" Kendall squealed. She broke into a delighted smile. "Why?"

"To visit awhile." Abbie didn't like lying to Kendall, even by omission, but she had no choice. She and Logan had promised they wouldn't say anything about the morning's events until all five of them were together.

"If we do say something," Logan had said, "that'll just produce questions we can't answer unless we want to tell them separately, and I don't think that's a good idea."

Abbie had agreed. A long time ago she'd read something about starting out the way you mean to proceed. So if they were to be one united family, that's the way they should begin.

"I think Mr. O'Connell likes you," Kendall said after a moment.

"Do you?" That was Kendall. Always the hopeful romantic.

"Uh-huh."

"Well, I like him, too. Very much. He's a very nice man."

Soon after, Kendall changed the subject and started talking about the art project she was currently working on and then about her new dance teacher and the program she was planning for the Christmas holidays.

Abbie tried to concentrate on Kendall's chatter, but the closer they got to Logan's house, the more nervous she became. She told herself it was silly to get all worked up.

After all, what was the worst that could happen? One or more of the children would be upset. Well, Abbie expected that, didn't she? Certainly Erin wouldn't fall into her arms. In fact, she would probably be hostile at first. Abbie was prepared for that. But Abbie would win her over. The child was crying out for a mother, and Abbie *was* her mother. Surely she could eventually get Erin to love and accept her.

But no matter how she talked to herself, she couldn't get rid of her jitters. By the time they reached Logan's house, she was strung tight as a fiddle string.

Logan opened the door immediately, and she knew he'd been watching for them. "That was fast." He gave Abbie an encouraging smile, then turned his gaze to Kendall. "Hi."

"Hi," she answered happily.

They walked inside and Abbie thought about her first visit to this house. It was hard to believe it had taken place only weeks ago. So much had happened since then. She swallowed. *This is my home now.* Suddenly, she remembered her wedding band and opened her purse to retrieve it. She slipped it back on her ring finger, then looked up to find Logan's eyes watching her.

"My mother would have noticed," she murmured.

He nodded, touching her shoulder briefly in silent support.

They walked back to the family room, which was flooded with sunshine. Rex, tail wagging, bounded over to Kendall and started licking her.

Giggling, she bent to hug the dog.

"Have a seat," Logan said. "I'll go get the kids."

Abbie was too tense to sit, so she walked to the French doors and looked out at the patio. It was obvious Logan had excellent lawn and garden help, because even now, in the worst heat of the summer, the flower beds and hanging baskets were filled with healthy, vibrant flowers. Turning around, her eye caught the family portrait above the mantel. She wondered if Logan would remove it once the children knew about their marriage. It might be touchy. Removing the portrait would probably upset Erin, and yet it would be awkward for Abbie if the portrait stayed there. She sighed. Just one more dilemma in the midst of many.

Footsteps alerted Abbie to Logan's return. *This is it.* Taking a deep breath, she slowly turned around. Patrick's smile was warm and welcoming, Erin's less so. As Abbie searched the child's eyes, she saw the fear, and her heart contracted. She wanted so much to go to Erin, to put her arms around her, to tell her it was all right, she understood exactly how she felt. Abbie tried to communicate her empathy with her eyes and smile, but Erin looked away, moving imperceptibly closer to Logan, almost as if she sensed that something was wrong.

Logan cleared his throat. "Abbie and I have something we want to talk to you about, so why don't we all sit down?" He walked over to Abbie and led her to the couch, sitting down next to her.

Three pairs of eyes stared at them. Kendall's and Patrick's were puzzled. Erin's were alarmed.

Logan reached for Abbie's hand. Abbie's heart thumped painfully. *Please, God, let it be all right.*

"This morning," Logan said softly, "Abbie and I were married."

For one long moment, there was absolute stillness as his words sank in.

Then Erin jumped up. "You can't be married," she said in a strangled voice.

"Are you really *married*, Mom?" Kendall said at almost the same moment. She grinned at Abbie.

"Gee, Dad," Patrick said, frowning, "why didn't you tell us?" He looked at Erin, whose face had turned a splotchy red.

Logan sighed and released Abbie's hand. Walking over to Erin, he put his arm around her shoulder. "I know it's a shock, honey, but it's true, and I hope once you get used to the idea, you'll be happy about it."

"No," she moaned, "you can't be married to her, Daddy. You can't!"

"Sweetheart, if you'll just sit down so we can talk—"

"I don't want to sit down!" Tears pooled in her eyes.

Abbie watched helplessly.

"Why didn't you *tell* us, Dad?" Patrick said again, and this time it was clear he was angry, too.

Abbie looked at Logan. He grimaced, then faced his son. "We didn't say anything to anyone because we wanted a quiet wedding. I'm sorry. I know it's a shock to you. Maybe we *should* have told you beforehand, but we thought we were doing the right thing."

"Yeah, well . . ." Patrick's voice trailed off. He looked uncertain and suddenly younger than his thirteen years. "You *shoulda* told us."

Abbie's gaze met Kendall's. Even Kendall, whom Abbie knew was thrilled by their news, looked disquieted by the reactions of Erin and Patrick.

Suddenly Erin wrenched herself away from Logan's touch. "I can't believe you did this!" she cried, tears streaking down her face. "I'm *never* going to be happy about it. Never! I hate you for doing it!" Then, sobbing hysterically, she ran blindly from the room. A moment later, giving his father an accusatory look that spoke volumes, Patrick got up and followed her.

Abbie sat frozen. Even Kendall's getting up and coming to sit next to her, sliding her hand into Abbie's in a show of love and support that would normally have warmed Abbie's heart and taken some of the sting out of Erin's words, didn't help. Erin's reaction was so much worse than Abbie had feared.

She finally turned her gaze to Logan, who looked as stricken as she felt. "You'd better go to her."

"Yes. But I—" It was obvious his normal self-confidence had been shaken.

"Don't worry about us. We'll go home." She squeezed Kendall's hand. "We have a lot to talk about."

Kendall gave her a reassuring smile and nodded.

Logan sighed and pushed his hands through his hair. "I'm sorry, Abbie. Maybe I should have talked to them alone first. But things will be better tomorrow."

She nodded, wishing she really thought so. All her doubts had come flooding back, and now they were even stronger than they'd been before. But there was no sense giving voice to them. The die was cast. They were married now, and they'd told the children. All they could really do was go forward and hope for the best.

Logan walked them to the door and gave Abbie a light kiss good-bye. "I'll call you later, okay?" His eyes were troubled.

She tried to smile but was afraid her effort fell short. "Okay."

He bent down to hug Kendall. Abbie swallowed against the lump in her throat as she watched the embrace, which Kendall returned wholeheartedly. She was happy that Logan and Kendall were already cementing their relationship, but her heart ached for the child crying her heart out in her bedroom. If only she could go to her. If only she could hold her and say what was in her heart. If only she could somehow push past the wall Erin had erected between them.

Oh, Erin, sweetheart, I have so much love to give you. Please give me a chance.

"Erin. Erin, honey, please open the door."

Erin squeezed her eyes shut tighter. "Go away."

This time her dad knocked harder. "Erin, come on, sweetheart. Open up. Let's talk, okay?"

She buried her head farther under her pillow. *Go away. Just go away.* Her father jiggled the doorknob a couple of times and continued calling out her name, but she didn't answer. Patrick had knocked a while ago, too, and she'd told him she didn't want to talk to him, either.

"All right, Erin," her dad said in a resigned voice, "I won't force you to talk to me right now. But later on, when you're not so upset, I'll come back, okay?"

No, it wasn't okay, she thought in despair. It would never be okay. As her father's footsteps retreated down the hall, she whispered, "I never want to talk to you again. I hate you." But even as she said the words, she knew they weren't true. She wished she *could* hate her father, but the truth was, she loved him. A lot. And she'd loved her mom, too. She had thought she and her dad felt the same way. Now she knew they didn't. He had forgotten all about her mom. He must have. Else why would he have married that . . . that *woman*? Erin couldn't even bear to think of that woman's name.

She remembered how happy their family had been when

her mom was alive. How on Saturday nights, when her mom and dad weren't going out—and mostly, they didn't go out, they liked staying home with Erin and Patrick—they would rent movies and pop popcorn or they would sit around the kitchen table and play Scrabble or Monopoly. Sometimes her mom made fresh lemonade. Other times, when it was cold outside, she'd make hot chocolate and put marshmallows on top. Erin remembered how sometimes they'd build a big fire in the fireplace and roast hot dogs, just like they were camping out. They'd had so much fun together. Her mom and dad had laughed a lot. Sometimes her dad told silly jokes, and her mom would get the giggles. Then Erin would get the giggles, too. The memories brought a fresh onslaught of tears. How could her father have forgotten all that? It was like Erin's mom had never existed, the way he'd married this other woman, who was nothing *like* her mom.

Why? Why had he done it? How could her dad have forgotten her mom so soon? *Well, you wanted him to marry Aunt Elizabeth.* But it would have been different if he'd married Aunt Elizabeth. Aunt Elizabeth was family. This woman was a stranger! And now . . .

Erin swallowed. Were that woman and her daughter going to move into their house?

That's what married people do. They live together.

Erin thought back to the night that woman and her daughter had come for dinner. How Patrick had seemed to really like Kendall. How the two of them had laughed and played video games together. How they'd all but ignored Erin. That night, Erin had felt so alone. Was that what it was going to be like here from now on? Her dad and that woman together? Patrick and Kendall together? And Erin all by herself?

She cried until she could cry no more. She didn't know what to do. She thought about calling her Aunt Elizabeth, but for some reason, she was reluctant to do so. Somehow she sensed it wouldn't be such a great thing to break this news to her aunt.

Sitting up, she rubbed her swollen, itchy eyes. And as she did so, she saw the blinking cursor on her computer screen. She had been playing a game when her dad called her and Patrick into the family room earlier, and she'd just left her computer on. Seeing it, she thought about Allison. Allison would understand. Allison always understood everything.

Erin got up and walked over to her computer. She logged onto AOL and checked to see if Allison was on-line. She was, so Erin sent her an instant message.

Allison, it's me, Erin. What are you doing? Do you have time to talk?

SURE. WHAT'S GOING ON? Allison wrote back.

You'll never believe what happened today. It's awful! My dad got married!

MARRIED? WHO TO?

Erin explained, fighting against the great lump in her chest and willing herself not to start crying again.

THAT SUCKS. THAT REALLY SUCKS. WHAT ARE YOU GOING TO DO?

I don't know. I still can't believe it's true.

WHAT'S YOUR STEPMOTHER LIKE? IS SHE NICE?

Don't call her my stepmother.

BUT MAYBE SHE'LL BE NICE. MAYBE YOU'LL LIKE HER.

I'll NEVER like her! I don't know why my dad does. She's nothing like my mom. My mom was so pretty and she was so much fun.

They continued to write back and forth for at least an hour, and by the time Erin logged off, she felt a little better. At least she could say what she was thinking to Allison. After switching off her computer, she sat there for a minute, trying to decide what to do now. She was thirsty, but unless she wanted to drink the lukewarm water out of her bathroom faucet, she'd have to unlock her door and go out and face her father. She wasn't sure if she was ready.

The thought had barely crossed her mind before she heard his footsteps in the hallway. A second later, there was a knock at her door.

"Erin?"

Erin sighed. She guessed she had to talk to him sometime. She got up and unlocked the door. One look at her father's face made fresh tears well into her eyes. He put his arms around her and let her cry, saying, "I know, I know," and "I'm sorry" over and over again.

When she was all cried out, he said, "Why don't you go wash your face and then come out into the family room? Patrick's there and we can talk."

Erin knew she looked awful with her swollen eyes and ugly red face, so she dawdled in her bathroom. Finally, though, she could stall no longer, and she reluctantly walked down the hall and into the family room. Her dad was standing by the French doors, and Patrick was sitting on the couch, head hanging down. They both looked up at her entrance. Her dad smiled, and Patrick shot her a sympathetic look.

Self-consciously, she walked over to one of the chairs and sat down.

"Do you feel better?" her dad said, sitting opposite her. She shrugged.

"I'm sorry about today," he said. "I realize now that it was a bad idea to spring things on you the way we did, but what's done is done. The important thing is, Abbie and I are married, and the five of us—you, me, Patrick, Abbie, and Kendall—are going to become one family. I know you're not happy about it, Erin, but I think, if you'll just give Abbie and Kendall a chance, you'll change your mind."

Erin wanted to say she'd never change her mind. Instead, she bit her bottom lip and looked at Mitzi, who was laying nearby in a puddle of afternoon sunlight. She wished Mitzi would come and sit on her lap, but even the cat seemed aloof today.

"I know how sudden this was and that you both probably have questions," her dad said.

Erin had a million questions, but she was sure he wouldn't like any of them.

"Erin?" When she didn't answer, her dad turned to Patrick. "What about you, son? Is there anything you'd like to ask?"

After a minute, Patrick said, "We're not gonna move, are we, Dad?"

"No, we're not going to move. Abbie and I talked about

it, and we've decided it makes the most sense for her and Kendall to move into this house. They're coming this weekend."

A new, horrible thought struck Erin. "I'm *not* sharing my room with Kendall."

"I don't expect you to," her father said.

"Then where is she gonna sleep?"

"I thought we'd give her the guest room."

"What about when we have company?" Patrick asked.

"It won't be a problem. If the company is yours, he'll share your room. The same goes for Erin or Kendall. And if we have adult company, they can either sleep on the sofa bed in the game room or we'll put them up in one of the hotels."

No one said anything for long minutes. Then Erin had another, even *more* horrible thought. She turned stricken eyes to the portrait over the fireplace. "Are you gonna take Mom's picture down?"

For the first time that day her dad seemed uncertain. He turned to look at the portrait, and when he finally turned back to her, his eyes were troubled. "It wouldn't be right to leave it there, honey."

Erin felt as if he'd just hit her.

"But we can hang it in your room," her dad continued. "That's a good idea, don't you think?"

She knew he wanted her to agree, but she just couldn't. "I don't know why you married her!" she blurted out. "Everything's going to be awful now. I s'pose you'll take down all Mom's paintings, too." She fought the tears that threatened to come again. "Weren't you happy with us? Why do we need *them*?"

Her dad sighed. "I know you don't understand. I hope someday you will, but in the meantime, I want you to think about something. Both of you."

Erin looked down at her hands. Patrick shuffled uncomfortably.

"Have I ever done anything to hurt you?" her dad continued. "Ever?"

Reluctantly, Erin shook her head.

"No," Patrick said.

"Well, this wasn't done to hurt you, either. I love both of you very much, and in marrying Abbie and combining our two families, I think, in the end, we'll all be happier. And if you'll just keep an open mind, before long I think you'll feel the same way." He smiled, looking first at Patrick, then at Erin. "Think about it, Erin. You'll have a sister. Somebody to pal around with at school, somebody to go places with."

Somebody for Patrick to like better than me . . . Erin thought about how Kendall looked. How pretty she was. How easy it was for her to meet people and talk to them. She would probably be the most popular girl in their class once school started. "I don't want a sister," she said miserably.

"Erin," he said sadly. "Won't you at least *try*? This isn't like you. You know, today, the way you acted, I'm sure you hurt Abbie's feelings. She probably thinks you hate her, and I know that's not true. You're not like that. You don't hate people." He sighed. "I don't expect you to love her right off the bat or to be thrilled about her becoming part of our family, but I *do* expect you to be polite and pleasant, the way you would be with anyone else. And the same goes for Kendall. And, I'm sure, if you do that, your feelings will eventually change, because Abbie and Kendall are both so nice, you won't be able to help liking them the way I do."

Erin bowed her head. What was the use of talking? She was so tired. Too tired to argue. Too tired to even think. She sighed deeply. Finally she raised her head. "All right, Daddy. I'll try. And you're right, I don't hate that wom—um, Mrs. Ber—" She stopped. She'd almost said Mrs. Bernard. But Abbie wasn't Mrs. Bernard anymore. She was Mrs. O'Connell. The thought was like a dagger in her heart. *Erin's* mother was Mrs. O'Connell. "I don't hate *her*," she corrected. "I'm sorry if she thinks I do."

Her dad smiled. "That's my girl."

"But what am I supposed to call her? I'm not calling her Mom," she added defiantly.

Her dad's eyes got that sad look she had gotten used to since her mom died. "You don't have to call her Mom," he answered quietly. "I think it would be fine if you called her Abbie."

"Good." Erin glared at him, because she knew the sad look was a lie. If it wasn't a lie, he'd have never married that woman. "Because she's not my mom, and she never will be."

Twenty-two

"You're what?"

Abbie couldn't help smiling. Laura's normally low-pitched voice had gone up a couple of octaves.

"You're kidding, right?" Laura continued incredulously. "You couldn't possibly be serious."

"No, I'm serious."

"But Abbie, how could you be married? Who *is* this guy and when did you meet him and why is this the first time I've even *heard* about him?"

Abbie had decided she would tell as much of the truth as it was possible to tell right now. "Well, I got this idea to do a story about the night Kendall was born. You know, I told you all about that night."

"Yes."

"Anyway, in researching the hospital, I got the names of the other babies born during the storm, and I contacted them. Logan was one of the parents."

"I take it Logan is the new husband."

"Yes. Logan O'Connell."

"And? Come on, tell me everything about him."

"Well, he's an architect. He's forty years old. A widower. His wife died three years ago. And he has a daughter Kendall's age—she's the baby born that night—and a son who's thirteen."

"Oh, jeez, stepkids. Abbie, are you sure you know what you're doing?"

Abbie smiled wryly. If Laura knew the entire story, she'd have even more reason to ask the question.

"Sorry," Laura said. "Go on."

"There's not much more to tell. We met. We liked each other. I like his kids, too. Very much. And, well, when he asked me to marry him, it felt so right."

"But how long have you *known* him? I mean, you just moved back to Houston two months ago. Did you meet him right away? And why didn't you *say* anything?"

Abbie did the best she could with the questions, but it was hard to make her actions sound sensible and responsible without telling Laura the whole truth.

"He must really be something to have swept you off your feet so quickly," Laura finally said. "I can't wait to meet him. You are bringing him to the wedding, aren't you?"

"We'll see. We haven't had time to talk about anything like that yet." Laura's wedding was scheduled for the week between Christmas and New Year's.

"Well, Abbie, I have to say, you're certainly full of surprises."

Abbie laughed self-consciously.

"But I'm happy for you, hon. I just hope your Logan is half as great as my Rich."

"He . . . he's really a wonderful man, Laura. I think you'll like him."

"Tell me, how did Mommy dearest take the news?"

"I, um, haven't told her yet."

"You haven't *told* her yet? Abbie! What in the heck is going *on* there?"

"You know how she is, Laura. If we'd told her ahead of time, she'd have gone ballistic. I just couldn't deal with it. I figured once the marriage was a fait accompli, she would have to accept it." She wondered what Laura would say if she knew Katherine didn't even know of Logan's existence.

"Oh, God, I'd love to be a little mouse in the corner when you do tell her. Promise me you'll call immediately and fill me in on every juicy detail."

Abbie rolled her eyes. "Laura, you're incorrigible."

"I know. That's why you love me."

"You're *what*?"

Logan heard the disbelief in his sister's voice. "I know, it's a shock."

"A shock! That's certainly an understatement. I mean, Logan, when? What? How? I-I don't understand. You . . . you didn't marry *Elizabeth*, did you?"

"Good God, no." Logan launched into an explanation, finishing with "I think you'll really like Abbie."

"Have you told Mom and Dad yet?"

"No, you're the first one."

"Do they even know you've been seeing Abbie?"

"No."

"Oh, boy."

Logan grimaced. "Think they'll be upset?"

He could almost see Glenna's shrug. "Dad'll just be bewildered. And Mom? Who knows? Sometimes she surprises me. When're you going to tell them?"

"I thought I'd go over there later tonight."

"Good." She laughed. "I'm not sure I can keep this secret much longer than that." Then her voice sobered. "How'd the kids take the news?"

Logan sighed and proceeded to tell her what had happened. He knew she was wondering how he could have done such a thing to Erin. He kept expecting her to ask the question, but she didn't.

They continued to talk for a while longer. Then Glenna said, "So when are we going to meet Abbie and Kendall?"

"Next week sometime. Let us get settled first, okay?" He was worried about this first meeting. Kendall's resemblance to Patrick was sure to be noticed. And then what? Would Glenna and Paul be suspicious? Well, if they were, he and Abbie would just have to deal with it then. No sense worrying about it now.

"Okay," Glenna said. "Oh, listen, I have an idea. Why don't I have a little celebratory party or something here? That way everyone can meet them at the same time."

"No, Glenna, don't do that. It'll be overwhelming for

Abbie if she has to meet everyone all at once. Tell you what. I'll call you Sunday night and we'll set something up." Jesus, the last thing he wanted was a party. And he was sure Abbie felt the same way. Things were tough enough as it was.

"Well, okay . . . if you're sure, but it would be so nice to have a party."

"I'm sure."

"You're *what*?" Katherine stared at Abbie. "Is this a joke?"

"No, Mother, it's not a joke." Abbie was mad at herself because her heart was thudding. When would she *ever* stop being afraid of her mother? She stuck her left hand out. "We were married yesterday afternoon."

Her mother's eyes nearly popped out. She grabbed Abbie's hand so she could take a closer look at the ring. When she met Abbie's gaze once more, there was grudging approval in her expression. Katherine knew good jewelry, so Abbie was sure she was impressed by the ring.

Even so, when her mother spoke, her voice was faint. "I think I need to sit down."

Abbie was immediately filled with remorse. She should have found some way to break the news more gently. After all, her mother was no longer a young woman, and this was pretty momentous news. "I'm sorry. I knew this would be a shock to you."

"Well, of course it's a shock," Katherine said indignantly. "I didn't even know you were *seeing* anyone, let alone considering *marriage*. Just who is this man?"

Abbie told herself not to get annoyed by her mother's demanding tone. Katherine had a perfect right to be upset. As confidently as she could, she attempted to explain the inexplicable.

"Are you saying you only met him since you moved back to Houston?" her mother cried when she'd finished. "And he has *children*? My God, Abbie, you couldn't have really *thought* about this. Why, this doesn't make any sense at all. What about Kendall? Do you *ever* think about your daughter's well-being and future?"

"Of course, I think about Kendall," Abbie said, stung, even though, on the surface, she knew it must look as if she hadn't considered Kendall at all. "She's the most important person in my life."

"I find that very hard to believe. How you can possibly think marrying someone you barely know, who already has two children of his own, will be good for Kendall, is beyond me. Why, she's just getting settled in, Abbie, and now there will be all this upheaval in her life. How can that be good for her?"

"Kendall is happy about this, Mother. She thinks Logan is wonderful." *And he's her father. If I hadn't married him, he might have taken her away from me. Then how would you have felt?*

"If she's so happy about all this, why isn't she here with you now?"

"She wanted to come, but I thought it would be best to talk to you alone first."

"Yes, because you *knew* what my reaction would be, didn't you? I swear, Abbie, I'll never understand you. I mean, of all the irresponsible, misguided things you've ever done, this really takes the cake."

Abbie had to bite her tongue to keep from answering back in kind. Someday her mother *would* understand, and maybe then, she'd apologize. Oh, sure. And maybe someday hell would freeze over, too, Abbie thought cynically.

She waited a moment before answering, and when she did, her voice betrayed none of her inner turmoil. "I'm sorry you feel that way, Mother. But the fact remains that Logan and I are married, and this weekend Kendall and I are going to move into his house. You will always be welcome there. But if you come, don't come with criticisms and negative comments. This is my family now. Mine and Kendall's. And I expect you to treat them with respect."

Logan knew it was cowardly, but he almost wished someone else would tell Elizabeth about his marriage. He'd put her off till last. He'd called his sister and his parents and each one of his brothers. Everyone had expressed the same stunned surprise, but they were all happy for him, he knew. Of course, he thought dryly, they had no idea what was *really* going on.

Now there was was only Elizabeth and his former mother-in-law left to tell.

Come on. Quit putting it off.

He picked up the phone.

She answered on the second ring. "Logan!" she said happily. "Hi! I was just thinking about you."

"Hello, Elizabeth." Unwelcome guilt made his voice gruff. "I, uh, I have some news . . ."

Elizabeth stared at the phone.

Married. Logan was married.

Her heart was pounding the way it did when she'd been running or when she was frightened. Elizabeth shook her head, as if the physical action of denial would make it not be true. She couldn't believe it. Logan had married Abbie Bernard. The woman he'd said was just a friend. No. This *couldn't* be true. It simply couldn't. It was too crazy.

Maybe she'd misheard. Logan *couldn't* have married that woman. Why, he barely *knew* her! He'd only met her, what? A month ago? Six weeks ago?

But even as she told herself this couldn't possibly have happened, she knew she hadn't imagined the phone call, and she hadn't misheard. Logan had been very matter-of-fact. He'd said he and Abbie Bernard had been married yesterday afternoon in Judge Dickinson's chambers.

Suddenly, the enormity of it all hit her—a crushing weight that pressed against her chest and made it hard for her to breathe. Furious tears sprang into her eyes. "Why?" she screamed, fists pounding the wall. "Why?"

She sank to the floor in a storm of turbulent weeping. She cried and raged until she was exhausted and her tears were dried up. Even then, she still sat there, too weary to move, still shell-shocked and disbelieving. A good part of the reason this out-of-the-blue marriage was so hard to believe was that it was so unlike Logan. He'd always been so sensible. As far as she knew, in his entire adult life, he'd never done anything reckless. And since Ann had died, he'd been so protective of his children, so worried about them and considerate of their feelings. And now, just like that, with absolutely no warning and in complete secrecy, with no regard for anyone, he'd gone and married a woman he barely knew.

Elizabeth remembered that day at lunch when she'd told him about Erin's phone call and how bewildered and disturbed Erin was about Abbie Bernard. He'd insisted that the only reason he'd invited Abbie and her daughter for dinner was so Erin could meet the daughter. Elizabeth recalled how uneasy she'd felt over his answer, how despite what Logan said, she'd sensed there was more to the situation than he was admitting.

And I was right.

Slowly, a cold determination crept over her. This marriage between Logan and Abbie Bernard didn't add up. Something was going on. Something very strange. And if it was the last thing Elizabeth ever did, she was going to get to the bottom of it.

A little after eight on Saturday morning, Elizabeth called Logan's house. Erin answered the phone.

"Hi, sweetie. It's Aunt Elizabeth."

"Hi."

Poor kid. She sounded completely dispirited. And no wonder. Lowering her voice sympathetically, Elizabeth said, "How're you doing?"

"Okay, I guess."

"Your dad called me and told me what's going on."

"Oh."

"Listen, honey, I was wondering. Would you like to come and spend the day with me today? You could even stay overnight, if you like."

"Really?" Finally there was some animation in Erin's voice. "But . . . don't you have to work?"

"I'm taking the day off." Saturday was normally one of Elizabeth's most productive days, and she'd had to cancel two appointments, but she figured this situation was a lot more important than a couple of possible sales. Besides, she'd rescheduled both customers for later in the week.

"I'll have to ask my dad," Erin said.

"Is he there?"

"Yeah. He's . . ." Erin lowered her voice. "Abbie's moving in today so he's got some people here taking away some furniture."

"Oh?"

"Yeah, Kendall's gonna have the guest room now."

"I see." Elizabeth's jaw clenched and it was an effort to speak lightly. "Well, why don't you go ask him and I'll wait."

"Okay."

A few minutes went by. Then Logan came to the phone, saying, "Hello, Elizabeth."

"Hello, Logan."

"Look, it was nice of you to invite Erin, but I really wanted her to be here when Kendall and Abbie arrive. I don't know if she told you, but they're moving in today."

Was that a touch of exasperation she heard in his voice? Well, wasn't that just too damn bad? "Yes," she answered sweetly, "she told me." Elizabeth could hear Erin in the background, and even though she couldn't make out the words, she knew by Erin's tone of voice that she was saying she wanted to come. "Even so, I think it would be good for her to get away from there for a while. I'm sure you realize how hard all of this is for her."

A long moment of silence went by. Then Logan said in a resigned voice, "Maybe you're right. Okay, fine. She can go."

Elizabeth's expression was resolute as she hung up the phone. After stopping by her office and returning a few phone calls, she headed for Logan's, pulling into his driveway a few minutes after ten. Erin ran out to meet her, flinging her arms around Elizabeth in a tight hug. The kid looked terrible, Elizabeth thought, pale and so obviously miserable you'd have to be blind not to see it.

When Elizabeth looked up, Logan was standing in the open doorway. Her heart contracted, and fresh pain stabbed her. It was all she could do to smile and say hello. His answering smile was strained, and she had a brief moment of satisfaction at the knowledge that he was feeling uncomfortable. Good. He deserved to feel uncomfortable after what he'd done to her and Erin.

They moved inside, and while Elizabeth and Logan waited in the entryway, Erin went back to her bedroom to get her things. There was an awkward silence. When Elizabeth trusted herself enough to speak without giving away her simmering anger, she said, "Have you called Mother yet?"

Logan nodded. "I called her a little while ago."

Elizabeth refused to ask what her mother's reaction had been, and he didn't volunteer the information. Elizabeth wanted to smack him. She couldn't even look at him, she was so afraid she would do or say something she would be sorry for later.

She felt enormous relief when Erin, carrying a duffel bag, reappeared. "Ready?"

"Uh-huh," Erin said. There was a bit more color in her face now.

"Bye, honey," Logan said, bending down to kiss her cheek. "Have fun."

Erin nodded. When Logan stood up, his eyes met Elizabeth's again. There was an unspoken appeal in them.

"I'll have her home sometime tomorrow afternoon," Elizabeth said stiffly. She hoped he didn't expect *her* to make things easier for him. She'd be darned if she would.

"Good, because we'll want to make it an early night for the kids. School starts Monday, you know."

Elizabeth didn't answer, just took the duffel from Erin and walked out the door. She didn't look back, and he didn't follow them outside.

"So are you doing okay?" Elizabeth asked Erin once they were on their way.

Erin shrugged. "I guess so."

Elizabeth reached over and gently squeezed Erin's hand. "I understand how you feel. And I just want you to know, if things get bad, you can always come to me."

Erin looked up. Her eyes were bleak. "I wish . . ." She sighed.

"I know." *Me, too.*

"My dad said I don't have to call Abbie Mom."

"I should hope not."

" 'Cause she's not my mother."

"That's right. She's not."

For a while, each was lost in her own thoughts. Then, in a hesitant voice, Erin said, "Aunt Elizabeth?"

"Hmmm?" Elizabeth braked for the light at North Piney Point Boulevard. Every time she passed through this intersection, she thought about Logan's parents, who lived in the neighborhood. Logan's parents, whom she'd expected to be her in-laws. Without warning, tears stung her eyes.

"Do you like Abbie?"

Struggling to compose herself, Elizabeth said, "I have no idea. I barely know the woman."

"My dad said she's really nice. That I'll like her when I get to know her. Do . . . do you think he's right?" she said in a small voice.

The light turned green, and Elizabeth stomped on the gas pedal with more force than she'd intended. The car shot forward, and she had to brake to keep from hitting the car in front of her. "Listen to me, Erin," she said when she had the car under control. "Just because your father married that woman and wants you to like her doesn't mean you *have* to like her." Her voice shook, but right now she didn't care.

Erin nodded. "I promised him I'd be polite to her, though."

"Yes, you must be very polite to her," Elizabeth said more calmly. "But no one, not even your father, can tell you how to feel."

Erin expelled a breath. "Good. 'Cause I don't think I'm ever gonna like her."

Elizabeth smiled grimly.

Twenty-three

An unexpected sadness crept over Abbie as she locked up the house Saturday afternoon. She was going to miss this place. Although she and Kendall had only lived there a couple of months, it already felt like home. Whereas Logan's house, even though it was so much larger and more beautiful, had been another woman's home.

The thought was sobering. For the first time, the knowledge really sank in that she would be moving into Ann's home, among Ann's things, where her memory was still very much alive. The realization brought with it a cascade of concern and doubts.

Thank goodness Kendall seemed to have no qualms about the move. All day, she'd practically been dancing in her excitement to get to Logan's. She'd chattered on and on about him (he's so *nice*, Mom!) and the house (it's so big and pretty!) and Patrick (I really like Patrick, don't you?) and Mitzi (now we don't need to get a cat, 'cause they've got one!) and Rex (and just think! I've got a dog like Bernie's now!). Every utterance ended on a rising note, an exclamation point of delight. Noticeably absent, though, was any mention of Erin, and although Abbie would have liked to talk to Kendall about Erin again, she had decided not to push it. It would be much better to let things take their natural course. After all, she couldn't force the two girls to like each other, and Kendall had already promised to make every attempt to get along with Erin. Erin, of course, was another story.

"Mom, *c'mon*." Kendall tugged at Abbie's hand. "Let's *go*."

Shaking off her worrisome thoughts, Abbie climbed into her car and motioned for the movers to follow. Because traffic was always heavy on Saturdays—all the eight-to-fivers were out shopping and running errands—it took more than a half hour to reach Logan's home. So it was after four when the little caravan pulled into Logan's driveway.

Abbie hadn't seen Logan since Thursday, but she'd talked to him several times. Each time they'd talked, he'd been comforting and reassuring, even when she'd told him about her mother's reaction to her news.

"She'll come around," he'd said. "Especially when she sees that Kendall is happy."

Abbie could use another dose of that reassurance right now, she thought as she got out of her car and saw Logan coming toward her. He looked great in his casual, yet obviously expensive, navy shorts, tan T-shirt, and Docksiders. Ruefully, she looked down at her beat-up jeans and dirty T-shirt, which she hadn't bothered changing after spending the day packing.

"You're earlier than I thought you'd be," he said.

"That's not a problem, is it?"

"No, of course not." He smiled down at Kendall. "Your room's all ready for you."

Kendall grinned.

"Are Erin and Patrick home?" Abbie asked. She saw no sign of them.

Logan shook his head. "No. Patrick had football practice and Erin's spending the weekend at Elizabeth's."

"Oh." Abbie wondered whose idea that had been. She hated to admit it, even to herself, but she was glad she had a reprieve before having to face Erin again. Glancing at Kendall, she could see her daughter felt the same way.

While they'd been talking, the movers had opened the back of the truck and started unloading. Logan noticed and walked over to the two men. "Why don't I show you where everything goes before you bring anything in?"

Abbie and Kendall followed Logan and the movers inside. Logan took them into the right wing of the U-shaped house. Abbie had been back here before, because the game room occupied the area of the wing that faced the front of the house. The room that would be Kendall's was next to it. "Erin's room is there." Logan pointed to the room on the other side of the intersecting hallway. "And Patrick's is down at the end."

Abbie could see Kendall was pleased with her room, which was larger than the one in the house they'd just left.

"We can have the walls painted or papered any way you like," Logan said. "And you can put up posters or pictures. We can have shelves put in, too. Whatever you want."

It almost hurt to see Kendall's smile, it was so filled with adoration.

"This is great," she said, practically bouncing up and down. "Mom, isn't it great?"

"Yes, great," Abbie echoed. And it *was* a nice room. Abbie didn't know why she'd suddenly gotten that awful, hollow feeling in her stomach. Maybe it was because in that moment everything seemed so real. She and Kendall were actually here. She and Logan were actually married. And one of these days, Kendall and Erin would know the truth about their parentage. Everyone would know.

"Do you have a computer?" Logan asked.

"Uh-huh."

"A modem?"

Kendall nodded.

"Okay. I'll call the telephone company and get them to send someone out. We'll put in a separate line for you."

"Oh, Logan, that's not necessary," Abbie protested.

"Patrick and Erin each have a line of their own. Kendall should have her own, too."

"But—" *She* was going to need her own phone line. That would mean five separate lines for the house. Abbie couldn't even imagine what the cost would be for all that. Well, she would insist on paying for hers and Kendall's.

Logan laid his palm casually against her back. "Don't worry about it, Abbie."

She nodded, too distracted by his touch to argue coherently. *Good grief,* she thought once he'd moved away. *I've got to settle down.*

"Now I'll show you where Mrs. O'Connell's clothes and things will go," Logan said to the men.

Mrs. O'Connell. Abbie swallowed. She was Mrs. O'Connell. This was her home. She really did belong here.

Logan led them through the living room. As they walked past the mantel, Abbie looked up. Her mouth nearly dropped open. The portrait was gone! What had Logan done with it? And what had Erin's reaction been? Abbie made a mental note to ask Logan about it once they were alone.

By now, they were in the other wing. In this part of the house, the dining room and kitchen occupied the front half. Opening the door that led into the back half of the wing, Logan revealed a large, sunny room that was furnished as a combination sitting room/office. Abbie wondered briefly if this was the room he intended for her use. If so, he would be giving up his home work area, because it was obvious he'd been using it as such. There was a large drawing table set up by the French doors that led out onto the patio, and stacked in the corner behind it were a dozen or so rolled-up blueprints.

But she didn't have long to wonder, because Logan continued on through a connecting doorway into the master bedroom, a beautifully decorated room in multiple shades of green which was dominated by a dark walnut, king-size four-poster bed.

"This is the closet," Logan said, opening louvered doors that revealed an enormous walk-in closet. Half of it contained men's clothes. The other half was empty. "I hope this will give you enough room," he added, looking at Abbie.

"More than enough," Abbie said, but the closet wasn't what she was thinking about. What she was thinking about was the bed. Were going to share that bed immediately? The prospect caused her insides to tense up with a combination of anxiety and excitement, and she couldn't look at Logan for fear he would know what she was feeling.

"What about her office stuff?" one of movers asked. "Where we s'posed to put that?"

"That's going somewhere else," Logan said. "Let's go out

this way . . ." He opened the French doors and everyone followed him outside and across the tiled courtyard. Their exodus startled a blue jay who had been drinking from the fountain, and he took off with a noisy squawk and flapping of wings. Rex, who had been sunning himself in a far corner, bounded up, coming over to give Kendall a welcoming lick.

By now Logan had reached the garage, which wasn't visible from the front of the house, and Abbie saw that it had a second level, reachable by an outside stairway.

"This room was Ann's studio," he explained as they climbed the stairs, the movers following. Kendall was still down in the courtyard playing with Rex. "She was an art major in college and painting was her passion."

He unlocked the door and stood back to let Abbie enter ahead of him. When Abbie walked inside, she sucked in a stunned breath and her eyes widened. The room was huge and filled with sunlight from half a dozen windows spaced around two sides. One of the solid walls was lined with shelves that must once have contained all of Ann O'Connell's painting supplies, and would be perfect for Abbie's research materials and office supplies. She looked around slowly. There was a small kitchen, separated from the main room by a bar. And on the other side of the kitchen was a partially open door that revealed a bathroom.

"Do you like it?" Logan asked.

"It's . . . it's wonderful," Abbie said, dazed. She couldn't believe how perfect this room was. Here she would have complete privacy—a place to work as well as a retreat when things became too much for her—as she was certain they would many times before she settled into her new life. It was big enough that she could have some of her living room furniture brought here, too. She could already picture the couch there in that corner and her rocking chair in the other.

When her gaze met Logan's, he was smiling. And yet, behind the smile she sensed a sadness he couldn't entirely mask. Some of Abbie's excitement and happiness over the room faded. Of course Logan would be feeling sad. This had been Ann's studio. He would be remembering happier times. "Thank you," she said. "This is a wonderful place, and I appreciate you letting me use it."

"I'm glad you like it."

As they all trooped back to the main house, Abbie's thoughts once more turned to their sleeping arrangements. She was dying to know what Logan had in mind, but she did not want to make an issue of the subject by asking him point blank. Thankfully, for the next forty minutes, she was too busy supervising the movers to worry much. And once they were gone, there were dozens of boxes to unpack.

"I'll help," Logan said. "Where do you want to start?"

"Let's get Kendall settled first," Abbie said.

So for the next hour, the three of them worked in Kendall's room. At six-thirty, Logan said, "Why don't we take a break? Patrick should be home soon, and he'll be starving. I thought we could go out and get hamburgers or something tonight."

Abbie looked down at her soiled clothes. "If we're going out, I'll need to take a shower and change."

"Me, too," Kendall said.

Logan grimaced. "Sorry. I didn't think about that. Maybe I should just go buy hamburgers and bring them back."

"Good idea," Abbie said.

Within minutes, as Logan had predicted, Patrick arrived and headed for the bedroom wing. He stopped at the open doorway to Kendall's room.

"Your room's looking cool," he said to Kendall.

"Thanks." Kendall looked around proudly. She'd made the movers reposition her spool bed, chest, antique dressing table, and desk three times before she was satisfied. She and Abbie had already made up her bed, and for the past ten minutes she'd been busy placing her stuffed animals in an artful arrangement on top of it.

"Wanna see my room?" Patrick said.

Kendall nodded happily.

After they'd gone off down the hall, Logan said, "Why don't you quit for tonight? You look tired." He smiled. "Tomorrow's another day."

Abbie nodded. She *was* tired. Yet once she stopped working, she would have to think. And although so far things had gone really well, there was still the little matter of where she was supposed to sleep tonight.

"While you put your feet up, I'll go get our food. Do you want a hamburger, a cheeseburger, or a chicken sandwich?"

Abbie made her choices and Logan headed off to Patrick's room to see what the kids wanted to eat. Abbie wanted to wash up and put on a clean shirt, but she was hesitant about using the master bathroom, even though her clothes and personal belongings were in that wing. Yet where else should she go?

You're being ridiculous. You're Logan's wife.

Finally, she decided she'd wait until Logan left to get the food, then she'd get cleaned up. At least with him gone, she wouldn't feel quite so awkward about invading his personal space.

After he left, she headed for the master suite. She quickly cleaned up and changed into a fresh blouse. Then she walked out into the bedroom and slowly studied it, as she hadn't had a chance to do before. It really was a lovely room. The kind where everything blended together perfectly yet looked warm and inviting. Abbie wondered if Ann had decorated the house herself, or if she'd had professional help. Somehow she had a feeling Ann was the one responsible. *Just one more way I won't measure up,* Abbie thought ruefully.

There were several silver-framed photographs on the dresser, and Abbie walked over to look at them. One was a photo of Erin and Patrick when they were much younger. Abbie would guess about five and seven. They were standing in the courtyard, with the fountain in the background, and they had their arms around each other. Patrick's grin revealed his two front teeth missing, and Erin—with traces of baby fat in her dimpled arms and legs— looked adorable in a ruffled pinafore and bare feet. Abbie's eyes misted. She had missed so much of her daughter's life.

Her gaze moved to the second picture. This one was an informal shot of Logan and Ann, taken on a beach somewhere. She wore a one-piece red bathing suit, and her honey-colored hair was wildly curly and wind-tossed. She was laughing up at Logan, who wore dark blue swimming trunks and a mischievous smile. Their expressions and the way they leaned toward each other, left no doubt about their feelings. Abbie twisted her wedding ring around and around and wondered if Logan would ever look at her like that. Then, angry at herself, she pushed the thought away. Theirs was not that kind of marriage, and hoping that it would someday be was simply setting herself up for heartache. Slowly, she set the picture back. She wondered why Logan had left it there, since he'd removed the portrait in the family room. Maybe he'd forgotten about this picture. He was probably so used to seeing it, it was just part of the background now.

The third photo was of an older couple. Abbie didn't have to be told these were Logan's parents. The family resemblance was too strong for them to be anyone else. Looking at his mother's serene face, Abbie suddenly knew exactly how Kendall would someday look. Now the ache she felt wasn't for herself, but for Kendall, who had also missed out on so much.

All that's going to change, Abbie told herself.

"Mom? Mom!"

Abbie hastily put the picture back and quickly walked out of the master suite. "I'm here, Kendall. What is it?"

"Nothing. I just wondered where you were, that's all." Kendall looked curiously into the utility room, which sat at the end of the hallway separating the master suite from the kitchen and dining room. "This is a big house, isn't it?"

"Yes, it is."

Together they walked out to the family room, where they were soon joined by Patrick. A few minutes later, Logan arrived with the food. Soon the four of them were sitting around the kitchen table with their sandwiches and fries and onion rings. The kids seemed perfectly at ease with each other, and when Kendall reminded Abbie that they still had to set up her computer, Patrick offered to do it for her.

"There's no phone jack in there, Dad," Patrick said.

"I know," Logan said. "I'll call the phone company on Monday. I'll ask them to change the line in your office to a separate number then, too," he added, looking at Abbie. "You might even be able to keep the number you have now."

"That would be great," Abbie said. She was amazed at how thoughtful he was. She hadn't even *thought* about trying to keep the same number, but it sure would eliminate a lot of problems if she did.

When they were finished eating, the kids took off for Kendall's room, and Abbie and Logan cleaned up, then Logan said, "We can get your office set up, if you like. Unless you're too tired," he added.

"No, I'm not too tired." She was, but Abbie preferred doing anything that would keep her from thinking about bedtime and where she was going to sleep.

It was close to nine o'clock before they finished, and by now Abbie was exhausted. The physical work of the day, added to the emotional stress, had taken its toll. Yet she was still reluctant to say anything. She couldn't stop herself from yawning several times, though.

"You're tired," Logan said as they turned out the lights and walked down the steps to the house.

"Yes." Her gaze slid to the doors leading to the master bedroom.

"Listen . . . Abbie . . . ," he said when they reached the bottom. He touched her arm. "Let's talk a minute before we go inside." The lights from the family room beyond cast a muted glow over the courtyard and backlit Logan's hair, giving it a halo effect.

"Okay," she said faintly. Her heart skidded.

"This is a bit awkward," he continued slowly, "but I want you to take the master bedroom. For the time being, I'll sleep on the daybed in the sitting room."

"But Logan, I don't want—"

"I insist. The daybed is comfortable. I've slept there a lot." The timbre of his voice changed, became softer, gruffer. "After Ann died, I couldn't sleep in our bed. I must have slept in the sitting room for six months before I had the courage to go back."

He looked away, and even in the muted light, Abbie could see him remembering the pain of those days. Watching him, she felt a welling inside, and an awareness of something she had only partly sensed but now knew to be true.

She could easily love him.

In fact, she was dangerously close to falling in love with him already.

Twenty-four

Abbie slept better than she'd imagined she would, even though it was a strange bed in a strange room, and despite the fact she was used to sleeping in the dark. At first she was disconcerted by there being no blinds or coverings of any kind on the French doors, but once all the lights were out, and moonlight flooded the room, it felt peaceful.

She lay in bed and listened to the soothing murmur of the fountain and the soft tinkle of the wind chimes hanging along the covered walkway, and slowly all the tension of the day seeped away, and she drifted off into a dreamless sleep.

The next morning, she was amazed to awaken and see that it was already seven o'clock. She'd slept nearly ten hours.

After splashing her face with water, brushing her teeth, and running a brush through her hair, she put on her robe and gingerly opened the door into the sitting room. She was chagrined to see that the daybed was neatly made up and that there was no sign of Logan.

She found him and Kendall in the kitchen.

"Hi, Mom," Kendall said, looking up from her plate. "Logan made waffles for me." Kendall was already dressed in shorts and a T-shirt. Her unruly curls were held back by a headband. She seemed perfectly at ease.

Logan, who was standing at the counter pouring a cup of

coffee, grinned. "No big deal. I just put them in the toaster." He, too, was dressed in shorts and a T-shirt.

Abbie felt self-conscious in her robe and wished she could go back to the bedroom and get dressed, but that would be even more awkward.

"Want some coffee?" Logan said.

"I'll get it." While she poured her coffee, he sat at the table and reached for a section of the *Chronicle*. She looked around.

"What is it you need?" he asked.

"Um, Coffeemate? Sweetener?"

"Sorry. No Coffeemate. There is some sweetener up there, in the second cupboard." He pointed to the one he meant. "And there's milk in the refrigerator. Tell you what, there's a grocery list over there on the wall. Write down anything you want, and we'll make a supermarket run later."

Like Kendall, he seemed perfectly relaxed, just as if having them there were a normal, everyday thing. *Just as if we're a real family.* "Okay."

"Mom." Kendall reached for the syrup and poured some on her last waffle. "I have to call Gran. We're supposed to go to the symphony today."

"Oh, that's right. I completely forgot about it." That would mean her mother would be coming here today, for Abbie was sure Katherine would never agree to having Abbie bring Kendall to her house. No, her mother would be dying to meet Logan and his children. Oh, God. Abbie wasn't sure she was ready. Yet maybe it was good to get this first meeting over with as quickly as possible.

"Can I call when I'm done eating?"

"Sure." Katherine was up by six every morning, so there wasn't any reason to wait.

Abbie sat down and Logan pushed the paper toward her. "Help yourself. And if you're hungry, there are eggs, um, some bagels in the freezer, and more of the frozen waffles. And Serita—that's our housekeeper, she's here weekdays— bought cantaloupe and strawberries. They're in the refrigerator, already cleaned and sliced."

"Thanks." Abbie reached for the front section of the paper. "I'm not hungry yet." So they had a housekeeper. She realized anew how many things about his and Erin's life she still didn't know.

For the next ten minutes or so, she drank her coffee and tried to concentrate on the paper, but her eyes kept straying in Logan's direction. He was such a good-looking man, almost *too* good-looking, with his square jaw, straight nose, and gorgeous eyes. Yet he was saved from prettiness by an aura of strength and solidity that inspired confidence and trust.

Her gaze moved to his hair, which looked wet, and she realized he had showered already. She wondered if he had used the master bath. It gave her an odd feeling to think of him walking through the bedroom while she was still sleeping. She hoped she hadn't kicked the covers off the way she usually did. She could just imagine the way she'd looked—sprawled over the bed with her nightgown bunched up. He'd probably been looking at her, thinking how much less attractive she was than Ann had been, probably wishing he hadn't had to marry her. *He'll never love you. You know that, don't you?*

Just then, he lowered the paper, and Abbie hurriedly returned her attention to the section she held. Her heart was beating too fast, and she was mad at herself. Negative thoughts wouldn't do anyone any good.

"Done?" he said.

"Hmm?" Abbie said, then realized he'd been talking to Kendall.

"Yeah, I'm finished," Kendall said. She drained her glass of milk, then picked up her napkin and wiped off her milk mustache.

"The dishwasher's there." Logan pointed to the corner. "We all rinse our own dishes and put them in."

"That's what Mom and I do, too," Kendall said. She stacked her utensils on her plate and carried everything to the sink. When she was finished putting her things in the dishwasher, she picked up the portable phone and punched in her grandmother's number. Then she walked out and into the family room, but Abbie could hear her saying, "Hi, Gran? It's Kendall." This was followed by silence, and Abbie knew her mother still hadn't picked up. Katherine kept her answering machine on at all times so she could screen her calls.

A few seconds later, Kendall said, "Gran? Hi."

Abbie listened to the one-sided conversation, which consisted of mostly "uh-huhs" and "yeahs" on Kendall's part. After a bit Kendall walked back into the kitchen and handed Abbie the phone. "Gran needs directions."

"Good morning, Mother," Abbie said.

"I wonder, Abbie," her mother said stiffly, "if you would have even *bothered* to call me if I hadn't made arrangements to take Kendall out today. If you had even *thought* about the fact that I had no *earthly* idea how to get in touch with you."

Telling herself not to rise to the bait, Abbie said mildly, "I planned to call you later and give you our new phone number and address."

"Really."

"Yes. Really. Now, do you have a pencil and paper handy?"

"Abigail, I am not an idiot."

Abbie bit back a smile. It didn't happen often, but occasionally her mother amused her. She proceeded to give her the phone number and address, then told her the easiest way to get to the house. "So what time are you planning to be here?"

"The program begins at two. I'll come at eleven-thirty because Kendall and I had planned to have lunch out before the performance. Does that suit you?"

"Of course. We'll see you then."

When Abbie hung up, she looked at Logan. "You'll be meeting my mother today."

He smiled. "I'm looking forward to it."

Abbie looked around to make sure Kendall was gone. Seeing that she was, she turned back to Logan and said dryly, "Let's see what you think *after* you've met her."

Logan was surprised by how good he felt today. He'd known it would be great to have Kendall living under his roof; what surprised him was how much he liked having Abbie there.

He watched her as she toasted a bagel, then buttered it. She looked cute in her bathrobe, with her hair tousled from sleep.

His gaze slowly traveled down her slender body to her bare feet. Logan had always been partial to feet, and Abbie had nice feet, narrow with delicate ankles and pink painted toenails. What was it about a woman's bare toes that was so sexy? he wondered as he studied them appreciatively.

Just then Abbie turned, and embarrassed, he quickly averted his eyes. His reaction amused him. You'd think he'd been caught doing something wrong.

She set her plate on the table, then moved to the refrigerator, where she proceeded to pour herself a glass of juice. But this time Logan studiously kept his eyes on the business section of the paper. It wouldn't do to make Abbie feel self-conscious. Their situation was awkward enough.

Once she was settled and eating her breakfast, he casually put the paper aside and stood. "I'll go back and get dressed while you finish eating. Then the bedroom and bathroom will be yours for as long as you like."

The faintest of pink tinged her cheeks. "All right."

Logan found himself whistling as he dressed. Maybe he was being completely unrealistic, but he had a good feeling about the future. A very good feeling.

"Mother, this is Logan. Logan, my mother, Katherine Wellington."

Even though Abbie was nervous, she couldn't help being amused by the blatant way her mother studied Logan. She looked him up and down imperiously, reminding Abbie of a queen sizing up a potential servant.

Logan bore her scrutiny with good humor, saying, "It's very nice to meet you, Mrs. Wellington." His smile was warm.

Katherine sniffed. "Yes, well, it's nice to finally meet you, too, Logan." Her tone said she wasn't ready to forgive Abbie or him.

"Please, come into the family room and sit down," he said.

"Yes, do, Mother," Abbie said. "Kendall's not quite ready yet."

"Would you like something to drink?" Logan asked as they entered the room. "Iced tea? Or some lemonade?"

"A glass of lemonade would be nice," Katherine said. She sat in one of the deep chairs flanking the couch.

"I'll get it," Abbie said.

"No," Logan said, "you sit. I'll get it. Do you want one, too?"

"No, thanks," Abbie said. She was too on edge to drink anything.

Katherine sat primly, legs crossed at her ankles, black linen dress discreetly covering her knees. She looked perfect—her salon-enhanced blond hair cut in a short, chic style, her sheath accented simply with a single-strand pearl necklace and matching earrings, her patent leather pumps shining and in perfect condition. It struck Abbie that she had never seen her mother with scuffed shoes or worn heels. Actually, she couldn't remember her mother ever wearing a soiled garment, not even when she was doing housework or gardening. She wasn't even sure her mother perspired.

Logan came back with Katherine's lemonade in one of the Waterford tumblers from the china cabinet in the dining room. Abbie bit back a smile. Even Logan was intimidated by her mother, or else why would he bother to try to impress her? Then again, maybe Abbie was wrong. Maybe Logan always used the good crystal for company.

He handed Katherine the lemonade, then walked over and sat next to Abbie on the couch. Casually, he draped his arm along the back. "Abbie tells me you're an enthusiastic patron of the arts."

Katherine smiled. "Yes. I've been a member of the symphony board for years." She took a dainty sip of her lemonade. "And Abbie tells *me* that you're a very successful architect." She looked around. "Did you design this house?"

"Yes, I did."

"It's quite lovely. I especially like the gallery effect out there." She nodded toward the courtyard.

"Thank you. Would you like to see the rest of the house?"

"Perhaps when I bring Kendall home this evening." She frowned. "What is keeping the child, Abbie?"

Abbie jumped up, glad for an excuse to escape, if only for a few moments. "I don't know. I'll go see."

"Do you mind knocking on Patrick's door while you're up?" Logan asked. "I'd like him to meet your mother."

"Is Patrick your son?" Katherine asked.

"Yes." Logan's smile displayed the pride any mention of his children always precipitated. "He's thirteen."

"And is your daughter home, as well?"

Abbie didn't hear Logan's answer, because she was now out of earshot, and knowing that her mother would soon meet Patrick and quite possibly see the resemblance between him and Kendall intensified her butterflies. Yet Katherine had to meet Patrick sometime. By now she'd reached Kendall's room, and she knocked on the door. A few seconds later Kendall opened it.

"Is Gran here?" She was struggling with the side buttons of her black skirt.

"Here, let me help," Abbie said. "Yes, Gran is here." Abbie buttoned the remaining button and stood back to look at Kendall. "You look very nice. That top looks cute with your skirt." It was a black-and-white silk-weave sleeveless sweater.

Kendall smiled. "This is one of the ones Gran bought me."

"I know. She'll be pleased that you wore it." Abbie straightened the rhinestone butterfly pins holding back Kendall's hair. "Are you ready?"

"Uh-huh." Kendall reached for the small black shoulder bag she favored.

"Well, you go on out and say hello to Gran. I'm going to get Patrick. Logan wants your grandmother to meet him."

Abbie found Patrick sitting at his computer. "Oh, okay," he said when she told him her mother was there. "I'll be out in a minute."

True to his word, he walked into the family room only seconds after Abbie had sat down again. Abbie held her breath as Logan introduced Patrick. To Abbie, the resemblance between Patrick, Kendall, and Logan was so obvious, she couldn't believe her mother didn't see it. But she must not, because she certainly didn't seem thunderstruck the way Abbie had been when she'd first laid eyes on father and son. Well, maybe it wasn't so strange that her mother didn't see what Abbie saw. After all, she had no idea the three were related.

"It's nice to meet you, Mrs. Wellington," Patrick said, shaking her hand and giving her his winning smile.

"I'm very pleased to meet you, too," Katherine said.

Abbie knew just by her mother's tone that she was impressed by Patrick. And why wouldn't she be? He was a charming young man, very like Kendall, and she adored Kendall.

"Your father tells me you're a student at St. John's."

"Yes."

"That's where Kendall's grandfather went to school."

Patrick smiled at Kendall. "She told me."

"Do you like it there?"

"Yes, it's a great school."

"You're a wise young man to realize it. Well," she added, turning to Logan and Abbie, "as much as I've enjoyed meeting everyone, I think it's time for us to be on our way."

When the door closed behind Katherine and Kendall, Patrick headed back to his room.

Logan said, "Now, that wasn't so bad, was it?"

Abbie shook her head. "No." But Abbie had always expected her mother to approve of Logan and Patrick. What she wasn't sure about—and the thing that worried her the most—was what Katherine's reaction would be to Erin, and vice versa. "This is just the first hurdle, though."

"I know," Logan said. "But let's not anticipate problems, okay? Let's just take things one step at a time."

Abbie nodded. She knew he was right. Even if the worst happened and Katherine and Erin disliked each other, there wasn't a thing Abbie could do about it right now.

Twenty-five

Katherine exited Logan's subdivision and entered the east-bound traffic on Memorial Drive. Once they were well on their way downtown, she glanced over at Kendall. "Well, Kendall, now that we're alone, you can tell me the truth. Are you *really* happy about your mother's marriage to Mr. O'Connell?"

Kendall smiled. "Oh, yes, Gran. From the minute I met him, I was hoping things would turn out like this. I mean, he's so *nice*. And so is Patrick. And I *love* the house and my room. You have to see my room later. It's bigger than the one I had before, and it has its own bathroom. I don't even have to share the bath with company. And Logan says I can have my room painted or papered or fixed up any way I like. He even said he'd have bookshelves built in if I wanted. And *Gran*! I'm going to have my very own phone!"

The child certainly *seemed* enthusiastic. "So you didn't mind moving?"

"Oh, no. Logan's house is a lot nicer than our old one. Besides, now I'm closer to my school."

"That's true." Katherine let a few moments go by. "What about Patrick's sister? Erin. Isn't that her name?"

"Yes. Erin."

A less astute person might not have caught the subtle change in nuance in Kendall's voice now that the topic of discussion had turned to Logan's daughter, but Katherine certainly did. "I'm sorry I didn't get to meet her this morning. What's she like?"

Kendall shrugged. "She's okay."

"Just okay?"

Kendall bit on her lower lip.

"Something tells me you don't like her."

Kendall sighed. "I wanted to like her, but she doesn't like *me*."

"Whyever not?"

Another shrug. "I don't know. Mom is trying to pretend it's my imagination, but I'm not *stupid*, Gran. I know when somebody likes me or not."

No, Kendall certainly was *not* stupid, and if she felt this new stepsister of hers didn't like her, she was probably right. Katherine could think of only one reason why a girl Kendall's age wouldn't like her, and that was if the girl were jealous of Kendall, because Kendall was a perfectly wonderful child. She almost said so, then thought better of it. After all, she didn't want to make things worse. "Well, darling," she finally said, "I wouldn't worry about it overmuch. I'm sure things will change once Erin gets used to having you around."

Katherine was sure of no such thing. In fact, it was this very possibility of friction that had concerned her when Abbie first mentioned Logan's children. Good Heavens, it wasn't easy for *adults* to cope with stepchildren, let alone the children themselves.

Poor Kendall, she thought. My poor darling. All the pleasant feelings Katherine had started to feel about Logan and his son were now replaced with worry about this daughter of his. Katherine's only hope was that perhaps Kendall had exaggerated the situation. "Do you think Erin will be home when we get back tonight?"

"Probably."

Good, Katherine thought grimly. She could see for herself if the girl was as disagreeable as Kendall had intimated. And if she *was*, Katherine would have a word or two with Abbie, because it would not do for Kendall to be unhappy. It would not do at all.

• • •

It was close to six before Katherine pulled into Logan's driveway. She parked behind a tan Mercedes that hadn't been there earlier. It was a lovely car, just the kind Katherine herself would drive if she didn't have her Cadillac.

"Erin's aunt is here. She just brought Erin home," Abbie explained when she answered the door.

Abbie looked tense, Katherine thought. Was it because of the girl? Maybe Kendall wasn't the only one Erin didn't like. Maybe she didn't like Abbie, either. Although Katherine couldn't imagine why she wouldn't. Abbie might be misguided in her ideas sometimes, but she was a very kind and generous person, as well as an excellent mother.

"You'll stay awhile, won't you?" Abbie said.

"Of course. I want to meet Erin. And Logan promised to show me the rest of the house."

"I've been telling Gran all about my room," Kendall said.

The three of them walked back to the family room, where Logan was standing talking to a smart-looking blonde. She turned as they approached.

"You're back," Logan said, smiling down at Kendall, who had gone straight to his side. "How was the symphony? Did you enjoy it?"

"It was great. Wasn't it, Gran? The program was all Chopin." Kendall's eyes sparkled. She gave the blonde a curious look.

The blonde's smile seemed stiff to Katherine. "You must be Kendall," she said. "Erin told me all about you. I'm her aunt Elizabeth."

"Hello," Kendall said. "It's very nice to meet you."

Katherine smiled proudly. Abbie had done many things wrong in her life, and would probably do many more, but she hadn't failed with Kendall. Of course, good bloodlines helped enormously. And Katherine's own influence shouldn't be underestimated, either.

The blonde turned to Katherine and held out her hand. "I'm Elizabeth Chamberlain."

"Katherine Wellington. Abbie's mother."

"I never would have guessed. You two look nothing alike."

For some reason, the remark irritated Katherine. "Abbie resembles her father."

"Ah. That explains it." Elizabeth's gaze moved to Kendall. "You don't look like your mother, either. Perhaps you take after your father?"

"Kendall is the spitting image of my grandmother Vickers," Katherine said haughtily. The very *idea* that Kendall might have any of Thomas's characteristics was ludicrous. The child was *nothing* like him. Nothing at all.

"My father is a famous archaeologist," Kendall said. "He's living in China right now."

"Oh, really?" Elizabeth said. "Imagine that."

Although she'd only been in the woman's company a few minutes, two things were quite clear to Katherine. Elizabeth Chamberlain didn't like Abbie or Kendall and the woman would probably do everything in her power to undermine Abbie's position, both with Logan and with his children. Katherine glanced at Abbie, but as usual, her daughter seemed flustered and totally incapable of coping. Honestly! Why *couldn't* Katherine have had a daughter with some backbone? Even though Katherine didn't think much of Thomas, she certainly wouldn't let Elizabeth Chamberlain imply that Kendall was a *liar*!

Just as Katherine opened her mouth to make a cutting reply, Patrick, followed by a young girl, entered the room. Everyone turned to look at them. The girl had to be Erin, but she certainly bore no resemblance to her brother or her father. Their hair was thick and black, and hers was a wispy, pale blond. Logan's and Patrick's eyes were dark blue, almost royal, whereas hers were a very light blue. Why, Kendall looked more like she belonged to them than Erin did. The girl must look like her mother. Too bad, Katherine thought. The father and brother were much more attractive.

"Erin, honey, come here," Logan said, beckoning her over. "I want you to meet Mrs. Wellington, Kendall's grandmother." He smiled at Katherine. "This is my daughter, Erin."

"How do you do?" Erin said.

She stuck out her hand, and Katherine took it. Well, at least she was polite. But good Heavens, would it kill the child to smile? Katherine was reminded of the way Abbie used to act when she was introduced to adults, how she'd shrink back and get all tongue-tied if they asked her questions. "Hello, Erin," she said firmly. "I understand that you and Kendall are in the same class at school."

"Yes."

"That's quite nice for both of you, isn't it?"

Erin nodded, but she didn't look at Kendall.

"You're lucky, you know," Katherine said, determined to get the child to respond. "Caldwell is a *wonderful* school. Kendall loves the art department there, don't you, dear?"

Kendall smiled enthusiastically. "Uh-huh. I especially like Miss Richardson."

"Are you an artist, too?" Katherine continued.

Erin shook her head.

"Erin likes to write," Patrick said.

"She's quite talented," Elizabeth added. "She wrote a poem for me last year, didn't you, sweetie?"

"Uh-huh." For the first time, the child showed some animation, smiling at her aunt and moving to her side.

"That's something we have in common," Abbie said. "I've always loved to write."

If Katherine hadn't been watching Erin so closely, she might have missed it, because the emotion only flared in Erin's eyes for a second, but in that brief instant, Katherine saw it and identified it. Her hunch had been right. Erin resented Abbie intensely.

More concerned than she wanted to admit, Katherine put her hand on Kendall's shoulder. "Well. I've enjoyed meeting everyone, but I'm going to have to be on my way soon. Before I go, though . . ." She smiled down at Kendall. "You were going to show me your room."

"I was going to give you a tour of the house, too," Logan said.

"If that's the case," Elizabeth said, "I'll be on my way and leave you to it. It was a pleasure, Mrs. Wellington." Her gaze moved to Kendall. "Kendall." Much more warmly, she said to Erin, "We'll talk soon, sweetie."

"All right."

"Good-bye, Abbie."

"Good-bye, Elizabeth."

If the situation weren't so serious, Katherine might have been amused by Elizabeth Chamberlain's pitiful attempt to

be pleasant to Abbie. Unfortunately for her, her gray eyes—
which Katherine guessed looked cool under most circumstances—were positively frosty.

"I'll walk you out, Elizabeth," Logan said.

"C'mon, Gran, let's go see my room." Kendall grabbed
Katherine's hand.

Katherine had to admit, the room *was* lovely. Of course,
she'd expected no less. The house itself—what she'd seen
of it—was incredible. Not just spacious, but beautifully designed. Monetarily, anyway, Abbie had done well for herself. Still, the whole situation bothered Katherine. And it
wasn't just that Erin was going to be a problem, or that Elizabeth Chamberlain disliked Abbie. Other aspects of this marriage puzzled Katherine, too. For one thing, Abbie and Logan
seemed so mismatched. And their marriage had been con-
ducted in such secrecy, almost as if they had something to
hide. But what that could be, Katherine couldn't imagine.

While Kendall was still pointing out things of interest,
Logan joined them. After that, he took Katherine around and
showed her the rest of the house. Yes, lovely, she thought.
Quite lovely.

"Why don't you show your mother your office?" Logan
said to Abbie when he'd finished giving Katherine the tour
of the inside.

"All right. C'mon, Mother. Out this way."

Katherine was glad of the privacy his suggestion afforded
them. As soon as the French doors closed behind them, she
plunged in. "Well, Abbie, I hope you're prepared for rocky
days ahead."

Abbie seemed startled. "W-what do you mean?"

Katherine sighed. Was Abbie *totally* dense? "You should
know perfectly well what I mean, and the fact that you don't
is alarming in itself. This hasty marriage of yours is not
likely to go smoothly. It was quite obvious to anyone with
any kind of perception at all that Erin dislikes you. Frankly,
that wouldn't trouble me except for the fact that her dislike
has spilled over onto Kendall. And that *does* trouble me."

"Oh, Mother, I think you're making too much of things.
Erin's just shy, that's all. She doesn't make a fuss over people. When she gets to know—"

"I am *not* making too much of things," Katherine said, not even trying to conceal her irritation. "This is serious and it's bound to cause all kinds of problems for Kendall. I'm sorry, Abbie, but it's just as I said. You could *not* have been thinking of Kendall when you married Logan."

"I was under the impression you liked Logan."

"I do like him. That's beside the point. My primary concern is Kendall, and it's quite clear to me that yours is not."

"That's not true. There . . . there are things you don't understand."

"Oh, I understand all right. Logan is a very attractive, very sexy man. I don't blame you for wanting him. I do blame you for putting Kendall in a situation where she can very easily be hurt."

Surprising Katherine, Abbie didn't back down. "Look, Mother, arguing about this is pointless. Of course, Erin is upset right now. Her whole world has been disrupted. But she'll come around. I know she will."

"And Kendall's world *hasn't* been disrupted?" Katherine replied indignantly.

"It's different for Kendall. She's always wanted a father, you know that. And she liked Logan from the very first. And she and Patrick have hit it off, too. But Erin, it's tough for her. It must seem to her as if she's losing her father, just like she lost her mother."

"Yes, well, let me tell you something, Abbie. Everything you say may be true. It probably is. However, if things *don't* work out well, guess who's going to lose out? It won't be Erin, I assure you. She is, after all, Logan's flesh and blood."

That night, as Abbie helped Kendall pick out something to wear for the first day of school the next day, she couldn't help remembering her mother's warning. But Katherine had been wrong. If Abbie's marriage failed, they would *all* be losers.

Logan couldn't fall asleep. He lay there on the narrow daybed and wondered if Abbie was still awake. He'd be willing to bet she was as wide awake as he was, thinking about the day and worrying about the future.

He wished they were sharing a bed. Not for sex, not if

she wasn't ready. Just to be close. To talk and share their hopes and fears. That's what he'd missed the most the past three years. The closeness and comfort of sharing and knowing he wasn't alone.

He eyed the door that separated this room from the master bedroom beyond. What would Abbie do if he got up and opened the door? For a moment, he was tempted. But he knew it wouldn't be fair to Abbie, for she was bound to feel he wanted more, and he knew she would never refuse him. No, she had enough to handle now. Time enough for them to work on their relationship once the kids were settled down.

Once Erin is settled down, he corrected, because Patrick and Kendall seemed just fine already.

Resigned, he closed his eyes and willed himself to go to sleep.

Twenty-six

The first day of school began exactly the way Erin figured it would. All the girls in her class made a big fuss over Kendall. In fact, she already seemed to be friends with some of them, including the other new girl, Heather Jamison.

Even Erin's supposedly best friend, Tiffany Dexter, couldn't stop talking about her. "Shauna says Kendall went to summer school here," Tiffany whispered to Erin during second period Spanish. "That's how she met Heather."

"Uh huh," said Erin noncommittally. She did not want to talk about Kendall. Bad enough she had to live in the same house with her. Of course, she knew she would have to talk about her eventually, because pretty soon someone was bound to find out about Erin's dad and Kendall's mom. And when they did, Erin could just imagine what they'd say. She dreaded it. Dreaded having to answer questions and pretend she was happy when she wasn't. Yet she knew she'd have to, because she and Aunt Elizabeth had discussed everything over the weekend, and she'd advised Erin to be very, very nice to both Abbie and Kendall.

"Don't give your father any reason to blame you when things don't work out," Aunt Elizabeth said.

Erin had felt so much better knowing that Aunt Elizabeth didn't think this marriage was a good idea, either, and that she didn't expect it to last. But in the meantime, her dad was married to Abbie, and Kendall was living in Erin's house, and everybody except Aunt Elizabeth was going to be talking about how Erin and Kendall were now sisters, and expecting Erin to be excited.

Why did people think she wanted a sister? She didn't want a sister. She certainly didn't need a sister. Not when she had Patrick and her dad. Erin's chest hurt thinking about Patrick and her dad and the way they seemed to like Kendall so much. Last night, after Kendall's grandmother and Aunt Elizabeth left, Patrick had asked Kendall all about the symphony, just as if he was really interested. Erin couldn't believe it. She knew darn well he didn't care a thing about stuff like the symphony. Then later, when they were watching TV in the game room, he hadn't paid any attention to Erin at all, just kept talking to Kendall as if *they* were the brother and sister and Erin was the outsider. After a while, Erin couldn't stand it anymore. She'd mumbled something about having stuff to do to get ready for school and escaped to her room. She'd spent the rest of the evening instant messaging with Allison.

Now today, it was last night all over again, only this time it was Erin's *friends* who were acting like Kendall was some kind of *goddess* or something. All morning they fawned over her until Erin wanted to throw up.

At lunchtime Erin couldn't find Tiffany, so she headed for the cafeteria without her. Then, when she got there, she saw that both Tiffany and Shauna were already sitting at one of the tables. She saw Kendall, too, but she pretended she didn't. Besides, Kendall was sitting with the new girl, Heather, so she had someone to talk to. She didn't need Erin.

After getting her food—macaroni and cheese, fruit salad, a roll, and milk—Erin headed toward her friends. She'd no sooner put her tray down than Tiffany said, "Erin! Why didn't you *tell* me?"

Erin's heart sank. "Tell you what?"

"About your dad! And Kendall's mom!"

Erin shrugged and buttered her roll.

"They *are* married, aren't they?" Shauna said.

"Yeah, they got married last week." She salted her macaroni and cheese and took a bite.

"Erin! I can't believe you didn't *tell* me," Tiffany said.

She had stopped eating entirely and was leaning forward with her mouth open. She reminded Erin of a fish. "Well," Tiffany said, "aren't you going to tell us about it? What's Kendall's mom like? Is she nice? Does she look like Kendall? Kendall's really pretty, don't you think?" She twisted around in her seat to look in Kendall's direction. She gasped. "Guess who's sitting with her!"

"Who?" Shauna said, practically falling out of her chair to look. "Ohmi*gawd*, it's *Madison*." Madison Singer was the coolest girl in the school. A seventh grader who usually pretended she didn't even *see* the sixth graders, she was tall and beautiful, with gorgeous long red hair, and she worked part-time as a model.

Erin refused to look. If Tiffany and Shauna wanted to gawk and act like giggling idiots, that was their choice, but Erin sure wasn't going to.

Finally they turned around again. "You never answered our question," Tiffany said. She took a bite of her tuna fish sandwich. "What's your stepmother like?"

Erin threw her fork down. "Don't call her that! She may be my dad's wife, but she's not my stepmother. She's not any kind of mother! I only had one mother, and she's dead!"

Tiffany stared at her as if she'd lost her mind. "I-I'm sorry," she stammered. "I didn't mean . . ."

It was all Erin could do to keep from bursting into tears. She knew she had to get out of there before she lost it entirely. Shoving back her chair, she jumped up, grabbed her purse, and walked blindly out of the cafeteria.

Logan was glad he'd decided to work at home today. His reasoning was that he thought it would be easier for Abbie if he was there, since she didn't know Serita and might feel awkward around her at first. What he hadn't realized was how nice it would be to have a quiet morning without the children around.

"You didn't have to stay home on my account," Abbie said as they sat over a leisurely breakfast.

"Tired of me already, huh?"

His attempt at humor brought a smile to her face, but her eyes remained pensive. "Yesterday was a strain, wasn't it?"

"Yes, but it'll get better."

"I keep telling myself that." She sighed. "My mother thinks we're going to have a lot of rough times."

Impulsively, he reached over and covered her hand with his. "We'll get through them together, Abbie."

She nodded slowly.

As they sat there, her warm hand in his, a stillness settled over the room. As he looked into her soft blue eyes, something stirred in Logan. Something he hadn't felt in a long, long time. Desire. He wanted Abbie. Maybe he'd wanted her all along. The realization jolted him, and for a moment he felt guilty and disloyal to Ann. But why should he feel guilty? There was nothing wrong in wanting Abbie. He was only human. And she was a lovely woman. Wanting Abbie took nothing away from what he'd had with Ann. Besides, Ann wouldn't have wanted him to be alone, just as he wouldn't have wanted *her* to spend the rest of her life alone if something had happened to him.

She would have liked Abbie.

The thought warmed him, and he smiled at Abbie. She swallowed, her gaze still clinging to his.

Afterward, he wondered what might have happened if Serita's off-key humming hadn't been there in the background, a reminder of her presence. And then, a few seconds later, she entered the kitchen, and the moment was lost.

For the rest of the day, Logan was acutely aware of Abbie up in her garage office. As he worked at his drawing board, he could look out the French doors and see her windows. A couple of times, he saw her moving past. Funny how last night he'd thought all he wanted was to feel close to someone again and how today everything was different.

More than once throughout the day, he thought about going up to Abbie's office and saying flat out that he wanted to change the terms of their marriage. But as much as he wanted to, he didn't. Altering the rules of the game in the middle of the game wouldn't be fair to her. Like it or not, he was going to have to give Abbie time to adjust before asking her for anything more.

At three o'clock, he finally did go up to her office, but only to say that he would pick up the girls from school.

Abbie looked up from her computer. "Are you sure? I really don't mind going."

"No, you stay here. I need a break, anyway."

Her smile was grateful, and he was glad he'd made the suggestion. Besides, he was anxious to see how the first day of school had gone.

He took one look at Erin's face when she got into the car and knew the day hadn't been a good one for her. Kendall, on the other hand, could hardly stop talking, she was so excited.

"And I *love* Mrs. Garcia, our Spanish teacher," she said. "Don't you, Erin?"

"She's okay," Erin mumbled.

"Are you girls in any classes together?" Logan asked with forced cheerfulness.

"Second-period Spanish and fourth-period math," Kendall said happily. "I like our math teacher, too. She's neat."

"How about you, Erin? Which class do you like best?"

"I don't know."

"What about English?" Logan said. "Last year you liked English a lot."

"I have Miss Freed for English," Kendall said.

It was like that the rest of the way home. Logan would ask a question, and Kendall would answer. Even when he talked directly to Erin, she either shrugged or mumbled. By the time they reached the house, Logan's patience was wearing thin. Giving Abbie a look that said *tell you later*, he followed Erin to her room and shut the door behind him.

"What's wrong, Erin?" he said. "Did something happen today?"

She refused to look at him, and a shrug was her only response.

"Honey, how can I help if you won't tell me what happened?"

Finally she turned. The unhappiness in her eyes made him ashamed of his earlier impatience. "It was awful!" she cried. "Everyone was talking about you and Abbie getting married and how great it was and asking me all kinds of questions. They all think Kendall is perfect. They like her more than they ever liked me."

"Erin."

"It's true. They do."

"Honey . . ." He couldn't think what to say.

"Patrick likes her better than me, too."

"Erin, that's ridiculous."

As if she hadn't heard him, she turned a tormented face to him, blurting out, "You probably like her better. You probably wish *she* was your daughter instead of me!"

Her words were like darts thrown at his heart. Pulling her into his arms, he held her close. At first her body was rigid, but gradually she relaxed and put her arms around his waist.

Stroking her head, he said softly, "Erin, sweetheart, I'll never like anyone more than I like you. I'll never *love* anyone more than I love you. You're my girl. You'll always be my girl. You know that, don't you?"

"Yes," she said in a small voice. She sighed deeply. "I just . . . I wish things could be like they were."

"I know you do, honey. But life changes. And we have to change with it."

Later that night, after the kids were in their rooms and ready for bed, Logan and Abbie sat in the kitchen and talked. He told her what Erin had said.

Abbie's eyes filled with sympathy.

"She's going to need a lot of reassurance from me," Logan said. "More than I realized."

"Yes. I . . . Maybe I should talk to Kendall."

"No. Don't do that. It's not fair to Kendall to put any of this burden on her. This is *our* problem."

"You're right, I know. I just feel so bad for Erin."

"Today was the worst day. Tomorrow will be better."

They talked for a long time, gradually moving from the problem of Erin to more general topics. Midway Abbie got up to make herself a cup of tea, and Logan sat back and watched her. She moved about the kitchen quickly and efficiently, the same way Ann had. For the first time, the remembrance of Ann brought no accompanying pang of sadness, which in itself made Logan feel sad.

But underlying the sadness there was an excitement about the future that Logan had never expected to feel again. And the reason for this renewed enthusiasm was the woman moving about the kitchen. He just hoped he wouldn't have to wait too long before he and Abbie could have the kind of marriage and family life he had once had and wanted again.

The key to everything was Erin. Sitting there, he vowed he would do everything in his power to bring about her acceptance of Abbie and Kendall as quickly as possible. Because now that he knew what he wanted, he didn't want to have to wait too long to get it.

Twenty-seven

"You're not sorry we got married, are you?"

It was an unseasonably chilly night in early November, two and a half months since their wedding. The kids had all gone to bed, and Abbie and Logan were relaxing before the fire with a glass of wine and Andrea Bocelli's latest CD.

Abbie didn't answer for a moment. "No, I'm not sorry," she finally said.

"You don't sound sure."

She sighed. "I just wish . . . Oh, I don't know." *I wish we had a real marriage. I wish you loved me. I wish I could acknowledge my daughter. And I wish I could see the same love in her eyes that I see in Kendall's when she looks at you.* Fighting a sudden wave of despair, she took a sip of her wine and avoided his eyes. She had about as much chance of him returning her feelings as she had of winning the lottery. There at first, she'd thought maybe he did have some feelings for her, but if that was true, why hadn't he said something? Made some move in her direction? He was always sweet, always considerate, but he kept his distance.

And Erin . . . The way things were going, Erin would *never* accept her.

Abbie thought back over the past eleven weeks. They hadn't been easy ones. There had been so many adjustments to make. Just the fact there were so many disparate people in their families, and so many feelings to consider—Erin's

Grandmother Chamberlain, for one—had presented a host of difficulties and awkward moments. To her credit, though, Celia Chamberlain had accepted Logan's marriage. From the beginning, she was very nice to Abbie—a decided difference from her daughter Elizabeth, who lost no opportunity to try to make Abbie feel like an interloper who would never belong. No, the weeks since Abbie and Logan had married hadn't been easy . . . not for anyone.

Even Kendall, who had settled in as if she'd always lived there, had been showing signs of occasional stress. And no wonder. Although Patrick had welcomed her and the two got along well, Patrick was now a freshman in high school. He had his own interests and was gone a lot of the time. Erin was another story. Whenever she could, Erin avoided Kendall's company. Her barely concealed dislike had to bother Kendall, whether she admitted it or not. Yet when Abbie broached the subject, Kendall always told her not to worry. "It's *her* problem, not mine," Kendall staunchly said. "I don't care whether she likes me or not."

But Abbie knew Kendall *did* care. How could she not? She just intuitively didn't want to say anything that might make the situation worse and cause her to lose the father she'd yearned for for such a long time.

Poor Logan, Abbie thought. He was having a tough time, too. His problem was opposite to hers. Kendall adored him, and he returned her feelings, yet he had to be careful not to show her too much affection, because each time he did, it hurt Erin immeasurably. He'd told Abbie he felt as if he were walking a tightrope most of the time, because no matter how much reassurance he gave Erin, her natural lack of self-esteem constantly undermined his efforts.

But of all of them, Erin was suffering the most. Abbie's heart ached for her daughter. She loved Erin so much, and she understood her so well. She longed to comfort the child, to tell her she knew exactly how she felt, to hold her and kiss her. If only she could. But Erin rebuffed every advance Abbie made.

What had happened that very afternoon was a perfect example. Because Charlotte Post had started a new book the middle of September, Abbie had been working long hours.

She was in the middle of an especially knotty research problem when the time came to pick up the girls—a chore Abbie usually reserved for herself, as it gave her time with Erin where Erin couldn't escape. But that afternoon she asked Serita to get them. Abbie did stop work when she heard Serita pull into the garage, though, so that she could spend a few minutes with the girls before they headed off to their individual rooms to do their homework. Then she'd go back to her own office and work until dinnertime the way she normally did.

As usual, Kendall sprang from the car exuberantly. She always had a lot of pent-up energy after being cooped up all day long. Erin, also as usual, greeted Abbie politely but saved her enthusiasm and the report of her day for her father's arrival later.

They walked into the house, and Erin headed straight for the kitchen, with Abbie and Kendall following closely behind and Serita bringing up the rear.

"Mom," Kendall said, "guess what? Miss Freed? Our English teacher? Today she told us about a statewide writing contest that's open to fifth, sixth, and seventh graders."

"Really?" Abbie looked at Erin, who had opened the refrigerator and was pouring herself a glass of orange juice. "Are you going to enter, Erin?"

She shrugged, not looking at either of them. "I don't know."

Behind Erin's back Kendall rolled her eyes. "You *should* enter, Erin. You're a really good writer."

"I'd love to help you with your entry," Abbie said eagerly. "I'm a great editor."

"I don't need any help."

The curt answer just missed rudeness, which surprised Abbie, because ever since that first night when she and Logan had announced their marriage, Erin had been unfailingly polite.

"You know, Erin," Kendall said, "my mom was just trying to be nice."

Oh, Kendall, Abbie thought. *Please don't. Things are bad enough.*

"I don't *need* any help," Erin said tightly. She looked at

Abbie. Her eyes had that cold look that Abbie had come to know so well—the look that said *I don't want anything from you, just leave me alone.* "But thank you for offering." Draining her glass, she carefully set it down in the sink. Then she picked up her backpack and said, "I'm going to go do my homework."

After she left the kitchen, Abbie tried to pretend that Erin's behavior was no big deal, because she did not want to discuss what had just happened with Kendall. She wasn't sure she succeeded, although nothing more was said, and Kendall soon went off to her room.

Remembering the scene now, it was extremely difficult for Abbie to keep believing Erin would someday accept her. And if Erin never accepted her, then what? Could Abbie really stay in this marriage under those circumstances? Wouldn't such an atmosphere eventually corrode even Kendall's happiness?

"Abbie, what's wrong?"

Logan's question made Abbie blink. She'd been so lost in her thoughts she'd almost forgotten he was there.

"Did something happen today?" he continued. "Everyone was awfully quiet at dinner tonight."

Sighing again, Abbie decided it wasn't fair not to tell him about the episode after school. Calmly, trying to keep her emotions out of the telling, she related the story. "I don't know," she said after she'd finished. "Today I haven't been able to shake the feeling that maybe things are hopeless. Maybe Erin will *never* accept me."

"I'll talk to her," Logan said wearily.

Abbie set her wineglass down. "No, Logan, please don't. It won't do any good. In fact, things will probably get worse if you talk to her, because she'll know I said something to you, and she'll hate me even more than she does now." Saying the words aloud caused Abbie's eyes to fill. Angry with herself, she brushed the tears away.

"Ah, Abbie," Logan said softly. "She doesn't hate you." He got up from his chair and moved over to the couch. Sitting down next to her, he took her hand and rubbed it gently.

Abbie swallowed, still fighting tears, which was a losing

battle. "Doesn't she?" If he'd seen the look Erin had given her today . . . A tear rolled down her cheek.

"C'mon, Abbie. It's only been a few months. It'll get better. She just needs more time."

Abbie wanted to believe him. She desperately wanted to believe him. She looked up. He smiled, his eyes sympathetic. The moment spun out, their gazes held, and Abbie was suddenly very aware of his hand holding hers. As the music in the background built to a crescendo, the expression in his eyes changed, and slowly, oh so slowly, his gaze traveled downward to her mouth and lingered there. His head moved imperceptibly closer. He wanted to kiss her—she could see the desire in his eyes—and for just the barest fraction of a moment, she thought he was going to. She could hardly breathe. *Oh, Logan, Logan.*

Then, startling them both, a pajama-clad Patrick shuffled into the room followed by Rex, who always hung out in Patrick's room when Patrick was home, just as Mitzi camped out in Erin's.

Abbie jumped, and Logan dropped her hand as if he'd been scalded.

"What is it, son?" Logan said a bit louder than necessary.

"I just wanted a glass of milk," Patrick said.

Abbie's disappointment was so sharp, it was almost a physical pain. Tonight was the closest she and Logan had come to any kind of physical demonstration of affection since that night in the kitchen right after they were married. For weeks now, she'd been hoping he would suggest moving into the bedroom, but he hadn't. Every night he slept on the daybed in the sitting room, and every night she occupied the king-size bed by herself. Several times she'd wondered what he would do if she opened the door and invited him in. But as much as she wanted to, she knew she never would. He had to make the first move.

She was beginning to think that he would not join her in the bedroom until and unless things changed drastically with Erin. Abbie knew this was probably subconscious on Logan's part. He was too honest to put conditions on their marriage that hadn't been fully discussed between them. Nevertheless, Abbie couldn't help feeling he would not move to consummate their marriage until he was certain it was actually going to last.

In the meantime, Abbie had been scrupulous about keeping her own desire from showing, because the last thing she wanted was Logan coming to her out of pity.

After Patrick had gone back to his room, Logan, who had gotten up from the couch to turn off the CD player, turned to her and said, "You look tired, Abbie. Why don't you go on to bed?"

She nodded. The spell had been broken. There was no sense prolonging her agony. She reached for her empty wineglass with the intention of taking it out to the kitchen.

"I'll get that. You go on. And quit worrying," he added kindly. "Tomorrow is another day."

Yes, she thought as she lay sleepless in bed. Tomorrow is another day for my daughter to hate me and my husband to wonder why he ever thought marrying me was a good idea.

Some of Abbie's sense of hopelessness had rubbed off on Logan, and once again lying alone in the narrow daybed, he wondered if they'd ever be a happy family.

It wasn't just Erin and her attitude toward Abbie that bothered him. His and Abbie's relationship didn't seem to be progressing, either. In fact, if anything, it seemed to be going backward.

If only she'd give him some sign that she wanted more from him than friendship. There for a minute tonight, he thought they were finally going to get past this invisible wall that seemed to have sprouted between them. But then Patrick came in, and by the time he left them alone again, that damn wall was back, bigger and more impenetrable than ever.

He expelled a noisy sigh and turned over, trying to get comfortable. Just before falling asleep, he decided he was sick of this limbo they were in, and that as soon as the holidays were over, he would bring the problem out in the open. Anything, even a rejection, was better than waiting.

Logan and Abbie and the children were invited to have Thanksgiving dinner at his sister Glenna's house. "The folks are going out to Denver to be with Tim," she explained, "so it'll just be us and Kevin and Debbie."

When Abbie reluctantly said she hated to leave her mother alone for the holiday, Glenna generously included Katherine, as well. To Abbie's surprise, Katherine actually seemed enthusiastic and accepted the invitation readily.

The day turned out to be one of the most pleasant days of their marriage so far. For one thing, Abbie felt completely at ease with Glenna and her husband Paul. She also liked Logan's younger brother, Kevin, a happy-go-lucky engineer, and his wife Debbie, an up-and-coming lawyer. For another, being with Logan's family brought out a different side of Erin. She smiled more in that one day than she had in weeks, mostly at Megan, Glenna, and Paul's five-year-old, but even so, it was progress and made Abbie feel hopeful again.

Even Katherine was on her best behavior. She was impressed with Glenna and Paul, that was obvious to Abbie, and because there were so many people around, she didn't have the chance to spend all her time observing Erin and storing up criticisms with which to bombard Abbie later. And when she discovered Debbie was a big supporter of the symphony, she mellowed even more. Abbie could have kissed Debbie, who seemed to really enjoy Katherine. After dinner, Debbie made a special point of seeking her out and talking to her, which left Abbie free to talk to Glenna.

"I'm so sorry we haven't had a chance before this to spend more time together," Glenna said to Abbie.

"Me, too," Abbie said sincerely. She really liked Glenna, a no-nonsense type of person who still retained a warmth and approachability that made people open up to her.

"But we'll correct that."

Abbie smiled. Glenna, more than anyone in either family, had made her feel welcome from the start.

"So how are things going?" Glenna said, her gaze moving to the men, who were engaged in a heated discussion of the Houston Rockets' recent losing streak. "Everyone settling in okay?"

Abbie shrugged. "We're trying."

Glenna gave her a thoughtful look. "Second marriages

can be tough, especially when there are children involved, but things seem to be working out fine with yours."

"Do they?"

"Yes, I think so. I know Logan seems happier."

"Does he?" Abbie wished she could believe that.

"I admit, I was worried about Erin for a while, but she seems to be doing okay."

Abbie wanted to say today was an exception, but she didn't. Therapist or not, Glenna didn't need Abbie crying on her shoulder. This was a social, family day, not a climb-on-the-couch-and-spill-your-guts day. Besides, to complain about Erin might seem petty to Glenna. So all Abbie said was "Yes, she does."

"And your daughter is lovely," Glenna said. She chuckled. "You know, when I first saw her, I had the weirdest feeling. I mean, she looks enough like Patrick to be his sister, whereas Erin, well, she's always taken after her mother's family."

Abbie should have been used to these moments, but whenever they came, they were always unexpected, and they always flustered her. She hated that she and Logan were deceiving their families, but they couldn't do anything else, not until they felt Erin would be able to accept the truth.

Not noticing Abbie's discomfort, Glenna continued. "She and Logan get along so well, too."

"Yes," Abbie said, on firmer ground now. "She adores Logan. Has from the very first."

"That must make you feel good."

Abbie smiled. "It does."

For a few moments, they fell silent. Then Glenna said, "Tell me about your work. Logan says you do all Charlotte Post's research?"

"Yes. I've worked with her for nearly eight years now." Abbie launched into a few of her choicer Charlotte Post stories, then the men joined their circle, after which Glenna decided it was time for dessert. Before Abbie knew it, the day had slipped away, and it was time to leave.

"Thank you so much," she said to Glenna, who gave her an enthusiastic hug. "It was a wonderful day."

As they were driving home, Abbie thought that if the rest

of their days could be even half as good as this one had been, she would be happy. Even if Logan *never* joined her in bed, she would still be happy.

But even as she told herself this, she knew it wasn't true. She would be happier, yes, but true happiness would only come when Logan was her husband in every sense of the word and when Erin was her publicly acknowledged daughter and accepted Abbie as her mother.

And today, for the first time, Abbie felt a glimmer of hope that things might one day happen just that way.

But as November segued into December, Abbie's hope faded and she recognized that Thanksgiving was an aberration, for Erin quickly fell back into her state of barely concealed misery. In fact, the only time Erin seemed happy was when she was with her Aunt Elizabeth or when Logan was home. When it was just Abbie and Kendall around, she spent as much time in her room, alone, as she possibly could. Even Patrick's presence didn't seem to make much difference.

Abbie continued to try to reach Erin, but nothing worked. It was like a physical wall separated them, and nothing Abbie could do was strong enough to break it down. Abbie and Logan talked about the situation constantly. Logan thought he should get Erin back into therapy, but when he suggested it, Erin pitched a fit, and he dropped the idea, at least for the time being. Abbie was glad. Forcing Erin to do something she didn't want to do would only make her resent Abbie more.

On a Friday in mid-December as Abbie was driving the girls home from school, she looked in the rearview mirror and, catching Erin's eyes, said brightly, "I thought we three might go Christmas shopping tomorrow. I know you girls haven't had a chance to buy your gifts yet."

"Oh, good," Kendall said. "I've been working on my list and I think I know what I want to get."

"Aunt Elizabeth is taking me to do my Christmas shopping tomorrow," Erin said.

I should have known, Abbie thought. Elizabeth never seemed to miss a chance to usurp Abbie's role. "Oh. Well, too bad. It would have been fun to do it together," she said lightly.

Erin didn't reply, and when Abbie glanced into the rearview mirror again, Erin was looking out the window, her face set in familiar, closed lines.

All at once Abbie knew this situation could not go on indefinitely. If something didn't change soon, she and Logan would have to take some action.

We were naive to think things would sort themselves out. Maybe with another child, they would, but not with Erin. She's too sensitive and she's been too hurt.

Oh, Erin, baby, I'm so sorry. The last thing I ever wanted was to give you more pain. Abbie's eyes burned with unshed tears. If she could, she would take Erin's pain and make it her own. All she wanted was for her child to be happy.

That's not all you want. You want Kendall to be happy. You want to be happy. You want Logan to love you.

What are we going to do? she thought in despair so profound it was like a great weight pressing on her chest. *Dear God, if you have any compassion at all, please, please give me some answers. Because right now, I'm truly at the end of my rope.*

Twenty-eight

"Where shall we go? The Galleria? Or Town and Country?"
Elizabeth smiled over at Erin.

"I don't care."

"The Galleria will probably be more crowded. Let's just
go to Town and Country."

"All right."

Elizabeth headed west on Memorial Drive and thought
about how to frame her next question. "So how have things
been going at home? You getting used to having Abbie and
Kendall around?"

Erin shrugged. "I guess."

Elizabeth barely suppressed a pleased smile. You didn't
have to be a rocket scientist to see that Erin wasn't happy.
And if, after all this time, Erin still wasn't happy, it couldn't
be much longer before Logan had to do something to rem-
edy the situation.

This whole marriage thing continued to puzzle Elizabeth.
She had seen quite a bit of Abbie and Logan since August,
because she made it her business to do something with Erin
at least once a week—not only because she loved the child,
but because seeing Erin gave her a good excuse to go to the
house. And in all the times she'd seen them, never once had
she gotten the feeling that Logan and Abbie were madly in
love. That might be wishful thinking on her part, but she
didn't think so.

"You know what, Aunt Elizabeth?"

"Hmmm?" Elizabeth shook off her thoughts.

"Daddy and Abbie don't sleep together."

Elizabeth nearly swerved off the road. "They . . . they don't *sleep* together?" She looked at Erin in disbelief.

"No." Erin's eyes met hers.

Elizabeth's mind raced. Could that be true? And if it *was* true, what did it mean? Excitement caused her voice to tremble slightly. "What makes you say that, honey?"

" 'Cause the other night I had a stomachache, and I got up and started to go get Daddy. Anyway, you know how you have to walk through the sitting room to get to his bedroom?"

"Yes."

"Well, I opened the sitting-room door, and when I did, I saw him sleeping on the daybed."

"Really." Now the excitement was mixed with a wild surge of hope. "Was Abbie sleeping in the bedroom, then?" she said in a studiedly casual voice.

"Uh-huh."

Maybe Abbie hadn't been feeling well, and Logan was just being considerate, and that's why he was on the daybed.

"You know what else?" Erin said.

"What?"

"I've never seen my dad kiss her, like he used to do with Mom. They don't laugh and tease each other, either."

Elizabeth could barely sit still, she was so galvanized by Erin's disclosures. She told herself not to read too much into this. After all, Erin was only eleven years old. She could easily have misinterpreted or misunderstood. Yet Erin was very perceptive, especially when it came to her adored father, and kids her age knew plenty about sex, given the environment they lived in nowadays. And added to what Elizabeth herself had observed about their relationship . . .

"I don't think Daddy loves her."

Elizabeth swallowed. Oh, God, if only that were true. If only Elizabeth thought she might be granted another chance. And yet, if Logan didn't love Abbie, *why had he married her?*

•   •   •

It was nearly six o'clock when Elizabeth brought Erin home. When they walked in, they found Abbie, Logan, and Kendall in the family room. There were bags from Dillard's and Macy's littering the floor.

"Well, it looks as if you went shopping today, too," Elizabeth said. The comment was addressed to Abbie and Kendall, but she turned her smile on Logan. She could tell from the expression on Abbie's face that her rival was less than delighted to see her, even though she was trying to pretend otherwise. *Don't worry, the feeling's mutual.*

Without even looking at Abbie or Kendall, Erin walked straight over to Logan and perched on the arm of his chair. He put his arm around her. "Have fun today, pumpkin?"

"Uh-huh. You'll never guess what I bought you for Christmas, Dad."

"No, I probably won't, so I'm not even going to try."

"Oh, *Dad*, you're no fun." But Erin was grinning.

"I hope we didn't get him the same thing," Kendall said.

"I don't *think* so," Erin said, finally looking at her. "You don't know my dad like I do."

Good for you, Elizabeth thought. *Put little Miss Perfect Britches in her place. Her and her mother, both.*

If Erin's remark bothered Kendall, she covered it up quickly, because neither her expression nor her voice betrayed anything. "We went to the Galleria. Where did you go?"

"We went to Town and Country," Elizabeth said. "The shops at the Galleria are a little too expensive for a child's pocketbook."

"You just have to know where to look," Abbie said.

Elizabeth pretended she hadn't heard the remark.

"We watched the skaters for a while," Kendall chattered on, and even though she was supposedly talking to Erin, Elizabeth could see that her remarks were really addressed to Logan. "There were some people there signing kids up for skating lessons, but Mom wouldn't let me sign up."

"You already do far too much," Abbie said. "I don't know how you'd have time for something else."

"But, Mom, the lady said they had Saturday lessons."

"Erin's always wanted to take ice skating lessons, too,"

Logan said thoughtfully. "Tell you what." He gave Kendall a fond smile. "Maybe you girls can have skating lessons for your birthday."

Elizabeth gritted her teeth. *Why* did Logan like that child so much? Couldn't he see how spoiled she was? And didn't he realize that every time he smiled at her like that, it hurt Erin?

"*Really?*" Kendall squealed. "Mom, did you hear what he said? And my birthday is only two months away."

Erin frowned. "*My* birthday is only two months away. When is *your* birthday?"

Later, Elizabeth would remember how Abbie had tried to interrupt at that point, and how Logan's face had flushed, but at the moment, these reactions didn't seem strange, given the strained atmosphere that already existed.

"My birthday is February seventh," Kendall said.

Erin's frown deepened. "How weird. Mine is February eighth."

"Really? How funny," Kendall said. "Mom, isn't that funny? Erin and I have practically the same birthday."

"Yes," Abbie said weakly, "funny." She looked at Logan.

Elizabeth was beginning to get an odd feeling. She would never know what made her ask the question. It just seemed to pop out of her mouth, unbidden. "Where were you born, Kendall? Erin was born in the middle of a blizzard in Hurley. But, of course, you knew that, Abbie. That's how you met Logan, isn't it? When you were researching that article about the Hurley hospital."

Kendall looked at her mother. "I was born in the middle of a blizzard," she said. "In Hurley."

"Yes, well, that's why I got interested in writing the article," Abbie said quickly.

Too quickly, Elizabeth thought. Something strange was going on here. Something very, very strange.

"It was because you were born in that blizzard that I thought it would be interesting to track down the other families," Abbie continued. She avoided Elizabeth's eyes.

Elizabeth looked at Logan again, but he, too, was avoiding looking directly at her. What was going on here? Was it possible Abbie and Logan had known each other ever since the girls were born? Had Abbie purposely tracked him down, using the article as an excuse to see him again? The idea seemed crazy. After all, how would Abbie know Logan was now a widower? Surely they hadn't kept in touch with each other all those years. And yet, *something* was fishy, or else why hadn't Logan mentioned the connection between him and Abbie before this?

Later, as Elizabeth drove home, she mulled over everything she'd learned tonight. In itself, the fact that both girls were born in Hurley during that blizzard wasn't that odd. After all, Abbie could have been telling the truth about why she'd first gotten interested in doing the article. No, the odd thing was that the information had been covered up. And added to what Erin had said earlier about Abbie and Logan not sleeping together and then topped off by the secrecy and haste of their marriage . . . well, something weird was definitely going on.

By the time Elizabeth reached her house, she had made a decision. As soon as the holidays were over, she was going to call the Hurley hospital and see if anyone there remembered that night eleven years ago. And if she found someone who did, maybe then Elizabeth would have some answers. Not to mention a few more questions!

"Oh, God, Logan, do you think she suspects something?"

It was eleven o'clock. The children were asleep, and Logan and Abbie were sitting at the kitchen table over cups of hot chocolate.

"I don't know," he admitted. "With Elizabeth, it's hard to tell."

Staring pensively into her cup, Abbie bit her bottom lip.

More than anything, Logan wished he could get up and put his arms around her, but he didn't dare. He knew if he succumbed to the temptation, he wouldn't be satisfied with simply holding her and comforting her. He would want to make love to her. And so far, she'd given him no sign she was ready.

She sighed and looked up. "If only we could tell the girls the truth." Her eyes were clouded.

Logan nodded. "I know."

"But Erin's not anywhere near ready to hear it."

"No."

"If . . . if Elizabeth *does* suspect something, do you think she'd say anything to Erin?"

Logan shrugged. "I don't think she would. She *does* love Erin, and I don't think she'd want to hurt her. What I think would happen is Elizabeth would come to me."

Abbie sighed again. "That's good. Then at least we'd have some warning." Her gaze met his. "She's in love with you, you know."

"Elizabeth?"

"Yes."

Logan wanted to deny it, but that would have been stupid. Abbie wasn't a fool. Grimacing, he said, "I know."

"She hates me."

"Yes, I think she probably does."

Abbie studied him thoughtfully. "Tell me something, Logan. If it hadn't been for our situation with the girls, would you have married Elizabeth?"

"I thought about it," he admitted. "But I never would have. I don't think I could have lived with Elizabeth."

A ghost of a smile tugged at Abbie's lips. "You know who she reminds me of? My mother."

Logan chuckled. "I wouldn't want to live with her, either."

Abbie laughed. The remark lightened the atmosphere, and for the remainder of the time they spent drinking their hot chocolate, they talked about the upcoming holidays and Abbie's trip to Chicago for Laura's wedding. When they finished their drinks, Abbie rinsed the cups and put them in the dishwasher while Logan walked around turning out the lights in preparation for bed. Then together they headed for the master suite. When they reached the sitting room, Abbie stopped.

Turning to him, she said, "If you really believe Elizabeth wouldn't want Erin to be hurt, maybe you should tell her the truth."

Logan nodded. "I might have to do that sometime, but I don't think we need to worry about it right now."

"All right."

But even though she agreed, the slope of her shoulders, her entire demeanor, said she *was* worried. Unable to resist, he put his arm around her shoulders and kissed her cheek. Her startled eyes met his. For a long moment, neither said anything.

Self-consciously, Logan removed his arm. And when he did, Abbie moved a few inches farther away.

Afterward, after they'd said an awkward good night and Abbie had disappeared into the bedroom, Logan wanted to kick himself. Why hadn't he followed Abbie into the bedroom? He'd had the perfect opportunity tonight, and he'd blown it.

For a while now, he'd realized he should never have agreed to a marriage like theirs. When he asked her to marry him, he should have made it clear it would be a real marriage in every sense of the word. Now there was this barrier between them, one that was getting more and more difficult to overcome.

But overcome it he must. And soon.

Twenty-nine

Logan couldn't decide what to get Abbie for Christmas. He discarded one idea after another. Everything he thought of seemed either too personal or not personal enough. He guessed his dilemma was a result of the fact that he and Abbie had been living more as friends than as husband and wife. Yet she *was* his wife.

In desperation, he called Glenna. Told she was with a patient, he left a message for her and forced himself to give his full attention to the elevation he was working on. About forty minutes later, Rebecca buzzed him to say Glenna was on the line.

"What's up?" she said, brisk the way she always was when they talked during working hours.

"Help," he said. "I can't think what to buy Abbie for Christmas. Got any suggestions?"

"Let me think about it for a while. I'll give you a call back. Or, better yet, why don't you meet me for a late lunch? I have from one until two-thirty free today."

"Sounds good."

They arranged to meet at a salad place close to Glenna's office near Memorial City. Always prompt, Glenna pulled into the parking lot a few minutes after one. Logan had just arrived, so they walked into the restaurant together. After going through the cafeteria-style line for their food, they found a booth and sat down.

"Did you come up with any ideas?" Logan asked once they were settled.

Glenna nodded. "Yes, but I have to confess, I'm puzzled as to why you need help. You never needed help buying anything for Ann."

"I know, but I'm out of practice." Logan ate some of his baked potato.

Glenna's eyes were thoughtful as they studied him. "Are you sure that's all?"

"What do you mean?" Logan said carefully.

"I don't know *what* I mean. I'm just getting some odd vibes from you."

Logan tried to laugh, but he knew the attempt was a poor one that wouldn't fool many people, least of all his perceptive sister with her training and fine-honed instincts about human nature.

Glenna put her fork down. Leaning forward, she studied him intently. "Logan," she said softly, "if something's bothering you, you know you can trust me."

"I know." He looked away. The temptation to tell her everything was nearly overwhelming.

"Maybe I can help."

He toyed with his fork. "I want to tell you. I wanted to tell you from the beginning, but Abbie and I made a pact that we wouldn't tell anyone until the time was right."

Glenna's eyes were curious, but she didn't say anything— just waited quietly for him to continue. Her therapist's technique, he thought with a twinge of humor.

He took a deep breath. "This is going to knock you for a loop."

She shrugged. The gesture said nothing surprised her anymore; she'd heard it all. Her eyes said she loved him and nothing he told her would change that.

"Okay. Here goes. Abbie and I got married so that we could be with our daughters."

Glenna frowned. "Be with your daughters?"

"Yes."

"I don't understand. You *were* with your daughters."

"No. We weren't. We thought we were, but as it turns out, we had each raised a child that wasn't biologically ours."

Glenna, eyes huge, clapped her hand over her mouth and stared at him.

Logan nodded sadly. "Yes. Kendall was born to Ann and me, and Erin was born to Abbie and her husband. The babies were accidentally switched in the hospital."

"Oh, my God," Glenna said. She sank back against the seat. "Oh, my God. H-how did you find out? *When* did you find out?"

He sighed. "It's a long story." For the next thirty minutes, their food forgotten, Logan told Glenna everything.

When he finished, Glenna was shaking her head. "Oh, Logan, my God. This is unbelievable. I can hardly take it in. It's . . . it's just incredible. What you and Abbie must have *gone* through."

"Yes, it's been rough."

"So *that's* why you two married," she said softly. "Everyone wondered, you know. Paul and I talked about it a lot, and Mom. Mom couldn't believe it when you told her, even though she put a good face on it. Oh, don't get me wrong, we all like Abbie, it's just that marrying someone you hadn't even told us about and then doing it in complete secrecy . . . Well, that's just so unlike you."

Logan smiled crookedly. "I know, but marrying each other was the only solution I could think of. After I found out about Kendall, I couldn't stand the idea of not being a part of her life, and Abbie felt the same way about Erin. But I'm not sorry."

Glenna smiled. "You like her."

"Yes," he said sheepishly. "I find I like her a lot."

"That's good."

He shrugged. "Maybe. Maybe not. Abbie's not very happy. This has been harder on her than it has on me." He went on to explain the problems they'd experienced with Erin. "I don't know who I feel sorrier for—Abbie or Erin." He shook his head. "Erin's miserable."

"She seemed to be doing well over Thanksgiving."

"That's because she was at your house. At home it's a different story."

Glenna's eyes softened in sympathy. "She must sense something. Feel some kind of threat."

Logan nodded glumly. "I wish I could talk to her about it, but Abbie doesn't want me to push her. She thinks talking to her will only make things worse."

"She's probably right."

"I don't know what we're going to do if things keep up like this. I'm not sure how long Abbie can take being treated like a pariah."

"This must be terribly painful for her."

"Yes."

"Oh, Logan, I am so sorry that you and Abbie are having to go through this."

"You and me both," he said with a wry smile.

"Do you mind if I tell Paul?"

"No." Logan trusted Paul.

Suddenly, Glenna looked at her watch and exclaimed, "Oh, good grief, I've got to run. It's quarter after two and I have a patient coming at two-thirty."

Logan gave their still-full plates a rueful glance. "I spoiled your lunch."

"Who cares about food?" She slid out of the booth.

When he had gotten up, too, she threw her arms around him and hugged him hard. "Remember," she said, "I'm only a phone call away."

"Thanks, sis." He kissed her cheek. "I'll remember that."

It wasn't until he was driving back to his office that he remembered she never had given him any ideas on what to buy Abbie.

Abbie, Logan, and the children spent Christmas Eve with his parents. It should have been a lovely evening, but Abbie didn't enjoy it the way she had hoped to. For one thing, she kept feeling as if people were watching her and wondering about her. Maybe they weren't. Maybe she was just so worried about the eventual outcome of her predicament, she was imagining something that didn't exist.

Logan's mother tried hard to make Abbie feel at home, but even Mary Margaret O'Connell's warmth and uncomplicated friendliness couldn't dispel the chill Abbie felt each time she was reminded of how little progress she had made in gaining Erin's acceptance.

She wondered if others noticed the way Erin always chose the farthest point in any room from where Abbie was located. Or how the child never looked directly at Abbie if she could help it. She continued to be scrupulously polite. But politeness bereft of any emotion was just as painful as rudeness. One could be polite to a stranger. One was rarely only polite to a person one cared about. So the sorrow Abbie felt was a constant—a deep ache nothing except Erin's love would ever assuage. Even the pleasure Abbie felt in Kendall's acceptance by Logan's family, the way his mother and father immediately took to her—just as if they knew she belonged to them—was dimmed by the omnipresent wall that existed between Abbie and Erin.

But if Christmas Eve was a strain, it bore no comparison to Christmas day, which was divided between the morning at home, with Celia and Elizabeth Chamberlain joining them for brunch, and the afternoon at Katherine's.

The day started out well enough. The children, including Erin, were excited. After all, it was Christmas. Erin was even friendly toward Kendall. Abbie knew, of course, that Logan had probably picked out the gift Erin gave her—a basket of fancy soaps, shower gels, and body creams from a local bath shop—but she didn't mind, because Erin actually smiled when she presented it, saying, "Merry Christmas, Abbie." And she genuinely seemed to like the sport watch and royal blue cashmere twin set Abbie gave her.

Kendall was delighted with her gifts: an identical sport watch and forest green cashmere twin set from Abbie, a nail care kit with assorted colors of polish from Erin, a Smashing Pumpkins CD and delicate silver earrings from Patrick, and in-line skates from Logan.

She opened Logan's gift last. No one was surprised to see the skates, because Erin had just opened her gift from Logan, and he'd given her skates, too. Kendall grinned and thanked him. "But I really want something else even more than I wanted the skates," she said.

Abbie stared at her, aghast.

Kendall got up and walked over to Logan. Bending down, she hugged him. "What I really want is to call you Dad," she said softly.

Her words brought tears to Abbie's eyes, and yet, as sweet and touching as they were, they also brought a corresponding dread, for Abbie knew how Erin would feel about them. Sure enough, when she glanced covertly at Erin, she saw hurt, disbelief, outrage, and resentment all mixed together in a portrait of abject misery.

And Logan's answer only deepened those emotions, Abbie was sure. "Nothing would make me happier," he said, returning Kendall's hug and kissing her cheek. His eyes were suspiciously shiny.

Abbie's heart felt as if someone were cutting it in two. Part of her was so happy for Kendall and Logan, the other part ached with pity for the child of her flesh, who must feel so betrayed. *Please God,* she thought, *please help her through this.*

Ever since their marriage, Logan had been extremely solicitous of Erin's feelings, never giving her any reason to be jealous of Kendall or to feel she was actually usurping her place in her father's affections. Until today, both he and Abbie felt he had succeeded. But now, with just a few words, the tenuous balance he'd managed to maintain had been jeopardized. Abbie knew Logan was painfully aware of the possible devastation the exchange with Kendall would wreak in Erin, and yet how could he have done anything other than what he'd done? To rebuff Kendall would be equally as abhorrent as causing Erin additional pain.

Abbie could hardly bear to look at Erin. The poor girl must want nothing more than to escape to the privacy of her room, but how could she? It was Christmas morning. She would only call attention to herself.

Finally, the moment passed, and Abbie and Logan opened their gifts from each other, which they'd saved for last. It had taken Abbie a long time to find something for him, and she'd finally settled on a beautifully made chess set, with hand-carved jade and ebony pieces. His smile told her how much he liked it. Then she opened her gift, gasping when she saw a double strand of creamy pearls and accompanying pearl earrings. "Oh," she breathed. "They are beautiful." She lifted the necklace from the box, and when she did, Erin made a strangled sound.

"You didn't give her Mom's pearls!" Erin cried.

For a few seconds, absolute silence reigned as everyone turned to look at her.

"Erin," Logan said gently, "of course I didn't give Abbie your mother's pearls. Those are put away in the safe and they'll be yours one day. You know that."

Abbie's hands were trembling as she put the pearls back in their box. All her pleasure at the gift was gone. For a second, Logan's eyes met hers. *I'm sorry* was the unspoken message in them. Abbie bit her lip and looked away. Suddenly all she wanted was for this day, with its heightened emotions, to be over.

Unfortunately, she was afraid the worst was still to come.

Elizabeth and Celia arrived promptly at ten. Elizabeth was dressed in a short cranberry wool dress with a wide band of cream silk around the neckline and hem. Diamond stud earrings and a diamond tennis bracelet completed her outfit. Celia wore a beautifully draped purple crepe dress and pearls. Both looked lovely. Abbie, too, had dressed with care, in a long brown velvet skirt and a dark gold tissue-silk blouse. Logan's pearls lay around her neck, and to show off the earrings, Abbie had lifted her hair back from her ears with tortoise-shell combs. For once, she wanted to be able to hold her own in Elizabeth's company.

Elizabeth gave Abbie a quick appraisal, accompanied by a cool smile and a perfunctory "Merry Christmas." Her warmth and hugs were reserved for Logan, Erin, and Patrick. Kendall was completely ignored.

But if Kendall minded, she certainly didn't show it. She was still basking in the glow of her gifts and Logan's pleased reaction to her request about calling him Dad, a form of address she now used as often as she could inject it into the conversation.

After the initial greetings, they all moved into the living room, and Logan took drink orders. Celia and Abbie opted for Mimosas while Logan and Elizabeth were having Bloody Marys. The children had fake Mimosas made with orange juice and ginger ale.

Erin seemed to have recovered from her earlier unhappi-

ness. Of course, Abbie thought wryly, the presence of her
beloved Aunt Elizabeth probably had more to do with that
recovery than anything else. As usual, Erin was sitting as
close to her aunt and as far from Abbie as she could manage.

After they all had their drinks, they exchanged gifts. Abbie
was amused to receive a gift subscription to *Vogue* from
Elizabeth. Was Elizabeth sending her some kind of subtle
message? Abbie and Logan had given Elizabeth a bottle of
Joy, which he said was her favorite perfume. Abbie didn't
ask how he knew.

Logan's gift from Elizabeth was a beautiful powder blue
cable-knit sweater. "I made it myself," Elizabeth said.

Why am I not surprised? Abbie thought.

Celia gave Abbie a lovely Hermes scarf in vivid shades
of green. Touched, Abbie impulsively got up and gave the
older woman a kiss on the cheek. As Abbie walked back to
her chair, her gaze briefly met Elizabeth's. In the other
woman's eyes Abbie saw such intense dislike, she actually
felt chilled. *You'd better watch your back,* Abbie told herself. *That woman will knife you every time she gets the
chance.*

Once the gifts were exchanged, they all moved into the
dining room, where Abbie had already laid out a spread con-
sisting of honeybaked ham, a casserole of potatoes with
cheese, deviled eggs, spinach soufflé, rolls and butter, fruit
salad, banana bread, and assorted pickles, olives, and rel-
ishes.

"How lovely, Abbie," Celia Chamberlain said. Her smile
was kind.

"Thank you." What a nice woman she was, Abbie thought.
It couldn't be easy to see another woman take her daughter's place, and yet—in marked contrast to Elizabeth—from
the very first Celia had been nothing but gracious to Abbie.

Erin sat between Elizabeth and Celia on one side of the
table, Kendall and Patrick sat on the other side, and Logan
and Abbie each took an end. Unfortunately for Abbie, that
placed her next to Elizabeth, who pointedly ignored her and
addressed all her remarks to her mother or Logan.

Abbie didn't care. She was content to sit and watch and

listen. Besides, she had nothing to say to Elizabeth. Erin had plenty to say, though. She chattered to her aunt and grandmother throughout the meal. She was more animated than Abbie had seen her since Thanksgiving.

When they'd finished eating, Celia offered to help with cleanup, but Abbie wouldn't hear of it. "The girls will help me later. Let's just visit awhile."

"I'm afraid we can't stay much longer," Celia said. "My brother and his wife are driving in from San Antonio this afternoon."

"Uncle Teddy's coming?" Erin said, clearly delighted.

Patrick grinned. "Are we gonna get to see him, Gran?"

"Of course," Celia said. "I thought maybe you children could come over tomorrow."

"Why can't we come today?" Erin said, looking at Elizabeth.

"You can if you want to."

"Erin," Logan said, "you know we're all going over to Kendall's grandmother's house this afternoon."

Erin frowned. "She's not my grandmother. Why do I have to go?"

"Erin," Logan said sternly, "we already talked about this."

"*You* talked about it, I didn't."

"That's enough, Erin."

"Logan . . . ," Abbie said. "Maybe—"

"No, Abbie. She's going with us, and that's that."

"I'm terribly sorry to have caused trouble," Elizabeth said in a sugarcoated voice.

I'll just bet you are, Abbie thought. *Trouble is your middle name.* But as irritated as she was with Elizabeth, it was Erin Abbie cared about. She didn't blame the child for not wanting to go to Katherine's. After all, why *would* she want to? In her mind, Katherine was part of the enemy and bore no relation to her. Katherine's attitude toward Erin hadn't helped matters. She clearly had no interest in Erin. Abbie had tried not to think how her mother would react when she finally found out the truth about her granddaughter. One step at a time, she kept telling herself.

After Elizabeth and Celia left, Logan and the children pitched in with the cleanup, and Abbie was guardedly relieved to see that Erin seemed to have gotten over her disappointment over not going with her aunt and grandmother. However, there was still the rest of the day to get through.

Later, as they drove to her mother's, Abbie sent up a silent prayer. All she wanted was an absence of tension for the next couple of hours. Just that, she pleaded fervently. A peaceful visit.

For a while, she thought her prayer had been granted. The greetings and exchange of gifts took place with no ripples to mar the surface serenity. But as the afternoon wore on, the children became restless. If Abbie could have, she would have made a move to leave, but Katherine—continuing a tradition begun by her own mother—had just served tea, complete with scones and cucumber sandwiches. The food kept the kids occupied for a while, but once they'd satisfied their hunger, they were ready to go. Even Kendall, who normally enjoyed being with her grandmother, seemed antsy. But Kendall—who always wanted to please—would never chance incurring Katherine's displeasure by saying so.

Erin had no such scruples. "I'm tired, Dad," she said, sighing. "When are we going home?"

Abbie darted a look at her mother. Katherine's lips were pressed together, her eyes cold with disapproval.

"Soon, honey," Logan said, squeezing her leg. He turned his smile to Katherine. "I'm sure Mrs. Wellington is tired, too." He glanced at the mantel clock. "It's nearly five."

"I'm not tired in the least," Katherine said stiffly.

Abbie jumped up. "Why don't we get these tea things cleaned up?" she said brightly.

Her mother grumbled something else, but Abbie paid no attention. Soon Katherine joined her in gathering up the plates and cups. When Logan rose to help, she said, "We can manage." Her tone left no room for argument.

The moment Abbie and her mother were alone in the kitchen, Katherine said, "I don't envy you having to deal with that unpleasant child."

Every time her mother made a disparaging remark about Erin, Abbie felt the same way she'd felt as a child who could never do anything right. "She's not unpleasant, Mother. She's just unhappy."

"Stop making excuses for her," Katherine snapped.

Abbie sighed. There was no sense arguing about this and she knew it. So she bit her tongue and didn't answer.

"All I can say is," her mother continued a few moments later, "I'm glad *my* granddaughter has some manners."

Abbie's stomach clenched. Suddenly all she wanted was to get out of there. She could not take another minute of her mother's disapproval, Erin's unhappiness, or the stress of having to pretend they were one big happy family.

We'll never be one big happy family, she thought in despair. *Never.*

Thirty

Abbie's plane touched down at O'Hare forty-five minutes late. As they taxied to the gate, she looked out at the snow that blanketed the landscape. More was predicted, according to the captain, who had given them a weather update a few minutes earlier. She didn't mind. She'd always enjoyed snow. Still, she hoped the weather wasn't too bad, because she knew if it was, it would impact Laura's wedding.

Thank God for Laura's wedding and the opportunity it had given her to get away. The strain of Christmas and having the children at home had just about done Abbie in. At least now she'd have three days away from her problems, and maybe by the time she went home, she would be better equipped to handle them.

The passengers began spilling into the aisles as the plane docked at the designated jetway. Abbie gathered up her purse, her book, her carry-on tote, and her winter coat, which she hadn't had an opportunity to wear for a while, and squeezed into the aisle.

"Good-bye. Thanks for flying Continental," the flight attendant said as Abbie reached the exit. Abbie smiled at her and at the captain standing behind her, then made her way up the jetway into the terminal. She spotted Laura almost immediately. Her red hair was a beacon that couldn't be missed. Not to mention the fact Laura was waving madly and grinning like a fool.

"Abbie!" Rushing forward, Laura gave her an exuberant hug. "Oh, it's *so* good to see you!"

Abbie smiled and hugged her friend back. "It's good to see you, too."

Laura looked great, Abbie thought as the two headed for baggage claim. Her brown eyes sparkled with happiness, making her look more attractive than she'd ever looked before.

"I'm *so* happy you're here, and I can't *wait* for you to meet Rich."

"When *will* I meet him?"

"Tonight," Laura said happily. "He's taking us out to dinner." She threw her arm around Abbie's shoulders. "Oh, Abbie, I'm so happy."

Abbie did her best to smile enthusiastically. "I'm glad." The sentiment was sincere. It was just so hard not to show her own unhappiness.

Laura talked nonstop all the way to baggage claim and while they waited for Abbie's bag to appear. Abbie was soon caught up in Laura's excitement and actually managed to forget about her troubles for a while. But when Laura pulled her Acura out of the parking garage and headed south on 294, she said, "Okay, that's enough about me. Now I want to hear all about you." She grinned at Abbie. "Is being married wonderful?"

"Oh, yes, wonderful." Oh, God, Abbie thought. She'd have to do better than that or Laura would suspect something. "Logan's a terrific guy. You'll like him a lot." There. She could be much more enthusiastic when she was telling the truth.

"I was hoping maybe you'd bring him with you."

"He wanted to come, but with the kids home for the holidays . . . well, he hated to leave them."

"Why didn't you bring Kendall at least?"

"My mother wanted Kendall to stay with her." *And I needed to get away alone.*

Laura grinned. "How *is* the old bat?"

Abbie laughed. "Laura!"

"I know. I'm bad. But—"

"That's why I love you," Abbie finished.

"Is she settled down about the marriage now?"

Abbie shrugged. "Sort of."

"What's that mean?"

"Well, she isn't crazy about Logan's daughter."

"Why not? Something wrong with the kid?"

"No, there's not a thing wrong with her. It's just that she's not real happy about Logan and me marrying." Abbie went on to explain about Ann and Erin's feelings of insecurity.

"Poor kid," Laura said softly when Abbie had finished. "I know exactly how she feels."

Yes, Laura would. Laura's parents had divorced when she was ten. Her mother remarried a year later, her father six months after that. Laura had grown up with two stepsisters, neither of whom she'd liked. "Actually," she'd said more than once, "I would have liked them if they'd liked me, but they couldn't stand me."

"What about Kendall?" she said now. "Is *she* happy?"

"Oh, yes," Abbie said. "She adores Logan and she and Patrick get along like a house afire. And she does her best with Erin, too."

"Yeah, she would. Well, you know, I think everything will eventually settle down, especially since the rest of you are making such an effort to see that it does."

"I hope so." *But you don't know the whole story.*

For the rest of the drive to Laura's home in Oak Park, they talked of other things: Abbie's mother, Abbie's job, Laura's job, Rich, and of course, the upcoming wedding.

The winter sun was lowering on the horizon when Laura pulled into the driveway of the seventy-year-old redbrick house that had been left to her by her maternal grandparents. It was a lovely place, with classic lines, but the expense of keeping it up was considerable.

"It's a black hole," Laura always said. "It gobbles up money." But the complaint was fond, for even though the house was in constant need of some kind of repair, she loved it.

"I've put you in the yellow bedroom," Laura said once they were inside.

"Okay. What time is Rich coming? Do I have time to shower?"

"Sure. He won't be here for at least an hour."

Forty-five minutes later, showered and dressed in black wool pants, a cowl-necked white sweater, and ankle-high black boots, Abbie headed downstairs. She found Laura in the small, cheerful kitchen. She had changed into khaki slacks and a black sweater and was arranging English water wafers around a bowl of artichoke dip.

"Want a glass of wine?" She pointed to an uncorked bottle of Reisling sitting on the counter. "Wineglasses are in the china cabinet."

Abbie poured her wine and stood sipping it and leaning against the counter while Laura got out a wedge of Brie and a package of toast squares. A few minutes later, the doorbell rang.

Abbie liked Rich immediately. A tall, rangy man with thinning sandy hair, intelligent hazel eyes, and a smile filled with warmth and humor, he would have been hard not to like. And Laura was clearly crazy about him. Her face shone with love every time she looked at him. Abbie wanted to feel nothing but happiness for her, because Laura deserved this, yet it hurt so much to see what Laura had in Rich and to know she would never have the same thing with Logan. Even the luxury of showing her feelings was denied to her.

For the rest of the evening, Abbie fought against an encroaching sense of hopelessness. For the most part, she felt she managed to hide her feelings from Laura. But when the evening was over, and Rich had deposited Laura and Abbie back at the house—declining Laura's invitation to join them in a nightcap, saying he knew they wanted time to talk and he would just be in the way—Laura turned to Abbie and said, "What's wrong, Abbie? I know you're unhappy. I can see it in your eyes."

Abbie swallowed, but the lump in her throat was lodged there, growing bigger with each passing moment. She blinked hard, willing herself not to cry, but the tears had been bottled up for so long, they refused to be contained.

"Oh, Abbie . . ." Laura jumped up and rushed to Abbie's side. Sinking down on the couch beside her, she enfolded Abbie in her arms.

Like a bursting dam, the tears gushed out.

"Is it Logan?" Laura asked when the first storm of weeping passed.

Abbie sniffed and nodded. Opening her wadded tissue, she blew her nose. "I'm sorry. I'm such a mess. I promised myself I wouldn't do this. It's your time. Your happy time."

"Don't worry about that. Good grief, I'm your best friend. Now tell me. You made a mistake, didn't you? You don't love him."

"That's not it," Abbie said brokenly. "He's . . . he's wonderful. And I do love him. The trouble is . . ." She stopped, took a long shaky breath, then looked her friend in the eye. "The trouble is, he doesn't love me."

"He doesn't love *you*!" Laura exclaimed. "What makes you think a thing like that? If he doesn't love you, why on earth did he marry you?"

She was obviously indignant and oblivious to the fact that her question was incongruous, seeing as how she was perfectly willing to accept that Abbie might have married by mistake.

Abbie was so tired. She wanted to tell Laura. She needed to tell her. And so, in a slow, halting voice, she began.

Laura sat quietly, listening and not commenting. The only indication she gave that Abbie's words shocked her was an occasional gasp. When she was done, Abbie put her head in her hands. She was completely drained.

"Oh, Abbie," Laura said softly. "I am so, so sorry." She rubbed small circles on Abbie's back. "I wish you'd told me sooner. You shouldn't have had to carry this burden alone."

Abbie slowly raised her head. "I don't know what to do." She sighed deeply. "Lately I've been thinking they'd all be better off without me."

"Abbie, you can't mean that," Laura said sternly, a look of alarm crossing her face.

"I don't mean I'm going to kill myself or anything. I just mean maybe I should forget about trying to share in Erin's upbringing." Fresh tears welled in her eyes.

"You know, you really haven't given this much time. It's only been, what? Four months."

"Yes."

"Abbie, four months is nothing when you're dealing with

something this major. I've told you about that gal I work with—Carolyn? Remember her?"

Abbie nodded.

"Well, you know she married a guy whose wife had died. It took a good year or more before his kids were even *civil* to her. I'm not kidding. They resented her so much. It was like they blamed her because their mother was gone. She nearly threw in the towel a couple of times, but she loved the guy, and so she hung in there, and gradually the kids came around. And now they're crazy about her. I think you just need to give it more time."

"The two situations aren't the same."

"I know that, but still—"

"No, what I *mean* is, her husband loved her. That's where the major difference is. If I thought Logan *loved* me, I could stand anything." She met Laura's eyes. "We don't sleep together."

Laura grimaced. "You don't?"

"No. Before we married, he said he wanted it to be a real union. We even joked about how we couldn't see ourselves going the rest of our lives without sex. But since then he's made no mention of it. The first night he said he knew I'd need some time and I could have the master bedroom. Ever since he's been sleeping on the daybed in the sitting room, and he's made no move to change things. A couple of times, he seemed close to saying something, but then . . ." She sighed deeply. "He didn't. Anyway, I figure he sees the writing on the wall. The marriage isn't going to last, so why make things more complicated."

"Oh, Abbie."

Abbie nodded dejectedly. "It's hopeless."

"Have . . . you thought about approaching *him*? You know, putting on a sexy nightie and just going into the sitting room? Maybe he *wants* to make love to you but he feels awkward about it now. That happens, you know. A situation goes along in a certain way, and then it's really hard to change it."

"I can't do that. Then I'd never know if he wanted to make love to me or if he felt sorry for me." She swallowed. "I couldn't take pity." Fresh tears threatened. "The thing is, I don't see how I can leave him, either." She closed her eyes.

"Oh, God, Laura, I don't know what to do. The only thing I do know is, I can't go on like this much longer."

Logan missed Abbie. Funny how you could get used to having someone around. Yet he had to admit the atmosphere had been a lot less tense the past couple of days, because with both she and Kendall away, Erin was her old self again.

But Abbie and Kendall would be home tomorrow. And he had decided that before they got back, he and Erin needed to have a talk. Tonight would be the perfect time. Patrick was out with friends, so Logan and Erin would be alone.

He walked back to Erin's room. The door was open, and she was sitting at her computer. He knocked on the door frame. Erin typed a couple of letters, then turned around. "Hi, Dad."

"I was thinking about ordering a pizza for tonight."

"Okay. But I don't like green peppers and mushrooms and onions and stuff."

Logan smiled. "I know. How about if I order a large and have cheese and pepperoni put on your half?"

"Okay." Her face and eyes were free of the misery that had been apparent for so long.

It saddened him to know what had brought about this change. He had hoped that by now she would have accepted, maybe even liked, Abbie and Kendall, that she might even begin to appreciate and enjoy the difference their coming had made to all their lives. But, if anything, her resistance to them had strengthened. "I'll call you when it comes."

"Okay. I'm just talkin' to Allison."

Logan walked into the kitchen and phoned the pizza place. When their pizza arrived, he called Erin. Once they were settled with drinks and had each eaten a couple of pieces, Logan said, "I talked to Abbie earlier."

Erin's face immediately took on that shuttered look he'd come to dread. She reached for another piece of pizza and made no comment.

"She said it was snowing there, but not too hard." He looked up at the wall clock. "The wedding should be starting about now."

Erin continued eating.

"I'll be glad to have her home again," he continued doggedly. The only indication that Erin even heard him was the stiffening of her shoulders. "Erin," he said softly, "can't you even *talk* about Abbie?"

For a long moment, she didn't move. Finally she looked at him. Her eyes were bleak. "I'm sorry, Dad. I've tried, really I have. But I don't like her. And I don't like Kendall. I just want us to go back to the way we were. Just us."

"Honey . . ." Logan felt as if he were in a minefield. One wrong step and there would be an explosion. "Remember how unhappy you were after Mom died? How you kept saying you wished we could go back?"

She bit her lip.

"And how I kept telling you the only way we could go was forward? How I kept saying things would get better?" He watched as her throat worked. "They *did* get better, didn't they?"

"Sort of." Her answer was barely more than a whisper.

"Well, honey, this will get better, too. Trust me. It will. And one day, you'll look back on everything and you won't even remember how unhappy you feel now."

She bowed her head, and as he watched, a tear rolled slowly down her cheek.

"Erin, sweetheart . . ." He touched her forearm.

"Why'd you marry her, Daddy?" she cried.

The look she gave him was so tormented, it nearly broke his heart. "Erin, I wish you'd give Abbie a chance. She's a wonderful person, and she loves you. If you'd just—"

"You don't love her! I know you don't. You don't even sleep together! When I told Aunt Elizabeth, she—"

"You told Aunt Elizabeth!" Logan stared at her.

The color drained from Erin's face. She swallowed. "I . . ." She stopped.

Logan told himself not to berate her. She was just a kid. A very unhappy kid. But the thought of her discussing his and Abbie's sleeping arrangements—and with Elizabeth!— was intolerable. "I don't know where these ideas of yours came from, Erin, but it was wrong to repeat them to Aunt Elizabeth. I am very disappointed in you."

Her lower lip trembled. "I-I'm sorry."

"You should be. What goes on here is personal. You know that."

"Yes," she said in a small voice.

"Besides, you obviously misunderstood the situation." He felt no guilt about the half lie. His and Abbie's sleeping arrangements were no one else's business. "Now I want you to promise me you won't discuss Abbie or me or our marriage with anyone again." He wanted to say *with Elizabeth again* but felt he'd better not.

"I-I promise."

The thought struck him that maybe it *was* time to tell the girls the truth. Maybe, if Erin knew Abbie was really her mother, she would no longer hate her. Maybe he and Abbie had been wrong to keep the truth a secret.

Soon after, Erin asked if she could be excused. Logan said yes with a heavy heart. He knew he hadn't handled the conversation well, yet what else could he have done?

She's coming home tomorrow, Erin wrote.

YUCK, Allison wrote back.

I wish her plane would crash.

ERIN! DO YOU REALLY?

Yes. I hate her.

BUT IF HER PLANE CRASHES, LOTS OF OTHER PEOPLE WILL DIE, TOO.

Erin reached for a Kleenex and blew her nose. She didn't really want Abbie to die. She just wanted her to go away and never come back. She sighed. *I know,* she wrote. *I didn't mean it. But I don't know what to do. Abbie and Kendall have spoiled everything.*

IS IT STILL BAD AT SCHOOL?

Yes! Tiffany and Shauna think Kendall is sooooo cool. It makes me sick.

WHY DON'T YOU TELL THEM HOW YOU FEEL?

I'm not telling them anything. If they like Kendall better than me, fine.

YOU'RE RIGHT. WHO CARES ABOUT THEM? I'M YOUR FRIEND.

For a moment, Erin felt better. Allison *was* her friend, and she could tell her anything. But the feeling didn't last long, because no matter how good it was to have Allison to talk to, talking wouldn't change anything.

Later, after she was in bed, she thought about her dad and how mad he'd been earlier. She guessed she understood why, but why couldn't he understand how *she* felt?

Sometimes Erin felt as if her dad didn't love her anymore now that he had Kendall. She thought about how Kendall was now calling him Dad. "He's *not* her dad. He's mine!" Her lip trembled, and her heart felt like somebody was squeezing it. "Mommy," she whispered. "Mommy, why did you leave? Why did God let you die?"

She fell asleep with tearstains on her face.

Elizabeth was so frustrated, she felt like screaming. She hadn't discovered a thing from the hospital in Hurley. No one seemed to know anything about the night Kendall and Erin had been born. The only information of any significance at all was the fact that the nurse who had assisted at the deliveries had died of a heart attack a few hours later. Unfortunately, the doctor who had made those deliveries was also dead.

The only other information she'd managed to uncover had to do with the blizzard itself, and the blizzard didn't interest Elizabeth. She tapped her pen against her desk while she thought about what else she might do or who else she might call. Nothing came to mind.

She thought about the problem all morning. It was a slow morning. New Year's Eve was always slow. It irritated her that Jack had insisted they keep the office open until one, especially since she was the one with floor duty.

A few minutes before one, the phone rang. She rolled her eyes and considered letting the answering service pick it up, then she thought, what the hell, and grabbed the receiver. "Turner Realty. This is Elizabeth."

"Aunt Elizabeth?" It was Erin.

"Hi, sweetie."

"Aunt Elizabeth," Erin said in a strangled voice, "I hate it here. Please let me come and live with you. Please." She started to cry.

Elizabeth murmured soothingly. When Erin's crying subsided, she asked gently, "Did something happen?"

"No. I just can't stand it here anymore. Patrick likes Kendall better than he likes me, and now I think Daddy does, too. I want to live with you."

Elizabeth considered how to answer. Her first instinct was to tell Erin that much as she'd love for her to come and live with her, it wouldn't be possible, because Erin's father would never permit it. Elizabeth wasn't at all sure she *would* love it. Yes, she cared for Erin and she was concerned about her, and she would have loved to be her stepmother, but having her here and coping with her alone—that was quite another story. So she answered cautiously.

"Nothing would give me greater pleasure than to have you come and stay with me, Erin, but I don't think your dad would let you. He *does* love you, you know."

"He'd probably be glad to get rid of me," Erin said bitterly.

"Now, sweetie, don't say that. Your father is probably just torn right now. After all, he has to try to make Abbie happy."

"I hate her," Erin said.

Elizabeth smiled. No more than I do, she thought.

"Will you just *talk* to him?"

Maybe she should. After all, if Erin *were* to come stay with her, even for a while, wouldn't that be the perfect way to put a wedge between Logan and Abbie, for wouldn't Logan blame Abbie for driving away his adored daughter? Elizabeth was sure it was Erin's imagination that her father preferred Kendall, but in this instance the child's paranoia could work to Elizabeth's advantage. "Well . . ."

"Please, Aunt Elizabeth."

"Well," Elizabeth said, purposely filling her voice with reluctance, "if you really want me to . . ."

"Oh, I do! I do!"

"All right, sweetie. I'll talk to him tomorrow."

Erin sighed. "Thank you, Aunt Elizabeth. I-I love you."

When she hung up the phone, Elizabeth no longer felt frustrated and she no longer cared whether she ever found out how Abbie and Logan had originally met. Soon that would be a moot point, anyway.

Thirty-one

Abbie came home resolved to talk to Logan about their situation. As much as it would hurt her to leave him, she had pretty much come to the conclusion that everyone would be better off if she did.

If he loved her, everything would be different. Just knowing he loved her would make her stronger and better able to cope with Erin's rejection.

But Logan didn't love her. He liked her, yes, she could see that. And for a while, she had thought friendship would be enough. And maybe it would have been, if only Erin loved her.

If. Such a little word to hold such power.

Face it, Abbie. Neither one of them loves you. And it doesn't look as if they ever will.

All right. She *would* face it. She would face it head-on. She would talk to Logan tonight. It would be the perfect opportunity. Patrick was baby-sitting for Glenna and Paul and was spending the night. Kendall and Erin had been invited to a sleepover at a classmate's house and wouldn't be back until midday tomorrow. So Abbie and Logan would be alone. Earlier, he'd asked her if she wanted to go out to celebrate the New Year, but she'd told him no. She had no desire to join all the crazies out on the road.

"Good," he'd said. "I've always hated going out for New Year's. We'll order some take-out Chinese and open a bot-

tle of champagne and watch the ball drop in Times Square.
How does that sound?"

"It sounds wonderful." But she felt none of the excitement an evening alone with Logan would have produced a
few weeks earlier. All she could think about was the very
real possibility that tonight would be the last night she'd
ever spend with him, alone or otherwise.

Her mind shied away from all the new problems her leaving him would create. Erin would be happy, yes, but Kendall
would be crushed. And Abbie and Logan would be right
back where they started, with neither having access to their
birth child.

And yet, what else was there to do? This was an un-
healthy climate for all of them—a no-win situation. And in
a no-win situation, the best anyone could do was the thing
that caused the least harm. And the thing that would cause
the least harm was for Abbie to remove herself from this
household.

Kendall would be okay, she told herself. She would still
see Logan whenever he wanted. As far as Erin was concerned, Abbie knew she'd have to content herself with hearing about her birth daughter from Logan, with maybe an
occasional glimpse from afar.

The children were gone by five.

Abbie showered and changed into the dark blue crushed
velvet pants and top that had been Laura's Christmas pre-
sent to her, spritzed herself with a generous amount of Plea-
sures, her favorite perfume, fluffed her hair, and took pains
with her makeup. After all, she told herself wryly, if she
was going down, she might as well go down looking her
best.

Logan had showered and changed into casual khakis and
a soft rust-colored sweater earlier. As always, he looked better than any man had a right to look.

He smiled at her when she walked out into the living
room. "You look nice."

"Thanks." She knew she was blushing, and she was irritated with herself. *He's just being polite.*

"Hungry yet?" he said as he switched on the news.

"A little."

"As soon as the news is over, I'll go pick up our food."

"Okay."

Abbie tried to concentrate on what the newscaster was saying, but her mind kept veering back to the upcoming conversation, and her gaze kept moving from the TV screen to Logan. Why did he have to be such a great guy? she thought with mounting sadness. And why do we have to be caught in this impossible mess?

By the time the newscast was over, she was near tears. Maybe she should talk to Logan now. Just get it over with. When he got up, saying, "Should I get the usual? Or do you want something different tonight?" she almost stopped him. Almost said, wait, don't go yet, we have to talk. *At least let the poor guy eat first.* "The usual's fine," she said instead.

Five minutes later he was gone. And thirty minutes after that, he was back. Abbie had set the dining room table, knowing that's what Logan would expect.

"I'll put on some music while we eat," he said.

"All right."

He selected Puccini, and the first piece, a melancholy aria of trembling violins and violas, seemed a fitting accompaniment to the aching torment in Abbie's heart.

While she transferred the food from the take-out cartons into serving dishes, Logan lighted the candles and poured them each a flute of champagne.

Abbie couldn't help thinking how romantic the scene would appear to someone looking in the window. The old cliché about appearances being deceiving was all too true in this case.

She did her best to do justice to the General Tso's Chicken and Moo Shu Pork, but she had no appetite. She kept watching Logan's hands as he ate—she was afraid to look at his face, afraid of what he'd see in hers. He had such beautiful hands. An artist's hands, with long, sensitive fingers. A sudden vision of those hands moving across her body caused her to experience a pain so sharp, she nearly cried out.

"Abbie," he said softly, laying down his fork. "What's wrong?"

The tears that had been so close to the surface all day threatened to spill. Abbie fought them. She had promised herself she would not cry. But the fight was in vain. She bowed her head, swallowing hard. And she could feel the tears coming, coming . . .

"Abbie . . ." He reached over, clasping her hand.

Don't! It was an agonized inner cry. If he touched her, she knew she would completely fall apart. But she didn't have the strength or the willpower to pull away. Nor could she speak.

Later, she would not be able to pinpoint exactly what happened or how it happened. One moment she was shaking and trying to gain control of her emotions, and the next she was standing and Logan's arms were around her, and he was murmuring against her hair.

It felt so good to be held. For a while, she just absorbed the comforting sense of closeness and the knowledge that he cared that she was unhappy. But soon other senses awakened, other feelings emerged and took over, and she was aware of how hard his chest was against the softness of hers, of the intricate design of their bodies and the way they fit together, of the smell of him—clean yet masculine—and yes, of those hands, those strong, supple hands against her back.

Yearning filled her, and involuntarily she pressed herself closer.

"Abbie," he whispered. His mouth moved against her hair, and then, slowly, oh, so slowly, drifted down. He kissed her lightly at first, then, as her mouth opened under his, with more urgency.

Logan . . .

As one kiss turned into another and yet another, as those hands she'd dreamed of roamed her body, Abbie was only aware of how much she loved and wanted this man. She was on fire from the wanting, and every kiss, every touch, fueled that fire. All else—her fears, her confusion, her torment—was wiped from her mind and all that remained was this blazing need.

When he took her hand and led her from the dining room to the bedroom, it seemed like the most natural thing in the world. Without speaking, they undressed, helping each other. And then they were lying together on the bed, and he was kissing her and touching her in all the ways she'd only dreamed of. Her breasts, her belly, her thighs, and then her secret places.

Slow hands.

The thought drifted through her. He had wonderful, slow hands. Lover's hands. She felt as if she were floating, as if these exquisite sensations couldn't possibly be real, and that feeling was intensified by the Puccini playing in the background and the moonlight silvering the room and spilling over their bodies.

Oh, God, was there ever anything more wonderful than this? she thought as the need built higher and higher, as his kisses and his hands became more demanding. When he entered her, pushing deep and hard, she gasped.

"Abbie." His voice was rough, filled with desire. He began to move.

I love you. I love you. It was her only thought as her body strained to meet his. *I love you.* And then, like a giant starburst, her body erupted with a shattering climax that took her breath away, and seconds later, after one last thrust, he cried out with his own.

When it was over, when the last spasms had passed, and their breathing had slowed, and their hearts had calmed, Logan put his arms around her and cradled her close. "I've wanted this for a long time," he said.

"Me, too," she whispered.

She still could hardly believe it had actually happened. Logan had made love to her. They had made love to each other.

He brushed her hair back from her face and kissed her temple. "Now do you want to tell me why you were crying?"

"I don't know . . . I just . . . I was feeling so hopeless about things."

"About Erin, you mean."

She sighed. "Yes." But of course, her hopeless feelings hadn't been just about Erin. They'd been about Logan, too. But now—she could hardly believe it—now everything was different.

"It's going to take more time than we thought for her to come around, but she will, Abbie. I'm convinced of it."

"I hope you're right."

His arm tightened around her. "If we hang together, this can work." With his other hand, he turned her face to his. Kissing her gently, he said, "I want it to work."

He hadn't said he loved her, but for the first time since their marriage, Abbie felt a stirring of hope that even that might one day happen. "I want it to work, too."

He smiled. "Good." He kissed her again and then, chuckling, said, "But right now I want something else." Taking her hand, he guided it down.

When Abbie first awakened, she felt disoriented. Something was different. And then, in a glorious torrent, everything that had happened the night before came rushing back.

She stretched, her body reveling in newfound well-being. Gradually, as her mind came fully awake, she realized she could hear water running. Smiling, she turned over to look at the closed bathroom door. Logan was in the shower.

She almost closed her eyes again. But then the idea of having breakfast ready when he came out took hold, and she scrambled out of bed and grabbed her robe. Unfortunately, her hairbrush was in the bathroom, so all she could do was run her fingers through her hair to make it look more presentable.

Fifteen minutes later, when Logan emerged from the master wing, the coffee was almost ready, and the first batch of pancakes sizzled on the griddle.

"Smells good," he said, walking over to her. He slipped his hands around her waist and nuzzled her neck. "Happy New Year."

Pure happiness flooded Abbie. "Happy New Year," she returned breathlessly.

"I think it's going to be a good one."

He smelled so good, she thought distractedly. Of soap and toothpaste and something else, something wonderful that was pure male. "Um, would you mind watching the pancakes while I go brush my hair and teeth?" She felt shy suddenly, and yet he didn't seem to feel awkward at all.

"Be glad to."

By the time she returned to the kitchen, she was more in

control. She'd not only brushed her teeth and hair, she'd washed her face, put on some lipstick, and hastily donned jeans and a red sweater.

While she was gone, Logan had set the table and put out butter and syrup. He'd also poured a mug of coffee for her, and Abbie was amazed to see he knew how she liked it, with Coffeemate and two packets of sweetener.

They ate their breakfast to the accompaniment of CNN—although Abbie couldn't have repeated a single word the newscasters said; she was too conscious of Logan across from her, too aware of how different things were this morning than they had been, and too caught up in her own world at the moment to care much about outside events. When they were finished with breakfast, Logan said, "You relax and have another cup of coffee. I'll clean up the dining room."

It was only then that Abbie remembered they'd never gone back to their meal the night before. She could feel her face heating. "I'll help," she said quickly.

Together they made short work of the cold food and dirty plates and utensils. Good thing, too, because it wasn't ten minutes after they'd finished putting the dining room in order that Patrick came breezing in.

"Hey, you're home early," Logan said.

"Yeah, Uncle Paul decided it was nice enough to play golf today, so he brought me on the way." He sniffed. "Do I smell pancakes?"

Logan laughed. "Pancakes don't smell."

"Sure they do."

"Didn't your aunt feed you?"

Patrick's grin was sheepish. "Yeah. We had eggs and stuff, but I love pancakes."

"Oh, come on," Abbie said. "I'll mix up some more batter." She liked Patrick. He was a good kid—a boy to be proud of. She felt they were friends.

Logan smiled and said he was going out to the garage to work on Erin's bike, which had a flat. After feeding Patrick, Abbie busied herself making the bed and cleaning up the bathroom. She couldn't believe how great she felt today. It was amazing what good sex did for you. Good sex? It had been terrific sex. Yet she knew her feelings stemmed just as much from the knowledge that Logan had wanted to make love to her as from the actual lovemaking itself. She was so happy right now she even felt capable of dealing with Erin, who would be home soon.

Less than an hour later, the girls arrived. Kendall was bubbling over with stories of what had gone on at their party and sleepover. Erin, although she didn't head straight for her room, said little.

"Didn't you have fun, pumpkin?" Logan asked, ruffling her hair.

"It was okay. Um, did Aunt Elizabeth call?"

"Aunt Elizabeth? No. Why? Was she supposed to?"

Erin shrugged and evaded her father's eyes. "I don't know. I just thought she might."

What was this all about? Abbie wondered. Some of her happiness faded. Anytime Elizabeth was mentioned, it always meant trouble. "You know what I was thinking?" she said brightly.

"What?" Kendall said.

"Well." Abbie smiled at Kendall, then turned to Erin. "Since school starts back again tomorrow, and since your dad and brother will probably spend the day watching football, I thought I'd take you girls to a movie."

"Oh, goodie," Kendall said.

"I have stuff to do," Erin said.

"Come on, Erin," Abbie said, "whatever it is, it can wait. We'll have fun. I'll even let you and Kendall pick the movie."

Erin shook her head. "I can't go."

When her face closed like that, Abbie knew it was useless to argue. She glanced at Logan and could see he was getting ready to say something. Giving him a mute appeal, she shook her head.

"I still want to go," Kendall said.

Abbie sighed. "Why don't we wait until Saturday? Maybe then Erin can go with us."

Kendall turned and glared at Erin. "She'll probably be *too busy* on Saturday, too." Then, mumbling something about her room, she stalked off.

"You know, Erin," Logan said, "I'm getting mighty tired of this atti—"

"No, Logan," Abbie interrupted, "if she doesn't want to go, she doesn't want to go. It's all right." Abbie knew she'd blundered. It wasn't fair to Kendall to constantly cater to Erin. "But I think Kendall and I will go anyway."

She could hear Logan say something else to Erin as she walked back to Kendall's room, and a moment later, a red-faced Erin rushed past on her way to her own room, and a few seconds later, her door slammed.

Oh, God. No matter what I do, it's wrong. "Kendall." Abbie rapped softly on the door.

"What?" came the muffled reply.

Abbie opened the door. Kendall was sitting on her bed. She wasn't crying, but she looked as if she might at any moment.

"Honey, I'm sorry. I changed my mind. Let's you and me go to the movie."

Kendall's shoulders slumped. "It's okay if you don't want to go."

"No, I *do* want to go. We haven't spent any time alone together in weeks. It'll be fun." She forced herself to smile convincingly.

Kendall brightened immediately. "Okay. Are we going now?"

"Let me go check the paper for the times, then we'll decide."

When Abbie walked out to the family room, Logan was standing looking out the French doors. He turned, and their eyes met. "I intend to talk to her," he said. "This behavior is inexcusable."

Abbie nodded. "All right. But why don't you wait until Kendall and I leave?"

An hour later, she and Kendall were driving through Memorial Park, on their way downtown, having decided on a movie playing at the Angelika Film Center located in the theater district.

"Mom?" Kendall said as they approached the light at Westview.

"What?" Abbie braked and turned to smile at Kendall.

"I'm glad Erin didn't come today."

Abbie didn't know what to say.

"I know I'm supposed to like her, 'cause she's my step-sister and all, but I don't."

"Oh, honey, I wish you wouldn't say things like that."

"I don't care, Mom. She doesn't like *me*, so why should I like *her*?"

When Kendall frowned, she automatically stuck out her lower lip, a habit Abbie had always found endearing. "Kendall, I know it's hard, but try to understand how Erin feels. Me marrying her dad has been very hard on her. Think about it. She lost her mother, and now—with you and me on the scene—it must seem as if she's losing her father, too."

"That's stupid. I'm not taking her father, and neither are you. He's still there. And the reason she lost her mother isn't because her mother didn't love her, it's because her mother died. What if she was *me*?" Her voice turned bitter. "*My* father didn't die. He just doesn't want me."

Abbie had imagined she was over hating Thomas, but Kendall's words—and the reminder that Kendall would never completely get over Thomas's rejection—caused that old, familiar anger to ignite.

All through the movie, Abbie kept remembering the look on Kendall's face and the way her voice had sounded when she'd said her father didn't want her.

All this time I've been worrying about Erin and thinking Kendall was okay. But now I know she'll never be okay until she's told the truth . . . and maybe not even then.

The happiness of the morning seemed naive. For could Abbie ever be truly happy if her girls weren't?

Thirty-two

Elizabeth couldn't call Logan until nearly five. She hoped they didn't have company and that he would answer the phone and not Abbie. He did. "Happy New Year," she said.

"Happy New Year to you, too."

"Listen, Logan, I must talk to you, but I don't want to do it over the phone. May I come over?"

He didn't answer immediately. And when he did, his voice was subdued. "Can it wait? This isn't a good time."

"No, I don't think it can wait. It concerns Erin."

"What about Erin?"

"I really don't want to discuss this over the phone. But if you must know, she called me."

"Today?" he asked sharply.

"No, yesterday."

He was silent for a moment, then she heard him sigh. "All right, Elizabeth. Come on over."

"I'll be there in an hour."

Exactly one hour later, Logan ushered her in. Walking back to the living room, she saw it was empty. "Where is everyone?"

"Abbie and Kendall went to see a movie."

"What about Patrick and Erin?"

"Patrick's at a friend's house and Erin's back in her room, sleeping. I just checked on her. I guess she was up half the night."

"I'm glad everyone's gone, because what I wanted to talk to you about is sensitive." Elizabeth lowered her voice sympathetically. "She was very upset when she called me yesterday. She wants to come and live with me."

"What?" Logan looked stunned.

"I'm sorry, Logan, I know this must be hard for you to hear, but she just doesn't like Abbie." When he didn't say anything, she went on. "She's not fond of Kendall, either, which I can certainly understand."

His jaw tightened. "Just what do you mean by that?"

"Now, don't get mad. I know you like the child, but she's just a little *too* perfect. I have a feeling that underneath all that perfection, she's calculating. She knows exactly which buttons to push."

"*Cal*culating? *Kendall?* That's the most ridiculous thing I've ever heard."

His vehemence took Elizabeth aback. "You're very quick to defend her, aren't you?"

"When she's the object of unfair accusations, yes."

"Well," she said, figuring it was time to back off that subject, "I didn't come here to talk about Kendall. It's Erin's welfare that concerns me. I've given this a lot of thought, and I think it would be good for her to come and live with me for a while."

He shook his head. "I know you mean well, and I appreciate your concern, but letting Erin live with you would only be postponing the inevitable. Eventually she would have to come back home, because this is where she belongs. With me and Abbie."

"You refuse to even consider the idea?"

"Yes, I do."

"I thought you were a bigger person than this. I thought you'd put Erin's welfare before your own, but I guess I was wrong." She could see her words bothered him. "My sister would be sick about what you're doing," she continued, pressing her advantage.

"Ann would understand. In my place, she'd have done the same thing."

"Oh, I don't *think* so. She would *never* have brought another man into this house if her children didn't like him.

Never. Her children were much more important to her than her own gratification."

"Elizabeth, please," he said wearily. "I know how it looks, but you don't have all the facts. Nobody does. If you did, you'd understand." He stopped. Seemed to be thinking about something. "Look. I'm going to tell you something, but first I must have your promise that you won't say anything to anyone about this. It's very important."

"Well, of course, I promise. I'd never repeat anything you told me in confidence."

"Once I tell you, you'll understand everything, and then I hope you'll help Erin adjust to life here instead of encouraging her in her unhappiness."

"I've never encouraged her. Coming to live with me was her idea."

"I'm not accusing you of anything. I'm just saying I hope you'll use your influence with her to help make things easier and better for her at home. She looks up to you, you know."

"Yes, we're very close."

He nodded, then ran his hands through his hair the way he always did when he was nervous or upset. A long moment went by. "Maybe I should wait until I can talk to Abbie before I tell you this."

Elizabeth frowned. "What does Abbie have to do with it? Erin is *your* daughter, not hers."

He took a deep breath. "Well, see, that's where you're wrong. Abbie is Erin's birth mother."

Elizabeth's eyes widened. She could not have heard him correctly. "You . . . you mean you *adopted* Erin?"

"No." He shook his head. "Ann and I thought Erin was ours. But the babies were accidentally switched in the hospital."

"The babies," Elizabeth repeated. "You mean . . . ?"

"Yes. Kendall was born to Ann and me. She's actually my daughter. And Erin was born to Abbie and her husband. So, you see, Abbie has everything to do with Erin, because Abbie is her mother."

A strangled gasp from the direction of the children's wing

caused Elizabeth and Logan to turn. And there, standing in the hallway, staring at them in horror, was Erin.

"Erin," Logan said hoarsely. He started toward her.

"No," she said, shaking her head back and forth. "*Noooooooooo*, she's *not* my mother! She's not! You're lying!"

"Baby . . ." By now Logan had reached her, and he tried to put his arms around her, but she flailed at him hysterically.

"My mommy's dead, she's *dead*, and she loved me! She told me I was her special angel and she'd always, always love me, no matter what." Tears gushed out of her eyes.

"Erin, sweetheart, of course she loved you." Logan managed to get his arms around her.

Elizabeth's mind was racing. She could hardly believe what Logan had just disclosed. *Kendall* was his daughter! No wonder he'd gotten so testy when she'd criticized Kendall, but how was *she* to know? Now that she *did* know, she wondered how she could possibly have missed the signs. No *wonder* Logan had married Abbie!

Erin still wept uncontrollably while Logan continued to try to calm her with soothing words.

Elizabeth couldn't think what to do.

And at just that moment, the front door opened, and Abbie and Kendall walked in.

Abbie took in the scene with uncomprehending eyes. But the moment Logan's eyes met hers over the weeping child in his arms, she knew. For one heart-stopping moment, there was silence as they stared at each other.

And then Erin, whose face had been buried against Logan's, looked up and saw Abbie. Face twisting, she moaned.

"Erin," Abbie whispered. Her eyes filled with tears. Blindly, she reached for Kendall. Her world was about to be turned upside down, too.

"Well, *this* is a fine mess, isn't it?"

Abbie swiveled. She had forgotten Elizabeth was there.

Logan looked at Elizabeth. "Listen, Elizabeth, maybe you'd better leave. I'll call you later."

At his words, Erin wrenched herself from his grasp and

flew to Elizabeth's side. "Take me with you, Aunt Elizabeth. I don't want to stay here." She flung her arms around Elizabeth. "I want to go with you."

"I . . ." Elizabeth looked at Logan helplessly.

Abbie's legs felt weak. *Please, God, help us.*

"Erin," Logan said. He walked over and, with Elizabeth's aid, gently unwound Erin's arms.

"Aunt Elizabeth," she cried.

"C'mon, sweetheart. Let's go back in your room and talk." He looked at Abbie with a question in his eyes.

She nodded. Yes, that's what needed doing right now. Logan was the only one besides Elizabeth that Erin would want. Later, when she was calmer, Abbie would try to talk to her. But for now Abbie needed to take Kendall into *her* room and try to explain things.

Elizabeth hurriedly gathered up her purse. It was obvious to Abbie that she was relieved to be going.

"Mom," Kendall said once Elizabeth was gone and Logan and Erin had gone back to her room, "what's wrong with Erin?" Her eyes were filled with concern.

"Let's go to your room, honey. I'll explain everything."

Abbie prayed for strength. When they reached Kendall's room, she sat down next to Kendall on the bed and took her hand. Slowly, she began to tell Kendall the story. At first, she wasn't sure Kendall understood what she was saying, because except for never taking her eyes from Abbie's face, she didn't react.

"So you see, honey, Logan really *is* your dad. And he's loved you from the moment he first saw you."

"But . . ." Kendall seemed bewildered. "But doesn't that mean you're not my mom?"

She swallowed, and Abbie knew she was fighting tears.

"Oh, honey." Abbie put her arms around Kendall. "I may not have given birth to you, but I'm your mom and I'll always *be* your mom." Kendall had started to cry, and Abbie tightened her hold, very close to tears herself. "I love you so much. I'll always love you."

They sat holding each other while Kendall absorbed the things Abbie had revealed. Finally she sighed shakily and pulled back. Her green eyes were still watery, but now there was an expression of awe, too. "That means Patrick's my brother," she said in wonder. "I have a brother."

"Yes, sweetheart, you do."

For the first time since Abbie had begun her tale, Kendall smiled. "I've always wanted a brother." Her smile got bigger. "You know, lots of people have said me and Patrick look like each other. And that's 'cause he's my *brother*!"

"Yes, you look very much alike." Abbie smiled gently. "You look like your father, too, you know."

"This . . . this means my dad really does love me, doesn't it?" Kendall said in wonder. " 'Cause the man I thought was my dad *isn't* my dad."

"No," Abbie said. "Thomas isn't your dad. And yes. Your real father loves you very much."

"But . . ." Kendall's smile faded. "What about Erin? Isn't . . ." She hesitated. "Isn't Thomas *her* dad?"

"No," Abbie said fiercely. "Logan is her father just as much as he's yours. Just like I'm your mother just as much as I'm hers."

Kendall thought about this for a while, and gradually her happy smile returned. "You're right," she said. "And that means Erin and I are kind of like real sisters, aren't we? And . . . and it also means we're a real family."

"Yes, darling. That's exactly what it means." Abbie's heart was so full of thankfulness. It was going to be all right. Oh, Abbie wasn't foolish enough to believe Kendall wouldn't still have some bad moments, but basically Kendall would be fine.

Now if only the same could be said of Erin.

The rest of the day was an exhausting ordeal for everyone. After leaving Kendall, Abbie joined Logan in Erin's room. But Erin didn't want to hear anything Abbie had to say—she kept covering her ears and shaking her head. Finally Abbie knew it was doing more harm than good to keep trying to talk to her. With a heavy heart, she left Logan with the traumatized child and rejoined Kendall.

A little later, Logan knocked on Kendall's door, and there was an emotional scene with the two of them, but at least this was a happy scene. Soon after that, Patrick came home, and Logan sat down with him and explained everything that had happened since he'd left.

"You mean Kendall is really my sister?" Patrick said in a dazed voice.

"Yes, son." Logan went on to emphasize how important it was that Patrick not let Erin think this made any difference in the way he felt about her.

"Dad, I'd never do that." Patrick ducked his head, obviously embarrassed. "It doesn't make any difference. I love Erin."

Logan's eyes looked suspiciously wet as he embraced his son. "I know you do, son. And I love you both."

"But it *is* neat that Kendall's my sister, too. I liked her from the first."

Abbie's own tears weren't far from falling throughout. She brought Kendall out then, and she and Patrick exchanged shy hugs. Logan tried to get Erin to join them, but she refused. Then Patrick tried to talk to Erin, but she did the same thing to him she'd done to Abbie—put her hands over her ears and refused to listen. Over and over she kept saying she wanted to go and stay with her aunt Elizabeth.

It hurt Abbie terribly to see the torture Erin was going through. And it frightened her when she thought about what would happen when it finally hit Erin that her beloved Aunt Elizabeth wasn't really her aunt at all.

At eight o'clock Logan told Abbie he was going to call Lois Caldwell and tell her there was a family crisis and the girls would not be in school the following day. He said he thought both Kendall and Erin needed some time to get used to everything before they had to face their schoolmates.

"The truth is bound to get out," he explained, "and it'll be difficult for them."

Abbie agreed. Patrick's school wasn't starting until the day after tomorrow, so he would be home, too.

After talking with Lois Caldwell, Logan called the therapist who had treated Erin after Ann died and left a message for her, asking her to call him in the morning.

It was only then Abbie thought about her mother. She would have to go and see Katherine tomorrow.

At ten o'clock, completely wrung out, Logan and Abbie

went to each child's room to say good night. Abbie was determined to tell Erin how much she loved her, whether Erin wanted to hear the words or not. But Erin was asleep, so Abbie contented herself with kissing her cheek and whispering, "I love you, baby."

That night, Logan and Abbie didn't make love. She didn't really expect that they would—certainly *she* wasn't in the right frame of mind, not when her child was in such pain. They did, however, sleep in the same bed, and Logan held her close for a long moment. Then, kissing her cheek, he said, "Try to sleep, Abbie."

It wasn't easy. Abbie lay awake for a long time, and she could tell by Logan's breathing that he wasn't having any easier time falling asleep than she was.

When the alarm went off at eight the next morning, Abbie groggily reached for it. Logan groaned and swung his legs out of bed. "I feel like hell," he said.

"I know."

After putting on her robe and thrusting her feet into slippers, Abbie shuffled out to the kitchen to put the coffee on. A few minutes later, Logan joined her. Rex, who had been sleeping on the floor in their bedroom, was panting at the back door. Mitzi sat in a patch of sunlight watching him.

Logan let the dog out. "Hey," he said, bending down to scratch the cat behind her ears, "what are you doing out here?" Mitzi always slept at the foot of Erin's bed and never emerged from her room until Erin herself came out.

Abbie would never know why, but his words caused a frisson of unease. As he straightened up, his eyes met hers. Her disquiet must have communicated itself, because he frowned. Saying, "I'll go check on Erin," he headed for the bedrooms.

A moment later, his shout caused Abbie's heart to turn over. Dropping the bread she was about to put in the toaster, she ran back to Erin's room. Logan stood in the middle of the room, his face white.

"She's gone," he said in a choked voice. "Erin's run away."

Thirty-three

Abbie gasped, her hand flying to her mouth. She looked around frantically. At first glance, the room didn't look any different. But then Abbie saw that Erin's favorite Beanie Baby, Congo, was no longer occupying the place of honor on top of her computer monitor, and her old Raggedy Ann doll, the one she'd had since she was a toddler, wasn't propped against her bed pillows— a place she'd always occupied.

"Her duffel bag isn't in her closet," Logan said. "I looked."

"Maybe she just went to Elizabeth's." But Abbie was so afraid.

"Elizabeth's. Of course. That's probably it." Some of the color returned to his face. He snatched up Erin's phone and quickly punched in some numbers.

"Elizabeth," he said after a minute, "it's Logan. Please pick up." He tapped his foot impatiently as he waited. "Elizabeth. Hi. Listen, is Erin there? No? Jesus." He shook his head at Abbie, mouthing, *She's not there.* "She's gone, that's why I'm calling. No. No. I don't know. No, don't come over here. Stay by your phone, because if she calls anyone, it'll be you. Yes. Yes, I'll call you back." He pressed the disconnect button, then punched in new numbers.

Abbie watched helplessly. She knew she should be doing something but she couldn't think what.

"Paul?" Logan was saying. "Paul, Erin's run away. Has

she called there?" Logan closed his eyes. "She found out about the switch, and she was very upset last night. She must have sneaked out after we fell asleep."

Abbie heard noise behind her and turned to see both Kendall and Patrick.

"What's wrong?" Patrick said, his eyes frightened.

"Mom?" Kendall said. Her eyes were enormous.

Abbie quickly told them what had happened. Both looked stricken by the news.

"Jeez," Patrick said angrily. "Why'd she go and do a dumb thing like that?" But the expression in his eyes belied his critical tone. He was scared. "I shoulda talked to her last night, no matter *what* she said."

Kendall looked as if she were going to burst into tears at any moment.

Abbie put one arm around Patrick's shoulders and one arm around Kendall's. "Listen," she said fiercely, "neither of you is to blame. What's happened isn't something you could have prevented. Maybe your dad and I might have been able to do more last night, but this *is not your fault.*" *No, but it's yours.* Pushing the thought away, she added with a confidence she didn't feel, "She can't have gone far. We'll find her." *Please, please God, keep her safe. Don't let anything bad happen to her. Help us find her quickly.*

Trying to tamp down her own fear, she steered Kendall and Patrick back to their respective bedrooms. "Why don't you guys get dressed and then come and have some breakfast?"

She figured giving them something concrete to do was the best way to calm them both, and the ploy seemed to work. Heading back to Erin's room, she stood in the doorway and waited for Logan to get off the phone.

Wearily, he broke his connection. "So far, no luck."

Abbie bit her lip. "Do . . . do you think you should call the police?"

He nodded. "I'm going to, but I don't think they can do anything officially, not until she's been missing twenty-four hours. But maybe they can give me some suggestions. First, though, I'll call her friends."

Thirty minutes later Logan, with Patrick's help, had called

every school friend they could think of with no luck. Finally, all other avenues exhausted, Logan called the police. The officer he talked to was very sympathetic and helpful. When Logan got off the phone, he told Abbie what the man had said, and in the middle of his report, Glenna and Paul showed up.

"We dropped Megan at Mom and Dad's," Glenna said. She hugged Logan hard, then threw her arms around Abbie. "Oh, God, Abbie," she said with tears in her eyes, "this is so awful. Where could she have gone?"

"I don't know." Abbie swallowed against the lump in her throat.

Logan started telling Paul what the police officer had told him. "He wanted to know if she had any money or charge cards. Because if not, he said she had either walked where she was going or she'd hitchhiked."

"Hitchhiked!" Abbie said in horror. There were terrible people out there who preyed on children. Oh, God. What if? But Abbie couldn't finish the thought. It was too frightening. Erin would be okay. She *had* to be okay.

"*Did* she have any money?" Glenna asked.

"She has a savings account, but she couldn't have gotten her money out in the middle of the night," Logan said.

"There's her bear bank," Patrick said. "She must have had a hundred dollars in it the last time she counted it."

"That's right," Logan said. "I'll go check it."

When he returned to the kitchen, his face was grim. "It's empty."

"So she could have taken a bus somewhere," Glenna said.

"I'll call the bus station," Paul said.

"Use Patrick's phone so we can keep this line open," Logan said.

"Why don't you try the cab companies?" Abbie suggested. "Maybe she called a cab."

"That's a good idea," Glenna said. "I can start doing that. Where's the yellow pages?"

Abbie gave her the phone book.

"You can use my phone, Aunt Glenna," Kendall said.

"Let's divide them up," Logan said. "I'll call some, too."

"What can I do?" Abbie said.

"Stay here by the phone in case she calls," Logan said.

An hour later they knew that Erin had indeed called a cab. The driver picked her up at five o'clock in the morning at the end of the street and drove her to Hobby Airport. Now they were busy calling the airlines to try to find out if she had taken a plane, and if so, where.

It was eleven o'clock before they had their answer. Erin had boarded an eight o'clock flight to St. Louis.

"How the hell does an eleven-year-old buy a ticket?" Logan demanded of the airline representative. "Isn't that irresponsible on your part?"

The ticket agent explained that the ticket had been purchased on-line with a credit card. "We have no way of knowing the age of the person buying the ticket, sir." Logan read off the numbers of the four credit cards he carried. Sure enough, Erin had charged the ticket to one of his VISA cards. "I still don't get it. Wouldn't she have to show some I.D. at the airport?" he fumed when he got off the phone.

Abbie knew he was really angry with himself, blaming himself for what had happened, just as she was blaming herself. After all, what did it matter how Erin had managed to get on a plane? What mattered was finding her.

"You know, Dad," Patrick said slowly. "She has that chat room friend. Allison? You've heard her talk about her."

Logan nodded. "Yes."

"I think Allison lives in St. Louis."

Logan's eyes brightened. "You know, I think she does, too. I remember once Erin said something about how Allison's uncle worked on one of the riverboats. But I don't know her last name. Do you?"

"No." Patrick frowned. "But I'll bet it's in Erin's address book."

"Address book?" Logan said. "I've never seen an address book."

"It's on her computer."

"Oh, that kind."

"Yeah," Patrick said. "And I'll bet we can access it if we try."

Everyone followed Patrick back to Erin's room. He sat down and booted her computer, then searched through her files until he found the address book. Five minutes later, he had Allison's full name and address, including a phone number in St. Louis.

Crossing his fingers, Logan called the number. A moment later, he said, "Mrs. Gibbons? My name is Logan O'Connell. Your daughter Allison is a chat room friend of my daughter Erin's?"

Abbie listened with her heart in her throat. *Please, God.* The expression on Glenna's and Paul's faces told her they were praying, too. Logan's eyes met Abbie's. Slowly, he shook his head. Abbie's heart sank.

"Would you mind if I talked to Allison?" His face fell. "Oh, of course. She's in school."

After giving Allison's mother his phone number and extracting her promise to call him if her daughter knew anything at all, Logan hung up.

"She said she'd call us back after Allison gets home," he said glumly.

Somehow they got through the next five hours. Logan paced, Abbie worried and blamed herself, Glenna and Paul tried to keep their spirits up by constant reassurance that Erin would be all right, and Kendall and Patrick were quieter than Abbie had ever seen them. Just when Abbie was sure none of them could stand the tension a moment longer, Allison's mother called. She told Logan Allison denied knowing anything. Logan asked if he could speak to the child directly.

"Please, Allison, if you hear from Erin," he said, "tell her how much we love her, and ask her to please call us."

"I'm going to St. Louis," Logan said when they'd hung up.

"What will you do when you get there?" Glenna said. "Where will you look?"

"I don't know. Go to the police. Hire an investigator. Hang out at Allison's house. Anything's better than sitting here."

He managed to get a seat on a flight leaving at seven. Leaving Glenna and Paul to call Logan's parents with an update, Abbie followed him back to the bedroom, where he threw some clothes into a suitcase.

"Logan," she said.

"What?" He didn't turn around.

Abbie swallowed. "When you find her, and you *will*, I'm sure of it, tell her it's okay. I'm not going to force myself on her."

He finally looked at her. His eyes were bleak. "Abbie, let's not talk about this now. There'll be plenty of time for talk when I get back."

"I'm just so sorry. I . . . Ever since I've come into your life, I've caused nothing but unhappiness. I wouldn't blame you if you hated me."

"Look, I can't even think straight right now." Grabbing his suitcase, he said, "I've got to go. Otherwise, I won't make the flight."

Long after he was gone, long after Glenna and Paul had left for home, long after Kendall and Patrick were in bed for the night, Abbie sat huddled on the couch in the family room and thought and thought. And just as the first rosy light of dawn crept over the eastern horizon, she came to a decision. She would stay until Logan found Erin. But once she knew Erin was safe, she would take Kendall and leave. Because no matter what anyone said, Abbie knew none of this would have happened if she hadn't tried to force herself into Erin's life.

Erin was curled up in the corner of Allison's dad's tool shed. She'd been there ever since the taxi had dropped her at the corner of Allison's street and Allison had met her and smuggled her into her backyard. At least Allison had managed to sneak out some blankets and food for Erin.

"I'm sorry," she'd said, "that you have to stay here, but if I try to hide you in the house, my mother's sure to find out."

"It's okay," Erin said. But she'd been cold and scared. Especially after it got dark and she could hear all the night sounds around her. She hadn't slept at all. But even if she'd been in a bed inside the house, she wouldn't have been able to sleep. How could she?

But now it was almost light, and pretty soon she would walk to McDonald's and get some breakfast and use their rest room. Allison said the restaurant was only three blocks away.

"And there's a shopping center right down the street from McDonald's. You can stay there until school's out. I'll meet you there, okay?"

"Okay."

So that was the plan. Erin would find somewhere to hang out during the day, and at night she'd stay in the shed. Allison had said she would try to come out to see her before she went to school this morning.

But at seven-thirty Erin heard the sound of the school bus, and she knew Allison was leaving. Allison had warned her the night before that she shouldn't show her face until she heard Allison's mom leave for work. And about ten minutes after the school bus had gone off down the street, Erin heard the click of heels on the driveway and the sound of the garage door going up. A few minutes later, she heard the car starting. Peering out a hole in the shed, Erin saw a blue car backing out of the driveway.

She waited about ten more minutes. Then, feeling it should be safe, she eased the door of the shed open. Taking only her purse, which she wore crossed over her chest, she walked down the driveway and out to the street.

Allison lived in a funny kind of neighborhood, Erin thought. The houses were old, mostly two-story, and they had front porches. Erin couldn't remember ever seeing a front porch on a house in Houston. Plus, there were no fences around the yards. Every house in Houston, practically, had a six-foot wood fence separating it from its neighbors.

Thinking about Houston, she got that awful feeling in her chest again, like she was suffocating. Did they miss her? she wondered. Did they even care that she was gone?

Daddy.

But he wasn't her dad, was he? He was Kendall's dad. Erin's father was some unknown man who lived in China. And her mom . . . Tears clogged her throat. No. She wouldn't think about it. She wouldn't.

Shoving her hands in the pockets of her jacket, she headed for McDonald's. After an Egg McMuffin and a big glass of orange juice, she cleaned up in the rest room, then headed for the shopping center, where she somehow managed to kill the day. And at four, just as she'd said she would, Allison met her in front of the yogurt place.

"Erin," she said breathlessly. She looked like she'd been running. Her cheeks were red, and her dark hair was all messy. "Your dad called yesterday."

"My *dad*? How'd he know where to call?"

"I don't know. But he talked to my mom first, and she asked me about you. And then she called him back, and I talked to him. That's why I didn't try to come out and see you this morning. I'm not sure my mom believed me when I said I didn't know where you were."

Erin's heart was beating too fast. "What did my dad say?" Even though she knew he *wasn't* her dad, she couldn't think how else to refer to him.

"He said if I talked to you to tell you he loved you. And to ask you to please call him."

"I'm not calling him." He wasn't her father, so why should he care about her? He probably just felt guilty.

"But Erin . . ." Allison looked unhappy. "You can't stay in the tool shed forever. What are you going to do?"

"I don't know." Erin stared at the floor. "All I know is, I'm not going back there. Not ever."

Thirty-four

Abbie spent two agonizing days waiting. Drinking coffee and waiting. Thinking and waiting. Berating herself and waiting. Talking to Elizabeth and Glenna and Logan's parents and waiting. And then, on Thursday evening, Logan called.

"I've found her." He sounded exhausted. "She's been at Allison's all along."

"Oh, thank God," Abbie said. "Thank God." Her knees were so weak with relief, she had to sit down.

"She was hiding in the tool shed."

"But I thought her mother—"

"Her mother didn't know. But this afternoon, she caught Allison sneaking food out, and Allison finally broke down and told her everything."

"Is Erin all right? Is everything all right?"

"She's fine physically. I'm not so sure about the rest. But listen, we can talk when I get back. We'll be home tomorrow morning. I couldn't get a flight out tonight. We're coming into Hobby at ten. Will you call everyone and let them know I found her?"

"Yes, of course." If only . . . But what was the use of thinking about what might have been?

Before placing the calls Logan had asked her to make, Abbie went to Patrick's room and told him the good news. He was so happy he gave her an exuberant hug. It was all she could do not to cry in front of him as she realized how much she would miss all of them.

"This is great," he kept saying. Then he added, "But I'm gonna shake her when I see her for scarin' us the way she did. She better never do anything like this again!"

Don't worry. Once I'm gone, she'll be fine.

Logan's parents were overjoyed, as were his sister and brothers. Abbie didn't try to call her mother, who knew nothing about the crisis. She would go and talk to Katherine in person tomorrow—a confrontation she was dreading. Lastly, Abbie called Elizabeth.

"Oh, hello, Abbie," Elizabeth said. "Do you have news?"

"Yes, I do. Logan just called. He's found Erin."

"Oh, thank goodness. I've been so worried."

To give the devil her due, Elizabeth *had* seemed genuinely concerned and had called Abbie at least twice each day Logan had been gone. "Yes, we're all very grateful."

"When will Erin and Logan be home?"

"About noon tomorrow."

"Please tell Erin how much I—No. Never mind. I'll just come over tomorrow and tell her myself."

"I'm sure Erin will like that."

Abbie spent a sleepless night. At three o'clock she finally gave up and got up. After making herself a cup of tea, she huddled in a corner of the sofa and stared out into the moonlit night. Shadows flitted across the courtyard, and even with the doors closed, she could hear the tinkle of the wind chimes and the splash of the fountain.

So lovely, she thought sadly. It would hurt to leave here, it would hurt unbearably, and yet nothing here had ever been hers. Not the house. Not Logan. And not Erin. *I should have known better. I never belonged here.*

She thought about all of Ann's paintings that still graced the house. Yes, Logan had started to take some of them down and she'd stopped him, saying she didn't want to alienate Erin any more than she already was, and certainly removing her mother's paintings would only fuel Erin's resentment and dislike.

She didn't cry. Tears wouldn't help. Right now she needed to be strong, if not for her sake, then for Kendall's.

At six o'clock, she went up to her office and typed a note of explanation for Logan. She sealed it into an envelope, wrote his name on the outside, took it to the master bedroom and propped it on the dresser where he'd be sure to see it.

By now it was time to awaken the children. After Patrick's carpool picked him up, Abbie drove Kendall to Caldwell, then returned to the house and calmly packed enough of hers and Kendall's clothes to last until she could make arrangements for the remainder of their things to be moved back to her house. She loaded everything into the trunk of her car, then went back inside to talk to Serita.

The housekeeper listened gravely as Abbie explained that she and Kendall were moving back to their old place. Abbie saw the questions in the other woman's eyes, but she didn't ask them and Abbie didn't volunteer anything further. Logan would talk to Serita.

"Mr. O'Connell and Erin will be home about noon. Tell him I left him a note in the bedroom."

And then, dry-eyed and resigned, she climbed into her car and headed for her mother's.

"Abbie! What are you doing here? Is something wrong?"

It didn't surprise Abbie that her mother knew something must be wrong. After all, it was mid-morning, a time Abbie normally would be working. Besides, she always called her mother before coming over, because Katherine was not the kind of person you dropped in on.

"Yes, something's wrong," she said wearily. "And I need to talk to you about it."

Katherine's face drained of color. "N-not Kendall?"

Abbie quickly shook her head. "Kendall's fine. This does concern her, but she's not sick or in trouble or anything."

"Oh, thank God," Katherine said in relief.

By now they had walked into the living room. As Abbie gathered her thoughts, she glanced around. As always, the room looked immaculate. Sunlight slanted through the bay windows onto the parquet floor, which shone from its twice-monthly buffing by Katherine's longtime maid. The Oriental rugs looked freshly vacuumed, the furniture smelled of lemon wax, and the aroma of baking bread drifted in from the kitchen.

"I'll ask Lottie to bring us some coffee," Katherine said.

"No, that's okay, Mother. I don't want any." That's all she needed, more caffeine. She was jittery enough.

Katherine sat in her favorite rocking chair. "Well? Are you going to tell me what's wrong or do I have to guess?"

Abbie sighed. "Tuesday morning Erin ran away."

"Ran *away! Why?*"

"Something happened Monday that upset her terribly. She . . . she overheard a conversation between Logan and Elizabeth."

"Hmmph," Katherine said disdainfully. "*That* woman."

If Abbie hadn't been so sick at heart, she might have been amused by her mother's barely concealed distaste for Elizabeth. Under the circumstances, though, what did it matter? "From what they said," she continued quietly, "Erin learned something that we, Logan and I, were going to tell her, but . . ." Abbie swallowed. "This is so hard."

"Abbie, for heaven's sake, quit beating around the bush. Just tell me."

Abbie closed her eyes for a brief moment of respite. Taking a deep breath, she said, "Erin learned that Logan and his first wife are not her real parents."

"You mean she's adopted and they didn't tell her?"

"No. She's not adopted."

"You're talking in riddles," her mother said impatiently.

"She . . ." Oh, God. Katherine was going to be devastated by Abbie's next disclosure, and Abbie could think of no way to soften the blow. "She also found out that Kendall is Logan's daughter. His and Ann's."

"*What?*" Her mother stopped rocking and leaned forward. "What on earth are you talking about?"

"Oh, Mother, I know how hard this is going to be for you. Believe me, I've been in torment for months over it. The truth is, Kendall and Erin were born in the same hospital, on the same night, during that horrible blizzard. You'll remember. I told you all about it. They were so awfully short-handed that night, and somehow, a terrible mistake was made and my baby—Erin—was given to Logan and Ann, and their baby—Kendall—was given to me."

Katherine shook her head. "That's impossible."

"I'm so sorry, Mother. But I'm afraid it's true."

"It's *not* true!" Katherine's face flushed a deep red, as if she had a fever. She stood, glaring down at Abbie. "It couldn't be true. Kendall is my granddaughter! She *is*! Don't you think I know my own granddaughter?"

Abbie's eyes filled with tears. "I'm sorry," she whispered again.

Katherine's voice, normally so controlled and modulated, shook. "You're *sorry*! You're *sorry*! You come over here, you tell me that my granddaughter is not my granddaughter, and you're *sorry*? You *should* be sorry. Why, Kendall is the spitting image of my grandmother Vickers. You know that. Of *course*, Kendall is ours. I hope you haven't filled *her* head with this nonsense."

Abbie brushed at her tears. "It . . . it's not nonsense. We . . . we had blood tests. Dr. Joplin did them."

"Ned Joplin?" her mother demanded. "He's a party to this . . . this *scam*?"

"It's not a scam," Abbie said sadly. "And to answer your other question, yes, Kendall knows."

Just as if Abbie hadn't spoken, her mother said, "Have you notified the police about Erin?"

"Yes, but they really didn't have a chance to do much. Logan found her. She was in St. Louis, staying with a friend."

"So she's home again?"

"Not yet. But she and Logan will be home this afternoon."

"That's good. Even though she's not a very likable child, I certainly wouldn't have wanted anything to happen to her."

"Mother," Abbie said incredulously, "Didn't you hear what I said? Erin is your *grandchild*. Is that all you have to say about her? That she's not very likable?"

"I don't care what you said. You're wrong, that's all. *Kendall* is my granddaughter."

"Mom," Abbie said softly. She never called her mother Mom. "No matter how many times you deny it, you can't change the truth. Erin is my child. My blood, *your* blood,

Great-grandmother Vickers's blood, runs in her veins. I know you love Kendall. So do I. And she'll always be ours, in all the ways that count. But Erin belongs to us, too." Abbie's voice broke. "And I hope, I pray, that someday she'll let us be a part of her life." Tears slid down her face. "Don't you want that, too?"

Abruptly, Katherine sat back down. She looked suddenly old. Her hands trembled as she raised them to her face. And then she started to cry.

Erin slept through most of the flight home. Looking at her, no one would guess the turmoil they'd all gone through the past couple of days. But the worst was over now. He'd found her.

She'd been overjoyed to see him when he'd picked her up at Allison's house. She had clung to him, crying as he'd told her over and over how frightened he'd been, how he couldn't have borne losing her.

"Don't you know," he'd said, "that you are my daughter in every way that matters? Don't you know how much I love you?"

"I love you, too, Daddy," she'd sobbed.

No mention was made of Abbie or Kendall. Logan figured that could wait until they got home. Somehow, he thought, they would work things out.

The important thing was, Erin was safe, and they were going home.

As her dad drove them from the airport to their house, Erin stared out the window and thought about the last couple of days. She was sorry she'd worried her dad so much. She could see he was telling her the truth when he'd told her how scared they'd all been.

All. She guessed he meant Abbie, too. She still couldn't believe it. Abbie was her real mother. Every part of Erin wanted to deny it. And yet her dad had said it was true. And when she thought about Kendall and how so many people had remarked about her likeness to Patrick, Erin knew it was true.

Tears blurred her eyes. *Mommy.* But the woman she had

loved so much, the woman she'd always believed was her mom, was dead, and her dad had married Abbie, and no amount of wishing was going to make any of these facts change.

And now she was going back home and everything was going to be so different. She had a sick feeling in her stomach as she thought about how everybody now knew about her and Kendall. Aunt Glenna and Uncle Paul. Grandma Celia. Aunt Elizabeth. Tears blurred Erin's eyes. Her Aunt Elizabeth wasn't really her aunt at all. Her bottom lip trembled, and she swallowed hard. She didn't want to start crying.

"Erin?"

Erin hurriedly brushed at her eyes, then turned to look at her dad.

"Sweetheart, we'll be home soon."

"I know," she said in a small voice.

"When we get home, maybe we can all sit down and talk."

She nodded.

Reaching over, he squeezed her hand. "Just remember that we all love you."

If she answered, she knew she *would* start to cry, so she didn't say anything.

"It's going to be okay, honey. It is."

Erin nodded once more, because she knew that's what her dad wanted. But down deep she knew no matter what her dad said, it would never be okay again.

The moment Logan entered the house, he knew something was wrong. One look at Patrick's troubled face told him he was right.

"Abbie and Kendall are gone," Patrick said after hugging Erin.

"Gone? What do you mean?" Logan looked at Serita, who had entered the room.

Serita nodded. "Mrs. O'Connell, she left this morning. She said to tell you there was a note for you in your bedroom."

Logan rushed back to the bedroom. Tearing open the envelope he found propped on the dresser, he read the note:

Dear Logan,

I've thought about this ever since Erin left. Our marriage was a mistake. I thought it would work, and I know you did, too, but obviously, we were wrong. So Kendall and I have left. Don't worry. You can see Kendall whenever you want, for however long you like. I won't stand in your way. And I hope that maybe someday Erin will want to see me, too. But if that doesn't happen, I won't force her. Her happiness is more important than mine.

I'll make arrangements for movers to pick up the rest of my things in a few days. Thank you for everything. You're a wonderful person and a terrific father. The girls are lucky to have you.

Best,

Abbie

Blindly, he sat on the bed. Gone. Abbie and Kendall were gone. Suddenly, his chest felt so tight for a moment he couldn't breath.

"Daddy?"

He looked up. Erin stood in the doorway.

"Daddy, Aunt Elizabeth is here."

Jesus, the last person he felt like dealing with right now was Elizabeth. But he guessed it couldn't be helped. Standing, he shoved Abbie's note in his pocket, then with his arm around Erin, he walked out to the family room.

Thirty-five

"Logan! Oh, it's so wonderful that you found Erin," Elizabeth gushed. "I've told her how worried we were and how happy everyone is now and how much we all love her." She walked over and threw her arms around him.

At first Logan was taken aback by her behavior, but it didn't take more than a moment for him to realize what was behind it. She thought, now that the truth was out and it was so obvious how shaken and upset Erin was, that his marriage would probably not last. And she was letting him know that none of it mattered to her. She still wanted to be Mrs. O'Connell.

So he hugged her back, thanked her, said yes, we're all very thankful, then invited her to sit and visit awhile, even though all he wanted was to think about Abbie's note and try to decide what to do.

"So where is Abbie?" Elizabeth said once she was seated. She beckoned to Erin. "Come sit by me, sweetie."

Curiously, Erin seemed to hesitate. But then she walked to the couch and sat next to Elizabeth, who put a possessive arm around her.

Logan considered an evasive answer, then decided it might simplify everything if he just told the truth. "She's gone."

"Gone?" Her eyes betrayed her excitement.

"Yes. She and Kendall moved back to their house this morning. She left me a note."

By now Elizabeth had managed to conceal her delight, and with a pathetically false look of commiseration and sympathy, she said, "Well, I know you're probably upset, but it's all for the best, I'm sure. After all, Abbie probably realized she didn't belong here and—"

Suddenly Logan couldn't stand another word. Cutting her off, he said, "Whatever Abbie thought, she was wrong. As soon as you leave, I plan to go and get her and Kendall and bring them back, because this is *exactly* where they belong. You see . . ." He looked her straight in the eye. "I love Abbie. And it's not just because she's the mother of my daughters. I didn't realize it before, but when I read the note she left me, everything became clear. I love her, and I don't want to live without her." Realizing how he truly felt about Abbie, and saying the words, made him feel lighter and happier than he had in years.

It was a long moment before Elizabeth replied. And when she did, her voice was flat. "I see. Well, I think you're making a terrible mistake, but if that's the way you feel . . ."

Logan almost felt sorry for her. And yet most of Elizabeth's problems were caused by Elizabeth herself. People who refused to see the truth, who always blamed others for their unhappiness, were doomed to a life of disappointments. A woman like Abbie, on the other hand, who was willing to sacrifice her own happiness for the sake of her child's, was the woman he wanted, and he couldn't wait to tell her so.

After Aunt Elizabeth left, Erin kept thinking about what her dad had said about loving Abbie. It was funny, but knowing this didn't hurt nearly as much as Erin had thought it would.

"Erin," he said softly. "Are you all right?"

Swallowing, she nodded.

"You're not gonna run away again, are you?" Patrick said.

She shook her head. She could tell Patrick had been really scared, because when she'd walked in the door earlier, he'd hugged her so hard he'd nearly squeezed all the breath out of her. It made her feel good to think he cared that much about her. Maybe it really *didn't* make any difference that she wasn't *really* his sister. She knew she'd always think of him as her brother, so maybe he felt the same way. Her dad had said he did.

"You'd better not," Patrick said, coming over to sit by her on the arm of the couch.

"Will you two be all right here while I go and get Abbie and Kendall?" her dad said. Although the question was addressed to both of them, he was looking at her when he asked it.

Erin sighed. "Yes."

"Sure," said Patrick.

"You're okay with this, aren't you, Erin?"

Although she wasn't sure how she felt about anything right now, she said she was.

"All I'm asking is that you give Abbie a chance. A real chance this time. Can you do that?"

After a long moment, she nodded again.

His smile made her feel good, and she resolved that, for her dad's sake, she really would try hard. She knew she would never think of Abbie as her mother—she'd only had one mother and she didn't want another—but maybe it could all work if she just thought of Abbie as her dad's wife.

For the first time in days, she smiled.

Elizabeth didn't cry. She was too angry to cry. This was unbelievable. Why, when she thought of all the hours she'd devoted to Logan and his children! All the evenings and weekends she'd spent providing him a shoulder to cry on. All the *dates* she'd turned down the past three years. And now *this* was the way she was repaid!

Fine, she thought bitterly. If he preferred that skinny, colorless, thoroughly *boring* woman over her, he was welcome to her. They were welcome to each other.

She'd show them. She certainly wouldn't sit around feeling sorry for herself. The next time Brian Keagan, that good-looking loan officer at the mortgage company she preferred to use, asked her out, her answer would be yes. In fact, she might just call Brian tonight and invite him to see the new play at the Alley Theater. It should be a simple matter to get tickets. She could say someone had given them to her. Yes, that's exactly what she'd do.

She would be better off with someone like Brian, anyway. Good grief, did she *really* want to be saddled with three children? Because even if Logan *had* broken up with Abbie, he would still be Kendall's father.

No, she was much better off with Brian or someone like him—someone who was unencumbered. Someone who would put Elizabeth first, where she deserved to be.

By the time she reached her town home, she had convinced herself she was actually lucky things had turned out this way.

Abbie was trying to decide what to do about dinner. She thought it might be a good idea to take Kendall out somewhere, get her mind off everything, for Kendall was upset. Not that Abbie blamed her. One day she gets a new father and brother, and three days later, she's told they aren't going to live with them anymore. That was a lot for a kid to handle.

Abbie herself felt numb. After the traumatic scene with her mother this morning and the equally traumatic one with Kendall this afternoon, Abbie's resources were exhausted. Still, she knew there would be many painful days and nights ahead and she needed her energy.

She wondered what Logan had thought when he'd read her note. She'd kind of expected him to call her, but then she sheepishly realized that would have been impossible. There was no phone here in the old house. It had been disconnected. It was probably just as well. What could Logan have said, anyway? At least this way they would each gain some needed equanimity before they had to face each other again.

Still thinking about Logan, she was walking toward Kendall's room when the doorbell rang. Sighing, she reversed direction. If it was a sales type, she'd make short work of him.

But when she peered out her peephole, she saw not a salesman, but Logan. Her heart contracted, and her thoughts careened wildly. She couldn't do this. Not today. Not now. She was still too raw.

As she stood there trying to think what to do, he rang the doorbell again.

Oh, God. He wasn't going to go away. He wanted to talk, and really, she owed him that much. Telling herself to be strong, to remember whose daughter she was—after all, whether her mother wanted to admit it or not, Abbie *did* have Katherine's determination and pride—Abbie opened the door.

"Hi." She gave him her best smile. "You're back."

"Yes, I'm back."

Something about his smile and the expression in his eyes made her heart knock painfully against her ribs.

"May I come in?"

"Oh, y-yes, yes, of course. I'm sorry. I-I wasn't thinking."

And then, so quickly she hardly had time to absorb it, he stepped inside, put his arms around her, whispered, "Abbie," and then kissed her so deeply and so thoroughly her head spun. When he finally broke the kiss, he held her face in his hands and looked into her eyes.

"You can't leave me, Abbie. I need you. I love you."

Abbie started to cry.

Gathering her close, he stroked her head. "Ah, Abbie, please don't."

"I-I'm sorry." Oh, God, it felt so good here in his arms. So right. If only she could stay here forever. But the specter of Erin's tortured face haunted her.

"When we got home and Patrick said you were gone, I couldn't believe it. Then I read your note. Abbie, it was like somebody had struck me in the heart, and I realized that I don't want to live without you. For better or worse, we're married, and I love you." He drew back, lifting her chin so he could look at her. Searching her eyes, he said, "Do you love me? Even a little bit?"

"Oh, Logan, of course I love you. I've loved you for a long time."

His face broke into a delighted smile and he would have kissed her again. She stopped him with "But . . ."

"But what?"

"But what about Erin?"

312 *Patricia Kay*

"She knows how I feel. I told her and Patrick both. I also told them I was coming over here and I wasn't leaving until you and Kendall came with me."

"What . . ." Abbie swallowed. "What did she say?"

"She said okay."

"She said okay? She's really okay with it?"

"I have to be truthful with you, Abbie. She's not ecstatic or anything, but she understands."

"You're sure? I don't want her to be hurt anymore. I-I can't take my happiness at her expense."

"I know that. But I really think it's going to be okay. She's pretty subdued over everything, and I think she's ready to try to make this work."

"Logan, I . . . As much as I want to believe you, if, when I talk to her, I'm not convinced she really is all right with this, I won't be able to stay."

"She needs you, Abbie. Whether she knows it or not."

She wanted to believe him so badly.

His arms tightened around her. "We all need you."

Oh, God. A person could drown in his eyes. This time when he kissed her, she allowed herself to think that maybe it really could work out.

"Now," he said when he finally released her, "where's Kendall?"

"In her room. She . . ." Abbie sighed. "She was crying when I left her. She was terribly upset about me leaving you."

"No more so than me."

Abbie smiled. "She's probably fallen asleep."

He grinned. "Well, then let's go wake her up and tell her we're going home."

Erin was in her room when the three of them arrived at Logan's house an hour later.

"I'll go get her," Logan said.

He was gone about ten minutes. When he returned, Erin was by his side. Walking straight up to Abbie, she said, "I'm sorry for the things I said, Abbie."

"Oh, Erin, honey, it's all right."

"My dad said it's not all right."

Abbie wanted so much to gather Erin in her arms. To make everything bad in her life go away. But she knew that it was Erin who had to make the first move.

"My dad said he loves you."

"Did he?" Abbie was so close to tears, she wasn't sure she could keep them from coming. Seemed like all she did lately was cry.

"He . . . he also said you weren't going to stay with us unless I . . ." She took a breath. "Unless I was okay with it."

"Yes, that's what I told him." Abbie's eyes met Logan's. In them she saw every emotion she was feeling.

Erin toed the carpet. For a long moment, no one said anything, and the only sound in the room was Rex's breathing. Finally Erin looked up. "I know you're my real mother and all, but you . . . you wouldn't expect me to call you Mom, would you?"

"No, honey. Not unless you wanted to."

"Then . . ." Erin swallowed. She looked at Logan, then back at Abbie. "I guess I'm okay with it."

It wasn't much, Abbie thought, but it was a beginning.

Epilogue

Two years later . . .

"Shall we tell them now?" Abbie asked. "Or wait until just before the party?"

It was the night before Erin's and Kendall's fourteenth birthday party—a joint affair that was taking place at a tea room in the Heights that had just been taken over by a friend of Abbie's mother. Katherine was in charge of the party; she had done a complete about-face since that awful day Abbie had told her the truth about her granddaughter. It had taken a while, but now Abbie's mother introduced the two girls as "my granddaughters" and seemed almost as proud of Erin as she was of Kendall, especially after Erin had won a statewide writing competition last year and been written up in the *Chronicle*.

Katherine had even mellowed toward Abbie, going so far as to compliment her on her appearance only a week ago. Abbie smiled wryly. *I guess she finally thinks I'm doing something right.*

"Let's tell them now," Logan said, putting his arm around her waist and nuzzling her ear. "I can't wait."

Abbie turned her head, and for a long moment, their lips clung.

"I love you," he whispered.

"I love you," she whispered back.

They kissed again, then he playfully patted her behind and went off in search of the kids. While he was gone, she thought about how happy she was. Her life was so different from what it had been before. Sometimes she had to pinch herself to convince herself she wasn't dreaming. Of course, everything wasn't perfect. Erin still kept her emotional distance, although even there, things had improved close to a hundred percent. She had accepted Abbie, and there were even times Abbie felt Erin might be beginning to feel affection for her. Just that morning, in fact, Erin had asked Abbie if she'd mind looking over a short story she'd written. Remembering, Abbie smiled.

Just then, Logan came back to the family room with the three children in tow. Sitting next to Abbie, Logan took her hand. Looking at each child in turn, he said, "Kendall, Patrick, Erin, we have something important to tell you."

"Gee, Dad," Patrick said with a cheeky grin, "the last time you said that was when you and Abbie got married."

Kendall grinned at him, and Patrick winked at her. Sister and brother had developed a deep love for each other, Abbie thought with quiet happiness. As always, her gaze then turned to Erin, whose smile held a combination of puzzlement and trepidation. *Please be happy, baby.* Abbie never worried about Kendall's or Patrick's happiness. Those two were so sure of themselves and such total optimists, life would always go their way. It was Erin—still so vulnerable—that tore at her heart.

As if he knew exactly what she was thinking, Logan squeezed Abbie's hand. He probably *did* know what she was thinking. In the past two years, Kendall and Patrick weren't the only ones who had forged such a close bond.

"C'mon, Dad," Patrick said. "Don't keep us in suspense."

Holding Abbie's hand very tightly, Logan said solemnly, "In six months, our family's going to grow by one."

Abbie held her breath and watched Erin's face. There wasn't any reaction. Obviously, she hadn't understood Logan's meaning.

When none of the children reacted, Logan chuckled. "I guess I have to spell it out. What I'm saying is, we're expecting a baby. You three are soon going to have a baby brother or sister."

"Dad! Cool!" Patrick said with a delighted smile.

"Mom!" Kendall shrieked. She jumped up and ran over

to Abbie, enveloping her in a hug. "That's so great! Oh, I hope you have a little girl."

Abbie hugged her back, but her eyes remained on Erin. Erin seemed bewildered as her gaze moved from Logan to Abbie and back to Logan again. *Please, God. Please let it be okay.*

A long, silent moment went by. Following Abbie's gaze, Kendall turned. Then, as the four of them watched, Erin got to her feet and walked over to the couch. Abbie braced herself. And then, in a moment Abbie knew she would remember always, Erin leaned over and put her arms around Abbie. Abbie was so stunned at this unprecedented show of affection, it was a few seconds before she returned the embrace.

Suddenly, Erin began to tremble, and Abbie felt her daughter's tears against her cheek. "I-I love you, Mom," Erin said brokenly.

For a long moment, Abbie was totally incapable of speech. Then her own eyes filled, and she kissed Erin's cheek and hugged her harder. "I love you, too, baby," she whispered. "I've always loved you."

Abbie's eyes met Logan's over Erin's head. Her heart was flooded with thankfulness. She was so incredibly blessed, she thought as she held her daughter and stroked her head. Out of pain and loss had come love and a new family—one that she now knew could weather any storm ahead.

And now, an exclusive preview of Patricia Kay's

The Other Woman

Available July 2001 from Berkley Books

Adam Forrester looked at his wife. He dreaded the next few minutes, yet he knew he had to do this. He had wanted to do it for weeks now, but had decided to wait until this weekend, when they would be at her parents' country home. That way, once he'd said his piece, he could leave, and Julia would be surrounded by people who loved her. Surely that would make his news easier to take than if he'd told her in New York, where—once he was gone—she would be alone.

Telling himself to get it over with, he said in as gentle a voice as possible, "Julia, there's something I have to tell you."

"Wasn't the party *wonderful*, Adam? And didn't Mother look beautiful? Why, no one would have *ever* guessed she's seventy years old if we hadn't told them, don't you agree?" Julia picked up the silver-backed, monogrammed brush that belonged to the vanity set her parents had given her on her sixteenth birthday and began to brush her long blond hair, which—until just a few minutes ago—had been twisted up into her usual chignon.

"Julia . . ." He walked over to the dressing table and stood behind her, placing his hand on her thin shoulder. "Stop that, would you?"

Startled, her pale blue eyes met his in the mirror. Then, frowning in bewilderment, she carefully set the brush down and swiveled around to face him. "What is it, Adam?"

Backing up, he leaned against the newel post of the canopied bed in this largest of the Hammonds' guest bedrooms. For a moment, the only sounds were the faint ticking of the Seth Thomas clock that adorned the marble fireplace mantel and the muted whine of the February wind as it buffeted this wealthy enclave in Westchester County.

Julia leaned slightly forward, and the pale pink negligee she wore gaped open, revealing a sheer matching nightgown edged in lace. It saddened Adam that the sight of her in the beautiful nightwear made him feel nothing but pity. He took a deep breath. "I want a divorce."

For a long, frozen moment, she said nothing. Then, in a voice that trembled, she said, "Y-you're joking."

He shook his head. "No," he said softly, "I'm not."

"I-I don't believe you."

"This can't be that much of a surprise to you." Now there was an edge of desperation in his voice. "Our marriage has been falling apart for years."

"No! No!" she cried. "That's not true. Why, we've been *happy*! You know we've been happy, Adam. Ask our friends! They're always telling me how we have the ideal marriage. And we do!" Tears gushed from her eyes, and she jumped up, coming over to him and flinging her arms around his neck. She pressed her mouth against his.

Adam closed his eyes. He didn't return her kiss. Couldn't. Yet his heart smote him, for he could feel how her frail body was trembling, and he knew her reaction wasn't an act. She really did believe they'd been happy. She would never have allowed herself to believe anything else, otherwise she might have had to face the truth—that he had married her because he'd been forced to out of a misguided sense of loyalty and obligation. Gently, he put his hands on her shoulders and pushed her away so he could see her face again. "Julia, we have to stop pretending."

"*I'm* not pretending! I love you, Adam," she said in a broken voice. The trembling increased. "I've always loved you. Ever since I was a little girl."

"Julia . . ." Adam felt like crying himself. The last thing he had ever wanted to do was hurt her. She *did* love him, in her way. But it was a love of dependency, a smothering love, not a mature love of equals. For a long time, he'd thought he could live with that. But now, after seeing Natalie again, the woman he'd loved before he'd ever married Julia, he realized it wasn't enough. He deserved more. Julia

deserved more. They all deserved more. He had given Julia
thirteen years. It was time to move on. Dissolving their marriage was the fairest possible thing to do—for all of them.

"I'm so sorry," he said. "But you'll be better off without
me, Julia. Now maybe you'll be able to find someone who
will love you the way you deserve to be loved."

"No! Don't say that! I don't want anyone else. I don't
care if you don't love me. I don't care! Please don't leave
me. I-I can't live without you, Adam."

"Julia, that's not true. Of course you can."

"No, no, I can't. You're everything to me! Everything!
You always have been. You . . . you're my whole reason for
being. Without you, I'm, I'm *nothing*." Her face contorted,
and she tried to put her arms around him again.

Telling her had been even worse than he'd imagined it
would be. And yet, as sorry for her as he felt, he wanted to
shake her, too. Couldn't she see that their entire marriage
was a farce? Couldn't she see that they would all be better
off once they admitted it? Why did she want him? Why
would anyone want someone who didn't love them?

Pulling away from her clinging arms, he walked to the
closet and removed his suitcase. It was best to just go. Talking about this would only prolong the agony.

"Why?" she cried. "Why are you doing this?"

This was the part he had dreaded the most. And yet, now
that she'd asked the question, he wouldn't lie to her. There
had been enough lies. He wouldn't look away, either. Meeting her gaze squarely, he said, "I'm in love with someone
else. We want to be together." Because he knew it would
accomplish nothing but to hurt Julia more, he didn't add that
he had alway loved Natalie, that Natalie was the one he'd
wanted to marry in the first place, until his father had black-
mailed him.

"No," she moaned. "No. You can't mean that!" Rushing
over to where he stood, she fell to her knees and wrapped
her arms around his legs.

Pity flooded him, but it didn't sway him. He had given
Julia too much of his life already. She would learn to live
without him. In the end, she would be better off.

Leaning down, he unwound her arms. Trying to ignore

her hysterical sobbing, he took his suitcase over to the bed and began to shove his clothes into it. When he was finished, he zipped it shut. "I'll be at our apartment tonight," he said. "But tomorrow I'll find somewhere else to stay."

Abruptly she stopped crying. Then, startling him, she whirled around, yanked open the door and, before he could even react, was running down the hall—the heels of her satin mules sounding like gunshots as they hit the oak floors. Dropping the suitcase, he ran afte her. Behind him, he could hear the door to her parents' bedroom opening.

"What the devil?" Julius Hammond said.

"Julia?" called her mother, Margarethe, anxiously.

Catching up with Julia at the head of the stairs, Adam grabbed her arm, but she wrenched it away. "Don't touch me!" she shrieked. "Don't you dare touch me!" She shrank away from him and, in an instant Adam knew he would relive in his nightmares for years to come, she lost her balance and toppled down the stairs.

"Julia!" screamed her mother.

The next few minutes would forever be a blur in Adam's mind. Racing down the stairs. The thundering footsteps of her father behind him. Margarethe screaming. Other voices shouting. And then, at the bottom of the stairs, Julia herself, lying so still, looking so fragile and so white.

"Adam?" she murmured when he reached her side.

"Oh, my God," Adam said, kneeling next to her.

"Get away from her," Julius Hammond said though gritted teeth.

"Daddy?"

"Julia, sweetheart. . . ." Her father's eyes filled with tears. He shoved Adam out of the way and put his hand under her, as if he were going to lift her up.

"Julius, don't touch her. She may have injuries we can't see, and moving her could make them worse."

Adam looked up. It was Peter Bendel speaking. He was not only an old family friend but also the family doctor. Moving both Julius and Adam aside, Dr. Bendel knelt beside Julia. While feeling her pulse, he said gently, "Can you move, Julia?"

"I . . ." Julia's voice seemed weaker to Adam. "I don't

know." She made a visible effort, grimacing as she did. "I-I can't feel my legs."

The doctor looked up. And in his eyes, Adam saw something that caused his stomach to clench with fear. Suddenly he knew with a certainty that came from somewhere deep inside that there would be no divorce. No new life with Natalie. No anything that earlier he had anticipated with so much hope.

His shoulders slumped as guilt and pity for Julia mingled with the bleakness filling his heart.

From the *New York Times* bestselling author
LaVyrle Spencer

- ❑ HOME SONG   0-515-11823-0/$7.50
- ❑ FAMILY BLESSINGS   0-515-11563-0/$7.50
- ❑ THE ENDEARMENT   0-515-10396-9/$7.50
- ❑ SPRING FANCY   0-515-10122-2/$7.50
- ❑ YEARS   0-515-08489-1/$7.50
- ❑ SEPARATE BEDS   0-515-09037-9/$7.50
- ❑ HUMMINGBIRD   0-515-09160-X/$7.50
- ❑ A HEART SPEAKS   0-515-09039-5/$7.50
- ❑ THE GAMBLE   0-515-08901-X/$7.50
- ❑ VOWS   0-515-09477-3/$7.50
- ❑ THE HELLION   0-515-09951-1/$7.50
- ❑ TWICE LOVED   0-515-09065-4/$7.50
- ❑ MORNING GLORY   0-515-10263-6/$7.50
- ❑ BITTER SWEET   0-515-10521-X/$7.50
- ❑ FORGIVING   0-515-10803-0/$7.50
- ❑ BYGONES   0-515-11054-X/$7.50
- ❑ NOVEMBER OF THE HEART   0-515-11331-X/$7.50
- ❑ SMALL TOWN GIRL   0-515-12219-X/$7.50
- ❑ THAT CAMDEN SUMMER   0-515-11992-X/$7.50

Prices slightly higher in Canada

Payable by Visa, MC or AMEX only ($10.00 min.), No cash, checks or COD. Shipping & handling:
US/Can. $2.75 for one book, $1 00 for each add'l book; Int'l $5 00 for one book, $1 00 for each
add'l Call (800) 788-6262 or (201) 933-9292, fax (201) 896-8569 or mail your orders to:

Penguin Putnam Inc.   Bill my: ❑ Visa ❑ MasterCard ❑ Amex _____(expires)
P.O. Box 12289, Dept. B   Card# _____
Newark, NJ 07101-5289   Signature _____
Please allow 4-6 weeks for delivery
Foreign and Canadian delivery 6-8 weeks

<u>Bill to:</u>

Name _____

Address _____City _____

State/ZIP _____Daytime Phone # _____

<u>Ship to:</u>

Name _____Book Total $ _____

Address _____Applicable Sales Tax $ _____

City _____Postage & Handling $ _____

State/ZIP _____Total Amount Due $ _____

This offer subject to change without notice.   Ad # B209 (5/00)